About the Author

Clara O'Connor grew up in the west of Ireland where inspiration was on her doorstep; her village was full of legend, a place of druids and banshees and black dogs at crossroads. Clara worked in publishing for many years before her travels set her in the footsteps of Arthurian myth, to Mayans, Maasai, Dervishes and the gods of the Ancients. The world she never expected to explore was the one found in the pages of her debut novel, *Secrets of the Starcrossed*, which is the first book in the The Once and Future Queen trilogy.

Clara now works in LA in TV. At weekends, if not scribbling away on her next book, she can be found browsing the markets, hiking in the Hollywood Hills or curled up by the fireside with a red wine deep in an epic YA or fantasy novel.

 twitter.com/clara_author

Books by Clara O'Connor

The Once and Future Queen Series

Secrets of the Starcrossed

Curse of the Celts

Legend of the Lakes

CURSE OF THE CELTS

The Once and Future Queen

CLARA O'CONNOR

One More Chapter
a division of HarperCollins*Publishers*
1 London Bridge Street
London SE1 9GF
www.harpercollins.co.uk

HarperCollins*Publishers*
1st Floor, Watermarque Building, Ringsend Road
Dublin 4, Ireland

This paperback edition 2021
First published in Great Britain in ebook format
by HarperCollins*Publishers* 2021

A catalogue record of this book
is available from the British Library

ISBN: 978-0-00-840769-8

Printed and bound in Great Britain by
CPI Group (UK) Ltd, Croydon CR0 4YY

The final touches of this book were done in the strange summer and autumn of 2020, when the gift of family and friends has never been more precious.

Thank you for being there (near and far).

Cx

Part One

THROUGH THE BLAST

It was a winter evening,
The snow was falling fast.
There was a little travelling wanderer,
Came trotting through the blast.

It had no covering on its head,
No cloak to keep it warm.
I ran to meet it on its way,
And save it from the storm.

*   — The Little Wanderer,* Esther "Hetty" Saunders

Chapter One

Londinium, Imperial Province of Britannia

In the reign of Caesar Magnus XVII

"Y ou are accused of crimes against the Code. How do you plead?"

The hood covering my face prevented me from seeing but I knew where I was. Underfoot was sand. The praetor's voice boomed out, silencing the roar of the crowd. We had been caught. Did I stand alone?

My thoughts were racing as my heart pounded. Was I here on the sands by myself? I was fully conscious of everything I had done, fearful of the punishment that would be meted out to me, but not sorry. Not regretful. I did not accept any guilt. Nor the right of the mob to judge my actions. I would not kneel.

The crowd's jeers and cries gained in volume as I remained standing in defiance, a great wave of sound crashing into me. Their fun could only be had if I knelt; my crimes would then be displayed for all the world to see and judge, collected from the cameras and microphones that dotted the city, pieced together and used in evidence against the accused. I was now that accused. Devyn had given me a charmed pendant that he promised would conceal me from the all-pervasive surveillance in the city. I guess now I would find out if it had worked.

Where was Devyn? Was he here? I wasn't sure. We shared a bond that allowed him to communicate with me as long as he didn't block it off to conceal what he was feeling. I didn't know whether or not I wanted to sense him here, now. With the handfast cuff on my arm, the range had been reduced to a few feet, so he could be here, caged, awaiting his turn at the other end of the arena, or he could be... My mind balked at the darker possibilities.

I had always believed in the transparency, the righteousness, of our judicial system. I knew now that there was a whole hidden world where the council chose who did and did not appear on the sands, one where people disappeared and left no record behind. I suppose it was harder to disappear an elite. My social visibility at least granted me the appearance of a public trial.

Why hadn't they started proceedings yet? Typically, by now Praetor Calchas would have moved on to telling the crowd what my crimes were, and I had to admit the list was probably long. Actually, I'm not sure the city had terms for some of the things I'd done in recent months. The crowd hushed in anticipation. My entire body tensed in reaction; this was all very off script. What was going on?

"You are accused of crimes against the Code. How do you plead?"

Was he talking to me again? I wasn't sure what was

expected of me. I looked around despite the mask preventing me from seeing, waiting for some indication from a guard or someone of what I should do. I couldn't breathe. I swayed. I bumped into a shoulder. A guard standing so close? No, another accused taking their place beside me; that was who Praetor Calchas was addressing.

A hand brushed tentatively against mine. Then more surely entwined our fingers together. Marcus. It was Marcus. I still wore the handfast cuff on my upper arm, so Marcus's presence made me feel better. My emotions over the last months swayed between two boys, like a pendulum swinging between two versions of myself, depending on which piece of metal I wore.

The cuff tied me to my old life, coded to make me long for Marcus, my city-mandated match, and to feel immediately better when he was near. And, as we found out too late, to cause intense pain if we were too far apart. The general desire to comply was only blocked by the charmed Celtic pendant Devyn had given me, the one that allowed me to remain the new me, the me who no longer did as her parents – and her city – wanted, but it had been rudely ripped from my neck weeks ago in Richmond. I realised I was not clouded by that urge to comply now, and my free hand found the familiar disc with its etched triquetra engraving. I was comforted to find it returned, however mysteriously. The crowd stilled again.

"You are accused of crimes against the Code. How do you plead?"

This time I could sense the approach of the latest accused taking his place beside me, could feel the rage and desperation and defiance rippling off him as he stepped closer. Devyn. I breathed more easily underneath the confining mask. He was here. The crowd roared as the third figure on the sand also refused to kneel. The growing displeasure of the mob at the unfolding events was evident in the noise that came at us like a tide of rolling surf. I had once sat in the audience here watching an accused take the sands, the masked and hooded figure cowed by the waves of sound coming from those seated in the arena as well as pouring down from the balconies high up in the glass and steel sky towers that encircled the ancient amphitheatre.

Another hand found mine. We were not cowed; we stood united. Like something out of a story. Stories of adventure sound so much more impressive from the outside. Guinevere, Elizabeth Tewdwr, Boadicea… Had their knees felt as unstable as mine did now? Had their mouths tasted of copper in their fear?

"Citizens, we are in uncharted territory here." Praetor Calchas addressed the mob. "These three are accused of serious crimes. Their story is shared, and their crimes are many. This extraordinary Mete has been assembled to deliver swift justice and punishment to these three who were captured attempting to escape the city last night."

Whatever happened to waiting until the city passed judgement? Was Praetor Calchas so sure that we would be found guilty? My mind raced. The charms must have failed to work. If they had enough on us to serve up to the crowd then we were indeed damned.

"The first is accused of repeat offences. He has been punished here before. Despite the mercy of the city, he has returned to the sands once more."

There was a shove from behind, and Devyn stepped forwards, breaking contact.

"You are accused of hacking. You have further offended the Code by aiding and abetting the escape of a convicted Codebreaker. Kneel to receive the judgement of the city."

There were the sounds of a scuffle. What was going on? In accordance with the law, Devyn had the right to refuse to face the city. By standing, he was choosing to go straight to sentencing. We would receive no fair trial, so why go through the charade?

"Your choice to refuse trial is dismissed. Your crimes are heinous and the city has the greater right here to bear witness. Begin."

I assumed Devyn's mask would still be on as the film rolled. Despite Calchas's unprecedented overruling of the most basic right of a citizen to refuse trial, the rules of the Mete were in many ways just; anonymity was total until the judgement was made. The accused's identity was protected by the mask and concealed in the evidentiary film that was shown to the citizenry. I could picture everything: the praetor on the balcony in front of us lifting his hand to indicate that the evidence should be played on the screens; the crowd turning their attention from the more commonly solitary figure on the sands to the big screens that allowed the audience within the ancient amphitheatre to watch the broadcast that was simultaneously being viewed everywhere in the city; the forum, highwalks, upper gardens – all public spaces would be empty as the citizenry assembled in front of hundreds of thousands of screens in homes across the city, from the hovels in the warrens of the eastern stews to the lofty, leafy levels of the towers in the western suburbs I had called home.

The crowd hushed as the film started. I heard the sentinels enter the civics classroom in the basilica and pull Devyn out. This was the moment when all this had started, when I took the illegal device from his pocket. There was a snippet of him being questioned and then a replay of the Mete I had attended, unaware at the time I was witnessing my classmate's sentence and subsequent flogging.

The crowd muttered, outraged to discover the accused was a known Codebreaker who had previously taken the sands and been forgiven for a capital offence. The film played on and the mob reluctantly quieted to hear the praetor's instructions that he be cleaned up and his memory wiped to see if they could get his accomplices.

Me. He had led them to me.

I heard my voice discussing the tech with Devyn, discussing what he planned to do with it. It was an early conversation before I had worn the triquetra pendant. The crowd was barely reacting; my identity must be concealed. I didn't understand. The praetor had referred to Devyn as having assisted a Codebreaker, but it couldn't be me because until convicted I was merely accused. Who was he referring to? I listened fiercely to follow the events unfolding on screen. There wasn't a great deal of audio; the charms must have worked for the most part, protecting our conversations from being captured despite what must have been close surveillance. The crowd gasped as they recognised a second person. It had to be Oban, the apprentice tailor to whom the mob had shown leniency on the same night Devyn was flogged. Then I heard Oban and Marina discussing Devyn's offer to forge papers and get them out of the city. Their home had a camera, so they would have discussed it somewhere they thought safe, but nowhere in the eastern stews was camera-free; the gaps in surveillance in the poorer sections of Londinium were few and far between.

They were twisting everything, making it appear as if Devyn helped Oban and Marina escape from the city to evade justice for using magic. Marina had magic? I had only been aware that it was a possibility, and I shook off the hurt that they had hidden this from me.

There was no mention of the illness that would have alerted the authorities to her status as a latent, and with it, of course, that she potentially had magic in her blood, making her a target for the sentinels to steal away as they had countless others in the stews.

It was difficult to guess at what was being shown – most likely whatever footage they had of Oban and Marina's escape from the city which would testify to Devyn having hacked the city's networks to get them out. Then there was the sound of horses – that must be my attempted escape the night I met Devyn in Richmond. But we hadn't got away. Devyn had, but I hadn't. His promise to come back for me echoed around the arena.

The roars started again as the film ended. The crowd had seen plenty. Now the praetor would be stepping forward, his outthrust thumb, held horizontally, an indication that it was time to vote to see whether the accused was deemed innocent or guilty. The seconds ticked away. It seemed endless. Was the minute always this long? Devyn's hand took mine again as he was allowed to stand. Finally, the gong sounded. Devyn's hood and mask would be removed now to face judgement. He would be displayed to all.

The crowd's jeeringly triumphant reaction indicated it was thumbs down.

"Devyn Agrestis, you have been found guilty of hacking for a second time as well as aiding and abetting the escape of two Codebreakers. In light of a 99.27% conviction rate, you are sentenced to our most severe sentence for your offences: your blood will be spilt upon the sand in full payment for your crimes. Death."

9

The crowd cheered its approval at the sentence. Capital punishment was rare, but when it did happen the condemned was granted a boon and a final night, returning to the sands the next night with the black-hooded executioner. I held Marcus's hand tighter. Which one of us was next?

A hush fell and I gripped the hands on either side of me tightly. Marcus's hand pulled away as he in turn was pushed forward.

The praetor's stentorian tones carried across the arena.

"You are accused of crimes against the Code, of using magic within the city walls, and aiding and abetting the escape of yourself and these others who stand before me. Kneel to receive the judgement of the city."

I didn't need to hear the crowd's reaction to know Marcus still refused to kneel. The mob exploded on learning that the use of magic was being tried here today, so that the praetor's direction to the sentinels to put the accused on his knees was barely audible over the din.

The clamour of the crowd faded as the evidentiary film began to play. I could identify the sounds of the hospital and could guess at what they would be seeing: a doctor with his face obscured, standing over patients who were dying of the illness. I had seen it many times myself: Marcus holding his hand above them when no one was paying attention and the patient clearly responding. I heard gasps and murmurings from the crowd, but it was impossible to know how this was being presented. Were they editing it to make Marcus look like he was making them worse? They surely couldn't try and blame the hundreds of ill individuals on one man? Could they? It wouldn't make any sense; those people were already ill when they came to the hospital. The film moved on, and I could hear the sounds of the pre-wedding revels as we sailed down the Tamesis less than twenty-four hours ago. It had been a cover for our ill-fated escape attempt.

"Marcus," a voice rang out from somewhere in the amphitheatre. "Marcus. That's Marcus Courtenay."

Pandemonium ensued. Marcus's name was on everyone's lips. His name was being chanted. He had been recognised. Of course he had. He was a well-known member of the elite, often featured in the social bursts and gossip feeds. Showing a film of a doctor and then clips of a party attended by members of the elite who were even now seated in prime spots around the amphitheatre made it inevitable that someone would connect the dots.

It was unprecedented. No one of Marcus's stature had ever taken the sands before. The usual measures taken to conceal the accused's identity were never going to be enough to keep justice blind in this case. In a regular case, a handful of people might recognise the events unfolding on the screens before them and be able to deduce who the obfuscated person might be. But that identity would mean little to the broader populace, even if they were named before the mask came off. Not so with Marcus. The city now knew their favoured son stood before them to be judged. The noise reached a crescendo. I couldn't hear the film anymore and had no way of telling what they were being shown. Our capture outside the city walls, possibly

Typically, the mob would quieten now in anticipation of the public vote, but there was no lessening of the din. It was deafening; there was outrage and certainty in their cries. They knew who stood before them and proceedings had descended into chaos. The council must be having a fit.

I sensed the sentinels push past me and I could hear Marcus struggling. What was going on? I felt something hit my feet. Marcus? Whatever was happening was quashing the mood of the crowd. There was a whoosh, like the sound of a thousand spectators gasping at once.

"Citizens," Calchas addressed the silenced crowd. "Kneeling before you is none other than Marcus Courtenay. Lady Justice prefers that her judgement be delivered blind. However, this time, one of your most privileged countrymen takes the sand. You have a right to know. A right to see who has betrayed you in this way."

Again, I could sense a scuffle in front of me. Had they unveiled Marcus? Were they making him stand? What was happening? The results of the vote were, as a rule, reflected in the sentencing. No capital offence had ever resulted in an execution where the public vote had less than a ninety per cent conviction rating. Would the city consciously vote to execute someone they knew? Was the council now cancelling the public's right to speak in judgement?

"Marcus Courtenay is a citizen like any other and his crimes will be voted on by you, the people," Calchas's voice sneered over the pandemonium. "Rise then, and face the justice of the city of Londinium. We will not call you doctor as that is the title bestowed upon the brave soldiers of science who stand as our defence against the illness they fight so bravely."

The crowd murmured at this. If Calchas's rousing words were supposed to turn the mob against Marcus's use of magic, then raising the flag for science which had been found wanting in its fight against the illness sweeping the city was not the way to go about it.

"Magic has always been the enemy of our great city. We refuse to resort to the weapons of that enemy, no matter how desperate the cause," the praetor quickly reframed, recognising his mistake. "Having used these methods, this coward tried to run from the lawful and proper judgement of the people of this city. It is a right that will not be denied. Friends and neighbours, vote now. Have you seen this man use magic inside these walls and then try to escape your judgement? The answer is a simple yes or no."

The seconds ticked by as the populace voted. There was no whispering, no anything, just a building tension as hundreds of thousands of people voted on the future of a boy they had watched grow to manhood in their newsfeeds. One who had lost his mother at a young age, who had grown into a man who chose medicine over taking his mother's seat on the high council. One the praetor urged them to condemn, though it was not Calchas's place to influence the crowd. Usually, the vote took place directly after the evidentiary film, before the accused was revealed. Oh no, the governor and the council would not be loving this. Calchas was not running the show with his usual aplomb.

The gong signalling the end of the vote finally sounded. There was a long pause. The crowd grew agitated. I felt the same. What was going on?

"Marcus Courtenay, you have been found guilty of breaking the Code through the use of magic, of attempting to flee the city and evade the righteous hand of the law, and of aiding others to the same end." Calchas paused for far longer than dramatic effect required. For far longer than my heart could take. Was Marcus also to be executed? For trying to help others? The crowd began to murmur again, as anxious as I to hear the verdict. "The mercy and wisdom of the citizens of Londinium is indeed great. Marcus Courtenay, you are convicted of your crimes at a rate of 62.84%."

The mob erupted. My knees felt like they would no longer keep me upright. The praetor would have no choice but to grant clemency; with a conviction rate that low there was no way he could inflict the ultimate penalty. Calchas liked to use these moments to praise and flatter the wisdom and mercy of the vote, to verbalise the weighting of the sentencing. I seriously doubted he would do so today. If mercy were to be granted, it was because Marcus was a much loved and admired son of the city, and the citizenry had deemed his magic, when employed to aid them, was not something they would punish him for. The hubbub of the crowd was at least partially subdued once more, presumably at some signal to which I was not privy from behind my mask.

"The sentence is fifty lashes."

Fifty lashes. Calchas was on the very edge of what would be deemed acceptable in light of a sixty-two per cent conviction rate, one of the lowest I had ever heard of for offences of this magnitude. The first and only time I had ever attended a Mete, Devyn had been flogged. Twenty lashes. This was more than double that. Could Marcus withstand such a beating? I wasn't sure how. I felt lightheaded, the clamour of the mob roiling through me. Perhaps Marcus would be able to heal himself. The crowd was a shrieking furious hive. Only a flogging, half the crowd cheered, but even louder were those baying for blood.

The use of magic was a significant offence and the punishment since the introduction of the Code centuries ago was singular: death by fire. Hatred and fear of magic was a central tenet of the Empire; sections of our society would be livid that he was being shown such leniency. But, given the low rate of conviction, there was no way Marcus could burn. Calchas's hands were tied; a capital punishment could not be meted out against the expressed desire of the citizenry implicit in the result of the vote.

Praetor Calchas was saying something, but it was impossible to hear over the cacophony of sound. He had to raise his voice to be heard across the agitated crowd, the most vocal of whom cried out for Marcus to burn, furious that one granted every privilege the city could offer had broken the Code in this way. Accusations of being a Wilder, a sympathiser, a coward for attempting to flee were hurled down from the thousands of people above and around us. Adding to the deafening din were pleas for mercy and objections against the harshness of the punishment.

My arm was grabbed and I was pulled unceremoniously from the sands. The Mete was over. We were being taken back to our cell.

"Citizens," Lord Calchas attempted to address the crowd once more. I couldn't make out what he was saying but, given the howls of outrage swirling over my head, it appeared the crowd was unhappy, and hungry for more. I was struggling to keep my feet as I was dragged across the arena to the howling of the masses at being denied immediate satisfaction.

I would not be accused today. I stumbled. More than anything I just wanted it to be over.

We were pulled and pushed, the sounds muffled as we presumably hit the tunnels under the amphitheatre until we were back in the holding cell from which we had been taken. We were released, footsteps sounded, and then the door slammed shut. I snatched the mask from my face as quickly as I could get it off. I couldn't bear to be stifled under it a moment longer.

Chapter Two

They were going to kill Devyn. I saw again the specks of blood on the sand from his last visit to the arena. His blood would spill there once more. We had been so close. And now... I couldn't think about it. I felt stunned by the noise and events in the arena.

What had happened? Why had the Mete been halted? Did it matter? We had been given a reprieve. One more night.

It took a moment for my vision to adjust after having been in complete darkness for so long, but the light in the cell was dim enough. I pulled in a breath of air as I was grabbed from behind and spun around, the black skirt of my accused's uniform swirling. Devyn's hands framed my face, his dark eyes scanning me for bodily injuries before holding my eyes with his as he did the same for internal damage. Satisfied, he lifted his head and turned to our fellow cellmate.

"Well, aren't you going to say something?" Marcus finally burst out, clearly unnerved by the lack of reaction.

"What do you expect me to say?" Devyn asked coolly,

under no doubt as to which corner Marcus expected an attack from.

"I don't know. Aren't you going to say getting off so lightly proves that I was in collusion with the authorities the entire time?" Marcus's point had merit, especially given how suspicious Devyn was already.

Devyn raised an eyebrow. "Were you?"

"No. I don't know how they were waiting for us. I was careful, but it was all arranged so quickly. I don't know." Marcus ran his hands through his hair.

"I may not remember the twenty lashes I took out there, but I've been beaten before. Have you?" Devyn asked. "Believe me, fifty lashes isn't exactly getting off lightly."

"Why didn't they hold my trial?" I asked quietly. "What happened out there at the end? I couldn't see."

"It looked like Governor Actaeon made Calchas call a halt," Devyn explained.

"After what happened with me..." Marcus trailed off.

An extraordinary Mete, Calchas had said. That it had been. Some of our most fundamental traditions had been overturned. Anonymity had been thrown out, both the government and the Code undermined by the clemency granted by the citizenry despite Marcus's conviction of the Empire's most vilified crime. An accused found guilty of using magic wasn't just burned at the stake, they were stripped of their citizenship; they were considered less than nothing.

The council would be incensed at the mercy shown by the mob towards Marcus. If Actaeon had objected to continuing, then it was to make sure my trial didn't repeat the leniency shown to Marcus.

"I failed," Devyn said, directing his soft words to me. My chest felt tight. He was blaming himself for this.

"No," I protested. "No. This is not your fault. You are not the reason we are here. *They* are. We shouldn't be here. *At all.* We don't belong in the city. We're not even citizens. We were born free. We were born with magic. They don't…"

I couldn't find the words to express that where we found ourselves was no fault of our own. They might as well condemn us for breathing. Our abilities were innate, the magic running through our veins the reason they had stolen me to begin with. We had been so close… We had been outside the wall with the smugglers' door closed behind us, the freedom of the night lying before us with its canopy of trees and the open sky above.

"Screw them." I lifted his head and held his dark eyes with my own. "I don't care. I would rather not live at all than live the lie I thought was happiness. I… We nearly made it."

Devyn pulled his head out of my hands, his fist clenched as he punched the stone wall. I could feel his frustration, his deep despair, pulse through the connection we shared.

He looked back at me over his hunched shoulder. "I'm sorry, Cass."

I smiled at him, opening the connection as wide as I could and allowing my feelings to pour through. I loved him. Fiercely. I was angry, but not at him. I was mad at the world, at the Britons who had failed to keep me safe as an infant, at the city that had stolen me. But not at Devyn. If my twenty-two years had meant anything, it was the gift of the precious hours I spent with him and the evening we were together, knowing what it felt to truly live. In his arms.

"Screw them," I repeated. I had lived.

Devyn grinned back. He always held back, always tried to maintain a distance between us. Now that we had nothing left to lose, now that it was all over, I felt what his true emotions were. They washed over me. They lit me up from within. They took my breath away.

We stood there like idiots, smiling at each other, for another heartbeat. Then I was in his arms and his lips descended on mine. He kissed me tenderly, hungrily. Like a lover. Like a soulmate.

"Cass," he breathed.

"Ugh," Marcus groaned. "Could you two stop it."

I pulled away, heat flushing my cheeks. I might have been in the clinch of my short lifetime, but I was still relatively new to all this and Marcus was officially my match, so it was pretty bad form. Life and death notwithstanding.

"Sorry, I forgot." We had discovered the incredibly mortifying fact that the handfast cuffs conveyed my passion to Marcus, who wore the partner cuff to my own, even when that passion was directed at another.

Marcus's brows pulled together, and his eyes narrowed as he looked down at the charmed wristband I had given him, then back at the chain around my neck.

"Actually, I didn't sense anything. Last night I could still... It seems that if we are both wearing charms then I'm not affected with the burning in the blood roused whenever you two..." He waved a hand in the air to indicate the embrace we had just shared.

"You couldn't sense my feelings just now? But I was wearing my pendant when I tried to escape through Richmond..." The handfast cuffs employed a push and pull technique. Presumably, in a more normal courtship, the attraction and passion felt by the couple fed the fire in each, a reciprocal desire building between the couple which acted to pull them closer together. It also pushed them together by punishing them for parting; being too distant from each other could cause physical pain... as we had learned during my failed attempt to flee, though only Marcus had truly suffered the pain of our separation. Thanks to the triquetra charm, I only experienced some light pangs when we were at our most distant. I was glad my pendant had been returned for me, and I felt for it now. "If we're both wearing one..."

"It's blocked," he finished for me. For all the help this new knowledge was to us.

"I don't suppose anyone has any bright ideas for how we get out of this one?" I asked, somewhat hopelessly. At which point, the light went out.

Marcus gave a short bark of laughter. "That's a little on the nose, don't you think?"

Fury at our powerlessness swept through me, a rage that usually found a response in nature since my magic had revealed itself. There wasn't so much as a flicker of the lights.

Why couldn't I feel the elements answer my call?

A snarl suggested Devyn couldn't reach his magic either.

"What?" came Marcus's voice.

"I can't use my magic," I said through gritted teeth.

Marcus let out a humph. "You think after that display in Richmond that everything you've eaten hasn't been laced with the pill they used to give you to suppress your abilities?"

Devyn pulled me close. "Marcus, you've still been able to help people. You did a shift before the party, right?"

He was referring to our pre-wedding revels, only yesterday. It felt like another lifetime.

"Yes" came Marcus's short answer out of the darkness.

"Then whatever they've been giving Cassandra probably wasn't served up to you."

"I suppose not," Marcus replied grudgingly, a little less

20

monosyllabic. He was curious as to where the Briton was going with this.

"Then we can have light." Devyn held me closer to his chest. After the events of the last twenty-four hours, I could do without the darkness. I needed some kind of outline, some relief from the dense black of our cell.

"How?" Marcus asked. "Magic? I only know how to use my abilities to cure the illness."

"Well, it's time you learned something a little more. With your bloodline, you should be able to do a great many more things than heal people. The Plantagenet line is one of the oldest and most powerful on this island," Devyn informed him. "I need you to close your eyes."

Marcus snorted. "What difference will that make? I can't see my hand in front of my face as it is."

"It'll stop you being distracted as the magic manifests itself. Trust me."

"Right, I'm going to trust you," Marcus flashed back. I couldn't blame him. Marcus didn't know Devyn; they had barely met before last night. And Marcus would not recall their earlier meeting with fondness as it was the same night he had learned not only that he had the magic so reviled by citizens, but that I was hoping to run away from the city with a Wilder.

Before Devyn came into our lives, Marcus and I had never been accused of so much as jaywalking; we wouldn't have dreamed of doing anything to disrespect the Code. Now we were the accused in what was undoubtedly going to become the most scandalous Mete in a century. Or ever.

"Close your eyes," Devyn repeated. An exhalation of breath presumably indicated that Marcus had complied this time. "I need you to focus. The power is within you. We gain magic from without, from natural resources most of the time; this is how you pull in energy. Here in the darkness, behind the stone and iron, you don't have access to that. You need to reach within to the power of your ancestors. Deep inside lies a light, a spark. I need you to bring that up to the surface. Raise it slowly, gently; it should be a delicate light."

As Devyn spoke, a glimmer appeared in the air beside Marcus. I stifled my reaction so I wouldn't disturb Marcus, his now visible face creased in concentration.

"The light is bright and true," Devyn coaxed him, and the glimmer responded, growing brighter. "That's it. Keep your eyes closed. Now, I need you to tie it off. Let it float free. Make it separate from yourself. You still control it, but it exists outside of you; you no longer need to sustain it."

The glowing sphere floated to the side, bouncing daintily in the air before steadying itself. It was beautiful, a manifestation of real magic, lighting what was quite literally our darkest hour. I was entranced. I watched as Marcus opened his eyes and took in what he had accomplished, his once ready smile tilting his lips and his green eyes widening at the thing he had created. His eyes danced to meet mine, the wattage dimming as he took in the sight of me in Devyn's arms.

I bit my lip. I didn't know what to say to him. It was my fault he was here. He would never have been in this situation if it were not for me.

"Thank you," I offered softly into the half-light of the cell.

My defiance, my fear, all the myriad jumbled emotions of the evening drifted away as we sat there in the cell, lit by the otherworldly glow hovering in the air.

A moment later, we heard steps outside.

"Quench it," Devyn hissed, and a startled Marcus looked up blankly at the light he had created and shook his head. Devyn had only supplied instructions on how to create it, not turn it off. Devyn lifted his hand and made a snatching grab at the air.

As the lock started to turn in the door, Marcus took a step and closed his fist around the light, wincing as he did so.

"No," Devyn exclaimed, too late. "In your mind. Not with your hand."

The room was in utter darkness once more, but I could feel him shaking his head. I shuffled to one side so I would not be discovered in his embrace. Devyn was moving to face the new arrival anyway. I still felt bereft despite the mere inches between us.

The door opened to a guard arriving with our supper, which he placed on the floor. He backed out, but, realising that to do so would leave us in darkness, he hesitated. Unsure of what to do, he stood in the doorway.

"Go on then," he said after a moment. "Eat."

The three of us surveyed the tray with its water and gloopy-looking mystery stew. The meal of champions.

"I ain't got all day," he said, torn between wanting to leave and making sure we were fed as had probably been his command.

"Is there anything in it?" Marcus asked in his most cordial manner, as if he were enquiring about the subtleties of the sauce being served with his meal at one of the city's most exclusive restaurants.

The sentinel looked at him in confusion.

"Why would there be anything in it? I was told to get you all something to eat. I got you something to eat. So bloody eat," he gestured again at the tray.

"You purchased this yourself?" Marcus pursued. We already knew Devyn and I had been dosed, but so far Marcus

23

had somehow been spared whatever they used to block powers.

"Look, mate. Eat, don't eat. No skin off my nose," he said brusquely. He obviously wanted to close the cell door and be gone, but it went against the grain to leave two of the city's most celebrated and loved citizens to eat their cheap meal off the floor in the dark.

Marcus looked at me and shrugged. "Might as well take the chance. What difference does it make now?"

He was right. Even if the food was laced with drugs, we were going to be dead before the previous stuff we'd consumed wore off. Even if it had worn off, we would be bound and blind when we were taken into the arena and therefore unable to wield what little magic we had. Marcus only knew how to heal people and create – though not quench – small lights. The only magic I had ever seen Devyn use was defensive and seemed to be integral to his role as Griffin, protector, helping him to pass unnoticed in the background, sense when I was in danger, and that kind of thing.

He also made me feel safe, though maybe that particular talent wasn't supernatural. Maybe that was just me. I had discovered that there was not a path he could tread where I would not follow. Those first times when he led me by the hand into his world, had he been using actual magic or had he just led and I simply followed? As for me, I could float away on a breeze, catch glimpses of the past, conjure up winds in a fit of pique, even rain down a storm given the right incentive; the only problem was I had no idea how I had done any of it.

At Devyn's insistence, I had stopped taking the little pills which I now knew suppressed the magic which flowed in my veins. But Devyn and I had never got around to talking about it, and he had never instructed me on how to use it the way he had with Marcus earlier. Devyn was usually more concerned with calming me and constraining the manifestations I experienced, which usually popped up at the worst time possible. So no, my magic wasn't going to help us any.

But as I picked up my bowl and lifted the spoon, I decided I wasn't hungry enough to eat whatever this was after all. Marcus likewise failed to eat more than a spoonful. Devyn didn't even pick it up. I guess he was unwilling to give up hope.

The guard's footsteps hadn't even faded when we heard him returning, this time with company: Matthias Dolon. Marcus's face went blank as he registered his father's unexpected appearance, his body entirely still. I had seen for myself how Matthias perceived the taint of Briton blood, a legacy of the marriage which sealed the treaty nearly 300 years ago. Now he had seen the evidence of how true that strain ran in his son's veins. I couldn't imagine having to face my mother now. I took a step towards Marcus, wanting to help him brace against the impending blow.

Matthias waited wordlessly until the guard departed and closed the door, having first provided a lantern which he propped up on the stool which also appeared out of nowhere in response to the presence of an exalted council member.

"You stupid, worthless child." Senator Dolon spoke directly to Marcus, ignoring our presence and foregoing any preliminary greetings or enquiries into his son's wellbeing, mental health or anything else regarding our general dire circumstances. "You've ruined everything."

Marcus drew himself up and stood tall. Taller than his father.

"I did what I thought was right."

"You have everything. I've given you everything and this is

how you repay me." As ever the doting father, worried less for his son than for his status in the city. "Why? What on earth possessed you? So much for your devotion to the poor masses."

"I was doing it for them. What I was doing wasn't enough. The Britons have a medicine that works; I wanted to find a way to help more people."

"Well, that's over now. You'll never set foot in a hospital again."

"What do you mean?"

"Governor Actaeon is furious that the mob and the praetor have shown mercy." Dolon's lip curled. "He never approved of the programme we set up to gain more magic within the walls and you've given him the perfect excuse to crush it... and you in the process."

"What programme?" I asked quickly. There was no way I was missing the opportunity to discover more about the mysterious manipulations which had directly led to us being here. Yes, there might be more pressing issues, but I had been obsessing over this for months and here was Matthias fully acknowledging that such a programme existed. An actual thing.

"Ah, our little cuckoo. What a waste. So many years waiting for you to grow up, all for nothing now." Matthias lifted the lantern from the stool and seated himself as if drawing up to a fire in a gentlemen's club to settle in for a leisurely conversation debating the issues of the day. "We had such plans. You see, there is a faction within the council that has argued for years that we should figure out how to harness magic rather than eradicate it. Our advances in technology are rendered useless once we hit the ley line at the border. We're still limited to the same tech there that has failed to gain supremacy for generations. We are tired of being trapped behind these walls. We want more. Following my wife's untimely demise, no real Courtenay sat on the council to stand in our way, and we had a child with magic at our disposal. All we needed was another Briton and we could breed a little litter to study, so we could find a way to defeat the Wilders once and for all. It's over now, of course."

I was aghast at his casual confession of what he had done, of how they had planned to use us. I knew it was true, but to hear him talk about it so frankly, so utterly shamelessly... How could he, his own son? Devyn's eyes met mine, wordlessly agreeing, conveying his contempt and distrust of a man who would do this to his own flesh and blood.

"You knew? They were planning to use me, to use my children." Marcus spoke slowly, his tone cold.

"You wouldn't have been harmed. Think of it. Rather than throwing your life away on a science already perfected, you could integrate it with native forms of healing."

"As *you* dictated. Under *your* control," I put in quietly.

I had seen Marcus in action at the hospital. He made no distinction between council member and sewer worker, but his father had never shared this view. Marcus had to know that any benefits of using magic would be made available to the elite first.

"Such a shame. There were so many advantages in a softer policy. Terrible waste, all that power. Actaeon is a fool. If we were to harness the power inside the city, we could achieve so much."

"But the Empire hates magic. They would never have stood for it." It was a central tenet of the Code.

"True, there have always been imperial zealots who wished to eradicate magic completely, who swept the city for any child unlucky enough to have a dormant gene show up. They thought they had thinned it down over the generations. Looks like they were wrong."

"What do you mean they were wrong? Wrong about what?" I asked.

"Why, the Maledictio, my dear." He used the name unknown to the public for the illness that wasn't nearly as new to the Empire as the council let on. "Haven't you figured it out yet? Who it is this illness attacks? "

Devyn believed there was a correlation between the illness and latent magic in the blood. Marina had been sick, and it seemed she was more than just a latent. But why let Senator Dolon know what we knew when it was so much more informative when he was doing all the talking? "I don't understand. The illness attacks at random."

Matthias looked at me like I was an idiot.

"Does it?" he huffed heavily. "Marcus, do I need to spell this out to you too?"

"No, Father. There was some basic genetic work done on Briton blood, but we don't have much of it." Marcus met my eyes; he had already informed me of the genetic testing back in the summer, encouraged me to get tested given my adopted status, but he betrayed no hint of that now. "In the tests on our own citizens, especially Shadowers and those who live near the walls, it seems there is an anomalous gene that lies dormant. It is often present in the ill; those with stronger bloodlines don't die as quickly. It can take years, like my mother."

"Bravo," Matthias applauded sardonically. "Sooner or later it comes for anyone with magic in their blood."

"Not in the rest of Briton. There is a medicine, something that treats the illness. People aren't dying of it in the Wilds,"

Marcus interjected. "If the governor would just talk to them... We have been at peace for centuries."

"Actaeon sees the illness as a solution, not a problem; a useful aid in cleaning house." Matthias paused before turning to Devyn for the first time since he entered the cell. "He'll only be happy when you're all eradicated."

Devyn smiled thinly at Matthias. I felt a pulse in the connection; Devyn wasn't visibly reacting but he had caught Matthias's slip as well: he knew Devyn was not a citizen. He knew he was a Briton.

"Why tell us now? You still have Marcus. Find him a new bride. It would be easily done. Back on course in no time," Devyn spat.

"Have you not been listening? They won't be able to do anything now that his magic has become such public knowledge. But it's never going to come to that. Marcus won't live long enough to have children."

"What do you mean? Why not?"

Matthias looked at his son as if he were mentally deficient before continuing in his familiar glacially scathing manner. "Actaeon is the head of the faction that has exterminated all latents identified within the walls for generations in order to ensure the end of magic. You think the verdict of the public vote is anything more than a stay of execution? He will come for you. Calchas may have used the mob to his advantage today, but Actaeon means to end you. Now, in a week, in a month. It is inevitable."

Marcus's shoulders slumped.

"But you are still my son. I will do what I can to keep you alive." He cast a lidded sneer at Devyn and me and was gone, the metal door clanging in his wake.

We were once more in the dark until Marcus repeated his

feat of earlier in the evening, after he had grudgingly asked for instruction on how to quench it without burning himself.

Despite all the new information Matthias had divulged, nobody broke the silence. What use was it to us now? Devyn was condemned, Marcus's relatively lenient sentence unlikely to stick. And it sounded as if the outcome of my own trial was a foregone conclusion.

"Shhh. Relax now." I sat back against Devyn, cocooned in the security of his arms. His hands were in my hair, soothing me, calming the turmoil surging through me. "Hush. The breeze lifts you, the current carries you, the earth holds you, and fire lights the way. Relax, be at one."

His odd chant soothed me, and, finally, I slept.

Chapter Three

I came awake slowly, stiff from lying on the cold stone floor. The awareness of the new day – and my new reality – slowly seeped in. It was a cold, unwelcome reality. Devyn had been sentenced to death. Today we would face the mob once more. My muscles tensed as if bracing against the day, protesting, sore from the waves of adrenaline that had surged and ebbed in response to the previous day's events. Devyn's arms were wrapped around me and squeezed a little tighter in response to my awakening.

I lay there, listening to the sound of my breath and his heartbeat, not wanting to open my eyes to acknowledge the day. I didn't know how to face a day like today. I was still reeling from the events of yesterday. Devyn had been condemned to death in the arena; that had really happened. Today we would be brought back out to face the city again.

When I did finally open my eyes, it was to find Marcus's glacially green ones staring over at us. My stomach whooshed downwards like a lead box falling from a high tower. I did this. I brought him to this.

"I'm sorry," I whispered when he didn't break his gaze. I should have got out with Devyn months ago. The night we helped Marina leave the city, we had both been beyond the walls. There had been Britons there to help her; we could have gone with them; it would have been so easy. I was being foolish. I wasn't ready then, would never have gone, too attached to the comfort and security of my cage.

Marcus blinked, leaning his head back against the golden stone wall. Our windowless room was still lit by the ball of light he had created the night before.

"For what?" he asked resignedly.

For not being his match, for not even being a particularly good friend. All I had done for months and months was lie to him. Like me, Marcus felt alone his whole life; his mother had died when he was very young and his father didn't really care for him. Being matched with me should have meant that Marcus finally had a person who loved him for himself. Instead, he got a girl ready to throw away all that the city offered at the crook of the little finger of the man in whose arms she now lay... in a cell, where we awaited the completion of the Mete that would send us to our ends.

I shrugged at my inability to adequately apologise to Marcus.

"I guess, I'm sorry for everything," I offered. "Without me, none of this would be happening to you."

Devyn stiffened and straightened up, slightly dislodging me.

"Without you, Cass, he would be dead," he defended.

Marcus's eyes snapped up.

"Looks like I'll be dead anyway," he snarled.

"And that's my fault? I'm not swinging the blade here. You are being executed by your friends because they don't like the blood running in your veins and because you are not one of them. Not really, even though all you've ever tried to do is be a good citizen. Help other citizens. They don't care because ultimately you are not one of them," Devyn threw back at him. "You never will be."

"That's not true. I used magic, the ultimate crime against the Code." Marcus sounded tired, resigned, as if overnight he had reconciled himself to his fate and his own part in earning it. "Magic is illegal for a reason."

"Is it? What reason is that?" the Briton at my back challenged. "Because they feel threatened by it? Because they can't control it? Enlighten me."

"Is magic the solution to everything in your world?" Marcus returned. "I don't think so, because magic doesn't run in everyone's veins, does it? Magic is held by the few to rule over the many. Control of magic is firmly in the hands of those at the top of your feudal society. The Empire is far more meritocratic. Your life isn't dictated by the colour of your blood or your skin; the intelligent, the strong, the driven can make something of themselves. Technology is available to all. Magic is not."

Devyn's head went back and he threw his arms wide.

"This society is a meritocracy? Do you truly believe that, Marcus Plantagenet Courtenay?" He emphasised Marcus's full name. "You are the single most entitled man on this island. A prince of the city, a prince amongst my people. What do you know of merit?"

Marcus stood abruptly, furious.

"My birth is not my fault." His voice was loud in the small space. "I have done everything in my power to do what I can to help others. And you're right. What has it got me? My Plantagenet blood is the reason I was matched to a Wilder foundling in order to give them control... over magic. My Courtenay heritage drove me to help my fellow citizens who will spill my blood on the sand for that very help."

There was no answer to that. He was right. Devyn didn't want to like Marcus, but that didn't mean he had done anything to deserve it. Silence descended on the cell, and Marcus swung away when Devyn had no response for him.

Eventually, footsteps heralded the arrival of our morning meal and Marcus quenched the light – mentally, this time. When the guard arrived and opened the cell door, he saw our food remained untouched from the night before. Throwing us a sour look, he put some unappetizing porridge on the floor and left immediately, unlike the evening before. He must have clarified his instructions on how to proceed; no dilemma today about whether or not he should leave us in the dark.

The hours ticked by slowly as we waited for the Mete to reconvene. We sat in silence, contemplating the evening ahead. So far, we had a one-for-two conviction rate with a death sentence. Marcus believed that the city might vote in my favour. I wasn't so convinced, and if Matthias was to be believed, it wouldn't matter anyway. Whatever happened out on the sand, there was no future in which Governor Actaeon would allow us to live if he had any say in it. Which of course he did.

The sentinels came to collect us at the allotted time, tying our hands in front of us – a new precaution against wielding magic, I guessed, now that we had stopped eating their food and thereby consuming the inhibitor they laced it with. Once we were secure, Praetorian Alvar entered the room, his head tilting as he surveyed us with satisfaction.

"Nice to see you all where you belong." He smiled his quick, fake smile – or rather, produced the baring of teeth he believed passed for a smile. "I'm informed that you failed to eat the food provided. Such a big day, are you sure you don't care for it?"

He pushed the tray towards us with his foot.

"Too kind," Marcus answered for us with impeccable manners. "We're all fine, thank you."

Alvar bared his teeth again. "I thought you might say that. No matter."

At that, Kasen, Alvar's ever-present sidekick, entered the room. Despite our current circumstances, I felt oddly relieved to see that Kasen had suffered no repercussions from having lost us the night of the pre-wedding revels. Although, as I now knew, he hadn't lost us at all. In fact, they had been in the exact right spot outside the wall waiting for us. How had they got there before us if they had been following us? It seemed that Marcus's defection to our cause hadn't been as much of a surprise to the authorities as it had to Devyn and me.

Kasen was carrying a covered tray which he presented to the senior praetorian. Alvar lifted the cover to reveal three syringes, one for each of us. Devyn immediately began to struggle with the guard holding him, and two more guards entered at the commotion. He pulled away from his guard and rushed at the two incoming sentinels but, bound as he was, he was no match for them, and was quickly tackled to the ground where the three of them pinned him down. He made no sound, but his dark glare was filled with hate and defiance as Alvar injected him in the arm through the sleeve of his black shirt.

"Hold him down," Alvar instructed as he turned away, and handed a fresh syringe to Kasen before turning to Marcus. "Do I need to invite more guards to join us?"

In reply, Marcus merely turned his shoulder towards the praetorian who had always been so courteous when he had been on my protection detail. Marcus stood unmoving, staring into the middle distance, as Kasen injected him in his upper arm.

Kasen picked up the last syringe and made his way to me. Devyn started to struggle against the guards who held him down. Alvar crossed the cell and kicked him in the stomach with his heavy boots. I felt the pain caused by the blow and whimpered.

"Wild animals will not be tolerated in the city, dog," he said, kicking Devyn a second time before he had managed to gain his breath from the first blow. I folded over at the second blow.

Turning, Alvar found Marcus now standing in front of me. He quirked a brow at my protector.

"Marcus, it's fine. I'm fine," I said, though I had backed myself up against the wall. Marcus ground his teeth and stood aside, letting Alvar pass.

"Donna Shelton." Alvar nodded to me as he pushed the syringe into my upper arm. I winced at the stinging sensation caused by the liquid as it made its way under my skin. My fears were quickly confirmed; it was indeed the inhibitor. I had started to recognise the difference in myself when it was in my bloodstream; the world felt a little less raw, my senses were just a little duller than they had been moments earlier. Perhaps, given the next hour or so, that was no bad thing.

Alvar nodded at the guards holding Devyn on the ground and they let go of him before hauling him to his feet. His eyes met mine, asking if I was all right. I nodded slightly, sending a reassuring pulse through our bond which seemed unaffected by the drug. Job completed, they untied our hands and started to march us to the door.

"No masks?" I asked Alvar, surprised.

"No," he replied shortly.

This was a considerable change in protocol. Nobody was ever brought into the arena unmasked; it was the way it had been for centuries. Calchas must not want a repeat of yesterday; Marcus's friends identifying him before the vote had caused uproar yesterday. It wouldn't take a genius watching my reel to figure out that the girl whose identity was obscured, the one standing beside Marcus Courtenay on the sands and accused of crimes not dissimilar to his, was his bride.

Making our way out to the arena for the second time was no less intimidating. If anything, the thunderous pounding was louder tonight. I felt weighed down by the thousands of eyes that stared down at us as we entered the arena. Behind my mask, I had known they were there, but it had made me focus on myself and on the hands that held mine. Now, my head bared, my face revealed, I felt the accusing stares, the appalled gasps, the whispering of the crowd as they conveyed their shock at my identity and speculated on my offences. Thousands in the arena, hundreds more in the balconies above, and in homes throughout Londinium, the entire city watched as I made my way across the sands. I looked around me,. Rows upon rows of faceless, nameless citizens salivated at the prospect of seeing my offences. My eyes flicked to the area at the side of the arena reserved for relatives and witnesses of the accused. Empty. No sign of my parents. Had they so easily washed their hands of me? I thought of Anna who served our family faithfully for years. Had they turned up when she was brought here to be judged and executed? Or had she meant as little to them as the girl they raised as a daughter? Had they turned their backs and publicly refused to support her by not turning up? Had no one turned up for me? I felt a wave of emotion from Devyn. I closed my eyes to savour it. The bond between us was vibrant with his strength, his belief in my ability to survive, and his admiration for who I was. I didn't need anyone else. I had Devyn. I would always have Devyn. Even when he had believed me dead, he had been there for me, risking everything to come and find me; against all evidence he believed in me. I could do this.

We stood in the late autumn sunshine, awaiting the council, which was another change in protocol. Typically, the council arrived first, events began, and the accused were the last to be brought in. The warm, soft light streamed down, turning everything golden. I looked at the proud, defiant profiles of the men standing each side of me. Devyn's dark curls waved in the breeze which swirled around the arena and his dark eyes stared straight ahead while his high cheekbones were accented by the play of the sunlight on his face. Marcus's chestnut hair was as impeccable as ever, and his green eyes caught mine, warmed, and told me to be strong. I smiled in return, looking around to see the last of the council taking their places as the praetor and the governor arrived and stood at the front of the balcony.

The governor and the praetor stepped forwards together.

"Friends, Romans, citizens," the Governor greeted as usual. "For two thousand years we have convened here to mete out the justice of the city. We are the first and last defence of the Empire. The walls keep us safe but the Code keeps us strong. Yesterday saw the trial of a young man who should have been the best of us. He has failed. We, in turn, showed him mercy he did not deserve. He failed us. He failed the Code."

A ripple ran through the arena. What was happening?

"We cannot let this stand. He used magic within the walls. He undermined everything we are and everything the Empire is. We thereby have decided to adjust his sentence to that meted out in all such cases. Death by fire."

I gripped Marcus's hand tightly. Matthias had been right. The crowd was silent, stunned by the unprecedented move. The governor had ignored the city's vote for clemency and overruled the sentence of the praetor.

"In the Code we are one."

The crowd returned, "We are one in the Code."

Today, nobody objected. The pandemonium, the division of the night before, had been quieted by the age-old response, the reminder that our unity as a province, as a city, was stronger if we were united as one under the law and customs of our Code. *Their* Code. Not mine; I was no longer protected or bound by the Code.

Calchas stepped forwards and raised his hands to quiet the cheering of the crowd.

"Citizens, welcome. Today you are returned to this special Mete to bear judgement on the last of these accused. We have dispensed with anonymity here today as it is our belief that you have a right to know when a fellow citizen has grievously and repeatedly broken the laws of our city. Cassandra Shelton has taken all the blessings bestowed upon her and thrown them back in our faces. For this, you have the right to look in her eyes and see her shame when you bear witness. She has forfeited the right granted to citizens by thus offending you all so mightily."

Woah, talk about leading the vote. By revealing my face and allowing the mob time to absorb my identity, Calchas ensured the result would not be fractured by any reflex of mercy that a late revelation of my well-known face and name might grant me, as it had for Marcus the previous day. Denying me anonymity as a privilege of which I was no longer worthy, he was making sure that the very fact that I was known to these people was proof that I had thrown all the privileges of my station and their good wishes in their faces.

He turned to gaze down his nose at me where I stood on the sands before him.

"Cassandra Shelton, you are accused of crimes across the spectrum, of aiding the Codebreaker Oban, assisting in his escape and that of his sister, a magic user. You have also betrayed your handfast by having sex outside of wedlock. You concealed and aided a hunted Codebreaker and, with him, attempted to escape justice, not once but twice. You persuaded an innocent citizen to aid you, for which they lost their life. And through the wilful use of magic, you destroyed citizen property in Richmond. How do you plead?"

I reeled from the list of offences of which I was accused. The crowd had reacted with increasing volume as Calchas dropped each one into the silence on which he insisted before continuing. By the end, the crowd were a seething morass of jeers with vile names being thrown down upon me from all sides. Calchas had staged it well; there was no need to go to a public vote. I was already judged. I was no longer the pretty girl on the arm of their golden boy. I was reviled, beyond redemption in the eyes of the crowd.

I would not throw myself on their mercy. There would be none for me. I smiled defiantly at Calchas, not breaking his gaze. I refused to sink to my knees. I lifted my chin. I was guilty. And proud of it.

The din of the crowd heightened as the mob screeched its anger at being denied the pleasure of informing me of their belief in my guilt. I did not doubt that if it went to the public vote, I would be convicted at one of the highest rates the city had ever seen. Many like me preferred to abstain from the capital cases. I'm sure even those people would make an exception for me. In truth, a part of me was shocked at the depth of the hate that was raining down upon me.

In moments, I ceased to be an obedient daughter of the city with a bright future who was matched to the city's most eligible bachelor. Calchas was right; I had been given so much. I was an elite, matched to a veritable prince of the city. Many of the populace wouldn't even aspire to a fraction of all I had thrown away. I had broken all levels of the Code, and they hadn't even been informed of my fraternisation with a Briton. Calchas had refrained from using that one; he hadn't needed to. But that was the crime of which I was proudest.

It was only now, as I stood awaiting the sentence that Calchas was about to pronounce, that I realised how unjust the system truly was. How unfair. I was offered no chance to defend myself. Despite its supposed transparency – the way justice appeared to be in the hands of the citizenry – it actually never left the hands of the praetor and the rest of the council. It was they who decided who should appear on the sands, they who edited the evidentiary reel to show unmitigated guilt or justifications for offences against the Code on which they chose not to frown for their own reasons. Calchas played his audience like a fiddle. Crimes that when punished would fill the council's coffers inevitably resulted in scant mercy. Crimes that didn't benefit them one way or the other were an offering spread beneath the feet of the city to condemn or not as they framed it, the final judgement of little concern to them. At the Mete I had attended, the sea captain who had evaded taxes had lost everything and would spend the rest of his life working to enrich the council further. Meanwhile, Oban, the apprentice tailor who had stolen from his master, was portrayed doing it because of undeniable talent and to aid his impoverished family; he had been duly raised up thanks to the wisdom of the manipulated mob. All hail the great people of Londinium. They were too blind to see that they merely participated in their own imprisonment inside the punishment and reward system of their prison guards.

"Cassandra Shelton, you stand guilty, ready to accept the sentence you so richly deserve. In doing so, I fear you seek merely to avoid having your shame witnessed before the city. You have broken the Code again and again in the most heinous of manners. You are a disgrace to this city. You have debased yourself by betraying your match and all that we stand for. You have offended the Code in ways that go against the very fabric of our society, employing magic to bring destruction upon the property of citzens. You are a threat to the wellbeing of everyone in the city. There can be no mercy for you. Death by fire."

I closed my eyes, unable to hold Calchas's malicious gaze any longer as the manner of my death was named. My stomach dropped. Fire. So I was to burn. No trace of me but ash and smoke would remain by the time they were finished.

The praetor raised his hands to quiet the crowd's cacophonous reaction to Calchas going straight to sentencing, reversing yesterday's policy of insisting we kneel and have our misdeeds displayed for the city's entertainment.

"People of Londinium and the Empire. Three among you have been found guilty and sentenced to death for their crimes. Despite the depth of their insults to the city, we shall offer them that which is always offered to the condemned on their last night on this earth."

My eye snagged on Governor Actaeon. His expression was thunderous. He clearly did not deem us entitled to the single last wish offered by tradition.

"Marcus Courtenay. Speak. What would you have on this, your last night on earth?"

Marcus looked miserable and in shock. He shook his head, asking for nothing.

My knees threatened to give way. I couldn't fall now. An arm reached under mine, steadying me. Unthinking, I turned to thank the guard for his assistance. The not unsympathetic eyes of Kasen met mine.

"Cassandra Shelton, what would you have as a boon on your last night on earth?"

I blinked, trying to extract a coherent thought from my scrambled brain.

"Lord High Justice, it is my wish to spend my last night in the arms of my lover." I spoke clearly, projecting my voice so my answer was heard. I smiled as I turned to my partner in amorous crime. "The Briton, Devyn Agrestis."

If I was going down, I might as well make sure that the full extent of my crimes was disclosed to the city. As the crowd erupted at this latest revelation, the governor grabbed hold of Calchas, forcing him to turn and face him, no doubt telling him how to deal with the unruly cat I had just let out of the bag. What would they do now that Devyn's true origin was revealed? Would he get a stay of execution? My aim had merely been to stick one in the eye of the oh-so-clever praetor, but I smiled as I realised the bonus effect of my revelation.

Praetor Calchas had not named Devyn as a Briton when judging him yesterday, calculatingly remiss for the sake of the peace. The Britons could not protest the execution of one of their own if the council could plead ignorance. Publicly killing Devyn as a Briton, while not in violation of the terms of the 1772 Treaty, would be diplomatically disruptive.

Calchas stepped forwards once more, raising his arms until the furore calmed.

"Donna Shelton, your claim appears to be a desperate attempt to delay justice being done. We found nothing to support such spurious claims in our investigations into your friend's activities. However, we would welcome anyone who can come forward and substantiate such a claim." Calchas smiled to the audience in what would appear to be a magnanimous manner; they had already begun hissing their displeasure at this perceived generosity, hungry for the promised blood. Calchas raised his hands once more to quieten the growing grumbles.

"Devyn Agrestis, unfortunately, there can be no last wish for you while this matter is open. For now, a stay of execution is in place." Again, his sodding pause for dramatic effect. "You have until noon tomorrow, after which your blood will stain the sands as your lover burns."

So much for my plan to outwit Calchas. Nobody would step forward, not if they valued their own lives. No one from beyond the walls would confirm his origins – word simply wouldn't reach them in time – but the Praetor would be seen to have tried to discover the veracity of my claims when the Britons came to learn what had happened. All too late, of course.

With a wave of his hands, we were pulled from the sands. I felt numb, disconnected from my body, slumping to the floor when we returned to our cell.

Marcus didn't recreate his light when the door closed. I was glad; I couldn't face them, couldn't have them see me. I needed the moment to fall apart. Devyn had risked his life to find me and Marcus had tried to help us escape. Now we were all going to die.

The heavy silence was broken by the sound of someone opening our door. But no solitary guard stood outside with our dinner. In his place stood many heavily armed sentinels with Alvar at their head. He was glaring in at us. Involuntarily, I curled in on myself away from the sliver of light coming in through the open doorway. It was too soon. I locked eyes with Devyn. I wasn't ready.

I wasn't ready.

Chapter Four

I stood up in the freestanding copper bath, its scented waters swooshing as I stepped out and reached for the towel. Laid out on a chair by the window was a beautiful deep-blue satin gown. I pulled it on and turned to look at my reflection. I barely recognised myself in the alluring, sophisticated gown. Unlike the usual gowns I wore on formal occasions, there was no hint of the innocent debutante to this low-cut dress. It was a thing of mystery and seduction. It looked like my last boon was actually being granted.

The brand-new cosmetics laid out for me by the sink were all my preferred colours and brands. I needed little though; my eyes sparkled, and my cheeks were flushed. Apparently impending death agreed with me, or perhaps it was anticipation of the night I had been granted. One last night with Devyn before the guards inevitably came to return me to the sands where I would be burned at the stake. My chest tightened at the reminder, the horror of such a death tingling at my flesh. I put it to one side. There was no point spending my last hours on this earth worrying about the pain ahead of me. I should enjoy what time remained to me. Time with Devyn.

After the Mete, the sentinels had taken Marcus, then an hour later they returned for Devyn, and an interminable time after that they finally came for me.

Calchas was too smart to transport us across the city together. Instead, he ensured that any escape attempt had to wait until we were reunited in our new prison. Or rather, in the praetor's residence. The White Tower was a building inside a fortress from more militant times. Built over a thousand years ago, it had for a time held Briton prisoners – or at least the noble ones captured in battle. Many of them had been executed in the grounds. The tower ceased to be used as a high-end prison in the last couple of centuries of peace and had more recently become the residence of the Province's commander of the legions, the highest judge in the land, whose hospitality we were enjoying this evening.

Finally dressed, I tried the latch on the heavy oak door and finding that it opened, I stepped through, where I was greeted by a waiting guard who indicated that I should follow him down the winding stairs.

We passed through stone corridors until we came to a dark wooden door which opened to reveal a warm room with tapestry-covered walls and a large formal dining table.

Devyn sat stiffly on one side with Marcus opposite. Praetor Calchas was seated at the head of the table. I looked around, half dreading to find my own parents – or at least Senator Dolon – here for our final evening meal.

"Yes, just us. The governor considers you vermin. His only concern is to have you wiped from the surface of the earth as soon as can be arranged." He had answered a question I had neither asked nor wondered at. Why did he think we would expect the governor? To have found ourselves at the praetor's table was surprise enough. "Particularly Master Agrestis here, who looks so much better than the last time we met."

Devyn's jaw clenched at this. He had no memory of the flogging he received on his last visit to the arena.

"I had my suspicions that you weren't acting alone, as you insisted," Calchas continued, gesturing to us to partake of the food spread in front of us, the picture of a gracious host. "No mean feat to persuade Governor Actaeon not to spill the blood of a hacker into the sands at his earliest convenience. Little did I think that removing your wounds and memories would reap such rich rewards."

His deceptively paternal countenance surveyed us each in turn, his manner that of a benevolent uncle.

"Such unexpected and unsettling rewards. The city's darling couple brought so low by a Briton." His lips turned down in false dismay.

Something about the way he said it caught my attention. He turned from Devyn to look directly at me, filling my glass as he spoke.

"Yes, Donna Shelton, I knew before your little announcement today that your boyfriend is a Briton; we've known since we brought him in. Had a citizen committed the crime of hacking, the sentence would have been instant death. When we captured Master Agrestis here, we did our usual thorough investigations and discovered his existence was a thing of fiction. No friends to speak of and no family – at all. Oh, they were recorded in our databases, but we had difficulty tracking down these people in real life. Turns out there was no real life up until ten years ago. So, what is a Briton doing behind the walls? Who is he working with? What is he doing here? We were curious... and it appears that curiosity has paid off." He smiled, beatifically, at the three of us. "As here we all are."

"So glad it worked out for you," Marcus commented sourly.

"Dr Courtenay... or do you prefer Lord Courtenay?" the praetor asked superciliously, as he filled Marcus's glass, in turn gesturing for him to eat his as yet untouched meal.

"Dr Courtenay is fine," Marcus gritted.

"Ah, the medical persona that drove you to betray your home." Calchas tutted. "Your mother's son, and, like her, destined to die before your time."

Marcus frowned, but our host had already turned back to me once more.

"Little Cassandra. You appear to be the focus of all this chaos." His eyes flicked to Devyn. "Our foundling whom we cared for as one of our own, our generosity so poorly repaid. How quickly you turned against us. Such a shame. We were going to create a new generation who had not only magic but technology under their control. We would have ruled the whole island. But our attempts will most likely lead to it all unravelling," Calchas sighed.

Praetor Calchas was part of Dolon's faction. Of course he was. This was who pulled the strings. I was quickly coming to loathe this man who was so impressed with his own cleverness. I had always felt like whoever was behind it all was a step ahead of us every time. I hadn't ever imagined it would all be explained with such insufferable smugness. It made me even madder that we had been so outwitted. As if someone who was about to lose their life could possibly be any more dismayed at having been caught.

"You did this to rule the island. You wanted to use our

49

children to wage war on the Britons?" I asked.

"Oh no, we didn't need your children to be full-grown to wage war; the war has already begun. Even now, change is sweeping through the country. Having your children would have ensured we controlled two of the greatest magical bloodlines. The Britons have weakened; they are not what they once were." Calchas took a sip of his drink. "With both of you under our control, we could finally take Britannia. But of course, we had reckoned without Actaeon's fervour. He is a true son of the Empire. Assimilate or die. If the Britons won't be subdued then he will eradicate them from the Earth. There will be no exceptions. The Maledictio has swept through the rest of the Empire so there are plenty of loyal citizens to occupy cleared space."

I frowned, trying to follow the politics of the power struggle within the council. Matthias had been involved with the faction that wanted to control magic and, presumably, ultimately the entire island; Actaeon wanted to rule the island too but was happy to empty it first.

"You wanted to have the greatest of our bloodlines under your control. It was quite the stroke of luck that Cassandra dropped into your clutches," Devyn observed quietly. He had noticed what I had missed. The two greatest bloodlines... Calchas knew I wasn't a random latent.

"Luck, ha! There is no such thing as luck; you make your own luck. Or not." He turned to me again. "We gave you all a girl could desire, all the comforts of the Empire, yet you threw it all away. And for what?"

My throat was dry, constricted. Not trusting myself to speak, I sat mutely. More than anything, I had wanted to be a long way from here, out of the tangle of streets and buildings, away from the overbearingly suffocating society I had grown up in; I wanted to return to the Wilds where, I had learned, my true home lay. Now, I would never see it.

I looked at Devyn. He had found me and revealed the truth to me. Tomorrow I would be executed, but at least I wouldn't die in ignorance. And there was still hope he would live a long life, that he would see days that were to be stolen from me. I set my jaw. It wasn't over yet.

"Ah. True love. It is enough for you to imagine he will make it back to whatever cave he crawled out of. How adorable." The Praetor failed to suppress a snigger. "Donna Shelton, really? You think your would-be rescuer will ever see the outside of the arena again? Much less the outside of the city?"

He intended to follow through despite my announcement to the world that Devyn was not an imperial citizen. It was over 200 years since the 1772 Treaty ended the centuries of war that had ripped the island apart. Devyn's presence behind the walls was in clear violation of the terms. But that didn't mean his execution would be accepted by those beyond the walls.

"You can't," I protested. From the moment I discovered that Devyn was a Briton, I had known that capture would mean death, but the recent Treaty Renewal had reminded me of something. The Empire was not alone on this island and Devyn had friends beyond the walls. He served a house in the north. Surely that meant something. "You can't know what the Britons will do if you kill one of their own."

"You think they will object? Perhaps," Calchas mocked. "But we did not accuse him of being Briton. There is no proof to be found of Master Agrestis's true origin. In fact, we have all

51

of that clever work he did in the city's databases that proves otherwise."

The insufferable Praetor Calchas actually smiled in his delight at the irony. "I do hope you're enjoying your meal. We've even got some rather delicious apple cake. I thought you might appreciate it, Master Agrestis – a final taste of home. I believe it is a seasonal speciality served at your Samhain celebrations. This is the last one you will live to see begin, even if you won't see it end."

Devyn hadn't spoken or even deigned to look at our host while his own imminent demise was so casually discussed; he had taken little interest in any of the proceedings, apart from Calchas's slip-up regarding my own origin. But now his eyes wandered to the sideboard where there sat a cake with dried apple on top, surrounded by hazelnuts and chestnuts; his interest piqued at the suggestion of a last taste of home. The city didn't usually mark the last night of October. Samhain, as the Britons called it, was a night for the Wilders and their superstitions; it had no place inside the city.

But it was clear that Calchas relished the idea of executing his captured Briton on a date that meant something to the rest of the island. Did someone as esteemed and preeminent as the praetor do something as juvenile as flick off the enemy? Before tonight I wouldn't have thought so. He had always appeared so righteous, but the man who sat crowing at our capture and imminent executions... of him I would believe it.

We ate course after course while the praetor chattered on about inconsequential city matters as if we had all the time in the world. This was how I was to spend my last night alive?

The last course was finally set on the table – a sumptuous lemon parfait – fresh plates laid out in front of all of us but

Devyn. A servant cut a slice of the Wilder apple cake and left the room, a sentinel entering as the servant exited.

"No Wilder food will ever grace my table. You are free to eat it elsewhere." Calchas's eyes rolled to the sentinel.

This left Devyn no choice but to leave the table after casting a last look at me. I had asked to spend what hours I had left to me with Devyn. Was that it? Would I never see him again?

"Don't worry, girl, I'll release you to join him shortly." Calchas finished his last mouthful of dessert while Marcus and I sat behind our untouched plates.

Odious man! I smiled in as close an approximation of gratitude as I could manage, even as every muscle in my body unclenched at his announcement.

"Marcus, would you care to join me for a drink while Cassandra enjoys her last wish?" Calchas said, pushing back his chair.

"Not really," Marcus replied flatly.

Calchas laughed as he made his way around the table to stand behind my chair, preventing me from pushing it out and leaving the table. "Did you think refusal was an option, Dr Courtenay? It was most gallant of you to allow your betrothed to spend her last night with her lover. Especially as you are so unlikely to enjoy it."

Marcus frowned, not following Calchas's latest gleeful pronouncement. "What do you mean?"

Calchas delayed answering. Instead, his fingers touched my bare neck and traced along my shoulder. I stifled a shudder of repulsion. "The last time the lovely Cassandra so wickedly betrayed you with the Wilder, you had yet to be handfasted, which you have been now for a while. At this point you would have been married. The wedding was scheduled for yesterday, was it not?"

I struggled to concentrate against the bile rising within me as Calchas allowed his fingers to traverse my shoulder and descend along my arm.

"Have you not felt the burning in the blood and passions rising?" Calchas asked Marcus archly. "But then, you have all been so very busy. Except, the handfast is not designed to handle a third wheel. You recall how you felt when your match encountered Master Agrestis in the hospital."

Enlightenment dawned and Marcus's eyes caught and held mine across the table. Calchas knew Marcus was affected when Devyn and I were together. It was Marcus's reaction to this effect that had alerted our security detail to Devyn's presence in the hospital after the handfast. What Calchas didn't seem to be aware of was our recent discovery that while we both wore our charms, this effect was almost entirely countered.

Our host's eyes flicked from me to Marcus, his delight in our feigned horror evident. He was a cat playing with trapped mice.

"You're disgusting." I pulled my arm away from Calchas's wandering fingers.

"Sorry, my dear, I don't mean to detain you any further." I waited for him to pull back the chair. His hands returned to my skin, touching my neck as he released the catch of the necklace I wore. In reflex I snatched at it; without it I had no defence against the effects of the handfast. In fact, they would have to drag me to Devyn's room. I held the rose gold pendant tight, my thumb worrying against the etched Celtic design on the back, as if I could imprint the triquetra charm onto my very flesh.

"Now, now, Cassandra, I think this little device has served its purpose, don't you? Such a clever little contraption. Our scientists haven't quite figured out how it manages to block the coding embedded in the cuff, but it has served its purpose."

It appeared that they figured out, as we had, that while wearing the charm the desire to comply with the city's dictates was countered. But it sounded as if they hadn't discovered its primary purpose: to hide its wearer from the cameras and microphones that covered the city. I hadn't failed to notice that in Marcus and Devyn's evidentiary reels, there was little coverage from those times the charms were activated. The triquetra charms succeeded in obscuring us from general surveillance but failed to deflect the focus when the cameras were directed at a specific subject, like in Oban's apartment; the rest must have come from physical tails who managed to capture us in public. This explained the sensation I had a few times of being followed. I refocused on Calchas's monologue.

"...After all, it was only fair that you should be fully cognisant of the events that brought you onto the sand. However, you failed to include it as a condition of your boon when you had your little fun this afternoon," Calchas crowed. His revenge for my revelation that Devyn was a Briton was to allow me to spend the night with Devyn knowing that as soon as he removed the pendant, my deepest wish to be with Devyn would become the last thing I wanted.

"Please," I whispered. I had to beg. Thankfully Calchas didn't know everything: as long as I allowed Devyn to get close enough, his presence alone would counter the effects of the handfast. Though, sitting with Marcus, Calchas would be able to tell that his plan to ruin our night had failed. Devyn would have to get close enough for me to tell him about Calchas's little game but then if I was to die tomorrow night, what difference did it make anyway?

Calchas peeled my fingers slowly off the pendant as I

stared across at Marcus. What should I do? Marcus's eyes flicked to his wristband; he would be protected from eavesdropping, as it were, while he wore it – to a degree anyway – so despite Calchas's repugnant games, we would have privacy.

The pendant removed, Calchas dropped it carelessly onto his dirty dessert plate and pulled my chair back, helping me to stand.

"Now," he said, his lips parting in a pout, "we must bid you goodnight. Time for you to make your appointment, Donna Shelton."

I blinked in confusion; the transition back to compliant citizen always left me dazed for a moment. Why was I arm in arm with the Praetor? I looked around the room. Servants were entering busily and clearing the table by which I stood, one leaning in front of the man who was sitting on the other side of the table to collect the plates in front of him.

"Marcus," I breathed in relief as the servant moved away.

Praetor Calchas smiled at me. "Marcus and I are going to have a little chat, Donna Shelton. His father is joining us for drinks. You are meeting a friend down the hall."

I looked to Marcus in confusion, and he nodded tightly. Lord Calchas instructed me to follow the guard who had just escorted Matthias Dolon into the room and I took my leave.

As we walked down the dark stone hallway, recent memories started to tumble into my mind. Preparing for my wedding, the night of the pre-wedding revels, Devyn appearing, Marcus, the warehouse, the arena, the cell in the amphitheatre. It all came flooding back in a bombardment of images. Death. I had been sentenced to death for my part in... Oh! I needed to go back to Marcus. How was this happening? I needed him to help me make sense of all this. I needed him.

The guard, noticing that I was no longer following him, returned and caught my arm. He marched me along the hall as I tried to process the scenes that were flooding my mind. Before I quite got a handle on it and was enough in my right mind to run back to Marcus, I was pushed into a room, and the door slammed behind me. I tried the latch but it wouldn't budge.

I needed to get back to Marcus. I looked around the room in which I was now locked. There was a decadent four-poster bed and a heavy brocade curtain on the other side of a room. There must be a window. Could I get out that way? I crossed the room quickly.

"Cass." A warm voice alerted me to the presence of another person in the room. I paused to take in the sight of Devyn Agrestis sitting in a large chair, his features highlighted by the play of the shadows cast by the fire. "I've been waiting for you."

What was he doing here? Ignoring him, I crossed to the curtain and pulled it back to reveal a lead-lined window. I opened the antique catch and leaned out into the night. My stomach dipped. We were many storeys above the ground. I looked out across the glittering lights of the glass and steel towers, the multi-levels of the city to my left. The old wall, low and wide, ran along to the right, and beyond that was the teeming warren of the East End. I could also see the crenellated walls on the far side of the cobbled courtyard below. I appeared to be in the White Tower. I had never been inside before. The lack of building in the air above us confirmed it; only a few of the oldest buildings in the city were so privileged.

I didn't understand what was going on. I wrapped my arms about myself. They had brought me here after the Mete, I recalled. The Mete where I... I stepped back from the cold air coming in through the window. None of this made sense. My progress was halted by a warm body behind me. Startled, I turned into a wall of bare chest. I looked up and my lips were caught. My hands came up to push him away but ended up tangled in black curls. My head tilted back to allow him access to my neck and the décolletage on display as a result of my wondrous dress.

His name was a sigh leaving my lips as his proximity worked its magic and reality returned. I turned into him. Kisses rained down on my bare flesh, my lips captured once more by his. It was like a spark catching on tinder, a kind of blue and red flickering passing across my skin, lighting me up from the inside out. He walked me backwards until I found myself folded onto a bed. A bed with a beautifully embroidered canopy. Devyn. Calchas. I was myself once again.

"Devyn, wait." I tried to catch my breath.

His fingers found the catch at my waist and the silken dress unhooked and fell off my body, allowing Devyn greater access. His skin, his torso were against mine, warm velvet heating me in the darkness of the room which was lit only by the flickering open fire. By the fire sat the remains of the apple cake, the cake Calchas made certain only Devyn ate. I could taste its heavenly flavour on the lips that danced with mine.

I tried to think. I needed to stop him, didn't I? But did it matter now? Why stop? I felt what Devyn felt, the fire, the heat surging through him. I could practically feel how delicious my touch on his skin felt to him, the drugging pull to surrender entirely to sensation. Need. Want. Our connection was oxygen to the flames, our bodies the fuel. We were here together. That was all. That was everything.

My fingers came back around to Devyn's face, so

exquisitely lit by the firelight, his dark eyes gleaming. The fire licked through me, the heat swooshing through my blood, stoked by the touch of his hands sweeping across my bare skin, touching my leg and following it up under the blue satin. I moaned at the blaze that swept through me. Deeper, deeper, I felt Devyn, his complete focus on me, on us, on this.

Something wasn't right. I arched back as Devyn kissed a trail down my skin. Our lives were in danger. I needed to think. I opened my eyes wide, trying to focus on something, anything, outside of my body and the maelstrom of sensation whirling within. The canopy... there was a canopy over our heads. Because we were in the White Tower, enjoying the hospitality of the praetor. We weren't locked in a cell; surely the security was laxer here. We needed to escape, or tomorrow we would die. Tonight was our only chance. I attempted to pull away and Devyn swooped back up, skin sliding on warm skin.

"Cass," he murmured as he caught my lips in his, his kiss deep and possessive, fresh fuel on the fire sending sparks flickering through my body. I couldn't breathe; I didn't need to. Devyn was my breath. I fell into his kiss, the drugging sensation bringing me back down, stealing my consciousness. I was mesmerised by the flame towards which he was drawing me. I no longer wanted to see. My pupils felt dilated by the sheer magic he caused within me. I looked up into the midnight eyes above me. Devyn's pupils were glazed, unfocused. I looked over to the blaze in the fireplace. My eye caught again the remains of food there.

Calchas sent me in here after taking the protection of the triquetra charm from around my neck. Devyn's kisses were mindless, fevered, as if passion were the only thing that drove him. The only thing that existed. Tonight of all nights. It made no sense. How could he be so singularly focused?

The bridal tea. The concoction they gave us before and during the handfast to stoke our passions… He had given it to Devyn. But why? It made no sense. Was there some motivation that I was missing or was it just that he couldn't resist manipulating us one last time?

I swung away so that I was above Devyn. I sat up, allowing the fresh air wafting in from the open window to wash over me, cooling my heated skin. Devyn's hand came up to pull me back down. I caught it in my own and held it to me. I adored his hands. I adored the strength in them, the slight calluses on his palm evidence of a physical past that gave away the truth of his childhood spent far from the city; I adored the sinews I could trace through his dark skin, the pulse of life at his wrist. I sucked in a breath. Think, I needed to think. Devyn's other hand came up, and I took both and pinned them either side of his head. He looked up at me, perplexed, allowing it despite his heated blood and superior strength. I sent a pulse of the fear I felt for tomorrow through me and his eyes cooled.

"Snap out of it," I urged him.

"What, Cass? Come here to me." He lifted his head to try to kiss me once more. I so badly wanted to be kissed. I leaned in, my grip lessening, allowing Devyn to wrap his hands into my hair. I groaned, giving in to it. My mind and body were pure sensation.

There was a commotion outside in the hallway. I sat up as the door burst open. Devyn pushed himself up and manoeuvred me behind him, his instinct to protect me always greater than anything else. I stared at the door, willing my foggy brain to clear. I pulled in a deep breath.

Marcus stood in the doorway, his burning gaze fixed on me.

"Get dressed," he snapped, his nostrils flared, his body all tension. "We need to go."

I looked at him in confusion.

"My father is helping us escape. Hurry."

Devyn was also slowly coming back to the real world. He shook his head as if to shake it off. The fire clearly still burnt within him, the embers hot ready to flare again.

"Devyn?" I called tentatively. He turned to look at me, his dark gaze still smouldering. My eyes flicked to Marcus in the doorway. Praetorian Alvar's second in command, Kasen, strode in behind Marcus. The normally diffident praetorian surveyed the room, taking in the scene, instantly understanding what I was still only starting to understand myself.

"Get dressed," he echoed Marcus, throwing a bundle at the bed. "Now."

I jumped out on the far side of the canopied four-poster, the curtain affording me a little belated privacy. My breath was still dragging through my lungs and my hands trembled as I pulled on the dark clothing Kasen had had the foresight to bring. My blue satin gown was not exactly the outfit of choice for a Codebreaker on the run.

I took Devyn's hand to pull him along with us as we followed Kasen, racing through the stone hallways, down winding stairs, and slowing to walk casually across the courtyard to the gate leading out to the river. Kasen and Marcus went to the side of the gate where a heavily caped Matthias waited, the trellis slowly lifting to reveal a boat beyond.

Devyn and Marcus leapt across the railing into the boat as I took Matthias's hand to aid my undignified scramble across the railing into the bobbing hovercraft.

I looked on in horror as the gate was lowered back down with Kasen on the other side watching as we pulled out onto the river.

I looked at Matthias for an explanation.

"He'll be fine." Matthias waved dismissively.

"What? But they'll know he helped us."

"No, they won't. While the praetor likes to keep an eye on the city, there are no cameras in his own home," Matthias explained. "Calchas will only blame me when he wakes up."

"When he wakes up?" I questioned.

"I slipped a little something into his after-dinner drink." Matthias nodded to his son. "All we had to do was wait until we were alone after dinner and servants were no longer coming in or out. And goodnight, Praetor Calchas."

"Why? How?" I asked Matthias, still slightly disbelieving that this was happening even as we swept through the night.

"Why?" Matthias repeated haughtily. "Marcus is my son. As for you two, he will need help once he crosses the border. As for how, once you were in the tower it was almost too easy."

"But it was built to be a fortress."

"True. A fortress whose main purpose has always been to keep safe the most important members of our society. Council members used to have automatic access to a number of public buildings via a biometric setting for use in the event of an attack that breached the walls. The practice has been abandoned in peacetime, and of course the tower is practically a private dwelling these days. I'm sure Calchas hasn't ever given it a thought. The thing with old biometric technology is that it was built not just for a single lifetime, but for the duration of that genetic line. He brought the key to get through the river gate inside with you."

"Marcus," I identified, recalling the way Praetorian Kasen had grabbed Marcus's hand to touch the lock when we arrived at the gate. His touch had released the catch.

"Indeed." Matthias nodded. "All chips were bet on the fact that Calchas wouldn't be able to resist bringing you to his home to have a little play with the dolls he hadn't been able to make dance to his tune."

"You knew he would bring us to the tower?"

"I was relying on it, did what I could to seed the idea after I left you all last night. It fell on fertile soil. Nobody has ever circumvented the handfast before. Calchas was fascinated by the fact that you had done so; he was obsessed with it. What had tipped Marcus off that Devyn Agrestis was in Barts? How had you gone from being a good, compliant citizen firmly in the grip of the handfast to one who was clearly lying? What was it between you and Agrestis that managed to bypass a compulsion which has enabled the city to dictate and socially engineer the population for centuries? After Richmond, when Alvar brought in the pendant, he had the tapes reviewed and he knew you hadn't been wearing it when Agrestis broke into the hospital," he explained grimly as he casually navigated the river. "Calchas loves control; he is the ultimate puppet master. Everything and everyone in this city is on a string, and he makes us dance. You broke free, and he had limited time to figure it out. The temptation to dress you up and have a little private, scripted theatrical night once he had all three of you in his power would have been irresistible to him. I encouraged it; all I asked in return was the opportunity to speak to my son one last time. I'm just grateful he didn't drug all three of you; I wouldn't have put it past him. Though I suppose there was only one of you he couldn't guarantee would play along, and after the events of the last months, he must have enjoyed ensuring he had control of your Briton. Speaking of which, there is a flask in that trunk over there. Give it to your Briton; it might help."

I retrieved the drink and handed it to Devyn. His dark eyes, a little glazed, still burning, were more interested in watching me than following the life-saving escape we were making across the city. Marcus appeared to have recovered more successfully, and he was far more interested in surveying the other traffic on the river as our hovercraft slipped silently through the night.

My hand reached for the comfort of my pendant, the gesture changing as I anxiously rubbed at the bare skin of my neck.

Matthias flashed his thin-lipped smile my way.

"I'm afraid we couldn't get the necklace back. We'll have to rely on the handfast to keep you with Marcus and ensure you don't try to make your way back to the city at your first opportunity, despite the fiery stake that awaits you," Matthias warned.

Even without the charmed pendant, I was confident I wouldn't be relying on the handfast to keep me with my companions. Devyn's presence was more than enough to negate the compulsion to comply with the wishes of my match and the city; as long as he was near I was operating under my own will. And that would never lead me back to the city. Marcus still wore the other charm and it seemed wiser to leave it in his possession in case the cuff did cloud his judgement and urge him to return to the city. As long as he had the charm, and I had Devyn, we would be fine.

"The handfast is not just technology, it's wrapped with magic and it will continue to work outside the walls." Matthias misread my confidence that I would be able to resist the handfast compulsion beyond the walls.

"I don't understand. There's magic in the cuff? But handfasting is codified." Even though we had suspected this was the case, it still came as a shock. The city abhorred magic, had fought wars against the magic-wielding Britons for millennia, had eradicated every trace of it within the walls.

"It was a joint venture between the Britons and us. The handfast was the glue that held the Treaty together," Matthias offered cryptically.

"What does it have to do with the Treaty?" Devyn had given me the short version of this but it couldn't hurt to play dumb and see if there was more to be learned.

"Without the Treaty, there would be no Marcus. Marcus's existence is living proof of the Treaty."

Matthias had grown bored with my questions and slipped back into being the supercilious ass with whom I was more familiar. I frowned as if I didn't follow.

Marcus took his eyes off the river to look at me. His hand came up to trace the etchings on the cuff that sat on his upper arm.

"They were created to ensure the Treaty would stick because the marriage that bound it together would itself be solid," he elaborated. I shook my head as if still not understanding, and Marcus went on. "Think about it, Cassandra. The Empire had been at war with the Britons for ever. My great-great-great-grandfather would have hated everything about the York princess he had to marry. And she him. They had spent their lives shedding the blood of each other's friends and families. Both sides were invested in that marriage holding, in them having children of mixed blood who would be living symbols to the city of the peace."

"Oh." This was pretty much what Devyn had been able to discover, that the handfast cuffs were a legacy of the marriage that had sealed the Treaty just as much as Marcus was. The device was created to bind together a couple forced into a union that both of them must have hated, then used to manipulate generation after generation of the city's sons and daughters. It was a band locked on your arm that instilled in you a desire to please your parents, to comply with the Code, to want to be with the partner your parents had arranged for you. It was diabolical. Our society was built upon lie after lie and it was a cycle that was repeated over and over. My chest tightened as I surveyed the banks of the river. The wall of towers constructed right up to the river's edge seemed to loom more oppressively than ever. I lifted my face to the night sky, closing my eyes to my last sight of the city that had been my home. I allowed the wind to whip through me, cleansing me of the last traces of the controlling clutches of the people who ran it.

We were already at the western wall, and because the hovercraft was flying the council flag, we were waved on without further inspection by the sentinels guarding the western gate through which I had passed on my previous escape attempt. The policy about passage through the walls being forbidden after dark did not apply to the council as it did to regular citizens.

Devyn had almost returned to himself and was listening keenly. He didn't trust Matthias; even now, as he helped us escape, the overriding emotion from Devyn was wariness. Had the senator changed sides so completely? I had witnessed for myself his lack of affection towards Marcus. Why throw everything away now to help him escape? Yet that was what he had done.

"Father!" Marcus's alarmed cry cut across us. He pointed to a boat coming around the bend behind us. "That boat has stayed with us all the way from the tower. It's following us. I'm sure of it."

"Let's put a little speed on and see what they do." Matthias pulled back on the throttle and the nose of the boat lifted, throwing us backwards. We watched to see whether the only other active craft on this part of the river responded. Because the river in the city was generally thick with traffic, citizens often joked that if you timed it right, you could walk across the Tamesis without ever needing a bridge. Around the docks was, of course, the busiest, but that traffic petered out as you went further inland. By the time you got to the inner wall on the east of the city there were no more great ships. There were plenty of barges delivering cargo to the warehouses, lots of little hackneys zipping about, but on the other side of the western wall, towards Richmond, boats were few and far between, especially at this time of night.

Matthias eased off the throttle as we came into Richmond. There was a long stretch here and still no sign of the boat that had been trailing us. I allowed myself to relax a little.

Devyn turned his attention back to Matthias, like a hawk hunting a mouse.

"How did you find Cassandra?" Devyn asked out of nowhere. Calchas had taunted us that finding me and matching me to Marcus had not been a matter of chance. Matthias and Calchas had plotted together. This man had to know the truth of my abduction.

Matthias ignored the question.

"Once we're back in our lands, I'm the only thing that's going to keep us alive. It's a long way to York."

"Touché." Matthias slashed Devyn with his snake-in-the-grass smile. He looked over at his son and back at Devyn; whatever he saw there clearly decided him. "You will see him to York. Promise me."

Devyn nodded. "Is that where your ally is?"

What ally? Did Devyn suspect a traitor? Did he suspect that someone had betrayed my mother, that someone had helped them steal me away? Was this why Calchas's earlier bombshell had sent him reeling?

Matthias shook his head, "No, I…"

"Look." Marcus grabbed his father by the shoulder, pointing towards not one but three boats that were now approaching us at speed. "We are caught."

"Not yet," Matthias pulled the throttle all the way back. The hovercraft shot forward, flying across the water. "If any of you have any tricks you can use, now would be the time."

I focused, willing the night to answer my call. I felt nothing in response.

"I still can't; it's not there," I yelled, raising my voice to be heard across the wind ripping my words away into the night. "At the arena, they injected us."

"We'll just have to hope our technology holds out then," Marcus shouted back.

We sped through the night. Richmond whipped by, and we were out, well past the furthest point I had ever been from the city. The pursuing boats chased us across the water, the sky behind them bright with the orange light of Londinium while we raced forwards into the black wall of the west. The only light was the tunnel made by the headlight at the front of the hovercraft.

Matthias glanced back over his shoulder. "We aren't going to lose them, and sooner or later the tech will fail. While we still have a lead, I'll pull in to one of the islands in the river.

You three jump out and hide, and I'll lure them further on. It will give you a chance."

Devyn nodded his agreement even as Marcus started to disagree. "No, Father. What about you?"

Matthias shrugged. "There was always a chance I would get caught. They may not actually be hunting you down. Maybe we just attracted the attention of a patrol. I may yet be able to talk myself out of it; I'm still a member of the council. Now, get ready. Grab the bags from the locker; you'll need them on the road."

Marcus protested, but his father just looked at him. "I said, go."

We pulled on the packs and prepared to jump.

"There." We had passed several small islands in the middle of the river, and a series of bends meant that we were also out of the line of sight of the pursuing boats. "Ready?"

He slowed the hovercraft and pulled in to the tree-covered island. We jumped into the dark. The water was freezing and I couldn't catch my breath. I felt a hand pulling me upwards and we all pushed through the tall reeds and pulled ourselves up onto the bank as the chasing boats flew by.

Matthias had lost his lead when he dropped us off; he couldn't be that much further ahead of them.

The noise reached us first. We turned in the direction of the boom as an explosion lit the night sky.

"No!" Marcus screamed, pulling his bag off, preparing to drop into the water and go to his father.

Devyn grabbed him. "What are you doing, you fool? You'll get us all killed."

Marcus pushed him away, every instinct – familial and medical – screaming at him to rush to the site of the fire. "That's my father. I have to help him."

"Marcus, Marcus." I stood in front of him, trying to get his attention as Devyn continued to hold him back. I grabbed his face so he would look down at me. "He's gone. I'm sorry, I'm so sorry. There is no way he could have survived. He's gone."

Marcus stilled, his stricken face ghostly in the night.

"You don't know that."

"Nobody could have lived through that."

Marcus slumped to the floor, all fight gone out of him.

Chapter Five

Marcus sat unmoving in his wet clothes, blankly staring at the night sky still lit up by after-effects of the explosion that had most likely killed his father.

"We need to move," Devyn urged. "We need to get through the borderlands as quickly as possible."

I looked over at Marcus. We had prevented him from going to his father, the father who showed him so little love in his lifetime but who ultimately gave his life to save his only son. Would the father whom I had always been so sure adored me have done the same? I had grown up showered with whatever my heart desired, but when it mattered, when everything I believed turned out to be a lie and I was sentenced to death, my parents had been noticeably absent. Meanwhile, the conniving power-hungry Matthias had risked and lost all to save Marcus. I couldn't even begin to imagine Marcus's pain at the loss, made so much worse by the twisted relationship he had with his father.

The sentinels' boats passed by us, making no attempt to scan the banks – a sure sign that they presumed all passengers had died in the explosion. One of the boats was towing the other, most likely because the power had failed this close to the border ley line. Once they had gone, the darkness once again was lit only by the fire further upstream.

Marcus continued to stare with unseeing eyes across the water. We had been here for hours, stuck in the immobility of his grief.

"We have to leave," Devyn whispered to me.

I nodded. I knew we needed to be on our way – the further away from the city we were the better. I had no desire to return there anytime soon. Honestly, it was past time that one of these attempts to escape just stuck.

I went over to Marcus and put my hand on his arm.

"Marcus…" No response. I repeated his name in the hope of getting some flicker of answer. Nothing. I turned back to Devyn. "Maybe we could give him another moment or two."

"We can't. It will be morning soon. We need to go north but the new day is Samhain – not a good time to be crossing the borderlands. Once the sun rises, it won't be safe to be here." Devyn shook his head, correcting himself. "While the sun is up, the borderlands will be perilous, but to be caught in them after dark will be suicidal."

I frowned. Admittedly, I knew very little about the world outside the walls, but I wasn't aware that the borderlands were dangerous to travellers. Not that there was much traffic; it's not like we had a trade agreement with the Britons. As far as I knew, the only people who ever crossed the borderlands were the Britons who came to the city every four years to renew the treaty that merely kept the peace. But surely meeting Britons would be a good thing.

"Are there sentinel patrols?" I asked. I was reminded of the one I had seen in my vision, the one that had cut down my mother when I was a baby.

"Not patrols; the borderlands are wide, and both sides monitor live movement," Devyn explained further at my frown. "If any sizeable force were to try to cross the borderlands, it would trigger magical alarms. Conversely, if a Briton force were to approach the city, there is no doubt it would set off a warning inside the walls. So it was during wartime, and so it is in peacetime too."

"How did you get into the city, then?" How did a sixteen-year-old intent on finding a lost child cross mile after mile of land rigged with alarms? No matter how determined or canny he was.

"On my own, I could likely have made it through the borderlands undetected, but it was easier to slip in on a boat that was coming from Calais," he explained.

"You've been to Gallia?" I was envious. This was the furthest I had ever been from Londinium – that I remembered anyway. But now, I was finally going home. An empty space within me fizzed in anticipation.

"Never mind Gallia, or how I got to Londinium." He halted me, his lips thin. "Worry about how we're going to get away from Londinium. The alarms and warnings will be the least of our concerns on Samhain."

"What does Samhain have to do with it?" I knew little more than that Samhain was one of the major festivals in the Briton calendar, a harvest festival held before the winter.

Devyn huffed, unimpressed with the know-nothing citizen. "Samhain is the day when the veil between this world and the next is at its thinnest, when those on the other side walk amongst us, and nowhere is more dangerous than the land

73

where generations have drenched the ground with their blood."

I couldn't help myself. I smirked. "Ghosts, Devyn? Really?"

He half laughed in reply. "Hocus-pocus, Cass."

Was it really only this spring that I had scoffed at the existence of magic? It seemed a lifetime ago.

He waggled his fingers in the air before walking behind me. "And things that go boo!" he whispered in my ear.

I looked at Marcus, hoping Devyn's antics weren't registering. "Shh, his father just died."

"And we will die too if we don't get a move on."

"Let's go then," Marcus said out of the darkness.

He stood up and went to his bag to change, as Devyn and I had earlier when we realised that we were going to be here for a while.

"Wait," Devyn stalled him. "There's no point. Cass and I will be taking these dry clothes off. We need to swim back to the other side of the river."

"Cassandra," Marcus grumbled, his emphasis on the all too often missing syllables. He hadn't said anything before about Devyn's shortening my name, but, perhaps because his mind was elsewhere, his irritation at the dropped half of my name came out.

We stripped down and pulled the bags onto our backs, then made our way through the tall reeds which glowed golden in the red dawn, stepping through them into the dark water of the Tamesis.

"Be careful, the current will be strong. Don't fight it; let it carry you but still make your way across," Devyn advised.

I squirmed my way into the freezing cold water. I'd had other things on my mind the first time we took a dip; this time there was no ignoring the intolerable temperature. With the boys hanging back so that I was in front of them, I had no choice but to brace myself against it and plough forward, knee-deep, hip-deep—the water seeping up the T-shirt I had left on for modesty's sake—shoulder-deep, and then the muddy, rocky riverbed was no longer reachable. I took one stroke and then another, my direction not as straight ahead as I had hoped; for each forward stroke, I was pulled several feet downstream by the current. Devyn's words repeated over and over in my mind: don't fight it, keep trying to move forward. The other side was getting closer, wasn't it?

By the time we pulled ourselves up the muddy bank on the far side, we had been swept hundreds of metres downstream. I hopped from foot to foot, trying to get warm as Devyn opened my bag; my attempts to release the zip with my frozen fingers had been feeble. He took a shirt out and roughly rubbed my body dry with it. I winced at the sensation but thanked him for his efforts. My skin felt raw, the cloth like sandpaper on my chilled body, but at least I could pull on some dry clothes.

Marcus started walking upriver along the bank before Devyn even pulled his boots back on. We quickly caught up with him.

"We don't have time for this," Devyn informed him.

Marcus didn't reply, just kept walking. The sky was now a beautiful aqua-blue and the sun had come up over the horizon behind us. It took longer than I would have expected to get to the place where Matthias's boat had been hit. It was stuck in the bank on the other side of the river, a burning husk. There was no way anyone had lived through that. If Matthias had been flung overboard, given the strength of the current, it seemed likely that he would have floated by us. Could we have missed him in the dark? It was a possibility.

Marcus pulled off the dry shirt he had donned only thirty minutes earlier.

"What are you doing?" Devyn asked sharply.

Marcus knelt to untie his boots. "What does it look like I'm doing?"

"It looks like you're being left behind. Come on, Cass." Devyn took my hand and started to move on. "Good luck."

"What? We're not leaving without him." I pulled my hand free.

"We're not waiting here while that fool crosses the river to confirm what he already knows." Devyn whirled round to shout at Marcus. "He's dead. Going over there... What's the point? If he isn't there, you have achieved nothing. If he is there, he's dead. And you'll have achieved nothing, except you will have killed us too."

Marcus glared at him with deadened eyes.

"The sentinels think we all died. Who do you think is coming for us now? Your ghosties?"

Devyn shook his head. "You're not listening. You're not in your comfortable lives behind the walls anymore. People all over the land will stay in their homes this day; they will carve out lanterns and light them in their window, so the dark doesn't cross their threshold. They will do that in the valleys, in the mountains, in the Lakelands. No one, but no one, enters the borderlands on Samhain. If we don't get moving, we will be here when the sun sets, and whatever chance we might have during the day, we have none at all at night. So you can do what you want, Dr Courtenay, but I am getting Cass out of here."

With that, he grabbed my hand in a painful grip and started marching away from the river across the field. Marcus stood watching us leave before he turned back to the shell of his father's boat and resumed taking off his boots in preparation for his next swim.

I gasped as pain shot through my arm. Devyn, unheeding, marched on, pulling me with him. My entire arm was starting to tingle before another shooting pain went through me. I bit my lip to keep from crying out, but Devyn must have felt it through our connection as he came to a stop.

"What is that?" In his single-mindedness, he had forgotten that Marcus and I were tied together.

I shook my head, unable to speak as the pain rolled through me and nausea followed in a wave after it. I crumpled onto the ground, my knees genuinely too weak to hold me up.

"Marcus!" Devyn roared as I closed my eyes, sinking into his arms. "Marcus. Please."

The pain started to ease until, looking up, I saw that Marcus had joined us.

"Are you okay, Cassandra?" he asked, not unsympathetically. "The handfast distance limit must have kicked in."

"Already? That doesn't make any sense," I said, recalling the previous time this had happened. "I was miles from you before it kicked in the last time. Here, you were still within shouting distance. In the city we lived further apart than this and nothing ever happened."

Marcus thought it over before offering, "My father mentioned that the burn in the blood gets stronger as the handfast goes on; most couples are bound for a shorter period than we have been. Maybe the distance gets shorter too."

"Or maybe it's the borderlands," Devyn said drily. "You've got to listen to me. This land is twisted; the war magic, the blood spilt... It's different here at the best of times. And at this

77

time of year, all bets are off. I am begging you. We have got to get out of here before nightfall."

Marcus surveyed him, weighing up his words. He looked back at the still smoking husk of the boat on the other side of the river before finally nodding his agreement.

"There's nothing you could have done," I said, contemplating my words carefully before attempting to offer what little comfort I could find in the awful situation. I went over and wrapped my arms around him. He stiffened before easing into the embrace and taking what was offered.

"Wait here." Devyn jogged back to pick up Marcus's backpack to save Marcus and me having to make the trip.

With one last look back at the burning boat on the other side of the Tamesis, Marcus finally pulled on his bag and we set off. We headed away from the city and the river, which I made out to be roughly northwest. Devyn set a cracking pace as we crossed fields of long green grass, so unlike the land tended by the Shadowers further east, where the fields were full of crops or livestock, stone walls marking out one farm from another. Here, there were no manmade boundaries, no signs of humans, except that I started to realise that certain dips and craters around which we wove were unlikely to be natural, but instead were signs of the fierce battles that had raged over these contested lands for centuries. Which side had created such holes in the ground? Were they the result of gunpowder and the limited technology that worked reliably this near the infamously destabilising May ley line, or were they the result of magical forces? I couldn't begin to discern.

Initially, Devyn had held my hand as we went along, picking out a path that only he could see, but as the hours passed and the sun rose in the sky, my legs began to tire and I started to lag.

"We need to take a break," Marcus finally announced. Devyn grumbled that we could walk and eat but eventually agreed to a five-minute break after looking at the heavily wooded hills ahead of us.

We perched on some rocks and rummaged through the well-provisioned bags Matthias had provided. As well as the clothes and waterproof boots of which we had already taken advantage, there were protein packs, hydration pills, pocket knives, rope, and other bits and pieces that I couldn't identify but which looked practical and survivor-y. At the bottom of each bag lay a primitive gun. Nothing as advanced as the laser-sighted weapons that the sentinels carried in the city – they would be unreliable out here – and Caesar only knew where he had managed to find such things. Matthias had done well by us. I marvelled again at the fact that he had done this for us, that a singularly ambitious and selfish man had, in the end, done right by his son. He saved us when all hope seemed lost. We were somehow alive and free.

I got up and, with a discreet smile, moved away to use nature's basic facilities. It might lack the faucet and lavatory of our cell, but I was okay with that. I was returning when Marcus let out a startled shout. I ran back, but he was standing looking at the ground, no sign of any sentinels approaching. Devyn too had stepped away and was returning at a sprint.

"What? What is it?" I cried as I ran up.

Marcus looked up and then back down at the ground.

"I don't understand," he started. "I was standing in... There was a pool at my feet."

We all looked at the spot he indicated. There was nothing there but grass and some fallen leaves.

"I saw it. It was up to my ankles. I was standing in..." Marcus shook his head.

"What did you see?" Devyn pressed.

"It was a pool of blood."

"Bags on. We have to keep walking," Devyn said, scanning the area, already moving.

Spooked, Marcus lost no time, more than happy to put distance between himself and the disappearing pool. I was less convinced, but the urgency flowing from Devyn was enough to hurry me along. As we headed into the trees, it became strangely dark; the day was golden, a magnificent late autumn gift, and the sun was evident in the sky, but under the trees, the dappled light was less bright than it should be.

My feet struggled to gain purchase as we trudged our way up the hill. I was bone tired: I was tired from the day before; I was already tired from tomorrow. My feet were raw, my legs ached, and my back was bowed in the effort of hauling myself up yet another hill.

To avoid a vast expanse of mud that the boys jumped across, I veered away to pick my way around a tree. I stepped on a pile of leaves and heard a too solid crunch. I looked down to see the sickening sight of a skeleton beneath my feet, then the wind whirled and the carpet of leaves swirled up in the air, clearing the copse and unveiling a sea of skeletons, bones stained with age, all rib cages and legs, skulls and reaching fingers. I shuddered and tried to pick my way through them; the boys had kept moving forwards and were now a few feet ahead. I hurried to catch them, biting my lip, navigating carefully, trying to get back to the path. My foot caught and, horrified, I looked down, expecting to discover that I had somehow been trapped by bones. I had, but not in the way I expected. I couldn't help myself and I screamed. Bony fingers attached to a skeletal arm were wrapped around my ankle; the dead hand was restraining me and I couldn't break free.

It looked like all the bones were starting to move. I screamed again as Devyn came up behind me. I pointed at the thing that held me, half hoping that, like Marcus, I would look like I had foolishly been imagining things, but no, the hand still had its skeletal fingers around me. Devyn lifted the long stick he had picked up earlier and whacked at it before prying it loose with his own live hands. The sound of bone cracking and crunching made me shudder as Devyn made sure the hand wouldn't be grabbing anyone again. Ever.

I shivered as he pulled me away from the glade of corpses.

"Don't veer off the path," he commanded before starting forwards again.

I was in shock, still recoiling from the experience. He looked back over his shoulder and, seeing that I was still unmoving, came back for me.

"Cass," he said, grabbing my shoulders and giving me a little shake. "I need you to move. That, that was nothing. Do you hear me? What just happened, what you saw, was *nothing*. Once the sun sets, that entire glade is likely to stand up and start following us."

I didn't want to move deeper into the borderlands. But he painted quite a picture.

"Let's not wait for them, then," I responded to his motivational speech.

"Good girl."

We pushed ahead once more, and this time, despite my screaming muscles, I powered on, matching the boys step for step. If we didn't make it out of here, it wouldn't be my fault.

As we crested the hills and started to descend on the other side, I had enough breath to ask how long Devyn expected it to be before we made it out of the area.

"We're crossing the Chiltern Hills now, then we'll go back

down through the valleys. We've come a good way since dawn, but if we want to be out the other side before dark, we're going to need to move faster than this."

"Let's go then," I urged. "I have no interest in meeting anything else out here."

"I'm with Cassandra," Marcus concurred. It was as much as he had said since we stopped to eat an hour earlier.

Chapter Six

The pit of my stomach continued to dwell somewhere much further south than it belonged as we trudged north. The sun had become a dim grey glow in a gloomy afternoon sky, barely glimpsed between the treetops, making the forest seem more menacing than it had in the golden morning. Earlier, I had revelled in the clean air and endless fields and forests, the beauty of the leaves carpeting the forest floor, and the dappled light snagging through the leafy boughs overhead. Now I worried endlessly about what might lie beneath the fallen decaying leaves on which we stood, and whether an unexpected warrior from centuries past was going to reach up and try to grab me again. I could still feel the trace of where the skeletal hand had clutched me about the ankle. The inconsistent lighting created shadows that crossed our path heavily, and the bushes in the darkness of the forest could conceal some unknown border-dwelling Samhain-raised ghoul or nasty that I never conceived of before stepping outside the city walls.

I edged closer to Devyn and put my cold hand in his.

Unfortunately, this seemed to have the effect of increasing the strength of our bond, and if my unease was at an all-time high then it was nothing compared to the reverberating dread coming off Devyn. I thought that the glade full of rustling skeletons had been the most terrifying sight I would ever witness, but Devyn's emotions promised that there was an awful lot worse out there.

We walked as quickly as we could across the uneven ground, the fading light making our trail harder to pick out. I stumbled, tripping across a branch and was caught and righted by a distracted Devyn.

"We should have been out the other side by now," he muttered, clasping my hand tighter.

"What?" Marcus asked, unable to hear as he was walking behind us.

A pigeon or some large bird burst out of the undergrowth, making us all jump. Devyn looked sideways at Marcus, unnerved by our recent scare. "We should have come out the other side of the forest by now, I'm sure of it."

Marcus jumped at the sound of a twig snapping from somewhere behind us. Or in front of us – the sounds here were distorted. "Let's walk and talk, shall we? What makes you think we should be out the other side? You've never been here before."

"No, but I know the lie of the land, we should have been across the Chiltern Hills and out into open space by now. It's getting dark. How long would you say it is since we left the river?" Devyn continued to set a pace that made my aching feet protest vehemently.

"I don't know, nine or ten hours?" I guessed. Marcus, nodded his agreement

"We should easily have covered twenty or so miles," Devyn

insisted. "We should be out the other side and seeing the lights of Oxford by now."

"We're going to Oxford?" I asked. I had never thought to see the Britons' centre of learning, a place which stubbornly remained at the edge of the borderlands, its reputation legendary. I had never been much of a scholar, but the city of learning was famed across Europe. Although Londinium, I knew, saw it as a nest of rebellion which spewed out young men and women who spouted their anti-imperial poison all over the Western World.

"That's where we're aiming for; we should be able to get help there, and supplies to travel north," Devyn explained, not pausing as he continued to pull me along. "But we're running out of time. The sun is setting and we are still inside the borderlands. We need to move, keep going in this direction, no matter what happens. Don't believe the things you will see and, whatever you do, don't engage with anyone or anything that approaches us. Do you understand?"

Now he did stop, turning to glare at us intently until we signalled our compliance with his commands. We might have been sceptical earlier in the morning but with the encroaching darkness and our earlier experiences, we were no longer so dismissive of his warnings.

I frowned as I caught the sounds of battle coming through the trees. The noises made by a large group of men attacking each other, faint clashes of swords and battle cries, roars of pain, screams. Had sentinels pursued us into the no-entry zone of the borderlands and been met by the Britons, alerted by their magical alarms? I looked at the boys to check that they could hear it too. Marcus looked similarly apprehensive.

"I was sure the city would think we were dead," he said to Devyn.

"They do," he assured us. If the noises weren't sentinels in pursuit and Devyn didn't indicate that it was Wilders looking for us, that only left things that went bump in the night. My heart started to sound awfully loud as we stood frozen in the darkness of the forest.

Hoofbeats had us whirling around. Someone was coming up the path behind us. I started to run to find cover, but Devyn gripped my hand and stood unmoving. My nerves jangled as I pulled at him to come with me. What was he doing? They were nearly here. I turned to watch the horses approach, my heart now beating so loud and fast it threatened to explode out of my chest.

The horse burst through the brush, its body covered in blood, its eyes wild as it galloped right towards us. I pulled Devyn with all my strength to step out of the way as the crazed horse surged past us. He stumbled at my unexpected burst of force.

"What?"

Was he losing his mind? Hadn't he seen it? If I hadn't pulled him out of the way, he would currently be lying broken in the path. Marcus and I exchanged glances. Had the man we were relying on to get us through this nightmare lost all sense of reality?

"I told you not to engage with them," he said, nodding at the retreating horse which was heading straight for a huge tree trunk. I cringed. It was going to hit... It sailed right into the tree, through, its body insubstantial. It wasn't real. I drew a shaky breath.

"Oh."

Devyn looked down at me, his dark eyes serious. "Yes, oh. The more we engage with them, the more attracted to us they'll be. That horse probably rides that course every year.

Nothing changes, but we just acknowledged its existence on this plane. That's what they crave; they want to touch the living. We need to act like they're not there."

I looked at Marcus to see if he was struggling to comprehend Devyn's lesson in the paranormal as much as I was, but he was looking at something behind us. Under a tree lay a little boy, wrapped in a blanket. He was unwell, and the larger shape beside him was still. Too still.

Marcus took a step to go to the boy before Devyn stood in his way. "No. Marcus, it's not real. We need to keep going."

Marcus dragged his gaze from the sick boy to Devyn.

"How can you be sure?" his voice was strangled.

"I'm sure," Devyn assured him. "It is Samhain. We will see a lot stranger before the night is through."

At this, he retook my hand and continued on into the increasingly dim twilight. I forced myself to look away from the boy who, noticing us, had reached a thin, pale hand out of his blankets to stretch it imploringly in our direction. Grimly, I steeled myself to ignore him. Marcus finally took a step to follow us, his mouth set as he, too, forced himself not to go to the boy.

We pushed forward. Unable to help myself, I glanced back just as we were about to lose sight of the child. The thin bundle raised itself up, and in the blink of an eye, the boy had sped through the air to hover in front of us.

"You could have saved me!" he shrieked, his eyes wide and accusing, his face all the paler for the dark crimson streak that ran from his mouth down his chin. And then he was gone.

Devyn ground his teeth in frustration at my action, which had triggered the boy. My entire body was trembling. I looked to Marcus who stood in shadow, his whole body tense in response to an accusation he must have thrown at himself many times over the last months. How could he bear it?

I glanced up through the trees. I could just make out stars in the sky; twilight was almost past, and the sun must have set. We were in real trouble now.

"I'm sorry," I mumbled to Devyn. "I promise, I won't look. I'll stop."

Devyn looked at me strangely. His eyes narrowed and he shook his head, as if dismissing my presence, before glancing around him.

"Cass?" he called into the cool air. "Marcus, where did she go?"

Marcus snapped out of the reverie that had held him since the bloodied child screamed at us. "What?"

"Cass," Devyn roared into the darkening woods. His entire body was tense, poised, as if he were about to break into a run. His eyes were searching wildly around us looking everywhere but at me.

Marcus frowned at me, then at Devyn. "Devyn, she's right there."

"She isn't," he gritted, his eyes flinching from where Marcus pointed to me.

"She is." Marcus looked at me, baffled. "She hasn't gone anywhere."

"No." Devyn shook his head, still scanning all around him, his movements growing frantic as he continued to call for me.

What was going on? I walked right up to him and he flinched, averting his gaze, stepping backwards and continuing to call for me.

"I have to find her," he muttered to himself, or to Marcus – it was hard to tell. "She's my responsibility. I will find her. I promise."

His head half tilted in my direction. "I promise."

With that, he started to move, his movements uncharacteristically uncoordinated as he picked up the pace to a near jog. His progress was louder than it had been all day as he crashed through the darkness. Marcus and I hurried in his wake, doing all we could to keep him in sight. My body was already aching from the walking we had done since dawn; it had been a crazy few days. Between the Metes and then our escape last night, and what happened to Marcus's father, I had never felt so weary. And now, Marcus and I were trying to keep pace with a man who had grown up in terrain like this, and I was exhausted.

"Devyn," I called as I pulled in a laboured breath. He had to slow down; I couldn't keep this pace up. If I couldn't keep up, he would abandon me. That was my last thought as I went flying. Marcus was too late to catch me as I tripped on some tangled tree roots that were hidden by the fallen leaves. I put my hands out in an attempt to save myself as I faceplanted onto the forest floor. I could hear Marcus calling for Devyn to stop as I tried to shake off the shock of the fall.

"Don't touch her." Devyn's voice was sharp as he turned to find Marcus trying to help me up off the ground. "Get your filthy city hands off her."

Stung, Marcus snapped his hands from where they were around my shoulders, turning to snarl in Devyn's direction. "You have no right to tell me who I can and cannot touch, Wilder."

Devyn strode across the clearing, coming to a halt inches from Marcus who stood his ground. "I said, don't touch her," he snarled, still not looking in my direction. "I have to find Cass. Where did she go?"

"Devyn, I'm right here. I didn't go anywhere," I whispered,

baffled and deeply disturbed by the dark emotions swirling through him: self-loathing, despair and an overwhelmingly frantic pulse. He really couldn't see me, which stood in total contradiction to his reaction to Marcus helping me off the ground. I stood and laid my hand on his arm. I was already terrified in my own right; I didn't need his emotions amplifying mine. As it was, my entire body was giddy with fear.

I attempted to push some reassurance of my presence through the bond, only to be resoundingly rebuffed as he blocked against me.

"I'm sorry, I'm sorry," he chanted, his eyes glittering in the dark. "I found her. Like I promised. I found her. I don't know how I lost her again."

"Devyn, snap out of it." Marcus pulled me back from the Briton who looked and sounded increasingly unstable. But this only roused him from his stupor.

"I said not to touch her," he shouted at Marcus, the tendons standing out in his neck, his eyes flashing.

He finally looked directly at me, his dark eyes almost wholly black. "I know I'm not worthy, I know it. I won't touch her again, but please give her back to me. I'll keep her safe, no matter what it takes," he implored me. "Please, my lady."

My lady? He never called me *my lady*. A mocking *princess* or a scolding *Cass*, but never *my lady*. He thought I was someone else. Devyn was seeing someone else; that's why he was trying not to look at me. He hadn't wanted Marcus to interact with me either, but it hadn't been like with the boy earlier. He had been enraged when Marcus had touched me; whoever it was he was seeing, she meant something to him. My lady... my mother?

"Ask him who it is he thinks I am?" I directed Marcus. Marcus frowned before his face cleared in understanding.

Devyn was muttering to himself, still searching frantically for signs of me, I presumed. He looked up as Marcus softly called his name.

"Who is it you're talking to?" Marcus asked quietly in the dark.

"You don't see her?" Devyn seemed confused. "But you were touching her. You can't touch her. She is… well, I suppose you are more worthy to touch her than I, even in death. I can never make up what was lost. He chose me over her. He shouldn't have done that. She was worth a hundred, a thousand, of me."

"Who?" Marcus pressed.

Devyn didn't answer. His focus was elsewhere, his eyes darting away, seeking me.

"Let's concentrate on getting out of here," I urged Marcus. "Maybe once we're out of this damn forest, he'll snap out of it."

"What did she say?" Devyn looked at Marcus suspiciously.

"She wants us to continue to Oxford. Cass is waiting for us there," Marcus supplied ingeniously.

Devyn's eyes lit up at learning of my location. "Let's go then." He moved off into the night. Marcus nodded at me but didn't reach out to take my hand as that seemed likely to set Devyn off again. We made sure we stayed close together as we trailed in his wake though; the last thing we needed was the handfast impacting me now, clouding my judgement at the worst possible time.

Was he seeing my mother? I saw again the woman in my vision cut down by the sentinels. Devyn told me his father had been her protector; he knew who I really was. If I had family, a place to be out here, I just had to get through this. I had to survive the night.

We moved slower now, carefully navigating our way in the dark, the crunch of our footsteps and heavy breathing unfortunately not the only sounds as we made our way, slipping and sliding down a steep incline. Occasional shrieks and screams split the air, as well as rustling in the undergrowth around us. Whether it was caused by real or imaginary creatures was impossible to tell. And none of us cared to investigate as we pushed relentlessly forward.

When the trees were finally thinning, a frail voice came out of the darkness.

"Help me…" I looked down to discover a teenage boy at my feet, the tell-tale signs of the illness on his wan face. I resolutely stepped over him. And the next one and the one after that – a small girl with the same dark skin and hair as Marina, the girl from the stews I had helped what seemed like a lifetime ago. The entire area was littered with the bodies of the dead or dying. None of them bore the signs of battle as the earlier ghost had. Instead, they seemed to be conjured up out of more recent victims. Looking behind me, I discovered Marcus had fallen behind. Devyn continued as if he didn't see anything.

I picked my way back to Marcus. While I knew I should step through the sick lying at our feet because Devyn had made it clear that acknowledging their presence increased their power, I couldn't quite do it. Marcus was frozen when I reached him.

"Come on, Marcus. We'll lose Devyn if we don't hurry."

"I can't," he said, his eyes scanning all the people on the ground. "I've got to try. Maybe I can save some of them."

"They're not real," I reminded him. I couldn't afford to lose another of my companions to the phantoms. If Devyn was anything to go by, once persuaded that they were real, it would be impossible to convince Marcus otherwise.

"I can't just leave them," he said. "I've got to try."

"Marcus, please listen to me." I looked back to where Devyn was still possible to make out on the moonlit path ahead of us. "They're not really there; you can't save them."

I watched as Devyn continued to walk away from us. He was leaving me, but I couldn't leave Marcus, even if the handfast weren't tethering us. He was now wandering from patient to patient and I could sense him pouring his magic into the phantoms. Not a good time for the inhibitor we had been administered in the city to wear off. If merely acknowledging the existence of the spectres made them more potent on this plane, what would pouring his healing magic into them achieve?

"Marcus, stop, please stop." I pulled at him, trying to get his attention. "Damn it, please, Marcus. They're not real, they're not real."

"So many... I've got to help them," he muttered, kneeling beside yet another who, if she wasn't already dead, looked like she was knocking on death's door. What was I saying? The form that lay on the ground looking up so beseechingly had come here from the wrong side of that door. He couldn't help her; he couldn't help any of them. They were already dead.

I shook him, and he barely noticed. Devyn had utterly disappeared into the night, and I was left alone with a maddened doctor pouring magic into ghosts who were faking illness and were unlikely to reward his efforts with the offerings the poor in the city had. His patients in the city... Devyn said that the dead were closer to this world than at any other time of year, that they could walk amongst us. Would the recently deceased answer my call? Perhaps if I couldn't reason with Marcus, someone else might have better luck. Someone dead. Someone who cared for the living still. I stepped away from Marcus. We were in a copse of ash trees; an oak had helped me see a vision before. Would the silvery ash respond to my plea for assistance? I squared my shoulders and walked over to the largest one in the area, laying my palm on its cold, pale bark. Only one way to find out.

I leaned into the silvery white of the tree, closing my eyes, focusing everything I had on my call through the veil. It had been nearly two days since my last dose of the suppressant. Surely it had worn off. I pushed the greyness aside.

Otho, I summoned, calling into the heavy darkness on the other side. *Come to me, Otho. Marcus needs you. Please help.*

I could sense something stirring, a whirl in the sludgy air, and there he was, old Otho, whom I had met only once when he had asked Marcus to let him go. He was the first patient I had witnessed Marcus unknowingly treating with magic. His smile was kind as he approached and stepped through the chink in the veil that I held aside for him. I opened my eyes and found myself back in the copse of stricken ghosts once more. Otho looked at me and went to Marcus, needing no direction.

"Boy," he spoke softly, his accent as strong in the afterlife as it had been when he was flesh and blood. Marcus paused at the sound of the familiar and profoundly unexpected voice.

"Otho?" he asked wonderingly, turning from the patient he was currently pouring energy into to the old man who stood over him.

"Yes, boy," he answered. "What new foolishness is this?"

Marcus looked around him. "They're sick... so many of them. I want to help them but I can't save them all. I have to choose. I have to choose, Otho. What if I've chosen the wrong ones to save?"

"You can only save them what can be saved. Some you got to let go." Otho indicated those around him. "Too late for me. Too late for these people. You got to accept that. Or they'll take you with 'em."

Marcus looked drained, as bad as he had been before he learned not to pour everything he had into the sick and dying. He looked desolate. I'd never thought about it before, but since we had told him that he had the power to save people – but only as long as he limited what he was giving – he had been made the saviour of a few and executioner to many. Fidelma had shown him how to protect himself, but he had been alone, alone to choose who to save. And who to let die. It must have been eating him up.

That was it. That was how the ghosts were trapping us into believing that their version of the night was real. They were preying on our deepest fears, on the actions and decisions that twisted our souls. For Devyn it was the guilt that had skewered him since the day I was stolen. And that, having found me, he had lost me again. That his promise to keep me safe was as broken as his father's to my murdered mother. It was a promise I knew he would gladly give his life to keep. He had given up everything to find me. His home. His family. He had spent years on the outside of my life waiting for proof that I was the girl he was looking for. Each day he had spent in the city, he had risked his life for the tiny hope that he was right, that I hadn't been killed on that road with my mother. Losing me again was his worst nightmare.

I looked around me. This, this endless glade of bodies dying of the illness that had swept the city, this was Marcus's nightmare. He bowed his head in defeat. The city's prince…

All that charm and promise utterly broken on the forest floor. I remembered him as he had been when we had first started to get to know each other properly at the beginning of summer – his health and vigour, a young man aware of his good fortune and generous to all around him. Vital and joyful, his easy smile and golden aura had meant that none begrudged him any of the gifts that luck and genetics had bestowed. Despite his social status, he had chosen medicine, and trying to help others had nearly broken him. His early successes in treating the illness had turned his colleagues against him. His later awareness that it was magic that allowed him to do so meant that he had to hide his true self from the prying eyes of those who wondered how he did it. I had been so caught up in my own stuff – by which I meant the boy I had rejected Marcus for – that Marcus had been left alone. My gaze drifted across the glade. I could hear the cries and moans of those lying beyond what I was able to make out in the darkness. It was endless... So many sick. So many for one man to heal.

I dropped to my knees in front of Marcus, cupping his cold cheek.

"They're not real."

He nodded, his head bowed. Talking to Otho had done the trick. He knew Otho was dead. Otho's death had hit him hard, and no matter how far gone he had been, that unassailable fact had remained true.

"I know." His voice was so quiet that I had to lean in to hear him, until we were leaning against each other, foreheads touching.

"It's not your fault," I added, wanting to give him comfort beyond this moment, wanting to give him words to soothe the pain he must have been feeling for weeks while he had to decide over and over who to save and who he had to walk away from. "You can't save everyone."

His empty eyes looked up at me, utterly drained, but aware.

"I can try."

"No, no. Their deaths are not your fault; you've saved so many." He had to see all the good he had done. Not just the ones he had walked away from.

"Sure." He pulled away from me and wearily levered himself up. "We need to keep moving. Find Devyn."

I knew he didn't want comfort from me, but his rejection smarted all the same. I scanned the dim clearing while we pulled ourselves together. Otho and the carpet of ill people had faded away, hopefully gone back to wherever they had come from, never to return.

"Devyn went that way." I pointed in the direction I had last seen him go. It was as good an idea as any and was still in the same general direction that we had been moving all day. Even though we should have been nearer to our destination by now than we were.

In Devyn's absence, I felt hyper-alert, my eyes and ears on the lookout for the next threat. We hadn't taken more than a few steps when Marcus stumbled; he looked a wreck. The magic had sucked out whatever strength he had left. I couldn't do this. This was not what I'd been trained to do. I could host a party or shop for an entire outfit for any occasion at short notice. Dragging a six-foot man through a dark and incredibly creepy forest with who knew what waiting around the corner was not something I could do on my own. I squashed down the rising panic, taking a deep breath. Devyn was out there being led a merry dance because his fear was causing him to lose me again. If it was the last thing I did, I would drag our sorry arses through this nightmare and find him.

"Come on," I said, wrapping an arm around Marcus, sharing my living warmth with him and encouraging him to lean on me. "We've got to move. We can't stay here. Procedite, centurion."

The old-school command to advance raised a glimmer of a smile and he put one foot in front of the other. We could do this. We had to do this.

I tried to keep our path as direct as possible in the direction Devyn had taken. Devyn had feared we were going in circles before he had left us. What hope two bedraggled, ignorant city-dwellers had of doing any better, I wasn't sure.

I was gradually able to sift through the noise we made as we shuffled forward, and the sounds we were not generating ourselves. The occasional scream and clash of battle remained distant, but I had an increasing sense of wrongness. The silence around us was unnerving. Used to the constant background hum of the city, I thought initially that maybe this was normal. It hadn't felt like this earlier, but now, when we stopped for a break, the only discernible sound was our own harsh and overly loud breathing. Not so much as a rustle was to be heard in our vicinity – no small animals, no birds. If there were worms in the ground, they were frozen in fear as we passed. I had been terrified many times in the last few days, but the very air seemed to be trying to warn me of our danger now. The sinister threat that seeped towards us was palpable, and yet nothing appeared.

We kept moving. I could feel Marcus flagging, his weight becoming heavier as he leaned on me more and more for support, and yet, by silent agreement, we pushed forward, unwilling to pause, desperate to get out the other side of this forest.

A flash of white slipped through the trees in front of us, causing us to stop still. Marcus looked down at me. I could barely make out his expression in the dark. I swallowed, a cold sweat breaking out on my face and back. We had to keep going. There was an increasingly foul smell; the forest no longer smelled of trees and fallen leaves but a gut-turning stench that had built up around us. Another pale streak snatched across the periphery of my vision as I looked at Marcus. I whipped round. There was nothing there, but whatever it was had allowed us to see it; it was coming for us, and it was fine with us knowing.

We stepped forward again. We had to keep moving. We continued in the direction we had been going, despite the glimpse of something we had seen. Whatever was out there, we couldn't outrun it anyway so why let it divert us from our path? We took the old-fashioned guns from our packs. The metal felt solid in our hands, even if the weapons' effectiveness against whatever was out there was questionable. Each step felt like it could be our last before the thing attacked. Dread built up in my gut like a stone until I thought it might paralyse me. When the thing did come for us, I was almost relieved.

Not entirely though… After all, who wants to meet a white hound the size of a small horse in a pitch-black wood, on a night when the dead can walk? We turned to face it as it slunk out of the night, its snarling visage dominated by teeth the size of my fingers. That was just what I needed, to put a visual of my delicate fingers and this otherworldly creature's fangs together.

It emerged silently out of the night itself. Its large feet padded towards us, its strangely prescient eyes malevolently fixed on us. There was an aura of death about it. The smell that had been heavy over the forest had its source here. Rotting and alien, the foetid, noxious stench was overpowering. It had a physical presence. My eyes watered as I held the blood-red gaze of the massive white hound slipping out of the shadows. It weighted itself backwards, its massive haunches gathering power before it leapt directly at us. We raised our weapons and fired in the direction of the pale beast. The sound of the gunshots snapped through the night. We fired again and again, and by sheer luck or horrifying proximity managed to hit the giant hound. We struck it mid-leap and it crashed sideways into a tree and lay there, unmoving. Another ghostly shadow lurked in the trees beyond it but with its partner down, the second one chose not to attack and slunk back into the night.

"What was that?" Marcus's hushed tones broke the returning normal quiet of the night.

"I don't know and I don't care," I answered, shivering in reaction to the adrenaline still coursing through my veins. I had been sure we were about to die a truly horrible death under the teeth and claws of that feral beast. I glanced uneasily at it. Was it dead? Did anything remain dead out here in this bloody endless forest? "Let's go before it decides to have another go."

We stumbled on, our near miss giving us a new surge of energy.

"Look."

I paused at Marcus's command and raised my head in the direction he pointed. Lights... or rather the glow of a town. We were finally out the other side. Now that I was paying attention to more than where to place my next step, I noticed that the trees seemed to be thinning. The hairs on my arms stood on end as I realised that the awful silence had started to gather around us once more. The hounds were stalking us again.

"We need to move faster." I urged Marcus on; whatever renewed strength he had shown after the attack had faded from him once again.

He sank to his knees, completely depleted.

"Go," he said quietly. "You'll have a better chance on your own."

"I'm not leaving you," I whispered back. It was too late anyway. The putrid stench seeped into the air around us. It was here.

We backed away from the approaching hound. Marcus was out of bullets. I raised my gun, aimed, and pulled the trigger. Nothing. I tried again. Still nothing. Devyn told us that even the most basic mechanical technology was known to fail in the borderlands; little had I realised that fact was going to cost me my life.

It was the same one as before. It was still alive. A dark wound marred the white fur of one shoulder. The beast was warier this time. It slunk towards us with deadly purpose, though not quite as confidently as it had done before. Marcus gathered a large stick off the ground and held it in front of us. I'm not sure it would hold the beast off for very long once it came at us, but at least we wouldn't go down without a fight. I would never see Devyn again, and all of this, making it out of the city and Marcus's father dying, would be for nothing. We were going to die within fifty miles of the walls. We hadn't even made it across the borderlands.

A crash came from behind us and I whirled in its direction while Marcus continued to watch the approaching hound. I expected to find another one of the hideous slavering beasts attempting to come at us from behind, but the sight that met my eyes sent my blood pumping around my body once again. An even larger dark shadow was making its way at speed through the trees. As it got closer, I felt a sweep of determination and sheer bloody anger roll through me as Devyn strode purposefully across the clearing to us, never taking his eyes off the beast.

"Begone," he commanded, carrying a great staff in his hand and taking a stance that indicated he knew how to use it. But that was all, no sign of the pack Matthias had supplied with our last remaining gun which might have had more luck than mine.

The hound took its eyes off the feast it had all but picked out seasoning for and took in the Celt, pausing in its approach. Weaving behind a tree, it contemplated the new arrival, its head low as it assessed our flimsily armed reinforcement.

A new sensation pulsed through me, the energy in the natural world responding to my fear. The trees rustled in response and a wind stirred. I shook my head to clear it; there was something off, a strangely distorted note clawing at the edges of the energy, but I let it flow through me. The trees around the beast swayed, just flickers in the dark moving towards it until the creature finally turned tail.

"You couldn't have pulled that out of the bag a little sooner?" Marcus said drily. But my focus was on one thing only.

"You found us."

"I'll always find you," Devyn growled and, sweeping me up, he captured my lips in an open-mouthed kiss as his tongue thrust in possessively, reassuringly. I pushed away the draining, corrupted energy; it felt wrong, twisted, as it seeped out of me.

He was back. I poured my relief, my stress, my joy into that kiss. Tears leaked out from beneath my lids. We were alive. Against all odds, we were alive.

Devyn finally straightened and gave Marcus a cursory glance. "What happened to you?"

"He tried to cure a forest full of dead people of the illness," I explained, when Marcus failed to answer.

Devyn raised an eyebrow but said nothing.

"And you? I left, you were... you're still you?"

I paused. He was right to ask.

"Yes, I'm still me." I thought about it a bit, further examining the effect of the handfast compulsion while Devyn had been gone. "I didn't want to comply with the Code and head off for the city. It never occurred to me. Perhaps out of the city itself, the handfast is reduced to its core purpose of binding a couple together?

"Good, good." He nodded.

"What happened to you?" I asked. How had he finally figured out that I hadn't gone on ahead as Marcus had assured him, but that *he* had actually deserted *us*.

"I felt your terror," he grimaced. "Even at a distance it broke through the enchantment. I'm sorry."

"That's okay," I said, reaching up to run my hands through his hair, a gesture that was as much for my comfort as for his. "You're here now."

His lips thinned in rejection of my reassurance. While I might be okay that he made it back in time, he was less happy that he had been lured away in the first place.

"It wasn't your fault." I attempted to dismiss the spell that had drawn him away. "You warned us."

"Not to believe your eyes, and yet that is exactly what I did. Like a fool."

Chapter Seven

W e made our way down the hill towards the town in the distance. As the sky began to lighten, my chest expanded and I finally pulled in deep breaths again. My feet were burning, my body was sore and stiff as the adrenaline left my system, but we were alive.

"We'll sleep here," Devyn announced, pulling abruptly to a halt.

"What?" I asked, stumbling with fatigue as I ordered my weary feet to stop. "But we're so close."

"If we go in now, we will announce our presence to the entire city. In a couple of hours, when the gates are open, we can slip in with a lot less fuss."

"Given the choice of waiting outside with all our friends –" I glanced behind us to the forest we had barely left in our wake, the unnatural sounds that haunted us all night still audible even in the growing dawn "– I'm happy to introduce myself to every person in Oxford as long as we are behind the walls."

"We wait," Devyn repeated. "The border alarms may have

been triggered by the gunfire. We don't need the attention that identifying ourselves as the owners of said imperial tech would bring."

That, it seemed, was that. Marcus offered no argument, wordlessly sliding to the ground. If Devyn wasn't practically carrying him, Marcus was going no further in his current state anyway. His eyes were closing before the discussion was even concluded. Great.

"All right then. Morning," I conceded, earning a half smile from Devyn at my begrudging tone at being outflanked.

"Sleep, Cass. It's been a long night. I'll keep watch."

"That's hardly fair; I'll take a turn." But my eyelids were heavy; the brief use of magic had emptied me of my last ounce of strength. My head barely hit my pack before I was asleep.

When Devyn shook us awake, the sun had lifted above the horizon. I felt worse for having rested; my body felt robbed of the proper rest that was far overdue. I scowled at Devyn as he put an arm around Marcus to help him.

"You were supposed to wake me."

"You'd have been happier if I woke you earlier, princess?"

I scowled harder.

"Am I?" I asked as I shook off the last traces of sleep.

"What?"

"A princess." The danger having passed, and realising I was on the edge of my new life, I felt curiosity about who I really was starting to bubble up within me.

He huffed a laugh. "No."

"Then stop calling me that." I braced myself. "Who am I then?"

105

Devyn's lips tightened before he lowered his voice for my ears only. "Not yet. I know you want to know more but it's not safe yet. What you don't know, you can't inadvertently let slip. You've got to be careful, Cass. You cannot mention to anyone that you were adopted, or in any way not city-born. Bad enough that we're travelling with him." He indicated the broken figure that Marcus cut. "Promise me."

"Why not?"

"Because the kingdoms are not all… It's complicated. News that you are alive will spread quickly and attract attention that we could do without. I will tell you. As soon as it's safe to do so."

"That who is alive?" I pushed. "Who am I really? Do I have family? Are you taking me to them?"

Devyn cast me a quelling glance as Marcus began to stir. As always, he had no intention of telling me anything more than he had to.

"Please trust me in this."

"You leave me little choice," I noted sourly.

Marcus sat up and blearily looked around for us.

"Fine," I grudgingly acceded. Devyn gave me a quick smile in thanks.

Matthias's bags had to be abandoned, their contents too identifiably imperial, before we made our way to join the people traveling along the road that led to the city gates.

At Devyn's urging, we pulled up the hoods of our cloaks as we approached the walls. The brightening sky illuminated the spires of the city that peeked above the defensive walls. So different to the soaring towers of Londinium, these were delicate and shaped in a variety of needles and domes, either crenellated or slender.

As we neared the walls, Devyn gave instructions on how

we should behave once inside. Marcus trailed behind, barely conscious, let alone paying attention.

When Devyn stepped forwards to speak with the guards at the city gate, I kept my head down and my face averted. Once we had been ushered through the gates, we followed Devyn silently through the quiet streets. I'd never been in a Briton town before. I wasn't sure what I had expected.

The buildings were low, many of them no more than two floors high, and constructed in a beautiful golden-coloured stone that was warm in the dawn light. Glowing lights that floated by the walls winked out as the new day began.

The streets were cobbled and there were already people out and about beginning their day. Some wore long hooded cloaks pulled up against the cold of the autumnal morning; others were bundled in wide woollen or tweed throws wound around their shoulders over tunics and tight-fitting trousers, with robust, practical boots. Some women wore long dresses with wide belts pulling them in at the waist, all in natural-looking materials. I felt a little conscious that the lightness of our temperature-regulating clothes was not helping us blend in on the rather brisk first morning of November.

Devyn stopped a couple of times to ask for directions, ignoring my questions as to where we were headed.

At last, we turned in through the high walls surrounding one of the buildings that Devyn told me was a college, and Devyn asked for a final set of directions from the elderly porter for how to reach a professor.

By this stage, Marcus was barely able to stay upright, despite Devyn's support, and managing the curving stairs was a struggle.

Our knock on the door was eventually answered by a large man with a tattoo curling from his temple down into his beard.

He was not the effete old professor I had expected. On opening the door at this early hour, he was grumbling deeply, but pulled up short as he took in the three exhausted strangers at his door.

His gaze snagged when he reached Devyn. His scowl deepened.

"Well, pup, what hour do you call this?"

Devyn's shoulders were hunched as we stood in the hallway. It seemed like he was unsure of his welcome. I took in the unsmiling face holding the door open as the bearded man contemplated us in turn. I held my breath; my legs felt like they were about to give way. I couldn't walk another step. If this man didn't take us in, I was going to sleep right here on his doorstep. I almost sobbed as he held the door open wider and took a step back, indicating we could come in.

"You had to land on my door," he said under his breath

Devyn helped Marcus onto a seat before turning back to the large professor.

"You expected us?"

"Expected is a bit strong. We knew you had left Londinium. The whole Empire probably knows you three have left the city, though rumour has it you be dead. But I heard tell you be dead before; seems it don't tend to stick. Figured there was a chance you might stop by. How many other friends do you have on the road north?" He spoke to Devyn, but he was still surveying Marcus and me, taking in our nondescript clothing, which was simple and neither recognisably Briton nor imperial in style.

"Are we friends?" Devyn challenged quietly.

"Can't say that we are, my lad." At this he grinned before sticking a hand out to me. "I expect we'll stand here all day waiting for himself to introduce us. I'm Callum Reed."

"Hi." My hand was engulfed by his shovel-sized paw. "I'm Cassandra, and this is Marcus."

"Yes, yes, indeed." He stopped studying me in detail, his gaze passing back to Marcus before he continued, "Isn't that something? The last of the Plantagenets at my door with his little city girl. Who would have believed it?"

He grinned again, his faded blue eyes creasing before finally releasing my hand. "Hungry, are we?"

I nodded. I could eat any one of the many books that lined the walls of his sitting room right now as long as it was served up hot. The cold of the night had seeped through to my bones. I felt like I'd never be warm again. Callum served us toasted sandwiches oozing with cheese and onions that I'm sure would have been incredibly tasty if we hadn't wolfed them down, barely taking the time to chew. Full and heated through, my eyes started to close as I listened to Callum attempt to get the tale of our escape from Devyn, who had reverted to his incommunicative default setting.

"I'll tell you after," I mumbled. "Never get anything out of him when he's in this mood."

"That's true." Callum smiled broadly at me. "I'll let you all have a little rest then, and we'll have a proper chat at dinner. You can be guests that actually talk back when your host asks you how you do."

This last came with a glare at Devyn.

"Follow me." Leaving the little sitting room, I followed him down the hall. "Only my own room here, I'm afraid. But you'll do all right here, and the boys, I'm sure, are happy where they are as long as they have a blanket. Your friend Marcus wouldn't even need that, I dare say."

I took in the large wooden bed with its many throws, and even more books littering the floor in higgledy-piggledy stacks. I felt a little vulnerable separated from the boys. It was crazy because they were only in the next room, and I could sense both of them. If anything were to happen to me, even if I couldn't cry out, Devyn would feel it. As I sank onto the bed, I wasn't sure I cared about any potential threat as much as I should. All I knew was the comfort of being fed and warm with a soft pillow under my cheek.

I woke to find the room in darkness, apart from a fire that had been lit in the neat fireplace on the other side of the room. It danced and crackled merrily as I slowly rose out of the deepest, most appreciated sleep of my life. Throwing off the covers and the last vestiges of sleep, I crept down the hall towards the light emanating from the sitting room. A creaking floorboard announced my entrance, and Devyn looked up from the window seat where he lounged, watching the courtyard below. He nodded to me briefly before resuming his activity. Marcus was still passed out on the chair which he had taken on arrival that morning.

"Where's Callum?" I asked quietly.

"Out."

I sighed. Now that our immediate futures were not in doubt, Devyn had reverted to his usual taciturn self. I walked over to him, hovering while I figured out my approach.

"He's going to help us?" I wasn't quite sure what to make of the giant professor; his welcome had been somewhat tepid.

"Maybe."

"Maybe? What does that mean? He's already helping us, isn't he? He's taken us in, anyway. How do you know him?"

"He was my tutor when I was young."

"He doesn't seem awfully surprised or pleased to see you alive," I observed, recalling the mixed emotions our arrival on his doorstep seemed to have evoked.

"I don't imagine he was. The news that I didn't die a decade ago will have filtered out by now. Not everyone will rejoice at the news; some may even seek to correct the situation."

When Devyn left for the city in search of me, many assumed he had died in the attempt. He was only sixteen when he ran off and he hadn't been heard from in years. The Briton delegates I met at the Treaty Renewal had certainly been mixed in their reaction to his reappearance.

"People out here want to kill you? Why?" What happened to my real mother wasn't his fault. What had he done that was so bad?

"I told you before, when I left I abandoned the fealty I owed to my lord. I broke my oath."

"So you broke a promise. You did it for a good reason. People would kill you for this?" I asked, aghast. "You think Callum might want you dead?"

Why on earth had he brought us here then?

Devyn smiled grimly. "No, I don't think Callum wants me dead. We may have had our issues in the past, but that's all bygones now."

I frowned, "Bygones?"

"In the past, I hope," said Devyn, explaining his use of a term unfamiliar to me. Since we had left the city, Devyn's accent had been slowly softening, nowhere near Callum's thick drawl but certainly much more Celt than it had been. Now it had a melodic quality to it that hadn't been there before.

"Because you've brought Marcus out to help with the illness?" I asked after a moment.

His dark head bowed.

"Having the last Plantagenet in tow may not entirely redeem my reputation, but it won't hurt. It looks like he thinks you are just Marcus's betrothed," he said, using an old-fashioned term I vaguely knew. A betrothal was a promise to marry, like we had before scientific matching... which it turns out was all a lie anyway. "I would rather keep it that way. He is a teacher, though; it might be useful for you to learn something of your power and how to control it."

"We can trust him?"

"I wouldn't go that far. Be careful. Callum has somewhat divided loyalties. While he served the house where I was fostered when I was a child, he is Anglian. He'll have loyalties of his own." Devyn's dark eyes were sombre. "And while I may hopefully be forgiven, I am not loved. He has no reason to suspect you are more than you appear: just Marcus's betrothed, with some latent talent."

"I see." Although I wasn't sure that I did. I thought once we made it out of the city, we would be safe – or at least once we had traversed the nightmare that was the borderlands. We had left the Empire behind and we were deep in Briton territory, yet we still weren't safe. I felt betrayed somehow. Devyn had promised that we would be.

Actually, I realised, he hadn't.

Devyn had never promised anything except that I didn't belong in the city and that we shouldn't be together. Two truths that I still struggled to accept, and both of which denied me the home I so desperately sought. Now it seemed he was telling me we were still far from securing refuge.

Without speaking another word or even looking at Devyn, I left the room.

Over dinner we told Callum about our escape from the tower along the river, about the death of Marcus's father and the terrifying journey through the woods, give or take some details.

He stopped us when it came to the hounds, his raised eyebrow aimed at Devyn during my stumbling explanation of how we chased off the hounds first with guns and then, less coherently, a second time.

"They chased off the hounds twice, eh?" He spoke directly to his former pupil. "You think I've lost what wits I had in the years since we last met? I know a burnout when I see one. Yon Plantagenet lad doesn't look like he'd have been much help; from the look of him he still ain't up to much. You telling me you and this pretty chit fought 'em off with a stick? Comes to mind that despite the boy burnt out like he was, they was still awful interested in a couple of city kids."

Devyn remained tight-lipped.

"What difference would Marcus being burnt out make?" I asked.

Again, Devyn said nothing.

The professor slashed him an irritated look before explaining. "They're hungry, but not in the way you might think. They don't go after most people, even on Samhain. With him being drained of magic, there was no reason for them to come for you."

"Cassandra has magic," Devyn said, shrugging in answer to the surprised question in my eyes. He had said that perhaps Callum could help me; it looked like he had decided to trust him. "There have been a small number of cases in the city of people displaying magic. The illness outs them. People like my mother, who were already in danger of being discovered before the sickness, displaying symptoms puts an even bigger target on their backs. I've helped a few of them out of the city before now. The Mallacht is now taking down latents as well, and there's a lot more of them."

"So I've heard. That girl you sent over this summer caused

quite the stir." The large man grunted before surveying me again with a little more interest. "How much you got, girl?"

"I don't know. I was blocked for years. I don't really know what I'm doing." I shrugged. "Sometimes when I'm distracted my consciousness can float away. Other times when I'm angry or afraid the elements respond."

"You were able to do something in the borderlands?" Callum asked.

I paused, recalling the strange, distorted energy that had come to me as the hound stalked ever closer.

"It wouldn't come at first; there wasn't anything there. I thought maybe the drug I was given in the city might still be blocking me. Then when it came it felt different to how I've felt before." I tried to answer as best I could, inner caution preventing me from giving him too much detail. "The borderlands, Samhain... Devyn said it makes magic unstable..."

Callum nodded, but his frown indicated he was dissatisfied with my answer.

"You were right on top of the May ley line; it has been corrupted by the wars," he explained. "It was stable for you? You could control it?"

"I don't know. I don't know that I've ever really controlled it. I don't usually intend to use magic... It just happens." I drew a shuddering breath to try and ease the tightness in my chest and looked to Devyn to help explain.

Callum watched me look to Devyn for answers, and his frown deepened.

"You did well to summon anything in the borderlands, but it sounds like you've been lucky so far," he observed. "Do you know what it is to properly summon magic?"

I sat still in my chair, my fork halfway to my mouth.

Thinking back, I wasn't sure I had ever formally summoned magic. It had just happened somehow, either when I wasn't focused or when I was all too focused on an imminent threat. The only time I did anything on purpose was asking Otho for help, but was that me wielding magic or the ash providing the aid sought? I had never stopped to think about how to call the magic to me; it just was. I dropped my fork back onto my plate, my appetite for the delicious pie disappearing. I had no control over the force that flowed through me; it came and went at its own whim, and it could not be relied upon, like everything else in my life. What if the next time my luck ran out?

"You'll stay a while. Your friend needs to gather his strength before you go anywhere. I'll teach you some of the basics. See if we can't get you started a little better," Callum decreed, though he waited for Devyn's nod before flashing his trademark grin, his white teeth flashing in the candlelight.

"The hounds of Samhain. It's a long time since anyone has reported seeing them. They're attracted by the scent of power, a power that has run ever thinner. There's not much that tempts them out on a hunt these days. What were you doing in the woods last night that attracted their attention and kept them coming for you despite being injured?"

There was silence at the table as we took this in. Magic was waning amongst the Britons. What would the council do if they had that information? It was the threat of the magic wielded by the Britons that kept our societies separate, that prevented the Empire from using its superior firepower and technology to dominate this island.

"This is no small matter. They have your scent now. How much power did you use to attract their attention and bring them to our plane?"

I looked to Marcus who had paused in eating too but kept

his head down. I wasn't sure what to do; Devyn had barely spoken since we arrived, and Marcus was scarcely recognisable. His gaunt, shrunken appearance showed the toll the last few days had taken on him – his father's death, depleting every last drop of his power in his desperation to try to heal those spirits, and then being hunted through the forest. As he met my eyes, his were vacant but he shrugged, giving his consent that I should tell the tale.

"It was Marcus. There were these people, so many of them… all showing signs of the same illness that's been sweeping the city. Marcus is a doctor. He's had some success in healing people, but he uses magic to do so. It comes from within him, and he knows he isn't supposed to go beyond a certain level; he knows he can only save a small number. Out there in the woods, there were so many, and Marcus kept trying to save them, one after another. He used a lot of power, more than he should have. That's how he got burned out," I explained.

"I see, but when they came, Marcus was a dried-up husk. You're the one that was the juicy bone, the one they'll be back for. I can't do much for him till he gets some energy back. Let's work with what you have and make sure you know how to give 'em a kicking they won't soon forget should they be foolish enough to return." Callum surveyed the table and, leaning across, heaped seconds onto our plates. "Now, eat up; you'll need your strength."

———

After breakfast the next morning, I followed Callum through the halls of the college, relieved to find my handfast tether to Marcus had extended to a greater distance now we were beyond the unstable border ley line. We wound our way through a labyrinth of stone passageways, some small and narrow, some wide and littered with portraits of stern men and women, no doubt professors and deans of generations past. Some wore elaborate Celtic dress while others were in simpler, more modern garb; most were distinctly Briton in style but occasionally we passed one with more exotic robes and colouring. In Londinium, people came from all over the Empire, which was why Devyn's darker skin fitted in so easily, but these people wore culturally rich clothing, indicating that they were from outside the Empire – Africans and Americans, though some dressed vaguely in the imperial style. I wondered if they might be people like Devyn's mother, people who fled persecution at home to live outside the reach of the Empire.

Our feet echoed on the flagstone – or rather mine did. Why did it seem like I was always the loudest person in the vicinity out here in the Wilds? Everyone walked like ghosts, barely making a sound. I supposed that, living in the city, I had grown up accustomed to the basic comfort of my own safety; even down in the stews I had never had to fear being attacked... Pestered by beggars maybe, but there was never any real danger that someone there would assault an elite. In the city, the danger wasn't being heard but being seen by the ever-present cameras. The same was not true out here in lands where it still held that the best insurance of one's safety seemed to be to tread lightly and carry a big stick.

Finally, we arrived in a courtyard. It was large and surrounded by stone walls with small casement windows higher up. The yard itself was divided up into quarters, each with its own unique characteristic. There was a large oak tree in the centre.

"Each section of this courtyard represents one of the four

elements of which magic is made up," Callum explained. "They are here to help you connect to them and train, but first we need to find out which of them you hold an affinity with."

I glanced up at the windows, uncomfortable at the thought that others might be watching.

Callum caught me at it and correctly interpreted my nervousness.

"Oh, don't worry about the windows; those are the halls of residence, and most everyone has gone home for the festivities."

"What festivities?"

"What festivities? What do they teach you behind those big walls? Don't you know anything about the people with whom you share this island?"

"Yes," I snapped back. "I know that it's Samhain and that the dead can cross over."

Which, admittedly, was fairly recently acquired knowledge.

"I can see that this might be pertinent information to someone crossing the borderlands, but it's a great deal more than that. It is the harvest festival. After all the work has been done and the fires are lit for the winter, there are bonfires and dancing and feasting. The beloved dead are invited to dine, and people disguise themselves from the dead who come with evil intent."

So maybe I knew hardly anything. At least it explained why the halls were so deserted. As long as no one but Callum was going to be watching me make a complete and utter fool of myself... I hated this, hated not being able to do anything well. I had striven my whole life to be perfect at everything, to do well at school, to have appropriate friends, to look good, to be deserving. To be worthy of my parents, of my betrothed, of everything I – outwardly at least – fitted into so beautifully while all the time feeling like a fraud. I had never felt entirely worthy or right in the life I was walking through. Now I knew why: that path hadn't been mine. Even the sodding shoes hadn't been mine. Too loud, too unaware of the world. I just needed to figure out how to walk in this one, besides being simply quieter.

"As I was telling you before, there are four elements: earth, water, air and fire. Each section helps you focus and hone the one that is your core element. Latents who display magic tend to have an affinity for only one or two, and usually it manifests as a very particular skill. For example, the city lights are tended by a woman with a small ability with fire and some air, but she has little skill beyond that." Callum led me over to the quadrant closest to us. It contained rocks of various sizes dotted around, from small pebbles to large boulders. "Let's see how you fare."

I picked up a smooth pebble and ran my thumb across it. Despite the coolness of the morning, it already retained some heat from the sun. I trailed my fingers across the considerable boulder that stood upright in the centre of the section, the white and pale-green lichen indicating that it had stood there for a long time.

"What now?" I asked, turning back to Callum.

"Breathe in. Focus. Centre yourself. You need to reach out and pull in the energy from below. There are currents deep down in the earth, streams of power that flow across the planet, all interconnecting with each other, and feeding the earth above, enriching it with life-giving power. Can you feel it? Let it come to you, absorb it into yourself." His voice was low, calming. "Relax, be at one. The breeze lifts you, the current carries you, the earth holds you and fire lights the way. Be at one. Repeat it with me."

Devyn said the same words to me in the cell in the arena. It wasn't the best association, but together we repeated it until I felt my body relax and grow calm. I wasn't sure I could feel any of this power he was talking about but I tried to do as he said. I felt a vague tingle, but nothing like the surge I felt in times of danger. But it was something.

"I'd like you to raise one of these stones off the ground."

"Right…" I put the small pebble on the ground. I tried to lift it, I really did. Or at least, I stared at it and sort of repeated over and over in my head that I wanted it to lift off the ground.

Nothing happened.

Callum shrugged. "Maybe not earth then. Let's try to do something with the water. Nothing too taxing, maybe just get it moving."

I focused on the pool of water in the second quadrant, again commanding it to move. Or to do something. No result; not even a ripple bothered the surface of the still water. We were there for what felt like for ever as Callum talked me through the techniques of how to command magic. He instructed me to breathe in and out, using the chant to focus. Sometimes I could feel something – a hum – but it seemed to draw energy from me rather than supply it.

I was exhausted when we finally sat down for our meal at the end of the second day. I could barely drag myself to the table. My eyes were practically closed as I mechanically lifted the much-needed food into my mouth. I felt as though I hadn't eaten in weeks. Trying to do magic was much harder than actually doing it. I had brought a storm down on Richmond without breaking a sweat; attempting to lift feathers and light candles, on the other hand, left me wiped out. *Attempting* being the operative word. I still had very little success in using whatever magic pulsed through my veins.

Finishing my plate, I reached out to scoop up seconds only to discover the three men had barely touched their own plates and were instead watching me devour my dinner in amusement.

"What?"

"Nothing, nothing." Devyn's lips were quirked in a half smile, and Callum was smothering what sounded suspiciously like a laugh. I scowled down at my plate.

"I'm hungry," I declared. They had a fair point. I had inhaled the food so fast it had barely touched my throat because I had been in such a hurry for it to reach my belly. I smiled sheepishly. "Yeah, okay. I'll wait for you lot to catch up, shall I?"

Even Marcus smiled at my barely contained dismay at having to civilise my eating style. Marcus had slept away most of the last two days, but he finally looked more like his old self. I sat dumbly, trying to think of a way to ask him if he was better without sounding like he should be better. His father had died and it was going to take more than a few days' sleep to recover from that, but it looked like he had recovered from depleting his power at least.

"Time to get you up and about, young fella." Callum's attention had also fallen on Marcus's revived form.

Marcus was slow to acknowledge the suggestion. It was too soon; he would quickly become exhausted once more if he joined in the training to which Callum was subjecting me. Not that he needed it. Marcus knew what he was doing; he already consciously used his magic.

"No, no." Callum saw that Marcus, like me, had assumed that he would be joining me. "You don't need to be using your magic yet, and you could do with a bit more rest. I've never seen anyone drain themselves like you did, boy. No, if you're going to empty yourself out like that, you need to be able to defend yourself by other means. I'm sure you didn't have too much call for fighting off man nor beastie in the city. Ain't so out here. You need to be able to hold your ground with or without magic. Devyn here can get you started with some sword skills."

"Swords?" Marcus's mouth twisted in disdain at the mention of the primitive weapons.

"Aye, swords. That's what you'll face out here. Even your legions train with swords. They know they can't always rely on tech. As you saw on Samhain the most basic mechanisms can fail you out here. Sharp pointy objects tend to be much more reliable."

"Right."

Devyn had gone still. He was closed off to me, increasingly so since we arrived in Oxford, but anyone could see he wasn't jumping at the idea. But neither had he outright refused. Devyn and Marcus hadn't spent much time together, certainly not alone, and neither seemed to be champing at the bit to do so now.

Callum picked up on the new tension in the room, his broad smile appearing.

"It'll be good for you boys to have a bit of a knockabout."

That was what I was afraid of.

The next day, the two of them took off together while Callum and I headed back to that sodding courtyard.

Chapter Eight

"**W**hy don't we take a break for a minute?" Callum's voice was patient despite the frustration I knew he was feeling too; we had been at this for days and I hadn't been able to command even the tiniest fraction of magic that I pulled into myself. "Maybe it would be easier if we knew a little bit more about each other, build up a bit of trust, eh?

"What's the point?" I asked peevishly. "In a few days we'll leave here, and I'll never see you again."

I would never see anyone again. I uprooted my life for some stupid Celt who was blocking me out, my parents had disowned me, I ruined the life of the man I was about to marry and, I paused in dismay, now I couldn't even do the thing that was the reason for all that and command a bit of damned magic.

"Life is long, little girl," Callum admonished me gently. For a big man, he never seemed to raise his voice or speak too loudly. He was at all times even-tempered, an erudite scholar in the body of a bear.

I exhaled, pushing myself to my feet and walking across the

well-worn rug to the window in the wide stone wall. I curled up on the polished window seat looking out across the warm stone of the city in the red light of the setting sun to the forest we had barely escaped. We *had* escaped though; we had made it and were still alive. I drew in a deep breath.

"You knew Devyn when he was a child," I prompted quietly, half turning back into the room and lifting my chin long enough to see Callum's raised eyebrow and half-smile. Damn. I wasn't supposed to show interest in Devyn.

"That's not really a question about me, but yes, I knew Devyn as a boy. I was a tutor to him and –" his hesitation was slight "– his friend. Mischievous boys they were, always up to devilment. Clever too, the pair of them. Always competing, pushing each other, but as likely to impress their tutor with frogs in his pockets as heed their lessons."

I smiled. I could see Devyn as a child getting up to no good and I had caught glimpses of the humour and restlessness that would have led a little boy into naughtiness.

"Once, I came on the pair of them having built a bridge across the goose pond. They were sending across his cousin, a little girl, to test the sturdiness of the bridge before they put themselves in danger. Oh, the uproar when her mother saw her darling daughter covered head to toe in mud." Callum chuckled at the memory.

"And when they were older?" I asked, curious about what Devyn had been like before I met him – or at least before he had taken up residence at the periphery of my life.

Callum sobered, the laughter washing out of his face. "Well, they weren't such good friends anymore... not like that." He looked away into the past, his dark eyes sombre in memory. "He's told you why he was in the city? What happened when he was a boy?"

I nodded casually.

"After what happened, Devyn didn't talk much, or at all really, for years after. Gods help him, I don't know that anyone much cared. With her ladyship lost, the light was gone out of our hearts, and the sight of him just made it darker. The other boys pushed him about a bit, and he took it – not the way for any boy to survive in a castle full of warriors."

"What about his friend? Didn't he help him?" I was horrified. It hadn't been Devyn's fault. His father was the one who had failed to protect my mother; Devyn had only been a child. A child who had watched as a lady he loved was killed, and the baby he adored was also ripped away.

"No, his friend didn't raise a hand against him, but he didn't help him either. I saw him watch as other boys – older boys – punched and kicked Devyn on a daily basis. He said and did nothing."

"What a little shit." My heart broke for the much younger Devyn, even as I noted that Callum hadn't mentioned intervening himself either.

"Humph. Wasn't a good time for anyone. Anyway, the time came some years on from the death of the lady and her daughter that they came to clear out the nursery. Devyn still attended lessons though he never did anything more than sit in his chair like a sullen pup. When he heard the men down the hall and realised what was happening, he tore out of there like his arse had been lit on fire. There came then the sounds of a fierce battle." Callum had settled into the story, clearly relishing this part of the tale. "That boy had set two grown men on their backsides and was picking up furniture and replacing it in the nursery. Two or three more men came running and took him on, and he fought them like a wild thing, doing a fair job of holding them off until they fetched a few warriors who were only too happy to be handed their chance at giving young Devyn a whipping. Most of them had argued that he be thrown out in the streets, that he was no longer worthy of being fostered. Oh yes, they were happy to help put some manners on him. But nobody had told Devyn he should give these mighty warriors any more respect than he dished out to the servants who tried to subdue him. Eventually, they overpowered him – he was still only a lad, after all – and, well, they set to give him a beating he wouldn't forget."

"What happened?" I asked intently.

Callum had paused his story, snarled in memory.

"What happened?" I asked again. The warming fire in the room we occupied suddenly blazed into a mini explosion which I knew would be more style than substance. It was a flash that set the little room alight with dancing colours that ricocheted outwards. It was a significantly more spectacular display than the spark we had been aiming for earlier during training.

Callum grinned at the evidence his ploy had worked. Distracted and emotionally roused, I had finally shown some ability. "Well, his friend went over and helped him. Sent them all away. He crouched down when Devyn collapsed on the floor and asked him what he was doing, why he wouldn't let them take the stuff away. Devyn told him that the little girl was still alive. His friend nodded, and that was that."

"What do you mean, that was that? He believed him? They went back to how it was before?"

"Nothing was ever as it was before. The two boys were close again but not as they were; that wasn't possible. His friend was a wild one, and as they grew older, Devyn was the shadow to his raging fire, always at his side, but... a shadow.

Until the day he disappeared. And left his friend behind." Callum indicated the dancing streamers playing around the room. "How's about we try doing something a little more practical then?"

Despite what had appeared to be a breakthrough, my progress continued to be patchy at best. I consistently failed to command the elements while inadvertently succeeding at one or two exercises. Callum's exasperation had turned to a more focused investigation as he threw test after test at me, by turns baffled, outraged and tickled by the results as no clear pattern emerged as to why I was so inconsistent.

"You really shouldn't be able to do that," he said, stroking his beard and surveying the results of a rare successful test – the smoking husk of what used to be a stone. "It defies the laws of physics. It shouldn't be possible."

"Isn't that why they call it magic?" I laughed up at him.

He shook his head. "That's not how it usually works."

I smirked, throwing out a hip and leaning against the tree in the middle of the circle. "And yet somehow I..."

I trailed off as my palm tingled in its contact with the great oak. The bark was intense against my hand, my eyelids were incredibly heavy and they closed as I swayed closer, leaning against the tree. And was transported...

A dark, thin boy railed against the servants who were attempting to take furniture out of a room. Another boy with fair hair stood silently by. The servants ran off and reappeared with guards... no, warriors, for these were Celts. They were tall and broad, and clad in dark leathers with their swirling tattooed arms and long hair. They pushed the boy away, but he grabbed a sword and somehow managed to lift it. His pale face was defiant and determined. I couldn't make out the words that were spoken, but it was clear he had no intention of letting anyone in the room – or rather of letting any furniture out. Another large man stepped forward. This one wasn't dressed like the others. He spoke softly and the boy let his guard down. The large man, Callum, stepped forward and snatched the sword away before backhanding the boy with a hard blow. The boy crumpled in the doorway, struggling to find his feet, his arm up not in defence but in his ongoing attempt to bar the others' entry to the room. Callum and the warriors were angry now and moved forward with violent intent. The fair-haired boy stepped in front of the fallen one, his face blank but determined. No one moved.

I snapped back to the courtyard as the vision faded.

"You lied. You lied to me," I accused the older, greyer Callum who hovered over me, concern in his eyes. "You beat him. It wasn't the warriors, it was you."

Callum stepped back, away from my anger and accusation, his face taut with regret.

"I know. How do you tell a girl that you struck a silent grieving child? For I see now that he was grieving. Devyn was supposed to be her protector..."

"He was no more than a child himself!" I cut across him.

"Not then. I mean, when he was older... when they both were older, as his father was for her mother. But the Griffin failed. Instead he saved his own son whose very existence was a constant reminder, and who sulked about the castle, not deigning to speak to anyone. We were all hurting, and he was there, always there. That day, they were clearing the room, but he wouldn't let them. He wouldn't let people move on with their lives. All he would say was that she was alive. The baby girl was alive. He needed to accept that she was gone, to let us all accept it. That day... I'm a teacher, Cassandra. I'm a big man. I've never struck anyone, and that day I struck a child. I've never been so sorry for anything in my life." Callum's voice was barely a whisper by the time he had finished, his hand shaking as he lifted it to brush his shaggy hair off his face. "Never been so sorry."

I couldn't blame him for hiding his misdeed in his telling. Why would he want to share that shame with a stranger? That said, why had the oak chosen to share that part of the story with me? I had already known about the incident... mostly. What was the point of telling me the rest?

"Have you ever struck a child since?" I asked.

Callum recoiled, horrified that I would even ask the question. "No, of course not. Never, never again."

"Have you done anything against Devyn again?" I pursued. There had to be a reason for the vision, there had to be. Oaks had shown me things before, things that gave me insight or information that was crucial for me to know so I could understand better what was going on.

Callum's face was closed as he turned away. He looked at the tree and then back at me as he realised where I had gained my newfound knowledge of the long-ago incident. His eyes widened.

"You're a crannoir, a type of seer," he breathed. "Such an unusual gift. But then, you've managed to reach the elements... but not with the kind of power that would have sent the hounds after you. You are a conundrum, child."

"Fidelma said that too." She also said I wasn't the girl Devyn sought. Was the reason why I was unable to control the power in my blood the same reason she had failed to see the truth? "She said if I made it out of the city I should go to her."

"She did, hey?" Callum pulled at his beard. "If Fidelma saw

129

a use for you, there must be more than just the ability to commune with tree spirits. Let's try again."

Some hours and little further success later, we made our way back to his rooms where I fell into a chair, exhausted. While Callum was a little distracted, I asked the question that had been building up inside me for days since he had let slip that Devyn had been fostered in the house into which I had been born.

I couldn't ask him directly because Devyn had warned me about showing interest in the lost lady and her child, but surely somehow I could figure it out myself?

"Magic is in the bloodlines, right? So somewhere in the past, before the Code, I must have a Briton ancestor. Is there a way to identify which family I might descend from?"

Callum didn't look up from the books he was rifling through, muttering under his breath and cursing at whatever elusive tome he was searching for. The question hung heavily in the air – on my side at least.

"Ah, there you are." He pulled a dark-green book off a shelf. "Yes, and I've only ever heard of the ability to see the past manifesting in the older bloodlines. Crannoirs are rare. Even with the increase in city latents like yourself, it shouldn't be too difficult to figure out which line you trace back to."

"Oh yeah?" I dragged a finger through the dust on the shelf I stood beside, trying hard not to appear over-eager. When my parents locked me up to prevent me escaping with Devyn, when they failed to turn up at my trial, thereby washing their hands of me, I had started to accept the fact that they, the only family I had ever known, were not really my family. They adopted me for profit, not for myself, and for the advantages the city bestowed on them for raising me until I was old enough to be married off to the groom of their choosing. My birth mother died trying to protect me, and I had lived my life under the false care of people who were merely doing their city a service. My family, my home, my city – everything I had ever believed in and loved – was a lie.

Devyn was all I had. And he was as hard to hold onto as water in a stream: mesmerising to watch, whether it was still and deep and simply reflecting its surroundings, or turbulent and boiling over in a storm and pulling me along in a current that I was powerless to resist. But every time I tried to hold on to him, he slipped away. I needed something I could hold on to, a new centre that would ground me. Something to give me a connection to this new life, this new world.

"It would have been generations ago, but I suppose you might be able to trace it," he acknowledged.

"Is it possible to trace what kind of magic a particular bloodline has?"

"Yes, there are only so many families with the kind of magic you seem to have. It should be possible to figure out with which family you have the most affinity. In fact, that might be the answer to why you struggle so. If we speak to someone in the family, we could find some answers, or, better yet, solutions."

"It's possible? I might have a living family?" I rushed, tripping over the words. My entire being bubbled with hope and joy. I wasn't alone out here. There was somewhere I could go. Somewhere I could call home. I had promised Devyn I wouldn't tell anyone that I was anything other than Marcus's betrothed, but if I could figure it out on my own... They used books out here, so it wasn't like I would leave an electronic trail as I would have if my research had been online.

"It depends. Latents with magic tend to have a single gift. The stronger, older bloodlines can have different strengths, but some affinities are seen again and again. The House of York is particularly strong at healing. They usually have an affinity with air and water. Their magic originated with a woman called Jacquetta, a refugee from central Europe who settled in Anglia. Her daughter married into the House of York shortly before Anglia was regained from the Empire so it's no surprise Marcus is gifted at healing. You could have a poke around upstairs and look?"

Of course. I was in a college and colleges had libraries. There must be some kind of record. I knew by now that the power flowing through my veins wasn't entirely common. Based on the magic I had manifested before, I seemed to have some touch of all four elements. I didn't feel overwhelmingly stronger in one over another, which would have helped to narrow it down, but it seemed my ability to connect to trees and have visions of the past was rare. Apparently, there were only a few families left on this island who had any real power, and they were amongst the most important in the land. Devyn and Calchas had both been sure of the identity of my bloodline. Surely there was some history book or lineage of magic that would have recorded something about my mother... and any other surviving family?

"It's worth a look," I agreed. "While we're here."

Callum, his interest already dragged away by the volume in his hand, nodded absently. "Good, good."

Despite the thousands of books at my disposal, I still hadn't managed to locate one that gave me the information I needed. It was incredibly frustrating; used to hundreds of instant answers at the touch of a few keystrokes, following the trail of references and misleading titles – not to mention incorrectly shelved books – was unbelievably slow. And distracting. I started with a clear objective: to identify families with magical bloodlines. But these were often the highborn Britons, and the genealogical tangle assumed some previous knowledge of the families, the events and the major battles. My understanding of magic itself was basic, so that was another avenue I got sucked down. Even when I did hit on something it was often obscure. It became apparent that most information about magic and its uses was held by the druids, and it had not been written down in order to protect it or to make it even more annoyingly mysterious. I could find little to nothing about how or why seeing visions was only truly strong in particular bloodlines, or why magic itself randomly manifested in people like Marina.

I lost an entire evening to a pile of books that I found in a small room off the library, awaiting the return of whatever holidaying academic had assembled them. It wasn't particularly helpful but the study was intriguing, involving a great many tomes on ley lines, as well as histories of the Empire. I even studied a large map on a wall that traced outbreaks of the illness the Britons knew as the Mallacht across a timeline. It appeared that what Devyn said was true, and the instances had spread across the Empire over the last century or so. In the Empire they called it the Maledictio, the curse of the Celts. They blamed the magic of the druids and had hunted them into extinction across Gallia and Iberia. While the number of Maledictio cases were fewer in the absence of druids, the crops still failed and records showed severely declining harvests in the last ten or more years. The last known major outbreak in the central Med was over two decades ago – this was the outbreak that had claimed the life of Devyn's mother – but occasional dots on the map signified more recent cases in the last decade. These were rare though, and in more remote regions, like the Alps and the Ethiopian mountains.

For all the thousands of books, I had little to go on and was unable to ask either Devyn or Callum for help without revealing what I was up to. I'd had little luck in identifying potential bloodlines, but while success evaded me, it did allow me to get away from the increasingly toxic atmosphere in Callum's rooms in the evenings.

Whatever good the sword and fight training was doing for Marcus physically, it certainly wasn't improving relations between him and Devyn, which had gone from frostily indifferent to downright antagonistic. I didn't understand why; it wasn't over me, I was pretty sure. Marcus and I were on reasonably good terms, and over dinner I chatted to him about the things I had learned that day, with Callum occasionally correcting my interpretation. Devyn had been subdued since our arrival in Oxford, but tried to be polite, at least in the evenings. But the new bruises that decorated them both every evening testified that training was anything but polite.

The next day we spent the morning down by the river. Callum had suggested that being closer to nature might help. While the results were the same as in the courtyard, it was a relief to have further evidence that, out of the borderlands, the handfast tether between Marcus and me had expanded to more normal distances. At lunch, Callum and I headed back to the college, passing by where the other two trained.

They were both sweating, their shirts discarded in the late autumn sunshine. Not that it mattered to me; it was foolishness to be playing at swords with no clothes on, if you asked me. Yet my eyes were snared by the play of muscles in

Devyn's chest as he disarmed his opponent, and not for the first time if Marcus's expression was anything to go by.

Devyn nodded in greeting as we passed, pushing his damp curls out of his face as he demonstrated a stance or something to Marcus. Wooden swords, I noticed; that explained the bruises. I didn't suppose you got too many bruises with real swords.

Back in the training yard, Callum was starting to look defeated as I failed yet again to command the elements. Frustration seeped out of every pore and his mouth was set in a grim line.

"Give me your hand." I did as commanded.

He took my hand in the traditional Celt grip – hands clasped higher on the forearm, pulse points at the wrist facing each other. He closed his eyes and concentrated.

His blue eyes opened, and he frowned.

"There's barely a glimmer in your veins, girl. Did he think he could fool me? That believing you had strong magic meant I wouldn't hurt you?" His broad smile was unnerving.

I attempted to step back, to pull away. Devyn was right: Callum was not to be trusted. Suddenly I glimpsed an echo of the angry man who had hit Devyn as a boy. I tried to escape his grip, unnerved by his strength, his size.

"Now, now, my dear, I don't think you'll be going anywhere." He started to drag me towards a different door to the one we normally used. I tried to pull away again, but he held fast. Turning, he raised his hand as if to hit me.

Suddenly, fire licked along his hand, and as he let go of me, a gust of wind pushed him off his feet, sending him to the other side of the courtyard. The sky darkened overhead. I felt powerful. Crackling with energy. It was too much. I needed to get to Devyn. We needed to leave. Now.

Before Callum regained his feet, I was away across the yard and racing down the long corridor.

"Wait!" Callum's shout behind me was off. He no longer sounded threatening. He was... laughing?

I careened headlong into Devyn who was running to find me, and I sent him flying. The sword that had been in his hand skittered across the flagstones, coming to a stop under the foot of the oversized professor. Devyn was on his feet in a second and quickly put himself between his former tutor and me.

"Hold on, let's calm down for a minute." Callum put both hands out, palms up, in a gesture of peace. He took his foot off the sword and backed up a few steps. "I'm sorry to startle you, lass, truly. But I was starting to doubt you had any real trainable ability beyond small arbitrary fluke results. It was one last test I needed to do before we gave it up for a loss."

"You deliberately tried to scare me?"

"We had tried everything else. It occurred to me that you have had more success when threatened," Callum said, casting a glance at the sky overhead, which was still darkly angry. My entire body was also still crackling with energy. Devyn took my hand, his thumb moving soothingly against my palm. "I knew you had more in you, but this... To take in that much energy, you must have a great affinity with the ley lines. I've never seen the like outside of—"

He stopped talking suddenly, his eyes looking directly into mine in startled certainty. "He's done it. You're not some random latent he found in the city."

Callum stepped forward, his arm reaching out, and Devyn stepped in front of me once more.

"Damned say-nothing pup. You found her," Callum growled. "You found her, and you have me teaching her without even... How is this possible? Is this real? Is it really her?"

Devyn flashed a glance at me, his face as cold as it had been all week, but his eyes glowed as he faced his former teacher.

"It wasn't for you to know."

"Foolish pup." Callum put both hands up to his face in a wearied exasperation. I felt a tad insulted at his dismay; I thought my being alive was a good thing, personally. "You should have told me. You've got to go, and you've got to go now." He waved his hands and, grabbing me, started to pull me towards the courtyard door. He turned back to find Devyn and Marcus standing still in surprise, unmoving.

"NOW!" he roared.

As we hurried through the corridors back up to the professor's rooms, he explained that he had sent word to York that we – or rather Marcus, Devyn and some city girl – had made their way to Oxford. Devyn was furious. A party was already on its way to Oxford. On reaching his rooms, Callum was like a whirlwind in his kitchen, preparing food for us to take as we hurriedly put new packs together. The packs Marcus's father had given us were replaced by Briton-style travelling packs filled with food and Briton clothing that Callum had obtained for us.

We donned our cloaks and Callum took us down through his tower and along more deserted passages, deep into the bowels of the college, until at last we came to a cellar door which he raised.

"This way," he urged.

Devyn backed up warily, his face tight. "The last time I trusted another with the exit, we were delivered right up to the people chasing us."

Callum ran a hand through his hair in agitation. "I swear to

137

you on all I believe in, on the life of this girl, on the love I had for her mother, *I am true*. Go this way. There'll be no record of your exit from the city, and it'll buy you a little more time."

I made my way down into the dark holding the torch, Marcus having led the way down. I turned around to thank Callum and wish him farewell to find he had grabbed Devyn and was whispering urgently to him. The force of his final words carried them to me, or perhaps it was the pain that made them echo off Devyn.

"You know she is not for you."

138

Part Two

LOVE DRIPS AND GATHERS

The lips of time leech to the fountain head;
Love drips and gathers, but the fallen blood
Shall calm her sores.
And I am dumb to tell a weather's wind
How time has ticked a heaven round the stars.

And I am dumb to tell the lover's tomb
How at my sheet goes the same crooked worm.

— The force that through the green fuse drives the
flower, Dylan Thomas

Part Two

LOVE DRIPS AND GATHERS

Chapter Nine

Devyn beckoned us over from the barn he had just checked out. I sighed in pleasure at the sight of the hay in the corner; it looked like it would be infinitely softer and warmer than the cold ground we had slept on as we trudged north in the increasingly cold and wet weather. I could barely remember the last time I felt warm. Devyn had set a punishing pace since we left Oxford, barely speaking as we trudged over never-ending miles, keeping away from small towns and avoiding travellers as we pushed on.

Sitting down with a sigh, I struggled to pull off my boots to begin what had become our evening ritual. Devyn would disappear to scout the area, and he would bring back firewood and foraged food – late autumn berries, nuts and such mostly, but occasionally some fish which he would then cook.

Tonight, he had nowhere else to be. We had leftovers from the bounty he had secured from a farm for dinner and firewood was piled in the corner of the barn ready for the winter.

I paused, taking off my boots.

"Aren't you going to light the fire?" I asked, unwilling to have him watch while I extricated my feet from the torture devices that were my boots.

"Later," Devyn said.

Marcus knelt at my feet. "C'mon then, let's get it over with. The sooner you do this part, the sooner it'll be better."

I nodded, bracing myself as he undid the laces before easing the boots off my raw and bloodied feet as gently as he could. I winced as my socks followed.

"What in the— What are you doing?"

I opened my eyes to see a furious Devyn looming over me.

Marcus gritted his teeth as he continued his unpleasant task of releasing my feet before he healed them back to blessed normality.

"What?" I asked back, all innocence, even though I had done everything I could to hide this from him as we trekked north.

"What?" he echoed, astounded. "What cursed foolishness is this, Cass? How long has this been going on?"

"Uh… since we left Oxford."

"You've been walking on bloody feet for most of each day and then hero boy here is fixing you up in the evening," he said, watching as Marcus ignored him and got on with the business of healing my feet. "How could you be so stupid?"

"Stupid?" I asked.

"You're never going to build up hard skin if you keep making it as new every night."

Marcus stood until he was face to face with Devyn.

"Excuse me, but you hadn't even noticed. You think she should sleep in pain each night and then push on with her feet still raw the next day?" Marcus's voice was barely controlled.

Devyn looked down at me, taking a breath, considering what Marcus was throwing at him. But Marcus wasn't done.

"You bring us out here and you don't tell us what's going on. Where are we going? Who's chasing us? Who is it exactly that Callum believes Cassandra to be? Why are you...?" Devyn stepped back, allowing the city boy to rage at him. Whether it was because he was still off balance at learning of my feet or in surprise at Marcus raging at him was unclear.

As Marcus backed him up against the wall, Devyn locked eyes with him and remained silent.

"I'm so sick of this. Of you. Of everything."

With that, Marcus went crashing out through the door of the barn into the already black night.

The atmosphere grew increasingly heavy after Marcus stormed out. It had been brewing for a while. The two were so different, and we were all struggling to come to terms with life since the city. The easy, charming Marcus I had known had all but disappeared in his grief at his father's death; their toxic relationship and his father's unexpected sacrifice must be tearing him up. He was already struggling with the responsibility his power to heal put him under in a land ravaged by illness, especially when his ability to help was limited to so few.

It was Devyn I most wanted to reach. Since Samhain and Callum's cryptic parting words, I could feel him pulling away from me. I needed to reach him, but I didn't know how. I still knew so little about him."Devyn," I started. This was my chance. The prickle that had started in my arm indicated that Marcus had gone further away than he should. News I wasn't planning to share with our surly guide anytime soon in case he decided we had to go after him. Marcus wouldn't go much further, knowing that it would hurt me. He might be angry but he was still at heart a doctor, and I believed in my friend.

Devyn lifted his head to look at me from where he was tinkering with his pack on the other side of the barn. His dark gaze was inscrutable.

"He didn't mean it," I assured him.

"Oh, but I think he did."

Silence descended once more. I ran over scenarios in my head, different approaches. How could I get him to tell me what was going on in his head? I had given him time, waited for him to tell me, but that hadn't worked. I got up and went over to him, my steps crackling on the straw. I laid a hand on his tangled dark head, his lengthening black curls a magnet for my fingers. I felt like I hadn't touched him in an eternity. Thinking about it, I hadn't really. He had taken my hand that first day, but since that night in the forest on Samhain, we hadn't been close. The space between us was growing.

"What's going on?" I asked softly.

"Nothing's going on." He continued about his task, putting everything neatly back into his pack. I crouched down beside him, reaching for his cheek to turn his face to me. He shrugged me off. "Cass, I need to do this."

"What?" My tone was sharp. "You need to refill your pack? I'll wait the two minutes and then we can talk."

"There's nothing to talk about."

"Really?" I leant in to kiss him, and he turned his head away.

"Are you still going to tell me that nothing is wrong?" I pushed at him now that I had evidence for my cause.

He was still focused on his pack. "Marcus could come back in."

"I don't think so," I returned, in my frustration.

"What do you mean?" *This* he was interested in talking about.

"He's not just outside," I grudgingly admitted, "he's gone far enough away that I can feel it."

Attention caught, Devyn abandoned his half-finished pack. "You're in pain? Damn him. I'll go and fetch him back."

"No –" I caught his arm "– let him have some space. I'm fine. It's not that bad. It feels like the longer we are together, the further we can wander from each other, and we've been in each other's pockets since we crossed the border. Let him go. He'll be back in his own time."

Devyn looked down at me as he considered my words before nodding curtly. "Let me know if you need me to fetch him back."

"I need you to talk to me."

"Cass, there's nothing to talk about."

"Really? Then kiss me."

His dark eyes surveyed me intently, then he turned away and bent over his pack once more.

"I thought that when we were beyond the walls, that you and I…" I whispered brokenly into the silence. He was doing it again; it wasn't just a mood or that he was busy, he was deliberately distancing himself from me. By now, I more than knew the signs. I moved away as my eyes began to burn. I would not let him see me cry. Screw him.

"Some things just can't be," he said quietly to my retreating back.

An unwanted tear fell down my cheek. I hated him. After everything we had been through, he was doing this to me again. For the last time. I would not throw myself at him again. Ever.

This was a vow I was to discover shortly was also

impossible to keep. I woke in the dark, stiff from the cold despite the cloak that Devyn must have placed on me after I finally fell asleep.

Exhaustion from the day's trek eventually won out over the screaming arguments and accusations that raged through my head in the aftermath of his most recent declaration that we couldn't be together.

It wasn't the stiffness of my bones that had woken me though, but the molten hum that was flowing through me. My lids felt languorously heavy. I looked across to the other side of the barn where Devyn slept, half sitting up, leaning against the rough stone wall. There was still no sign of Marcus. I exhaled as another wave of warmth ran through my length, coiling inside, sinuous and sexy. I stretched, letting it flow through me. It felt good... which made no sense. I had dozed off, feeling despondent, miserable that Devyn had pulled away from me yet again.

Now I didn't mind so much, though I was slightly disgruntled at the distance between us. I made my way over to Devyn in the dark, pausing to take in his sleeping form as I stood over him. The faint slivers of moonlight that worked their way through the slatted door highlighted his high cheekbones and fuller lower lip. I had been so angry at him earlier, so utterly disappointed, but that feeling had drifted away and was replaced now by a tugging urgency. I needed him.

It no longer seemed so important whether Devyn spoke to me or kept his promises. What was important was getting closer, touching him. My hands lifted of their own volition, my fingers tracing his face, moving softly across the silvery path of his cheekbones. Leaning down, I touched my lips to his.

I was all sensation. I could feel the heat coming off his body,

I could inhale deeply the combination of smells that was uniquely Devyn. I ran featherlight kisses across his face.

His breathing changed and I knew he was no longer asleep but he didn't open his eyes, delaying the moment when he would have to acknowledge what was happening and push me away.

Taking advantage of his momentary lapse, I sat down beside him and, lifting his blanket, snuggled in. I tangled myself around him, chest to chest, hip to hip, our legs entwined. My hand wandered across his broad shoulder and down along his muscled arm, falling to his waist and then under his shirt. My fingers crept up his spine as I pressed myself closer.

I touched my lips to his again, and this time he responded, sleepily, warmly rolling his tongue with mine. His hands came around me. We kissed slowly, unhurried, enjoying ourselves. But the burn in my blood grew stronger and would not be denied. I turned up the tempo on our kiss, making my will known. The kiss heated up in response. I pushed Devyn so that he was lying on his back and moved with him, so I was lying on top of him. Our lower bodies were joined, my body yearning for that connection. I needed more... more contact, more heat. I was on fire.

Breaking off the kiss, I sat up, pulling my top over my head. If my purpose was to stop Devyn thinking and encourage him to just go with the moment, it seemed that taking things a notch higher served only to bring him to his senses. As I leaned in again to kiss him, his whole body stilled under mine. I was losing him. I knew it. I used what connection I still had to press my invitation. I needed this, needed him, the burning in my body assuaged only by contact with his. I could feel him through the thin cloth that separated us. He was not unmoved. Definitely not indifferent.

Not entirely on board either though. He turned us so that I was now on the ground and he could pull his hips away from mine. His eyes glittered down at me as he sucked in a breath to regain some control as I wriggled frantically beneath him. I needed more. Fire licked through me, seeking oxygen, and I lifted my head to kiss him once more, to bring him back into the inferno with me. The need pulsed through me. He groaned as he pulled his head out of reach, his hands restraining me, holding me down as he maintained what distance he could.

"Cass." His voice was tortured, questioning. "What is going on?"

"Please," I answered in reply, twisting my body up to regain contact.

He freed one hand to retrieve the blanket and attempted to cover me with it. I used that hand to grab a fistful of dark hair and pull his head back to mine, and now that he was caught, he responded once more, his tongue dancing with mine in the dark.

The blanket he had pulled between us fell away again and, untangling my hand from his hair where it was no longer needed to hold him to me, I pushed his shirt up and away. My skirt was tangled up around my waist as I sought and found as much skin to skin contact as possible.

I sighed, exhaling from sheer want and need. Devyn groaned in my ear.

"Cass…"

He was as caught up in the heat as me as the flames burned down the mental wall he had built between us.

We were both frantic with it, heat pulsing through us as we sought to get closer and closer, his flesh, mine, one body. The fire raged and burned us up, engulfing us both as we exploded together. Consuming us from the inside out.

I came to, shivering from the aftermath as well as the cold on our sweat-slicked skin in the chill of the night air. I could still feel Devyn, could feel our hearts fluttering in synch. I laid my hand across his chest to lie on top of his heart. And I felt him flinch.

Not again. How could I have been so stupid? Nothing had changed; he didn't want me. Nobody wanted me. I curled onto my side into a ball as my body physically attempted to protect me from the crushing pain wafting through me.

"Cass?" His voice came out of the darkness.

I couldn't answer. I didn't know how. The blaze that had consumed me was utterly gone, and in its wake lay the bitterest of ashes. My soul felt like a wasteland. I kept believing in what was between us in spite of the evidence he presented again and again that he didn't want this. That he didn't want me.

"Cassandra." His voice came again, stronger this time, demanding an answer. He put his blanket around me. "I'm sorry."

A sob bubbled up from deep inside me. I shook my head. No. I didn't want to hear his apologies. Didn't want to listen to his explanations of why he didn't want to be with me.

Unable to help myself now, the sob broke through, followed by a devastating torrent of them. I couldn't hold them inside any longer, and they consumed me. Devyn wrapped himself around me as they took me over. I cried all the tears that I had in me, for the storm of flame had burned down all my defences. I cried for the life I had left behind, the family and future that were no longer mine, for Marcus who had lost his father, for Devyn who had lost everything to find

149

me. For the heartbreak I felt inside at this second devastating rejection.

I had known that Devyn was pulling away. I had known I needed to go softly, to figure out why he was doing it, to fix it. The balance had still been in my favour. What had possessed me? Why had I pushed so hard? I needed to tread carefully, instead of which, out of nowhere, I had backed him into a corner. I thought back to my behaviour and my cheeks burned as I recollected my advances. I had jumped him in the middle of the night.

"I don't know what came over me," I began to apologise.

I tried to pull out of his arms, unable to think, unable to make any sense of his words as my skin crawled in self-disgust. In shame.

He held on to me tighter.

"I don't think it was you," he sighed in the darkness.

I shook my head. I didn't understand.

"Whatever is going on in your crazy mind right now, stop it. What just happened, it wasn't you."

Some part of me surfaced through the roiling shame and ashes, and I didn't understand. What wasn't me? What did he mean to imply, that I was not responsible for throwing myself at him? That made no sense; of course it was me. I was the one who got up in the middle of the night and practically forced myself on him, even though I knew that was the last thing he would welcome at the moment.

"Marcus," Devyn said, lifting my chin to look him in the eyes. I couldn't hold his gaze. "This was Marcus. We know that the handfast band leaks desire. It wasn't you. Marcus must be..."

He didn't need to finish. While Marcus was shielded by the charm he still wore, without my pendant, I was vulnerable to the effects of the handfast. Devyn's presence allowed me to think clearly, but he couldn't protect me from the leaked passion and the pain we felt on seperation. I understood. But I didn't care. Why it had started was now less important than how it had finished. With the proverbial crash.

"Leave me alone."

"But Cass, this wasn't your fault. It was—"

I couldn't look at him. "Leave me alone."

I did not want to debate this, not now, I felt raw and empty. I closed my eyes to shut him out. He unwound his arms and went over to my blankets for I was now wrapped in his. I lay there dry-eyed, listening to the wind and rain hammer down until the first rays of dawn broke through.

"Where have you been?" Devyn's angry snarl alerted me to Marcus's return as the grey dawn light entered through the open door with him.

Marcus pulled his sopping wet hood down and unwrapped the scarf from the lower half of his face to reveal a taunting smirk. "What business is it of yours?"

Devyn's glance over at me was more revealing than it needed to be. Marcus followed his gaze and immediately realised something had happened. Whatever he read in my face was presumably the cause of the flash of guilt that crossed his before he squared his shoulders and stuck out his jaw.

"No fun, is it?" he threw at me pugnaciously. He didn't care that his actions of the previous night had made their presence felt here in the barn. Rage flooded through me. He knew what he had done to me and how bad things were between Devyn and me and he didn't care. Two short steps had me face to face with him, and the next thing I knew he was looking back at me with a shocked expression and the palm of my hand stung from its contact with his smug, handsome face.

"No fun," I replied belatedly.

The resounding silence was punctuated by the sound of the door crashing as Devyn exited the barn. There wasn't room for three of us in here right now. I felt like the air had been punched out of my lungs as I watched my red handprint light up Marcus's face.

I winced as I met Marcus's gaze, expecting to find anger there, but the look in his eyes was one of loneliness. The rage seeped out of me. What he had done was ugly, but he was in pain.

"I'm…" Was I sorry? What he had done was unforgivable, no matter how understandable. "I shouldn't have… It's just all so messed up."

I felt dreadful. Marcus had needed to blow off some steam. Who was I to be so bloody self-righteous? He had been on the receiving end of me being with Devyn. Marcus had every right to be mad at me. He put his hand on mine in acknowledgement of my apology before pulling away to start putting his pack together.

"Where did you go?" I asked softly. Whatever the answer, Devyn was unlikely to approve, so I kept my voice low.

"There's a village a mile or so back that we passed yesterday. I went to the inn there."

I nodded, absorbing the risk he had taken when he stormed out of here last night. Scratch Devyn being unlikely to approve; he would be livid if he knew what Marcus had done. There was a reason we weren't sleeping in soft beds every night. I swallowed my annoyance at Marcus's selfishness, reminding myself that I'd had months to get used to the idea of leaving the city for the wilderness. Marcus had only faced the inevitability of this new life a couple of weeks ago.

"You can't just go off on your own like that." What had he been thinking? We were only a few days out of Oxford. Whoever was chasing us was unlikely to be on foot. "Anyone could have taken you, and we wouldn't have known."

"You'd have figured it out sooner or later," Marcus replied, indicating his arm. The distance we could get from one another had extended back to the levels we had been used to in Londinium but that was all. Who knew what would happen? If anyone had tried to take him, there was only so far that distance would stretch before I would start to suffer. The cursed handfast cuffs.

"An inn?" I lowered my voice despite being reasonably certain Devyn wasn't within earshot. It was one thing for Marcus to wander off in a huff; it was another for him to engage with the locals. Devyn did all our talking on the rare occasions when we had to interact with anyone so we wouldn't give away how very strange to these lands we were. "What were you thinking?"

Marcus raised an eyebrow at me. "It's okay for you and him to get up to whatever you feel like. It's the first time I've ever been with someone who wasn't faking it. Unlike some, I never betrayed my match. I've never been with anyone but you. And you were only with me because of the handfast and because Devyn told you to." I stilled in my packing but couldn't raise my head and face him, even though I could feel him looking directly at me. Marcus had been on the receiving end of my emotions whenever I tangled with the Briton who drove me crazy, emotions that he had never inspired in me. What little chemistry had surfaced between us had been engineered by the handfast and was a pale imitation of what I had with Devyn.

Something that Marcus must realise now. If he had found something of his own with some local girl, who was I to begrudge him? "Didn't she notice that you aren't a Briton?"

"I told her I was from Kent, a Shadower looking to trade anything I could find. Besides, we didn't do much talking." He winked.

"So I noticed," I said sourly. He might think it was fun but I had never intentionally set out to hurt him with the effects of the handfast. Could he say the same?

Marcus raised his eyebrows, probably wondering what exactly his actions had incited back at camp. My face burned. Let him wonder. Toad. All I needed to complete my humiliation was for Marcus to know what had happened last night.

"Well, if you're finished regaling Cass with tales of your tomcatting, we'll get moving, shall we?" Devyn sneered, having caught the end of our conversation.

Marcus's head whipped up and he turned to face down the Celt standing in the doorway.

"My *what*? How dare you! Like you can talk. I heard Callum: you shouldn't be anywhere near her. There is no chance for you and her, yet you took her from me. When we were out in the borderlands, you said you wouldn't touch her again. I don't know why but I'm pretty sure you'll never be allowed to be with her. So who and what I get up to isn't something you get to have any say in." By the time he had finished, there were mere inches between them, each daring the other to strike the first blow.

"Is he right?" I asked into the charged room. I had hoped it was just a temporary thing while we were with Callum, but he had remained distant.

I was so tired of being in the dark. I knew that Briton society was much more strictly hierarchical than the society I had grown up in. I didn't know where I fitted into that society because Devyn still wouldn't tell me, insisting it was safer for me not to know. From the glimpses I'd seen of this world, I thought Devyn was in the same class, a nobleman, so why would they not allow us to be together? Whatever the reason, Devyn clearly knew it. He had tried to stay away from me from the start and he continued to push me away.

"Is that true?" I demanded again.

Devyn tore his macho eyeballing away from Marcus to give me a tormented look. His walls were still up so I couldn't sense his emotions, but they were writ loud on his face: pain, shame, truth. The same emotions that had run through him after we had been together that first – and until last night, *only* – time.

"Right," I said to no one in particular. I needed a minute to process this. Or rather, I needed more information to fight whatever it was that would keep Devyn and me apart.

Marcus shoved against Devyn as he collected his pack and exited the barn into the morning light. Devyn stood unmoving, never taking his eyes off me as I processed this new information.

"You're not going to explain any of that, are you?" I asked. It was all I could do to keep my voice from breaking.

He pushed his fingers through his dark curls. "Cass, I can't. I—"

He broke off, his attention caught by something outside. His voice rose to carry out to Marcus.

"Where are you going?"

I couldn't hear Marcus's reply, but it gave Devyn an excuse

not to answer my question. "We need to go. Marcus is halfway down the road already."

"Of course he is," I huffed in annoyance as I gathered my pack. How convenient.

I drew the hood of my cloak over my head as I stepped out into the pouring rain, wrapping my scarf as high up on my face as I could. Devyn preferred us to travel like this. That way, if anyone asked, we were just three nondescript travellers on the road. Not a fair-haired woman with two darker-haired men. Even during what little interaction we had with people on the road, Devyn did all the talking, a scarf wrapped around his lower face, for while he spoke with a more pronounced Briton accent out here, he was also the one who was most likely to be recognised. Devyn was from here and those who chased us knew what he looked like, so he took extra precautions to remain concealed.

I knew nothing about them, these shadowy figures who were pursuing us across the countryside. I sighed as I trailed after Devyn, who ensured he stayed a few steps in front so I couldn't engage him in conversation. Marcus also kept quite a way ahead of us as the path wound through the woods, and I only occasionally caught glimpses of him before the trees obscured him once more.

Chapter Ten

W e had lost sight of Marcus after he crested a hill ahead of us when suddenly we heard raised voices ahead. Devyn indicated that I should stay quiet and then we hurried up the hill. As ever, to my annoyance, my efforts to make as little noise as possible were substantially less successful than I wanted them to be. Arriving at the top of the hill, we could see Marcus in a clearing below surrounded by half a dozen men on horseback.

The smaller man at the front dismounted and strode towards Marcus.

"I told you, I'm a Shadower looking to trade."

We couldn't hear what the man said as he was facing away from us but he was making a big show of looking around.

"I don't have anything with me. I'm scouting," Marcus protested in response. "If your bed was cold this morning, I'll be happy to warm it again when I come back this way."

Not a man. His lady friend from last night. Perfect.

Devyn's eyes narrowed as he learned more of Marcus's escapades of the night before, and he muttered under his breath at Marcus's arrogant ham-handed answers. He indicated that I should stay hidden while he dealt with the situation. I shook my head; I wanted to go with him. But he glared me down and I retreated behind a particularly wide tree trunk as he wound his scarf higher around his face.

"Ho, friends," Devyn hailed the group as he walked into the clearing.

Spooked by his unexpected appearance, the riders drew their swords, their horses skittering at the charged atmosphere. The dismounted cloaked woman pointed hers directly at Marcus while the rider closest to Marcus nudged his horse forward, blocking Devyn's route.

"Good day, friend," he responded sardonically. The warrior's hood was down and his long hair tied back, revealing, even from this distance, that he was exceptionally handsome despite the scar that tracked down his right cheek. "Can we help you?"

Devyn looked up at him and alarm pulsed through the connection. Whoever he was, Devyn recognised him, and he was most certainly not someone he considered a friend.

"Just looking for my travelling companion," Devyn replied, coolly edging his way around the horse in order to reach Marcus's side. "'All's well?"

Marcus tore his angry eyes from the armed rider in front of him.

"Fine. I was just telling these folks that we are merely passing through, on the lookout for new trading opportunities." Marcus repeated his story. I couldn't see Devyn's expression from here, but I'm sure he was less than pleased with Marcus right now for attracting the attention of these riders. Were they the ones that Callum had said were coming for us?

"Long way from the shadow of the wall out here," the scarred warrior on the horse nearest Devyn answered. "Don't get too many traders this side of the borderlands. Spies, perhaps."

Devyn laughed, raising his hands in a placating gesture. "Spies? My friend here ain't clever enough to be a spy, and I am from Powys; I'm a Celt through and through. I have no love for the Empire."

"That so? You folks been on the road long?"

"Not too long. We were in Bath for Samhain. Been on the road since then," Devyn continued to saunter across to Marcus, stopping when he reached his side. He stood ever so slightly between him and the dismounted warrior's drawn sword.

"Your friend said you were in Oxford," the woman said, raising the sword so it lightly touched Marcus's chest. She had a scarf wrapped around the lower half of her face against the driving rain, but you could hear the flash of false smile in her voice.

"We stopped in at Oxford on our way," Devyn explained, his voice betraying none of the irritation I sensed through the bond; he had let the barrier between us down a touch, no doubt to use it as a way to tell me to run if things went badly. Run. As if I would leave them. Where would I go without them? Marcus, I couldn't leave. Devyn, I wouldn't.

"Quite the circuitous route." The tall warrior nudged his horse menacingly forward, hedging them in. His skill was apparent as he manoeuvred his horse with a featherlight touch of his big tattooed hands.

"No crime in that." Devyn smiled back. "We got plenty of time, nowhere in particular to be."

"You meet many others on the road?" a third rider asked.

Like the others, he wore a dark cloak with the hood up, but long red hair was visible from underneath.

"Some, aye," Devyn responded shortly.

"We're looking for two men and a girl," the red-haired rider said. "Probably dressed as Shadowers. You seen anyone like that on your travels?"

"Can't say that I have," Devyn replied calmly. "Now, if it's all right with you, friends, we'll be on our way."

Devyn started forwards and Marcus moved to follow him. The sword against his chest held firm, and Marcus was forced to stay put.

"But it's not all right with us," the woman at the other end of that sword said softly. "Your Shadower friend is going to come with us. I'd like to enjoy his company a little longer."

"Didn't get enough last night, did you?" Marcus taunted the hooded figure. The rider was holding the pointy end of a reasonably substantial looking sword to his chest, and he thought the best way to defuse this situation was to offend her further?

"That's right, and I decide when a man leaves my bed. Can't recall any man sneaking out before. That makes you... interesting. So, we'll hang on to you for a little while. See if you don't get a little chattier with some of my friends here."

"I do apologise for my friend's poor manners but we have to be on our way." Devyn drew the sword Callum had supplied from its scabbard and the dismounted rider somewhat reluctantly pulled her sword away from Marcus's chest to defend against the new threat. What was Devyn thinking? It was six against one. If you didn't include Marcus, which I didn't. In fact, at this point, I'd happily beat the crap out of him myself.

At a gesture from the woman on the ground, who seemed

to be their leader, the riders pulled back, making space for the pair to fight. Rather than use their extra numbers, they seemed happy to let her have at it, confident that Devyn and Marcus, two humble travellers on the road, proved no real threat to any of their company one on one.

She and Devyn circled one another, each taking in the other, the terrain, and the space available. The girl feinted first, Devyn easily deflecting her strike. Then they went at it, trading blow for blow. The girl was fast and, despite the size of the sword she wielded, never seemed to tire. Her footwork was better than Devyn's. Devyn had spent the last decade in the city; when was the last time he had used a sword properly? The few days he spent showing Marcus the basics were not going to count against this warrior's evident skill.

Marcus's attempt to fade into the trees while the group's attention was on the fight was blocked by the scarred rider who smiled wolfishly down from his horse as soon as Marcus took his first couple of backwards steps. I needed to do something. Devyn was not going to beat the girl, and even if he did, I sincerely doubted that her friends would be happy just to let them walk away.

Callum had said I should try to avoid using powerful magic when I was out in the open. The hounds of Samhain had my scent, and he felt they were unlikely to give me up so easily. Apparently, they were not bound to either the borderlands or that night. Nor would they be caught unawares as they had the first time. But what choice did I have?

I sucked in a steadying breath and stepped out from behind my tree. I focused, as Callum had taught me, letting my consciousness flow out as I exhaled and dragged in energy from the forest around me with each breath. Devyn's consciousness distracted me from my task; he could feel me trying to summon my power. I shook him away. I needed to concentrate. I breathed in and out, but still it wasn't working. Despite my recent training, I continued to fail to command the energy to come to me. I opened my eyes and lifted my head, taking in the scene below me. Devyn was pushed back against a tree. He was tiring. What was worse, he had ceased to attack and had retreated to defence only. As if he could sense my approach, his head snapped towards me. I made my way down the track, drawn helplessly to a fight I could not possibly hope to assist. He shook his head at me and I stopped, confused. What had I missed? Why, when he was so clearly losing, was he taking the time to wave me back?

With the bond open I realised I couldn't sense any fear, though there was some fatigue. What was oddest of all was the mischief I could suddenly identify, and in the same moment, he pounced forward, new energy in his arm as he feinted and parried with his sparring partner.

The girl danced backwards, their struggle taking on a new rhythm as she wove her way back across the clearing. I couldn't quite understand what was happening. One moment Devyn had been fighting for his life and now it felt like he was playing a game. Confused, I looked around at the rest of the people in the glade. Her fellow riders clearly didn't like the change of tempo and were leaning forward, watching uneasily. But it was the scarred rider who caught my eye. I looked back at the girl fighting Devyn; she too was starting to flick glances at the rider. It felt like she was warning him off.

Her footwork was slowly growing clumsier while Devyn pressed her harder, and then she was on the ground. From where I stood, I could finally see her face as her scarf had drooped around her neck in the fight. Her eyes widened as she fell, but looking back up at her opponent from the ground, a familiar mocking grin spread across her face. Devyn turned slightly towards where I stood and winked.

I glared back, and our eyes held as I saw his widen with shock and pain. I flinched at the echo stabbing into my own body. Across the clearing, the rider who stood in front of Marcus had a second knife ready in his hand.

"No." The scarred rider had decided to disobey his leader's instruction not to intervene. His knife was now sticking out of Devyn's shoulder. The girl on the ground turned to the rider, attempting to rise and put her body in between them, her long dark braid falling loose.

Devyn fell back, his hand going to the injured shoulder. Rage and fear surged through me. I had rained a storm down on Richmond in his defence, and I would flatten this forest, this entire island, if he died. I ran forward, my sights set on the rider still nonchalantly weighing his next throwing knife, delaying his follow-up in light of his leader's defence of Devyn.

"Cass," Devyn called. "No, stop."

He took a few faltering steps towards me, but I was only half aware as the hum of power surged through me, alive and vengeful. He stumbled past the girl who had dropped her sword to the ground.

She swore as she too stepped towards me, her hands raised in surrender. Well she might surrender; I would leave nothing of any of them but red mist on the grass.

"Damn, no. Cassandra." She knew my name. How did she know my name? These were the people who were chasing us and I was so bloody tired of being hunted. I would become the hunter. Let these people be a lesson to the next who came to try and hurt us.

But as I took in the scene before me, Devyn stood between me and my prey.

"Get out of my way," I snarled, not even registering that his injury could hardly be fatal if he had made his way towards me. He had one hand pressed to the bleeding handle, the other raised palm up towards me. The leaves rustled angrily as my power swirled around the clearing.

"No, Cass. Hush, it's okay," he said soothingly. "It was a mistake. They're friends. Friends. It's okay."

His certainty pulsed through the bond.. His walls were fully down, his emotions flooding through to me, damping the rage that surged through my body. I looked back at him, confused. These people were not my friends. I narrowed my gaze at the woman he had been fighting. The one who started all this. Bronwyn stood there, his friend from the Treaty Renewal, wearing the clothes of the rider he had fought. Her scarf was pulled down, framing her pale, fine-boned face, wisps of dark hair whipping free of her braid and across her face in the wind that surged around us.

Devyn stepped closer, his palm cupping my cheek, dragging my attention away from my targets. I didn't understand. I wanted to take them down.

"Shhh, everything's all right." His dark eyes were gentle and I couldn't follow what he was trying to tell me, the power swirled within me, demanding release. I was aware of Devyn's closeness but remained tense and ready for action. He had left himself vulnerable – his back was to our enemies – and I shifted to put them back in my view. At a gesture from Bronwyn, the mounted warriors dropped their swords, the one with the scar slow to sheathe his second knife. I allowed the storm to swell and the trees by him swayed precariously; he was the most significant threat, the one who would be first to strike. Had already been the first to strike. He had hurt Devyn.

Devyn, whose lips were gently touching mine, his whispers gentling me, distracting me as they had that first time that nature responded to my call, deepening his kiss, sweeping in, my being lighting with a different kind of fire. The winds gentled as his kiss deepened, his lips moving across mine, then nibbles at my jaw and soothing whispers in my ear. I wrapped my arms around him, my fingers as always anxious to wind themselves through his hair. My hand ran down his back, his hand awkward at his side, a jarring note in the new song that he had started in my body. His shoulder. I gasped, pulling back. He was bleeding. Finally, coming to, I reached for his hand to see how bad the injury was. He had closed the connection between us and I had lost all sense of it.

"Marcus," I called urgently. "Marcus, please."

He shook his head, his green eyes coming alert as he ran to his bag and carried it over with him. The scarred rider sat unmoving, watching the scene.

"Well, well, if we haven't caught our three little mice," he drawled, his eyes on me.

I glared at him before turning on Bronwyn who still stood hesitantly a few feet away. "What have you done?"

"It wasn't exactly me," she sighed, indicating behind her at the unrepentant rider.

"The two of you," I rounded on Devyn. "You knew and kept going anyway."

"It had been a while," he said. "I wanted to see if she had improved any."

He hissed as Marcus examined the hilt of the knife in his shoulder. Bronwyn watched worriedly.

"Dammit, I'm sorry. I didn't know. I didn't see his face.

There were two men and we were looking for three of you. I thought they might be from the city in pursuit," she gabbled, tripping over her words in an attempt to explain. "I'm sorry, Devyn."

"Don't be. It wasn't you who did it," he snarled towards the now dismounted rider as we helped Devyn to the ground.

"What? Like I was going to sit there and let some Shadower scum scratch up my favourite princess," Scar said as he stood over Devyn.

"I wasn't going to harm her."

"No way for me to know that," he replied. Leaning down, Scar wrapped his hand around the knife where Marcus had removed Devyn's shirt and was cleaning the entry site and pulled it roughly from where it sat just below Devyn's shoulder.

The pain lanced through me, and I launched myself at the dark swirl of leather and cloak.

He caught me and we tumbled to the ground, his grip on my wrists holding my clawed hands at bay.

"Now, now, kitty cat, put your claws away... or do you want me to kiss it better?" he soothed, laughing in my face as he held me. I pulled and kicked ineffectually, wishing for a spark of magic to light within me. But with the real danger having dissipated, there was no sign of it.

"Let her go, Gideon, or I will end what's left of your pretty-boy looks," Devyn's face growled from above us.

"Spoilsport."

I was free and scrambled to stand and regain what dignity I had left.

I looked aghast at the blood trickling down Devyn's torso before turning back to my recent wrestling partner. I pulled my arm back, tucked my thumb on the outside as Callum had taught me during a more practical session, and struck with full force right on his elegantly straight nose. His head reared back and when it righted, blood was pouring down his face, giving me the strongest sense of satisfaction I had known in a very long time.

"Ha," he said, "it looks like your little kitten here can scratch, after all."

"Good for you, Cass," Bronwyn approved, turning to the tall, broad-shouldered warrior. "Enough, Gideon. Walk away."

With a smirk in my direction he bowed out.

I glared at the oaf and, turning, caught the glance that Bronwyn and Devyn exchanged.

"It's got to be said, I nearly had you." Devyn smiled up at his recent opponent from where Marcus had seated him in order to tend his wound.

"Hardly," she retorted.

"I held my own," Devyn defended himself.

"Ha. Some champion," Bronwyn bantered, while Marcus mopped blood from the wound to get a clear view.

A sadness haunted Devyn's dark eyes as he watched the knife-throwing ass attend to his horse. "The path not walked."

Bronwyn's lids lowered to cover her eyes at her faux pas. "We'll have to train you back up now though, hey?"

"He's going to need stitches," Marcus announced.

"You can't just heal him?" I asked quietly.

He shook his head. "No, I've already tried. I don't know how to treat open wounds with magic, and I don't think I've recovered enough yet anyway. We're going to need a fire," he informed Bronwyn, her cold gaze reminding him that she hadn't forgotten that they had unfinished business. "And a needle and thread."

"Sounds fun," Devyn murmured. His hand felt cold in

mine and I wrapped both of mine around his, whether to warm him or reassure myself I wasn't sure.

Devyn gritted his teeth and showed little sign of his pain as Marcus pulled the needle in and out of his flesh, stitching back together what Gideon had sundered. At Devyn's warning glare, to show less concern I was forced to retreat out of the glade under the pretext that I was squeamish. Instead I walked off the tightness that wound every sinew and muscle in my body, before we mounted or doubled up on the horses to continue north.

I felt hollowed out as I watched Devyn sleep in the light of the fire while Bronwyn and scarface-ass Gideon argued over what to do in the morning. Frustrated by the pace of our travel with a wounded member, Gideon was arguing that we split up, with him taking Marcus and me ahead while Bronwyn could travel slowly behind with Devyn.

"No," I said quietly across the fire, repeating it louder until they finally turned to look at me. "No, no, no."

Gideon raised a brow, the arch pulling at the scar on his face.

"No?" he queried, the smirk I had begun to recognise as habitual playing on his lips.

"No," I repeated. "We will not be splitting up. Devyn has got us this far and we are not leaving him behind. "

Gideon narrowed his eyes. "Fine, you stick with the Griffin. It's him that's wanted anyway." He nodded in the direction of Marcus's sleeping form.

Marcus, despite his claims that he wouldn't be able to help Devyn with his magic, had overextended himself again, if his renewed exhaustion was anything to go by. Marcus did not trust our new travelling companions in the slightest, but he had barely made it off his horse before falling asleep.

"You're not splitting us up," I repeated once more, in the hope that this time the smirking hulk might finally comprehend what I was saying.

The smirk widened into a full-blown grin before he turned back to Bronwyn, continuing to outline his plans as though I hadn't interrupted.

"I don't think I'm making myself clear," I said quietly. "Marcus and I actually cannot be separated. It's not a matter of choice."

They turned to look at me once more. Gideon frowned.

"We're handfasted," I rushed on, before I lost their attention again. I pulled up my sleeve to show them the distinctive armband. "Marcus and I won't survive being more than a few miles away from each other for an extended period."

"Fine. Then I'll take you too, city girl."

Gideon leaned back, satisfied at the return to his original solution.

"I'm not leaving without Devyn."

"Nobody is splitting the group up," Bronwyn stated, flashing me a warning glance and a quick shake of her head. There it was again, that flash of a hint that my being with Devyn was not okay and that I would do better to hide our... whatever it was.

"The Anglians want Marcus Courtenay. The Mercians want the Griffin. It makes sense to split up. You want me to throw the Griffin over the back of a horse and drag his arse north, with York chasing us, we can do that." Gideon paused for emphasis. "It'll probably kill him, but maybe that would be a kindness compared to what awaits him."

"What? What do you mean, what awaits him?"

"Shut up, Gideon," Bronwyn said. "Of course it won't kill him. He has a wound to the shoulder; despite your best efforts, it was far from fatal."

Gideon snorted.

"If that were my best shot, the Griffin would be dead. Besides, I wasn't really even in the queue; it would hardly have been right to have robbed so many others of the pleasure."

Bronwyn stilled, her eyes icing over as she surveyed the languid length of the warrior laid out on the other side of the campfire.

"You knew it was my cousin when you threw that blade?"

Scar snorted again, pulling his cloak around him as he settled back to sleep for the night. I absorbed this new snippet of information. I had been jealous of Bronwyn from the first time I had seen her with Devyn. Admittedly, she'd had her hands all over him, which would be hard for anyone to take, even if Devyn and I hadn't exactly been talking at the time. Cousins.

"Gideon." Bronwyn was coldly furious.

"Perhaps."

"What? Why would you do that?"

There was no answer from the other side of the fire.

Bronwyn threw her cup and a grunt indicated she had found her target. It wasn't enough for me. My grip tightened on the knife in my hand. Right now, I could quite cheerfully plunge it into the intricately tattooed neck.

"Sheathe your claws." His soft lilting drawl indicated he somehow knew my intentions. "If you're going to go for blood every time somebody touches your boy, you're going to be a busy girl."

"He's not my boy," I corrected.

"Good." He rolled over, away from the fire. "A city latent and the damned Oathbreaker, what a mess that would have been."

"What does that mean?"

There was no answer. It seemed Gideon was done talking. Arrogant ass. I looked to Bronwyn for an explanation, surprised to see the sad look on her face as she glanced over to where Devyn lay.

"What does he mean?" I demanded. I couldn't let it go. Why could Devyn and I not be together? And what awaited him when we arrived? I knew he was not loved – I had seen that much – but Gideon implied much worse lay ahead.

Bronwyn cast me a quelling look and shook her head. But I couldn't leave it. Since we had crossed the borderlands, Devyn had pulled away from me and Bronwyn knew why.

"Bronwyn."

The pale Celtic girl glared at me now, tight-lipped. "Just go to sleep, Cassandra."

"What my lady doesn't want to tell you, city girl, is that your guide may have a very short future, and what does remain certainly doesn't involve playing happily-ever-after," Gideon finally spoke again.

"Gideon." Bronwyn's voice cracked, whip-like, across the dying embers.

"Well, he did break his oath. You think the welcoming committee is breaking out the party food? Sharpening the knives, more like. The Griffin used up his second chance. He was a child last time. He'll be lucky if they consider his carcass worthy of throwing to the dogs when they're done with him."

Chapter Eleven

As we rode on the next morning, I mulled over what I had learned the night before. We made better time on horseback and my feet were grateful, even if I despised the man who sat behind me. The three of us had been on foot and the group did not have extra horses to carry the recent additions to their party. Marcus rode with the smallest of Bronwyn's men, while Devyn shared with his cousin. So far, so much sense. Why I had been lumbered with the most offensive warrior in the group was beyond fathoming, but he had insisted. Neither Devyn nor Marcus had seemed too happy with the idea either.

When Bronwyn and I had gone down to the brook to wash up before we broke camp, she had taken the opportunity to speak privately to me.

"Cass, you must be careful. I don't know what's between you and Devyn, but you are here as Marcus's betrothed. The countryside is teeming with warriors searching for Marcus; he has value to them and as his bride, you too will be safe. But it sure looked like you were with Devyn rather than Marcus yesterday. It cannot be," she whispered, her hand gripping mine tightly in warning.

"Why? Why can't I be with Devyn?"

What was it that made it impossible for us to be together?

"Devyn's future is not certain. He has enough problems – keeping himself alive is more than enough." She eyed me assessingly. "That was a lot of power you pulled in yesterday. I know Fidelma didn't think you were more than a latent but…"

I bit my lip. Fidelma had been wrong. I had to count on the likelihood that Bronwyn didn't know in any great detail what had happened in Londinium. But she knew who Devyn had been in search of and if she had realised I was indeed the one he had sought, she would have said something already. I wanted to trust her but I had promised.

"I'm not sure what happened or if I could actually have done anything with it."

Bronwyn inhaled deeply before pursing her lips and returning to the topic of Devyn's fate. "Whatever hope he has is in getting back to Mercia quickly and then delivering you and Marcus to York."

"What's in Mercia? Will we be safe there? Will Devyn? Why can't we be together there?"

Bronwyn looked at me, her face lined in concern.

"You just can't. He left a mess behind him; it will be enough for him to deal with that. The last thing he needs is to turn up with a city latent on his arm. Especially one he thought was…" She shook her head. "Devyn is helping Marcus and you're merely along for the ride. Whatever was between you is a complication he can ill afford."

"If that was supposed to clear things up, it really hasn't," I told Bronwyn sourly as she turned and started to head back up the hill, making her way across the golden leaves on the forest floor.

Bronwyn turned, her mouth pulled down. "I'm sorry. I know it's confusing. Oh, and Cassandra… you mustn't reveal your magic any more than you already have. That girl you helped escape the city was one of the most powerful latents we've ever seen. Her discovery was a surprise, and there are those who fought over her bitterly. The arrival of a second one of you could be seriously disruptive to the balance of power. It's just best if you keep it hidden for now. Especially from Gideon."

"Why Gideon?" Gideon had hurt Devyn and seemed to follow no one's orders but his own, but he was with Bronwyn, so why couldn't he be trusted? "Isn't he your friend? Don't you trust him?"

We were almost back at the camp and she stopped once more, looking in the direction of the tall cloaked figure striding across the glade, his long hair loose in the breeze.

"My friend? Maybe. Do I trust him? Not at all."

I looked over at Devyn, sitting on the black horse ahead of us with Bronwyn. Yesterday had taken its toll on him. We had made good progress, the Britons paying little heed to his injury. He had been exhausted when we finally made camp last night and was asleep as soon as he had eaten. Given his natural propensity to be taciturn, and with the injury as well as our argument, I wasn't sure I had seen him utter a word since Marcus had closed his wound. He barely looked my way, and had given no sign that he thought at all about what happened the other night. I, on the other hand, was a mess. My stomach folded in on itself every time I recalled what had happened in that tumbledown barn, and while my conscious mind was aware that Marcus's leaking passions had ignited the incident, it was impossible to draw a line between what had come from Marcus and what had come from me.

Whatever had precipitated the whole mess, it was the aftermath that washed over me like unrelenting waves crashing against the shore. The rejection from deep within Devyn hit me again and again, sometimes soaking me through, sometimes threatening to knock me over with the unexpected force of it. Screw him. Screw all of them. Particularly the handsy giant who held me close to his chest in the misty rain of the late afternoon. I elbowed him and turned to throw at him the ire and bile that consumed me, directing it at Gideon for lack of a more deserving target. Gideon's eyes creased and he pulled me tighter to his hard chest. Oaf.

I wasn't the only one reacting to Devyn; the dozen or so warriors in Bronwyn's group all watched him. While ostensibly Marcus was the prize that everyone in the country was looking for, it was Devyn who attracted the most attention. Gideon's lack of repentance at wounding a man he knew was no real threat to Bronwyn was baffling; it was as if, once the opportunity had presented itself, he had been unable to resist taking the shot. The others also reacted strangely to Devyn's presence. When they weren't busy staring at him, they pretended he wasn't there at all. Was this an indication of what awaited him? Was the treatment he had received as a child as nothing to the reception he would receive now?

Why was I still worrying about the turd?

My bones hurt from the jolting sway of the horse, and holding myself stiffly away from the body behind me wasn't helping. Though I was certainly grateful that my feet were being given a day off. Being in company also allowed me to relax; what I realised now was that constant vigilance against the next attack was exhausting.

I tried to piece together what little I knew to make sense of it all. The Britons were not as united as they had appeared from the other side of the wall. The country beyond the imperial province was divided between various kingdoms. Devyn was from Cymru which was to the west of us, while we were headed north towards Mercia.

I had assumed Anglia and Mercia were allies. They had both been ruled by the same house for a period; the two Houses of Plantagenet had joined forces to form the Rose Union, the central force that had finally pushed the Empire back, leading to the dominance of the Tewdwr dynasty. It appeared that alliances had shifted in the centuries since.

It sounded like reaching the Mercian capital would see us protected from the York forces who pursued us. I didn't know a great deal about the Mercians. They didn't usually attend the Treaty Renewals, mostly keeping to themselves, and as far as I knew were little involved in the warring that frayed the Anglian–Cymru border. Mercia was left alone by the other kingdoms, no doubt for fear of the famed power of the Lady of the Lake. Devyn hadn't spoken of Kernow to the southwest, but I knew that was where Bronwyn came from. But was she here as a representative of her region or as Devyn's cousin? What her relationship was to the Mercians was unclear, even as she rode in their company.

I ground my teeth in frustration at how ill-informed Marcus and I were. Devyn had barely spoken on the road since Oxford, apart from instructing us as necessary. Marcus had also been totally shut down. I sighed. Maybe our current circumstances were an improvement... or not, I thought, as a slice of pain leaked through my connection with Devyn when Bronwyn's horse's gait jarred his shoulder. It caused me, in turn, to stiffen and pull away from the thug who had injured him.

Explanations from Devyn as to what the Anglians wanted had been met with tight lips, though he had admitted that Marcus was their primary interest and they would mean him no harm. He had warned that falling into their hands would not be ideal for either of us though, especially with the risk that more people might discover my true identity. No more had been forthcoming. Devyn had promised Matthias that he would deliver Marcus to York, where his ancestors were from, but he was insistent that we should get to Carlisle first, then deal with York from a position of safety.

I wondered if I should try to interrogate my travelling companion but I didn't want to give him the satisfaction. I combed over the titbits of information to see if I could make any more connections as we made our way across the countryside in the wintry grey light of the day. Bronwyn had said that this Gideon was a friend, though not one she trusted. Why didn't she trust him?

My head hurt. Devyn was barely speaking to me, Marcus had retreated into his grief once more and wasn't talking to anyone, and I certainly wasn't going to ask the warrior behind me, with his scar and his glinty, watchful eyes. I would just have to wait and try Bronwyn when we made camp. In the meantime, my mind played with the facts like a nagging tooth.

I had completely melted into the broad-chested warrior by the time we stopped to make camp.

"Wakey-wakey" was whispered into my ear, the breath

warm against my cold skin. I started awake; we had ridden on in the dark, the early evening an inconvenience we could ill afford. We had continued on in the pitch-dark countryside, moving more slowly with a view to caring for the horses, but we had not been able to camp as early as the winter sun had set.

As he dismounted behind me, I sat helplessly on the horse, pretty confident that when I got off this creature, I was going to crumple in a heap on the muddy ground.

Gideon looked back up at me, assessing my situation, and without asking put his great paws around my waist and swept me off the horse. He held on to me while I found my balance, using the moment to step into me, crowding me against the horse. I glared up at him. What did he think he was doing? He leaned down to me.

"You're welcome," he said, mocking my lack of thanks for his help. Exhausted beyond measure, I just glared harder. He chuckled as he released me and stepped back.

Back on solid ground, my eyes did what they were best at and looked for Devyn. I didn't need the connection to read the anger emanating off him at Gideon's little display; his fists were clenched as he watched, narrow-eyed.

Good.

I looked up and to Gideon's surprise flashed him my choicest smile, my hand coming up to touch him lightly on his chest as I stepped around him. He instantly looked suspicious and, somewhat cynically, I felt, for a man who had only just met me, surveyed the camp to see who that little display had been for. I cursed myself for my tired stupidity. So much for not drawing attention to myself and Devyn, but hopefully our little byplay had been missed by the rest of our audience. I steeled myself not to seek him out and made my way over to

Marcus. To my shame, I realised that after all the drama yesterday, once he had stitched Devyn up, I had no idea what had happened to him. I wasn't sure I was yet over my anger at him that it was his fault Devyn had been in a fight at all. Or at his escapades of the night before. I didn't know what to feel. It was exhausting and, once I met his eyes, irrelevant.

Marcus looked deeply unhappy. I slipped my hand through his to give him comfort, and immediately felt guilty that it crossed my mind that doing so helped with our official story that we were together. Motives within motives within tangled webs.

That ceased to matter as Marcus's hand wrapped around mine, and he responded with a slight smile.

"Hey, there."

"Hey yourself," he returned, as he watched the warriors bustle around, prepping the camp. "What're a couple of citizens like us doing out here in the wilderness with this lot?"

Bronwyn's men were busy tying up the horses, putting up canvases between the trees, and collecting firewood. But then again, as I thought about it, I realised that they weren't Bronwyn's men... They were Gideon's. It was Gideon they looked to for instruction. My assumption had been based on the way the group had followed her lead yesterday. But that could have been because she was the one who had picked up the trail or because, title-wise, she was the most senior, but she was most definitely in the company of the Mercians rather than in charge.

"I have no idea." I smiled at Marcus. The Briton outfits supplied by Callum had been appropriate in the more refined collegiate parts of Oxford, but they did not help us blend into this group at all. They were the Celts that I had envisaged as a child come to life: large wild men with long hair and beards

179

and tattoos liberally adorning arms and necks and, in some cases, faces. Even Bronwyn looked like she belonged with them with her long, wild black hair and cloak, striding about busily. Marcus and I stood apart. Always apart.

"How are you?"

Marcus looked taken aback at the question, which stung. Was it so hard to believe I was checking he was okay? That was unfair. For the first time really since we had left Londinium, both Marcus and I were not on the edge of exhaustion. The days trudging north in those awful boots had most definitely taken their toll on me, but dealing with the effects of that while still recovering from burnout had pretty much depleted whatever energy Marcus had left at the end of every day.

"Marcus." I laid my hand on his arm. "I'm sorry. I've been so caught up in my own stuff. You've had… I'm sorry. Truly."

"For what exactly?"

I looked at him, and around at the camp. I shrugged. What could I say? He hadn't wanted any of this. He didn't deserve it. He was a good person and all he wanted was to treat his patients and be left alone. Now, because of me, he was here amongst these Mercians who told us nothing and being hunted by those who I realised might actually be his allies. While Devyn and I couldn't fall into Anglian hands for some specific, secret reason, Anglia was likely to be Marcus's destination. His Plantagenet ancestor had been from the House of York.

I tried another tack. "Are you feeling better?"

It was his turn to shrug as he leaned against the trunk of the tree sheltering us from the never-ending rain.

"Yeah, mostly. Better than I was in Oxford."

"But not well enough to deal with Devyn's injury?" I asked.

He pushed himself away from the tree angrily.

"I might have known that this show of concern for me was really about him. It's always about him."

"No, no, I didn't mean it like that," I started. I honestly hadn't, but I couldn't deny that most of my day had been spent worrying about Devyn. I grabbed his hand as he made to stride off.

"Please wait, Marcus. I really was asking." I stopped and tried again. "I mean, of course I'm worried about Devyn; we're travelling hard and he is wounded." *Through no fault of his own*, I added darkly in the privacy of my mind. Apparently it wasn't so private as the look on Marcus's face and his tug to get me to release him indicated that my thoughts were pretty evident on my face.

"Which is not my fault."

"What? If you hadn't gone off and—"

I pushed down my anger. There was a series of events that had led to Marcus storming out of that barn and we did not need to get into a full-blown argument here in full sight of the Britons, who already seemed far too interested in our conversation.

"Marcus," I sighed. I had spent my life waiting to be with this man, had spent the summer getting to know him. We were friends, but the burn in our blood at this late stage of the handfast made it difficult because our tempers rose too quickly to the surface.

"I don't think I'm jealous of you and her." I spoke the thought unguardedly as the idea swirled in my brain. It was easy to dismiss the night he'd spent in the arms of another woman as Bronwyn made excessively clear she had no desire to repeat the experience.

"What?" Marcus struggled to follow the tangent in our conversation.

"I think the handfast is making us both a little crazy. We're friends... or we were," I amended, at the slightly sceptical light in Marcus's eye. "I want you to be happy. I know things are all over the place right now, and my uh... interactions with Devyn haven't helped. But we need to get through this by sticking together."

Marcus paused before replying, contemplating what I was saying. His hand came up to cover mine where it still rested on his arm and his thumb rubbed thoughtfully along it.

"I really was just asking if... Are you okay?"

He nodded, looking down at me, his green eyes transparent and open.

"I know you're worried about Devyn," he said. "Truth be told, I am myself. I don't know why I wasn't able to do more to heal the wound. I felt pretty good the last few evenings when I was helping you. But your blisters were superficial; Devyn's wound is deeper, and it just doesn't seem to want to respond. I know that sounds odd, but it's like it's blocking me."

He dropped his hand from mine, looking uneasily over to the camp.

"I'd better get my paws off you before he does more damage by trying to come over here and kick my arse," he said on a lighter note.

"Well, actually, I need to talk to you about that," I said, drawing a deep breath. Marcus was not going to like this. "We can't let anyone know I have magic and we need to act like we're together. That is, we can't let anyone know that Devyn and I... They think I'm here as your match anyway... or betrothed, as they call it."

His face darkened with each word that fell out of my mouth.

"I'm sure they don't. Not after that little display yesterday."

"Nothing happened." At least, nothing had happened because despite having a knife in his shoulder, Devyn had hauled himself off the ground to my side before I could unleash my rage.

"Yeah. Just as well they don't know what happened in Richmond," he said, referring to the storm I had rained down on the sentinels who had pursued us in our first failed attempt to leave the city. Failed because of the handfast bond which had led to Marcus inadvertently alerting them to my departure.

"Right," I said. "I would do the same if they hurt you."

"Would you?" His eyes were hollow.

This time when he pulled away, I didn't try to stop him.

Chapter Twelve

I rejoined the rest of the group at the camp, such as it was – some waterproof coverings strung from tree branches providing cover from the relentless rain. I don't suppose it rained more here than in Londinium, though it certainly seemed to. I couldn't remember the last time I had been in fully dry clothes. The completely natural materials didn't help either and I thought wistfully of my city clothes. The only room left around the fire that the Britons had got going – in a remarkably short time – was either beside Devyn, who was stretched out against a fallen log, or by his attacker. With an inward grumble, I chose to sit beside the ass who had put the hole in the man I loved.

Gideon cast me a strange look as I eased my aching bones down beside him. Damn. In trying to appear as if there were nothing between myself and Devyn, I had overplayed it. Gideon knew I couldn't stand him, a reaction with which he seemed to be familiar. He seemed like the kind of person you had to get used to, if Bronwyn's interactions with him were anything to go by.

"Miss me?" he joked, as I proceeded to ignore him, his long legs stretching out to the paltry heat from the baby flames which were struggling to take hold of the damp wood.

I smiled sourly at him. "Couldn't last another minute away from your side."

The evening meal was barley and meat stew, substantially better fare than we'd been managing on our own. The chatter around the group was subdued, with glances continuing to assess us, their reluctant guests.

"How long will it take us to get to Carlisle?" I asked. The sooner the better for Devyn's sake. He had barely touched his meal, and when Marcus had redressed the wound, I hadn't missed his wince at what he found under the bandage.

"A few days," Bronwyn said. "All being well."

"We need to get there sooner," Marcus said. These were the first words he had spoken all evening.

Bronwyn cut him a dismissive glance. "We aren't exactly taking a leisurely stroll. Are we keeping you from something, my lord? Or are our accommodations just not up to standard?"

Marcus narrowed his gaze. "There's something wrong with Devyn's wound. We need to get him to help."

"What's wrong?" I asked. So much for appearing unconcerned.

"I don't know. It's not deep, but he's developing a fever."

Unable to help myself, I scrambled to my feet and crossed to where Devyn lay sleeping. Developing a fever was putting it mildly; his cheeks were flushed and, laying my hand to his forehead, I could feel that he was burning up. This close, I could also hear that his breathing was laboured.

"Marcus, do something."

"I can't. He's not responding to anything I try."

Bronwyn had joined me and, pulling back his shirt, lifted

the makeshift bandage. Dark tendrils crept outwards from the inflamed mark. Bronwyn laid her hands around the site and frowned grimly.

I glared across at Gideon who was less concerned with Devyn than the state of the fire, which he was nudging with his great oversized boot.

"What did you do?" There must have been something on the knife. What little knowledge I had of sickness came from my brief stint working in the hospital with Marcus, and I had never seen anything like this.

"Me?" He had the gall to play at innocence. "Nothing. I can't be blamed for what's inside the Griffin. Maybe I just gave it a way to get out."

Bronwyn pulled the bandage back before straightening up and walking away into the dark. Devyn was her cousin and she cared so little? Marcus gave a slight shrug; he had little faith in our new friends. My anger boiled up inside me. I knew I wasn't supposed to draw magic to me, but what did it matter if Devyn was going to die? Was he going to die? It was just a shoulder wound, but it looked nasty. I felt the power flood through my veins, warming me, making me feel whole. I turned back to Devyn and, after checking nobody was near enough to see, I laid my hands around the wound as I had seen Bronwyn and Marcus do. My eyes slid closed as I focused on Devyn, on the oily, grim foreignness that slimed through his blood, lighting it up, but it just slithered further into the shadows. I tried again and again to draw it to me, to push it away, to burn something. I refused to let it defeat me. It felt wrong, and my skin prickled each time I got close to it, as if every atom of my being was repulsed by the dark matter that eluded me.

"Stop, Cassandra."

The voice seemed so far away. It was distracting me. I needed to focus.

Arms grappled me, pulling me away from the oily tentacles I chased.

"Cassandra, you have to stop. You're hurting him." Marcus's voice was low but I heard him. I blinked and looked down. Devyn's entire body was strained and rigid, arching in protest. I pulled back. If my power couldn't help me fix him, then it would help me break someone else.

I whirled on Gideon, whose attention I had now thoroughly caught.

"What did you do?"

He tilted his head to one side. "You have an awful lot of juice for a latent."

"You haven't seen anything yet."

"No, Cassandra." Bronwyn stepped from the shadows, bow in hand, the arrow already drawn. "I've got this."

All the men had risen and were poised to attack, but Bronwyn had chosen her position well. She was at the edge of the firelight, well away from all the warriors.

"Gideon. What did you do?"

The laconic Briton smiled up at her from where he sat, the only one who seemed unconcerned by the danger he was in.

"Bronwyn, is that any way to treat a friend?" His scar caught the flickering light as he smiled across at her.

"I have plenty of friends." She shrugged. "Cousins though... Well, I've only ever had the one and, what can I say, I missed him."

"You were the only one who did," Gideon said.

Bronwyn's face grew cold and blank.

"Maybe so. But I have him back now, and you have no right. Why would you do this?" Bronwyn seemed to take a pause at her own question, catching the eye of one of the tall warriors who had been backing away from the light and closer to her. He stilled as she shook her head to indicate he should move no further. "Rion most certainly didn't command this."

A flicker of something flashed across the face of the previously impervious warrior.

She looked around at the men. "Think about it. Gideon was to bring Devyn and his travelling companions north. You think Rion wants him dead?"

She paused at this as a couple of the men grunted in assent and exhaled in annoyance.

"Poisoned on the side of the road. If he wanted Devyn dead, don't you think he would want to do it himself? Think, you idiots."

The men shuffled uneasily, a few of them taking surreptitious steps towards Gideon who had decided to get up on his feet in light of the new atmosphere in the camp that grew tense and shifted out of his favour. Enough that his hand now rested lightly on the hilt of his sword.

"Poison?" The dark-haired Briton shook his head, his other hand raised in protest. "No, Bronwyn. I would never kill a man like that, even him."

I took a step towards him, the fire flaring as I advanced. Gideon's eyes widened, his brows drawing together before he turned his attention back to the armed woman facing him on the other side.

"You know me. Is this my style?"

"I don't care. The fact is that it has been done. By your hand." Bronwyn pulled back on her bow.

"Wait." He took his hand off the hilt of his sword and pulled at his belt, letting it drop to the ground. "If the blade was poisoned it was not with my knowledge. Maybe something was put on it to slow us down."

"Slow us down?" Bronwyn repeated. "So that York can catch us before we can reach Mercia?"

Gideon ignored her accusation, nodding his head to Marcus. "He belongs in York anyway. Let the steward have what he wants, give us a cure, and then we can be on our way and deliver Rion's oathbreaker back to him. No harm done."

"No harm done?" I practically screeched, every fibre of my being wanting to lash out at him. How could he be so indifferent to the fact that Devyn's life hung by a thread? Was this really his justification for delivering Marcus to the people who were chasing us? If Bronwyn didn't kill him, I would.

Bronwyn didn't even glance in my direction.

"You did this at the Steward of York's command?" she asked Gideon quietly.

His face shuttered.

She hissed, her dark eyes flashing. "You would betray Mercia this way?"

Gideon stiffened. "I have betrayed no one. Our priority should be to get Marcus Courtenay to safety. Whether that is York or further north is not my concern. My allegiance is to the Lakelands. Rion wants the Griffin. If there was something on my blade, I did not put it there. I know it plays into York's hands that we go slowly and that York has a grudge against the old Griffin. Call it an unfortunate coincidence or bad luck, I don't care."

And with that he ended the argument, striding away from the paltry comfort of the campfire. Once Marcus had done what he could to cool Devyn down, we curled up beside him for the night.

As the first light softened the darkness, I felt myself drift slowly awake, as if I were one with the floor of the forest. My mind swept out across the land, through the soil laced with roots and its covering of dried leaves and twigs, kernels of life already readying themselves for the spring that lay ahead. My mind wove and melded with the great trees and their steadfastness, winging across babbling brooks and around solid boulders, delighting in the freedom and sheer life of it all. Outward and beyond. It was a luxurious meander through the life of the forest and I revelled in the organic life, feeling a sense of belonging that I yearned for as I danced along. Ever outward, mile after mile of it, none of the smothering, teeming populace of the city, just hill after hill, clean, crisp air, the warmth of the trees, and life that cared not at all for our momentary passing.

Until I hit a sense of wrongness that seemed to catch me and pull me towards it by its gravity, a dark and swirling menace. An unforgettable foetid smell, creeping our way.

The hounds were coming.

I started awake, sitting up and gasping for breath. Was it real? Were they tracking us?

"What is it?" Marcus's voice came softly through the morning from where he lay on the other side of Devyn.

"The hounds of Samhain." I felt compelled to tell him what I had seen, what I knew to be reality. "The hounds are coming."

Bronwyn's voice came from the far side of the camp. "The hounds of Samhain are tracking you?"

"Yes," I confirmed quietly. There was silence as the waking group absorbed the new threat.

"Devyn won't make it to Carlisle," Bronwyn mused aloud. "We need to get him help. Now."

"Chester?" Gideon suggested.

"They may not have a druid in residence," said Bronwyn dismissively, "and even if they do, there's no guarantee they will help us. What about Conwy?"

"No," Gideon said flatly, already starting to break camp. "Anglia and Gwynedd are never on the best of terms. York will interpret us taking their heir to the prince as an act of war. No."

"Fine." Bronwyn nodded curtly, agreeing with the tall warrior's assessment as she kicked over the traces of the fire. "Dinas Brân then."

"Dinas Brân?" Gideon arched a brow. "Didn't the pup Griffin disown his father?"

"Yes." Bronwyn's lips thinned. "But Rhodri didn't disown him, and there is always a druid there to tend him."

"Dinas Brân it is then. But we have to go now," Gideon urged. "The Griffin is slowing us down, and the hounds are following the magic. We'll ride west with Marcus and the girl and once we've got some air between us, we'll turn north and meet you."

"This all plays rather neatly into your suggestion from the first," Bronwyn said stonily.

Gideon swung around. The scar flexed as his handsome face tightened.

"I did not poison that blade," he repeated. "I will meet you. I will see the Griffin to Carlisle. The hounds want the magic; what little the Griffin holds will not attract them. We have no chance if we all ride together. I can lead them away and... Dammit, Bronwyn, I will be there."

The sickening feeling of being stalked by those awful creatures was a deadweight in my stomach. Marcus's eyes sought and held mine. The hounds were coming for me, but the Mercians weren't to know that, and as long as Marcus and I stayed together they didn't need to know. Devyn's best chance lay in my going as far in the opposite direction as possible. His cousin would take care of him. I knew Devyn wouldn't be pleased to wake in his father's home, but if that was what it took then that was where we had to go.

The thought of riding away made me feel like I was abandoning my only anchor. I had no family, no home. I only had Devin – or at least I hoped I still did. I didn't belong in this world any more than I had belonged in the one we left behind. It didn't matter where I was as long as I had him. But first he had to be alive. And if I had to leave him to ensure he lived, then that was what I would do.

Bronwyn laid her hand on my arm. "I will get him to safety, Cassandra, I promise, but you have to go now. We have to get Devyn to his father's castle, where he can get proper help. There's no time and we can't afford the delay a fight would take."

I whirled back to Gideon, his tall, broad shape a dark shadow under the trees.

"I want your vow." The camp around us stilled at my words. I knew little enough about Briton society, but that they took vows seriously was certain; Devyn's future here was threatened because of the vow he had broken by leaving for the city.

Gideon stepped towards me.

"I owe you no vow, city girl."

"Then I'm not leaving with you, and if I don't leave, Marcus can't."

"Can't?" Gideon had spotted the *can't*, not that Marcus *wouldn't* leave without me.

"Can't," I repeated, raising my sleeve to show him the handfast cuff on my upper arm. "I told you before. As soon as you get any distance from me, he will be as incapacitated as Devyn."

"What's to stop me throwing you over a horse and making you come with us?" His dark smile glinted in the firelight.

"I will," Bronwyn stated flatly. "Why the hesitation, Gideon? You just said you would meet us, so why not vow it?"

Gideon smirked. "It's an uncertain world, Bronwyn. What makes you think I can deliver on such a promise?"

"Vow that you will do everything in your power –" I paused to think through the wording carefully; it had to be something he could deliver on but also something that couldn't be twisted in such a way that it served him better than it did us "– to see us safely reunited with Devyn and Bronwyn and able to continue to Mercia."

Gideon's eyes bore into mine, unblinking, a muscle ticking on his jaw.

"I give my vow to no one, and ask for no one's in return. If you want my help, it is yours. If you don't, you are welcome to continue to bring the hounds to the Griffin." Gideon raised a lazy brow. What choice did I have? His lip quirked as he inclined his head to Bronwyn before turning on his heel and striding to his horse. "Now, let's go."

Dawn light lit the camp palely as we hurriedly broke camp. The trees seemed more vibrant in the early light, the leaves more splendidly alive – in stark contrast to Devyn.

Devyn was barely conscious as I bid him a constrained goodbye in full view of everyone. His glazed eyes hardly registered what was going on, and I couldn't read him as we had closed off the bond on both sides to protect me from his pain. Actually, it was less pain than a sense of weakness and deterioration. He hadn't even been consulted when Bronwyn had decided his childhood home was our best bet. He certainly wouldn't be happy about it. But if he was well enough again to be angry at our decision, then it would be worth it. We just had to get him home where I would see him again. And I *would* see him again. I knew it in my bones. This shabby farewell would not be the last time I saw him. I pressed a light kiss to his forehead, running my hand across the damp black curls. Then I stood and, taking Marcus's hand, walked away.

Chapter Thirteen

W e had ridden for hours. At least for the moment I was sharing with Marcus and not the obnoxious Gideon. The warriors had all gone with Bronwyn and Devyn, whose slow pace made them more vulnerable, but one of them had given his horse to Marcus so we had two between the three of us. This meant that I spent a couple of hours on one before being transferred to the other in order to keep up the punishing pace that Gideon set.

Bronwyn was heading directly northwest to get Devyn to the druids at Dinas Brân as quickly as possible. We were taking the somewhat longer route southwest into Powys to lure away the hounds before turning north again.

As the sun set, we hit a river that Gideon told us was the Severn. Its dark waters looked icy in the wintry evening. We stopped to allow the horses to drink and I gratefully eased my aching bones off Marcus's horse. It was a momentary relief as I stretched my legs in the chilly evening air, wrapping my cloak tighter around me.

"How much further before we stop for the night?" Marcus asked while Gideon led the horses over to the river to drink.

His face slanted towards us, then beyond us contemplatively. "We need to put as much distance between ourselves and those creatures as possible."

"That's not an answer," I said.

His lips curved up to the scar on his cheek. "We keep going."

"What do you mean, we keep going? You plan to ride all night?" I asked. The horses were already tired; it had been a long day, and horse riding was new to Marcus. We would kill ourselves if we kept going in the dark.

"Not all night." He smirked. "There's a town south of here. We can rest there for the night."

Marcus and I looked at each other. Could we trust Gideon? So far on our journey we had avoided towns. The one time that rule had been broken, we were discovered, and now Devyn was injured. Bronwyn had warned me that Gideon's interests were not necessarily aligned with ours.

Our suspicion was clearly not too well hidden as Gideon rolled his eyes.

"You think I'm leading you into a trap?" he asked. "I'm less concerned with the Anglians who are looking for him than the hounds which are coming for you, city girl."

I swallowed at the reminder of the menace that was hunting us. I didn't miss that Gideon saw me rather than Marcus as the real magical magnet.

"We'll be safe in the town?" Marcus asked.

"They're stronger at night," Gideon explained. "They won't attack us in the daytime so being behind town walls surrounded by people will be safer, yes. Whether we are entirely safe depends on how determined they are."

I tried not to think too hard about how determined those eerie beasts were once they were in pursuit. I had caused this. Callum warned me that the hounds were unlikely to forget me and that I shouldn't do anything to attract their attention. Well, pouring everything I had into Devyn to try and heal him had caught their attention.

I sat down on the bank, watching the swirl of the great waters. A terrifying thought occurred to me.

"What if they went after Bronwyn and Devyn instead of us?"

"We should be so lucky," Gideon said grimly.

"It's not possible or it's not likely?" How could he wish that on them? They couldn't travel quickly with Devyn so ill, and they would stand no chance against the hounds.

"Both."

We waited for him to explain, but in typical fashion he had turned away to tend to the horses rather than expand on his reply. Gideon didn't do much of that, I had noticed. It was still unclear to me why he'd thrown that knife at Devyn in the first place, when he'd already realised that he bore no threat to Bronwyn, much less why the blade had been tainted with whatever was making Devyn sick.

I had had enough. Anger burned through me as I picked myself up off the cold, damp ground and strode over to Gideon. My arms were already outstretched to push the hulking warrior but he turned at my not so stealthy approach, and I ended up with my hands pushing against his chest. However, as a trained soldier, he was braced for impact, and I just crumpled against him.

I looked up to find him smirking down at me. Fury blazed through me, but he held his ground. He had to be able to feel my anger.

"Easy," he gentled me, his amusement fading.

Energy pulsed through me, looking for an outlet. Gideon's eyes widened as he seemed to sense the power snapping and crackling beneath the surface.

"Dammit," he cursed, and picked me up before striding into the river up to his knees.

The energy in me paused, unsure of its target, his actions having bewildered me.

"Put your hands into the river and let the water take it," he ordered me.

Who was he to tell me what to do? He hurt Devyn, forcing me to leave him behind while he carried Marcus and me off to gods knew where.

"Listen to me," he barked, pulling my attention outward once more. "Your power attracts the hounds. You need to release it as gently as possible, do you hear me?"

I nodded.

"Lean down and put your hands in the water. The Severn goddess will take it; you just need to release it," he counselled me.

I put my hands down into the icy water and felt the heat burn through me and out through my hands into the water. The water seemed to sigh as it took the power I released, sending out a feeling of gratitude and love at receiving the gift I gave it. The anger that had ignited the power had transformed into a blessed energy. Usually Devyn distracted me, grounding me somehow while the power dissipated.

This time, as the energy was released, my body seemed to go limp, until I was unable to tell where the power I was giving ended and my own personal energy began. I couldn't stop myself feeding the energy into the river. It flowed into the water that journeyed the course of this land and out to the sea where waves embraced it, the land-born water joining with the salty pull of the tides that washed it away.

"Stop her." I heard Marcus's urgent voice come from the bank.

Gideon scooped me higher, my skin losing contact with the rushing, swirling waters. I moaned softly. I wanted to go back. I felt abruptly cut off from the loving force that had taken the power I poured into it. I didn't want to leave. I struggled in the arms that confined me as they swept me up to the bank where Gideon laid me down on the ground far from the water's edge because the lapping swirl still called to me.

"Cassandra," Marcus cried. I lifted sleepy eyes as he ran his hands over me, pressing against my pulse points. My head swung back, too heavy to hold up as he attempted to lift me.

"What in Hades have you done?" he snarled at Gideon. But it seemed Gideon still wasn't in the mood to explain himself and his footsteps faded then returned with the accompanying sound of the whickering horses.

"Lift her to me."

"No." Marcus spoke sharply. "I don't know what you just did to her, but she stays with me."

"You thrice-damned fool." The warrior's voice was a low growl in the gloom of approaching night. "We're trying to sneak away from the beasts that hunt us, and she throws out a gods-damned beacon that any hound within a hundred miles will have felt. We need to be elsewhere, fast. Now, stand up, hand her to me, get on your horse, and we ride for the town. Keep up or don't, I couldn't care less, but when those hounds get here, I will be long gone. Do you understand?"

I tried to help as Marcus lifted me into the waiting arms.

Gideon's hands gripped my upper arms as he hauled my almost entirely limp body up onto the horse in front of him.

He took the reins and, taking care to ensure my cloak was wrapped tightly around me, his arms settled in a warm band around my waist. Unable to help myself, I slumped against the warmth of the broad chest behind me.

I still loathed him.

Without waiting for Marcus to mount, he turned his horse's head and started to ride.

We flew through the night, the horse surefooted as its master guided it across the obstacle course of trees and bracken that was barely lit in the fading evening light. Finally, the lights of the town could be seen in the night sky and we joined a road that headed directly towards the closed gates.

Our arrival caused a commotion and there was some argument with the guards. Gideon of course overruled them with some no doubt terrifying threat, but I was too tired to follow it. My only real awareness grasped that Marcus was still with us as I heard his soothing voice temper Gideon's aggressive approach.

———————————

When I opened my eyes again, it was to the soft firelight of a bedroom, the feel of blankets, and the security that came with Marcus's proximity in the bed with me. A bed. I was unresisting as sleep pulled me back down into its comforting arms.

I woke again as the grey light of dawn slipped into the room. I surveyed my surroundings – it seemed we were in a house or an inn, perhaps. Nothing too fancy – bare floorboards and barer walls – but it was inside, though a little cold now that the fire seemed to have gone out. I raised my head to see if I could solve that particular situation. There, beside the still glowing embers of a fire, was Gideon, stretched out on a chair, his long legs before him, his head uncomfortably rolled to the side.

I lifted the arm that Marcus had wrapped around me and crept out of bed and across the dusty floorboards. I gently poked a couple of logs onto the fire and watched as they caught from the embers and flame began to lick up the side of the lower one. Backing away, I flicked a glance at the long-legged warrior, the hard planes of his face stern even in rest. The tangled tattoo winding up his neck was exposed by the awkward fall of his head and his long dark hair was free and trailed loosely over his shoulder. I winced as I caught sight of his trousers. They were still wet on the side that had not been exposed to the heat of the fire.

I took a blanket from the bed and returned to place it over the large sleeping man; it was the least I could do. What was wrong with me? Had I really tried to…? I paused. How had I pulled all that power into myself? What had I thought I would do with it? Obliterate him? I realised I could have; that possibility had flickered before me in the moment. What had I been thinking? But I hadn't been thinking, and the power had surged in response to my fear for Devyn and my annoyance at Gideon. Instinctively, it had wanted to strike… In anger or in defence, I wasn't sure. I could have killed him.

Draping the blanket gently over him, I realised the hooded lids weren't entirely closed and my activities were under the flinty gaze of our unwilling guide.

"I'm sorry." The words just popped out of my mouth. I

didn't know if I meant to apologise, but I had tried to attack him and I'd put all our lives in danger by pulling in magic, the one thing I had been warned not to do. The words felt heavy in the air as he made no acknowledgement that I had spoken at all.

"To Hades with you," I threw at him as I whipped away. It was his own damn fault that I had wanted to kill him; he was the one to blame for this in the first place.

His hand caught and held me, wrapping around my wrist. I stalled but didn't turn back to look at him. My body was stiff.

"Are you okay?" he asked, taking me by surprise.

I nodded.

"Your trousers are still wet," I said, turning back and indicating the leg furthest away from the fire where the leather looked darker as far up as his thighs.

His lip tugged up at the corner. "Yes."

"You should dry them while we have a fire," I admonished. Why he hadn't done it overnight was beyond me, but maybe he had tried to stay awake on guard. I guessed it would have put him at a disadvantage had hound or man burst in here to attack us. I smiled as the image of him fighting with his scrawny legs exposed amused me.

One eyebrow rose and he levered himself out of the chair. Watching me, he proceeded to open his trousers at the waist before peeling them off. His thighs were as wide as tree trunks and were wrapped in more of those twirling Celtic tattoos. A tree encased one muscled calf, its branches reaching up and wrapping themselves around his thigh. I wondered how far its pattern played over his body.

And my cheeks proceeded to heat as I realised what I was doing – the type of full-body flush that I knew had my face glowing red in the grey light of dawn. I refused to look up to see if he had noticed. Of course he would have. I grabbed the damp trousers and busied myself with straightening them out. They were still warm from his body as I draped them over the arm of the chair on the other side of the fire.

I hesitated.

"How did you know what to do?" I asked softly, not wishing to disturb Marcus.

"I have a friend with some of your talents," he returned equally quietly, his voice a low rumble in his broad chest.

My eyes flicked to his. I so badly wanted to know more but I was damned if I would ask him for anything, no matter how desperately I wanted it. I gnawed at my lip as I considered my options. I could return to the relative warmth of the bed while it was still available... but I couldn't resist. What he had revealed was not nothing. Would he tell me more?

I perched on the edge of the chair that held his trousers towards the growing heat of the hearth. The damp leather had a particular earthy smell as it heated.

"He wasn't trained?" I asked, "I mean, if he was trained why would he...?"

"Need a way to release power he wasn't sure how to use?" he finished for me. "We were teenagers together, and he occasionally had moments of temper; he wasn't always in control. When that happened, he had to figure out a way to release it without having to go to his teachers who would have reprimanded him for such reckless pulling of power."

I settled back into the chair, sifting through the information he had just given me.

"Drawing in power when angry... That happens to other people?"

Gideon exhaled a huffed breath. His tone was wry as he answered.

"*Other people* implies there are lots of people who can do what you do. Outside of the druids, I know of only one or two others in the whole land who have anywhere near the level I felt in you."

"Who?" I asked. Maybe this other person, or people, could help me, or at least tell me how to control my magic… or tell me who could teach me. I needed to learn to figure out what I was doing because I had seriously endangered us last night. If the hounds had found us, I would have been depleted, completely unable to fight them off. Though it remained to be seen if I could do anything at will, whether fully conscious or not. The odds so far weren't in my favour that I would be able to draw on my power as opposed to just stand there, entirely defenceless.

"Rion Deverell," Gideon answered me. The Rion they spoke of was of House Deverell, and we were headed to Carlisle, seat of the ruling family. House Deverell wasn't just any house of Mercia, it was *the* house of Mercia.

"You grew up with the Prince of Mercia?" I asked. I'd assumed that Gideon was an Anglian from the way Bronwyn had spoken of his divided loyalties. His father, at least, was Anglian.

Gideon blinked, then answered.

"Yes, my father and I had a disagreement. I offered my services to the Deverells."

"Does Devyn also serve them?" I asked. Devyn had given the impression that he had served a minor Mercian house. Apparently not.

"Supposedly."

Then Devyn and Gideon both served House Deverell, the ruling family of Mercia.

"But you hurt Devyn."

Amusement lit his face. "It's complicated."

"Explain it to me," I gritted.

His head tilted to the side, the dark sheath of hair falling over his face as he contemplated me from across the hearth. The stoked flames brought the scar that slashed across his face into stark relief. He pushed his hair back as he turned his gaze into the flickering firelight.

"I barely knew Devyn as a child; he was a few years younger than me. We met a few times at some of the great gatherings. His father was the greatest warrior on this whole island. Devyn was just this dark, intense kid, but he was the beloved son of the Griffin. I was so envious of him. My father cared little for me. I don't tell you this to make you feel in any way sorry for me. I lived a life of enormous privilege, and I trained with the best warriors in the land. But the son of the Griffin… he was adored. By his father, by his house and by the Mercians."

"And you hate him for that?" I asked, confused. Devyn had known real family; he'd had a true home where he was loved. While I understood all too well Gideon's envy, why that would cause him to strike almost twenty years later was beyond my comprehension.

"No, I hate him for what he left in his wake, and for what it cost everyone who loved him. His father betrayed all that he was for love of that child. Saving that child cost Mercia, all of us a great deal."

"Devyn wasn't to blame for that; that was his father's choice," I objected, seeing again the scene on the river. Even as a boy Devyn had not agreed with what his father did.

"Maybe so. But Devyn made his own choices. I would lay my life down for Rion Deverell," he stated flatly. "And your friend betrayed him. After everything, he broke his vow to serve him. Rion stood by him even though Devyn was responsible for the death of his mother and sister and even though he deserted him."

The pieces started tumbling into place. My breath quickened as my mind pulled the scattered information together.

Devyn and his father were blamed for the death of a lady and her baby daughter. Devyn in a castle with a golden-haired boy, whom he left behind when he ran off to find that lost girl. A foundling girl with the old blood of the Britons in her veins, growing up in the heart of the Empire. The Briton lord who had been angry at Devyn at the masquerade ball.

Rion Deverell.

The Mercian Prince.

My brother.

Could it be? I tasted the idea in my mind, letting it roll around. It felt right. It felt true.

That was why Devyn was trying to get us north to Carlisle instead of heading to York with Marcus. And that made me the daughter of the Lady of the Lake. The Lady of the Lake was legend, even in Londinium. She held power of serious magnitude. But still it made no sense. She wasn't dead, and the threat of her power was one of the main things that maintained the balance of power between Britannia and the Empire.

"But the Lady of the Lake is alive," I breathed. Was my mother alive? My heart leapt in my chest, even as I recalled the sweep of power that was released as the lady from my vision was cut down.

Gideon shook his head, casting a glance at the sleeping figure in the bed.

"Why do you think everyone wants your princeling so badly? The lady has been dead a long time, her death a secret hidden from the wider world, and especially from Londinium. Rion isn't a prince, he is the king, and though he has yet to marry and have children, his daughter will not inherit his mother's precious gift. The power of the Lakes is gone, lost for ever, as it was always passed down directly from mother to daughter. The Plantagenets are one of the few true bloodlines left in the land. And in case you had missed it, the land is dying. I'll bet Mother Severn kissed your hand last night when you released that power. Seductive, was she? Desperate for more?"

I recalled the swirl of love and relief that welcomed the power I had loosed into the waters last night, the eddy that had tried to pull more and more of my energy down into its depths. It had sucked my very life-force, the impact of which had afterwards left me semi-conscious for the rest of the night.

"I thought you said that your friend, that is, the King of Mercia, had power?"

"Yes, he's still of the Lakes bloodline." Gideon's dark gaze levelled on me directly. "But what I felt coming off you shouldn't be possible outside the old blood. It's unheard of for a latent to have power like yours, especially not to just turn up out of nothing and from nowhere."

Light dawned in his eyes, and his face blanched.

"Not out of nothing…"

He stopped, and I watched the play of emotion over his face: disbelief, hope, anger, the very mesh of feelings I had seen flash over Callum. That was who they believed me to be, I realised now, the lost daughter of the Lady of the Lake. Come back from the dead.

I shook my head. Bronwyn had warned me not to trust Gideon.

"Well, it's happened. Marina is much stronger than me – you know, the girl I helped Devyn get out of the city," I babbled. "Like her, I'm a citizen of Rome, but I'm a latent. I must have some mixed blood, that's all."

"I met your friend and her brother. She told us that you were the one who got them help." His head tilted to one side as he eyed me. "How did you meet Devyn?"

"He was in my class at school."

"Was he now?" His amber eyes gleamed. "In the whole of Londinium, he happened to be in the same class as a girl some years younger than him who just happens to turn out to be a latent hiding enormous power. How old are you, city girl? Twenty-one? Twenty-two?"

I mutinously refused to answer. I didn't want to give him any more clues. But Gideon knew, I could see it in his eyes; he was surer of my true identity than I was.

He leaned across and took a lock of my bright hair and rubbed it between his fingers.

"Catriona Deverell..." he breathed. "Alive."

He trailed the backs of his fingers softly down the side of my face, his eyes lingering, studying every feature. *Catriona Deverell*. That was my name. It rolled around inside me, lighting me up. That was who I really was.

His face was inches from mine. At this distance, I could see through the ordinarily impenetrable mask with which Gideon faced the world. Behind that granite wall, he was considerably shaken by his discovery. Everything in his world would change when the news was revealed.

I exhaled shakily.

"Cassandra," Marcus's voice called to me from the other side of the room. He was sitting up in the bed, his eyes as wide as mine no doubt were. I stood up warily and made my way back to his side, taking the hand he offered.

"Is it true?" he asked.

"I don't know," I admitted. His fingers tightened on mine.

"We'll figure it out," he reassured me. I didn't need reassurance though. I needed time. Time to understand what all of this meant.

If what Gideon said was true then I was the Lady of the Lake. It felt true. I kept seeing the woman I glimpsed in that vision. The devastation in the very earth as she had fallen to the ground. Her love for the baby in her arms... me. I had been loved so very much. Why had she been so near Londinium? How had the Britons managed to hide her death all this time?

"What does this mean?" I asked. Gideon was still frozen in position by the fire.

Finally, he took a deep breath and leaned back in his chair.

"Right now, not very much." He shrugged. "We still need to keep ahead of those cursed hounds. And we need to keep ahead of York. They want their prince back, but if they could lay their hands on both of you..."

He trailed off.

"Well, that would be a lot of power to control," he finished.

He stood and pulled on his trousers, which could hardly be dry. "We need to ride. The sooner we get you to Carlisle, the safer we'll all be."

"You will take us to Devyn's father's castle?" I don't know why I needed confirmation. He served Mercia, he had said he would meet Bronwyn... Where else would he take us?

He nodded curtly.

"And then north to Carlisle?

Gideon smiled broadly.

"Nothing would give me more pleasure."

We ate a sombre breakfast in the common room of the inn. Unused to visitors, the barkeep and the serving girl attempted to engage us in conversation to hear what news we had of the wider world.

I was too inside my head to do more than spoon the salted porridge into my mouth, swallow, and repeat as their mellifluous voices rippled around the room. Marcus was his usual charming self but had little to offer in the type of news that would pass as typical in this remote town. Unsure of what to say, he opted for saying very little.

They didn't try too hard with the stern-faced warrior who sat silently waiting for us to finish our meal, eager to be on the road.

I chose to ride with Marcus, allowing myself to sink into the false security and feeling of home offered by the handfast cuff. Mostly, it made me feel tethered to a lie. The lie that the Empire was my home, that Marcus was my mate, that I belonged to someone and something as I had been raised to believe, that the handfast bound me to something real.

None of it was real though. All of it was a lie built to fence me in, to control me. Well, built initially to fence in Marcus's ancestor, the princess who had been given to the city to seal the truce by marrying a man she must have detested to the core of her being.

The truth of who I really was washed through me, like waves rolling against the shore, inevitable and repeated, crashing on arrival each and every time.

This was why Devyn had come to the city, and why he had

wanted me to leave with him. Not because he wanted me, but because others did. My brother. His sworn lord.

This was why he couldn't be with me. The Lady of the Lake was a being of legend, a keeper of magic, the source of power among the Britons. Devyn wasn't just any personal guard; he was sworn to protect the Lady of the Lake. His line was hated because their one purpose was to protect her, and they had failed.

Devyn had told me that his family were in disgrace, that he was seen by many as unfit to breathe the same air. It was no longer a question of being allowed to be together, but whether he would even be allowed near me once he had delivered me to the Mercians in Carlisle.

Home. I supposed it would be. A brother awaited – the tall golden masked prince of the Britons who prevented Devyn from revealing himself the night of the masquerade ball in Londinium.

Devyn had known then that I stood within touching distance, no, that I danced in the arms of my own full-blood brother. And he said nothing. My better self conceded that to have revealed who I was then not only would have started a war that would have consumed us on the spot, but I wasn't sure anyone would have believed him – least of all me. I had only just started to accept that I was a Briton and not a citizen. That I was the heir to the Lady of the Lake? The very idea would have been laughable.

What had she been doing in the borderlands? I chewed on my lip as the thought hit me anew. Why would the most protected person on the island have been riding with her sole protector and two children so close to the city? They hadn't expected to be attacked. But why were they there in the first place?

We stopped briefly to eat some lunch, and I ate mechanically, looking out on the sweep of the countryside before me. It was a green that rolled on for ever, with snow-covered mountains to our left and the Severn running somewhere in the distance to our right. I had long wondered what Devyn's home was like, and now I was here.

Glorious, luminous light broke through the clouds to bathe the vast, open countryside, the hills and valleys, in pale sunshine, and it sparkled off the water droplets nestled within the russet golds of the autumnal leaves. I heard the crackle and crunch of twigs and leaves under the hooves of our horses. I wished I could be here with Devyn. My heart dragged at the pain of it. Where was he? Had they crossed over into Cymru yet? Had he heard the sing-song voices of his home?

"Did you know?"

"What?"

Marcus stood leaning against a tree behind me as I surveyed the open world before us.

"Did you know?" He hadn't spoken of this morning's revelations all day.

I lifted my hands as if I had an answer and then let them drop helplessly to my lap. I had known nothing, suspected nothing.

"How could I?"

"You knew who he was." He spoke of Devyn.

"I knew bits and pieces," I admitted. "That Devyn came to Londinium looking for a girl, a Briton, who had been stolen away somehow. But I didn't know she was…"

The truth sat in my mind, waiting for me to summon up the nerve to say it out loud.

"The Lady of the Lake," he supplied when I didn't.

"Exactly." I was no happier with him saying it out loud, if I was honest. "How could I suspect? As far as I... as far as any of us knew, she was safe and well in Mercia. Could you imagine if the praetor had known? No need for his crazy plan with us. He could have ridden out and crushed the Britons at any time."

I paused, my breath snatched as if someone had punched me in the gut. It was true. If the Empire had known, they would have destroyed the Celts. It was the threat of magic that kept the Empire confined to Londinium. Without the main source of that power, with the lady gone, they would have been practically defenceless.

"They wanted a baby they were fairly certain would have magic. What luck to have found me." I stopped. *You make your own luck.* Was this what Calchas had referred to? Sentinels had taken me from my mother's arms. Chance? Coincidence?

"It wasn't luck," I said finally.

Marcus looked at me in confusion.

"Calchas knew exactly who I was," I breathed.

"Of course he knew. Marrying us, the York line and the Lakes... Imagine the power he would have held."

"But he was going to execute you... No, not Calchas." I thought it through. "He never planned to pour that power into the sand. He never planned for you and me to die. He sentenced you to a beating. The governor forced his hand. The governeor was the one who wanted us dead."

What if Calchas hadn't finished playing his hand? Master manipulator of the mob, would he have conceded defeat to Actaeon so easily? His plan had been decades in the making.

How could he have spun it to save Marcus and me? I'd seen him do it time and again at the Metes. Justice was doled out to victim and villain alike, according to how he framed it.

But it had been over. We had already been sentenced as

Codebreakers, as the villains of the piece. Unless he had planned to reframe it with a new villain, making us the victims somehow, as he had done with Oban and countless others. But how? Nothing would have changed by the time we took the sands the next day. A night in the tower would...

Wait.

"Calchas sent me to that room after he took my charm away. I didn't want to be there. Devyn had been dosed with the bridal tea and he was all over me the moment I walked into the room." I picked through his strategy, and the details of how it had actually played out. "He didn't know that Devyn's proximity cut through the handfast and that I would come to my senses. If things had played out as he expected them to, then the scene would have gone very differently."

"My bride being taken against her will by a Briton," Marcus finished for me.

I nodded, stunned. "Right. Did anything happen? Did he say anything to you when you talked? He must have had a plan to reprieve you too in the eyes of the mob."

Marcus shook his head.

"How did you find me? How did you break free of him?"

"I... My father put something in his drink."

"But if things had played out according to Calchas's plan, what would have redeemed you?"

"Killing your Briton attacker?" Marcus suggested.

I nodded. If I had managed to get away... No, not that. If Calchas had taken Marcus's wristband from him, my match would have come for me. It would have been easy to arm him, to show him the way.

"Win-win," I said. "I'm redeemed. You're redeemed. Calchas has the mob in the palm of his hand, and we've just proven our loyalty. Actaeon couldn't have us executed then."

'If all that is true, then why haven't they come out to crush us already? Why didn't they follow you?" Gideon slunk out from the cover of the trees.

My eyes narrowed in annoyance at his eavesdropping; I got an innocent look in reply. Or at least as innocent as his darkly handsome, scarred face could pull off.

"If he knew what he held in his hands, why didn't they chase you through the borderlands? If they had finally figured out how weakened we are, why wait?"

"I don't know. Actaeon hates Britons." I caught my breath. "He doesn't know. Actaeon doesn't know. *Calchas* is the one pulling the strings. *He's* the one who wants to control everything."

"Then why didn't he follow you?"

Put like that it seemed obvious.

"They did chase us," Marcus reminded me flatly. "My father died making sure they didn't think there was anything left to chase."

As far as the praetor was concerned, we had died in a fireball on the Tamesis with Matthias as we tried to flee.

"The York troops tore up Oxford trying to find you," Gideon informed us. "So, if the city thought you dead, it doesn't anymore."

"How would they know what happened in Oxford?" I asked.

"Don't be so naïve. Shadowers earn their entry into the city by keeping the council well-informed about what happens in the borderlands. Why do you think there is so little information about the Lady of the Lake? Carlisle is too far north for what little word might have leaked beyond the Lakes to have reached the ears of anyone deemed to have divided loyalties." Gideon slanted us a mocking smirk. "That's why your disguise as Shadowers was useless once you left Oxford. Shadowers are deeply discouraged from crossing too far into our lands since she died. Now mount up, we need to go."

We rode hard for the rest of the day, Gideon pushing us even harder as the winter sun lowered in the sky. Suddenly, riders appeared in the gloom on the road before us. There had to be twenty of them. I looked to Gideon for guidance. The hounds were behind us and armed warriors were in front.

What did we do now?

Chapter Fourteen

"They're York troops," Gideon confirmed.

"How can you tell?" Marcus asked.

"I can tell."

I could feel his body tensing as his head turned from side to side, his gaze sweeping the road in front: mountains to our left, ever darkening forest to our right.

"At least we'll have company when those bloody dogs catch us." He shrugged. His arms went to my waist. "You'd best ride with your boyfriend."

"Why?"

"They're looking for Marcus. He's their prince and they will protect him with their lives; let's hope that protection extends to his little city girlfriend." And with a mocking "M'lady," he swooped me down to the ground. I took the step back to Marcus's horse and in a moment was up on the horse in front of him.

I ran over Gideon's reasoning for changing our arrangement. If riding with Marcus gave me more protection, then what did that mean for him? But it was too late to ask as the York riders had gathered pace and were on us in moments.

The York riders wore similar leathers to Gideon, but their tunics had something like a breastplate to them. Where the Mercian warriors we had ridden with had been wildly Celtic, the Anglian troops were somewhat more martial in appearance.

Any hope I had that we could hide our identity was blown out of the water as a familiar bearded man sat at the head of the troops.

"Callum," I gasped in dismay. I had thought him our friend, but he had clearly led this troop in pursuit of us.

"My prince." He bowed his head to Marcus before turning to Gideon. "My lord."

My lord. Gideon was a lord. He certainly didn't act like a noble. I retraced that thought. Actually, he had no shortage of the arrogance of one privileged from birth.

"Callum." Gideon knew him too, it seemed. Had he also been Gideon's teacher? But no, that made no sense; Callum had been Devyn's teacher in Carlisle. Gideon hadn't arrived there until he was a teenager. "I see you've disappointed my father recently."

A small cut marked Callum's cheekbone. I looked at the similar location of Gideon's own much older injury. Who was his father?

"Why didn't he kill you?" Gideon asked.

"I guess he must still have some use for me," Callum answered drily.

"Like hunting a member of the blood?" Gideon nodded at Marcus. At least I hoped that's who he meant.

"Seems I'm not the only one following the fresh scent of

magic across the countryside," Callum said as another howl rang out in the distance, echoed by the rest of the pack.

"We need to ride," a dark-haired warrior spoke up, addressing Callum but nodding respectfully at Gideon.

"Let's move then." Gideon urged Marcus's horse forward. He had clearly assessed the competing threats and deemed the York riders the lesser of two evils as he dropped behind to ride between us and the pursuing hounds.

"City girl, ride with Callum," he ordered.

I turned to look at Gideon. "No."

I was tired of him ordering me about. And what was with the *city girl* moniker again? Now that I thought about it, it had been *m'lady* all day. Not a hint of the dismissive nickname with which he had christened me on sight.

"He's right, girl." Callum spoke up. "If we need to move fast, having the pair of you, as has barely ever ridden before, on the self-same horse is going to give them hounds an easy target."

Marcus was obviously not the best rider, but I felt Callum had an ulterior motive in splitting us up. If the hounds came, I was their target, not Marcus. It would give Marcus a better chance if we separated. Callum was effectively tying his survival chances to mine.

For the second time in a few minutes, I changed horses. We took off again, the York troops putting Marcus in their centre while Gideon moved to ride behind Callum and me.

It was a move that did not go unnoticed by my former teacher, who caught the younger man's eye for a moment before meeting mine contemplatively. I inclined my head, confirming his suspicions. His eyes narrowed in response, clearly not happy that I had company in my new-found knowledge.

"We ride," Gideon called out and the entire troop headed into the oncoming night as if the bats of Hades were on our tail. If only. Bats would be preferable to the horse-sized hounds that were in pursuit.

It felt like we rode for hours at that terrifying speed, but eventually, we were forced to slow as the horses tired.

"Dismount." The call came from the warrior in the lead.

Walk? Was he crazy? Did he think the hounds were walking too? I had no doubt the vile beasts could run for ever if needed.

Callum dismounted before reaching up to help me down.

"The horses will get fresh legs sooner if they are not bearing our weight," he explained.

A whimper escaped me. The hounds were closer and their calls to each other had become less frequent as the net closed. Now there were more of them than the two that had followed us through the borderlands at Samhain.

"Why are there so many, Callum?" I whispered to the bearded man.

He slanted me a crooked smile in the moonlight, checking to see if anyone was near us before speaking.

"Girl, you are the juiciest thing they've caught wind of in many years; they will pursue you to the gates of Avalon in high summer, if they must."

"That's not very reassuring," I returned. What girl being hunted by mystical slavering beasts that wanted to devour her would be pleased to hear that they would never give up?

"I wasn't aware you were looking for a bedtime story." He laughed back, wincing as the movement tore at the injury slashing across his face.

"What happened?" I asked, indicating the cut.

His bearded face creased. "My lord steward was –" he

paused, raising a hand to the tender wound "– he was disappointed to have missed you."

"Me?" I asked. Did he also know who I really was?

Callum glanced at the other warriors walking behind us before shaking his head almost imperceptibly. "Marcus."

"Marcus plans to go to York. Why chase us?"

"Because you're running. He knows you travel with the Griffin, and he doesn't know why you aren't travelling directly to York. It makes the most sense – at least to him. The Anglians have the strongest army, and Marcus is the heir to their crown. As Marcus's betrothed you would be safe there. As for Devyn, his fate is less certain, no matter where he goes." He looked back at me. "Speaking of our friend of few words, where is the boy?"

"We had to separate." I wasn't sure how much to reveal to Callum, but perhaps he could help. "He was poisoned and the hounds were coming. Bronwyn, his cousin, is with him, along with a handful of warriors, but they have to travel slowly, so we took a separate route to draw the hounds off."

"Poisoned? How?"

I cast a dirty look at the tall man walking behind us.

Callum raised a bushy brow so high it sought to meet the tattoo that ran along his hairline on the left side of his face.

"Gideon?" he asked on an out breath. "Not really his style."

"Well, apparently it is."

"How?"

"He put a dagger in him."

"Where was the hit?"

"What?" I asked. "In the shoulder. What does it matter where the knife hit him?"

"Well, if he wanted to kill him, why not take a more direct route and put it through his eye?"

I shook my head, bile rising as I remembered the moment the dagger had sunk into Devyn's shoulder. "Because he's a lousy shot," I threw behind me.

"Humph." Callum's grunt indicated this was not his belief. "Gideon is many things, Cassandra, but he wouldn't poison a blade. If he wants a man dead, he'll do it with steel; he has no need for tricks. Tricks are for men who care what others think of their actions."

I thought back again to the scene; he had claimed not to have known of anything on the blade.

"Gideon backs down to no man. Apologises for nothing. How do you think he ended up in a rival household as a teenager? If he hadn't left when he did, either he or the steward would surely be dead by now."

"The Steward of York is his father?" My voice rose in my surprise. They had spoken before of Gideon's father but my mind was a whirl and I hadn't pieced it together.

A growl came from behind us. "Are you two planning to gossip all the way through the night?" a sour voice asked. "It's not like we're being hunted by beings with supernatural hearing or anything."

Point taken.

Callum and I fell silent, but my mind spun at the revelation that Gideon was the son of the Steward of York. York was no friend to Devyn, that much I knew. York had been pursuing us from the moment we left the city, but did they want Marcus in order to restore his crown or was the steward more interested in clinging on to power for himself? How had he known so quickly that we had left the city? What if he was somehow in league with the council? Was it crazy to consider the idea? Someone must have betrayed my mother to the city for them to have found her. Had it been someone here who had an interest

222

in the balance of power being off? But why had she been so close to the imperial border in the first place? It made no sense.

As to Gideon being an Anglian, was he a plant in the Mercian court? A boy sent to replace the friend that Rion had lost? Were we all caught in a web of York's making? I didn't know Gideon, and what little I did know, I didn't like. I remembered his gentle touch when I had drawn in magic. Was it only yesterday? He had helped me. But he had also known who Devyn was when he threw that knife and now Devyn was dying.

A howl ripped through the air.

"Time to mount up." Gideon's low voice carried across the group.

The horses had barely had time to catch their breath, much less restore enough strength to race across the dark countryside, but what choice did we have?

Gideon stepped forwards and put his great paws around my waist, lifting me up behind Callum with ease. I scowled down at him as he released me, receiving a flash of white in reply. I was getting seriously tired of being manhandled by him.

The hounds were coming and there were more of them. My heart thudded in my chest. At least now we had Callum and the other warriors, but I had no idea if it would be enough. Suddenly, I felt a pull come over me, a tug that called me to go right.

"Callum, we need to go that way," I whispered, pointing east.

"Why?"

"I don't know."

He considered me gravely for a moment before he gave the order.

We flew through the night, the barely rested horses surprisingly surefooted in the moonlight. Each howl raised the hairs on my flesh and flashes of the memory of slavering jaws only added to my terror.

I held on to Callum's solid torso and buried my head in his back, my stomach churning. What could I do? I had been useless last time, but this time surely I could be more help. I silently prayed to the world around us, the air, the earth, the water, as Callum had taught me. This time, I would not be defenceless.

The howls were closer now, and while they were infrequent, they weren't just behind us anymore. When the eerie hunting calls began to split the night, they were identifiably coming from different directions.

One was directly behind, another, higher-pitched, to the right somewhere in the dark. Two more behind and to the left. One, now two more…

"Callum, they… Was that one in front of us?" Were they now all around us?

The road in front of us went uphill and the horses were visibly tiring, even as they too trembled at the sound of the hounds.

We crested the hill and took in the sight of the Severn in front of us.

A howl tore through the dark. Closer.

No one said a word.

I had led them this way. My mouth went dry. I had led all these men to their deaths.

"Well, city girl, where to now?" Gideon's voice was dry, rather than the castigating sneer I deserved. He was genuinely asking, as though I might have the answer.

But maybe I did have the answer. The glitter of moonlight

across the wide expanse of the river was a path and the path spoke to me. Not literally, not out loud, but it called to me and I had to follow it.

Callum turned his head.

"Girl?" he prompted.

"I..." My mouth was so dry I could barely get the words out. "To the river."

Another howl. Closer still.

The lead warrior nudged his horse forward.

"The river is suicide; we'll be trapped," he objected.

"And yet, that is the way we go," Callum stated flatly, and he started down the hill, Marcus and Gideon following closely behind.

Was I losing my mind? The Anglian was right; I was leading us into a dead end. Yet I felt sure that this was where safety lay.

As we approached the river, it became clear that we had stumbled upon a crossing point, the road leading right up to the gravel bank. However, there was no sign of a ferry or footbridge.

"It's a ford all right," Gideon said after leading his horse several feet into the rushing water. "In the summer, sure, but this late in the year, who knows how—"

The howl was closer and I spotted two sets of twin red lights waiting unmoving on the other bank. Their vile stench came across on the wind. They had surrounded us.

"I've counted four, maybe five behind," Callum assessed.

"Do we cross?" Marcus ventured.

There were two on the far bank, and four or five behind. Surely twenty men could take on two of these things? We had managed to chase them off the last time, but back then, one had been injured and power had flooded my veins. But now, nothing. I commanded nothing.

We stepped out into the river, the cold water swirling ever higher up the horses' legs as they took each tentative step.

One of the hounds in front was visible now, its white coat flashing as it stalked the water's edge... waiting for us.

Two more sets of eyes had become visible on the road behind, another appearing from the trees to our left as the rotting smell closed in on us.

We were nearly in the middle of the river now and the water was as high as the horses' chests so our legs were submerged in the icy waters. Yet here we were safe, I was sure of it. The river fairly sang to me to *stay, stay*.

"Stop," I whispered.

My voice was barely audible over the babble and whoosh of the water, yet everyone stopped.

A snarl came at us from the fourth hound on the bank behind us as he entered the water, his fellows following, spreading out as they came.

The York warriors took position around us, their swords glinting in the moonlight as they waited for the hounds. The two beasts on the bank facing us grew tired of waiting and slipped into the dark water, their white heads visible as they made their way to us. They seemed to be swimming more slowly than I would have expected. Their path was clearly more difficult, the fight against the current on that side more challenging perhaps. But still, the flash of white and the glint of their eerily bright eyes came inexorably closer.

The river pulled at my focus as the soldiers in the front drew closer together. One of the horses descending the bank behind us screamed as it disappeared under the water, its Anglian rider surfacing once and then disappearing into darkness. The water glittered where once the mounted warrior had been.

There was a flash of white in the darkness of the bank and a horse reared. Another flash and more screams. The warriors still on the bank urged their mounts into the water, bunching together to close the gaps in the circle around us. The water suddenly seemed louder and there were more cries from behind. More men disappearing into the darkness. I was somehow calmed by the lulling rhythm of the river as it flowed past us, past this momentary disruption in the eternal flow from the hills and mountains towards the sea. Inevitable, timeless.

I was barely aware of the hounds now; all I could feel, all I could hear, was the river. The Severn whispered to me of the hills, of the moon, and of its journey to the wide, open sea. The hounds were mere flashes of white, as were the pockets of moon reflected on the bubbling water's surface that tugged ever more forcefully around the bodies of our horses. The current rushed by my legs, the drag pulling at the horses. Soon we all would be gone, taken by that current, washed away, lost in the darkness...

Until it suddenly wasn't there anymore. We stood in the middle of the rushing, foaming river, yet where we were had quietened to the glassiness of a pond. It was all still, so still.

We were fewer now. Not everyone had made it to the waiting stillness. The hounds were now nearly impossible to see as they slipped into the river. There were fewer of us left to fight them off as we stood motionless and vulnerable in the water. And then all of a sudden a roar came towards us, a boom exploding upriver, a surge of water, and high on the surface of the river was a wave, endlessly frozen in an almost cresting state, coming straight for us, many feet high in the air.

It would surely take us all, drown every last man and beast beneath its foaming wash, but from nowhere came a certainty that it wouldn't. I slipped off the back of Callum's horse.

Calm, I was calm to my very soul, and the Severn was grateful for the power I had given it yesterday, welcoming of the magic I had drawn and then released, given back, to the water. Now, I stood in the icy depths and closed my eyes, savouring the purity of the exchange.

The colossal wave whooshed by us, the heavy surge of the water going against the natural flow of the stream, and suddenly the hounds were tumbling and thrashing in the white water as its icy grip surged and pushed and sucked the vile beasts down, down into its depths. And then all of them gone. Gone. In moments.

And the roar continued north, against the stream, carrying the beasts with it.

Silence descended once more as the warriors scanned the banks. We were alone.

"City girl." Gideon said no more as he reached his hand down to pull me up and out of the freezing water.

I blinked. It was over. The taut, pale faces of the warriors who remained circling us stared down at me. The river had saved us. I was cold and incredibly tired.

I clasped Gideon's wrist, and he hooked me out of the river and sat me in front of him in one fluid motion, leaving me sitting sideways rather than astride.

We had survived.

Three men had been lost though, taken by the river. But the river would take care of them, I knew. She would take them into the depths or return them to shore.

I rested my head on Gideon's chest as he pulled his cloak about me. My clothes were wet and heavy against my icy skin.

He smelled of cedar and the leather of his moulded body armour. My eyelids felt so heavy and I let go...

———

When I woke, it was to find myself stretched out on the ground in front of a fire, my cloak still wrapped around me. My clothes were dry, though I could still smell the tang of the river on them. Callum. His talents were with fire and air.

I felt bone-tired.

Marcus lay stretched behind me, his warmth against my back, and Gideon's long legs stretched out to the fire at my feet. I followed them back to find him sitting up, contemplating me. Did he never sleep?

"Are they gone?"

He shrugged. "There has been no further sight of them."

I looked over to the dark huddled shapes of the York troops.

"What happens now?"

"Callum and his men are going to escort us as far as Castle Dinas Brân, and then he is going to York to tell my father of your miraculous return."

"What?" Why would he betray me like that?

"Callum was given a clear objective to find Marcus and his girlfriend and take them to York and there is no reason he can't follow through on that," Gideon explained in answer to my dismay. "However, re-routing Marcus and his city girlfriend away from Cymru and taking them to York is one thing, but forcing the returned Lady of the Lake to do so... Well, I convinced Callum that that would perhaps not be the wisest course of action. If you want to continue deeper into Cymru, the price is revealing your identity."

"There has to be another way." I wasn't ready, wasn't even close to ready. I had barely absorbed the news of my new status myself, but if Callum and Gideon's reaction was anything to go by then as soon as this news got out…

They would know. Everyone would know. That was what he was telling me. No more hiding. I wasn't entirely sure I was ready to face the expectations that came with the title; I wasn't sure I was prepared for any of it, especially as my magic was a long way from being something over which I had control.

Bird calls were starting to chirp through the darkness, heralding the dawn. It was a new day. We had survived the night and I was going to meet Devyn, and telling my truth would allow us to do that. So, the truth they would have. Anyway, it would take a while for the news to arrive in York and spread. Maybe by then I would be ready to face it.

Callum and his remaining warriors rode with us for most of the day, only turning back just before we reached Devyn's father's home, where Callum assured me they would not be assured of a welcome.

Callum had chosen not to tell the troop who I was; this was a piece of information he would reserve to deliver to the Steward of York himself. Even so, I had found myself the subject of many stares as we rode together through the countryside – contemplative, curious gazes that yesterday had focused on Marcus. They knew I had power. Did they wonder how or why? And would any of them manage to put the pieces together as Gideon had?

"I will delay for as long as possible," Callum assured us when we stopped in anticipation of our separation. I had ridden with Marcus, needing the comfort of his closeness, however false it was, to keep at bay the memory of the night before, the men and horses disappearing screaming into the night. The unnatural eyes of the hounds. The feeling of power that had surged through me as the Severn responded to the threat against us. "If I wish to keep breathing, I will have to explain why I let you go as soon as I arrive so I will endeavour to arrive slowly." His broad smile flashed beneath his beard.

He glowered in Gideon's direction. "You keep her safe."

Gideon raised an eyebrow in my direction before a smirk tugged at his lips.

"Of course, Callum. It is my pleasure and my duty," he said formally, with a glint that belied his tone. Annoying man.

Callum's mouth thinned but he chose not to react, turning to me with some final advice.

"Get to Rion as soon as you can. Once you are in Mercia, you are protected. Until then, you're fair game. Whoever gets to you first will have the advantage, and their interests may not align with yours." He glanced at Gideon. "York would use you, and the Albans would keep you. Londinium has agents this side of the border, and when they realise you are alive, they will be coming for you both. You should be reasonably safe here; Gwynedd and Mercia have long been allies, though Devyn's return may stress those ties some. Best you keep who you are to yourself as long as you can."

My mind was reeling at the download of new information. I had been confused by the different factions on the Council, but the politics between the Briton nations was entirely new to me. I nodded absently at the one constant direction I had been given: keep my identity secret. Got it. Hide my abilities. As Callum well knew, my command of magic was far from under my control. Keeping it concealed would be easier if our lives stopped being threatened.

"Swear to me," he insisted.

"Swear what?" I asked, distracted by my swirling thoughts.

"Swear that you will not reveal who you are to anyone unless your lives are at risk," he said.

"Who would I tell?" I had a hard enough time digesting the information myself, and I had only the loosest idea of who and what the Lady of the Lake was. Why on earth would I go blabbing to strangers, especially since I had nowhere near her legendary power?

"Fine. I swear," I conceded, under Callum's unwavering glare.

Marcus echoed my promise.

Gideon lifted a brow at Callum. "Promises are for fools. I do not give them."

"Gideon," Callum growled.

"It's her secret." Gideon lifted a shoulder carelessly. "I will not reveal it before she does."

That, it seemed, would have to suffice. We would be in Carlisle before long anyway. Where my brother lived. And there the truth must all, surely, be revealed.

Chapter Fifteen

W e rode for miles, and I was uncomfortably aware of Gideon, who had barely acknowledged my presence. Finally we came into view of Dinas Brân and, from our vantage point high on a hill, we looked down into the golden valley spread out before us; the stone tower was the most welcome sight I could recall seeing in my life. The sun cast soft light across the wooded valley and a slight evening mist was starting to seep across the meadows. The fallen autumn leaves rustled as we made our way through the dappled light under the trees. My mind began to tumble with worry. Were they here yet? Had his condition worsened? Was he…?

I glanced over at Marcus as we arrived at the entrance to the castle, which was a lot less welcoming up close. The outer wall was high and solid, and the central tower loomed over us in the growing dark.

Gideon hailed the sentry, who was no more than a dark shadow peering down on us from above the gate.

"Ho there! Open the gate," he called up.

"Who goes there?" the voice called down. The tone was flatly unfriendly.

Gideon huffed a laugh in my ear. "Well, lady, what name would you have us enter under? I assure you mine is unlikely to gain us entry."

"Tell him we are…" I racked my brain for inspiration. "Weary travellers," I finally offered weakly.

I could practically feel Gideon's eyes rolling in his head.

"We travel in the name of the King of Mercia," he called up, ignoring my suggestion. "We have a message for Lord Rhodri."

A second man-shaped shadow appeared above the gate, no more welcoming than the first. "The Lord of the Lakelands is no friend to those who dwell here. If you have a message, deliver it and begone."

"You will deny weary travellers a bed and food, my lord?" Gideon challenged the newcomer, using my words despite his scoffing. I sat straighter in the saddle, unable to let the moment pass unmarked.

The second figure disappeared and the shadows grew longer. What if they refused even to let us in to explain. Should we announce to all here at the gate that we were here to meet Devyn? Was Devyn already here? Was that why they were so unfriendly to strangers? No, that made no sense. If Devyn were here then they would have expected us. My stomach sank, the expectation that had been building since morning fizzling slowly out of my tired body.

"He's not here," I said out loud, to myself as much as my companions.

"How do you know?" Marcus's face was in shadow as he started to utter the unspeakable. "Maybe he isn't…"

I frowned at him, seeking Devyn through the bond that

stretched thin between us. I couldn't feel anything, but I also couldn't feel a dreadful nothingness either.

I shook my head.

"He's not here; we are not expected." I twisted my body to take in the silent warrior behind me. "We should go out to meet him."

"Our horses are exhausted. We were to meet here. Bronwyn will bring him."

"And you just don't care," I threw at him. After all, it was his fault Devyn was sick. Why would he do any more than he had to?

Voices came from the other side of the gate and the heavy wooden barrier in front of us opened slowly, the grand oak entrance yielding unwillingly. Gideon nudged our horse forward, and we made our way under the wall and into the courtyard in front of the tower, dark figures of armed men edging forwards from the shadows.

Gideon scanned the men appearing in our wake as the gate closed shut behind us, his body tensely poised at my back. I leaned forward, aware that my presence hindered him should the lack of welcome here become something more life-threatening. Though his odds against the ten or more guards that surrounded us couldn't be good. I steadied myself, tensing in anticipation of the attack that felt imminent.

"An odd group of messengers," came a dry voice from a slightly bent figure who I could now see was walking towards us across the courtyard.

Gideon turned and inclined his head.

"My lord."

The grey-haired man stopped as he came alongside us, his eyes shifting from one to another of us in measurement. He grunted what I supposed amounted to acceptance and with a swing of his head indicated for us to follow him to the main entrance of the tower.

Marcus dismounted first and made his way to me to help me down as. With two of us astride, there was no easy way for me to get down without help and I was typically somewhat unsteady at the end of a long day of riding.

I hesitated before swinging a leg over in readiness to slide off the tall black stallion, bracing for the impact of his touch. Awareness flared as he put his hands on my waist, his green eyes a mixture of heat and denial as I slid to the ground. I looked down, fighting the chemistry ignited by his touch and the damned handfast cuff, shame at my involuntary response curdling in the pit of my stomach. I felt like my reaction was broadcast to everyone in our vicinity. Yet the guards continued to back away and go about their business. Gideon dismounted behind me and gave the reins to a stable boy who had run up to take care of our horses.

Marcus's corresponding reticence was the only visible sign that the strength of our response to each other was not a figment of my imagination. Last night, in my exhaustion, I had felt only safe in his arms, but this morning, the burning in my blood had returned in full force. Worry for Devyn, fear of the hounds, and exhaustion from what had happened on the river had dulled the handfast-elicited desire but this morning I had felt it strongly enough that I had actually volunteered to ride with Gideon.

Each day that I was separated from Devyn, my defences against the handfast bond weakened. The urge to comply with the Code and return to the city thankfully remained absent. Given that we needed to convince people we were together, my desire to be close to Marcus wasn't all bad... as long as it didn't become overwhelming.

Marcus lowered his eyes, sucking in his cheeks in acknowledgement of my rejection. He turned to stride after the older man, not waiting for either Gideon or me. The pull to stay close to him was almost tangible. I forced myself to lag back, earning a dark glance from the ever-observant warrior, who stopped to wait for me.

"Stay close," Gideon said quietly as I rejoined him. His warning brought me back to the broader present and the fact that we were neither welcome nor safe in our latest surroundings.

Part of me wanted to almost dismiss this knowledge in anticipation of the fact that for the first time in what felt like forever, we would not be sleeping on the ground. At least I hoped we wouldn't, I amended, taking in the rather forlorn appearance of the inside of the tower as we made our way through the dark entrance hall with its tired tapestries and tatty furnishings; dust and dirt tracked in from outside remained undisturbed in this unkempt space. My experience of Briton buildings was limited, given we had avoided them as much as we could on our journey north. The odd barn was the only structure I had seen the inside of apart from the beautiful golden stone of Oxford's great buildings of learning. Despite being relatively empty of students when we had been there, the halls had been well cared for, warm and welcoming. This building had a coldness to it that went beyond its grey granite stone; what once might have been a home felt hollow and abandoned, despite being occupied.

Exiting the darkness of the hall, we came into what I supposed was the great hall of the keep. At least, I supposed it had once been great, but the long, dusty tables and dirty floor added to the general feeling of neglect. Were it not for the fire crackling in the hearth at the top end, I would have easily believed no one had lived here in decades.

"Well, what is your message?" came that dry, raspy voice from a high-backed chair that faced the fire. Was this really Devyn's father? His grey hair hung limp about his face, and his eyes, while dark, did not have the intensity of his son's; they appeared, instead, endlessly tired. His shoulders were slumped, as if the energy to stand tall was beyond him, though underneath this they appeared to be broad and his long body hinted at former power. His face was lined, pale and unshaven but his clothes, unlike the hall, were clean; small hints of mending suggested that someone here at least took better care of him than he did of his home.

Gideon walked forwards until we stood within range of the warmth of the crackling fire, my entire body absorbing the heat as it hit the skin on my face and started to warm my clothes.

"No one has arrived before us?" Gideon asked in his turn.

The man in the chair cocked an eyebrow at Gideon's failure to answer the question asked, his eyes narrowing as he looked up at the tall warrior. He had to be Devyn's father, or at least some relative, because I recognised the guileless look that masked the detailed threat assessment that was taking place. But while Devyn was always coiled in preparation for a fight, I could see the muscles of the man before me start to gather as he took in Gideon before surveying Marcus and me rather more slowly.

"Who are you?" His question was directed at me as he finally met my eyes fully.

"We are weary travellers seeking hospitality at your door," Gideon responded, taking an almost imperceptible step to place himself slightly in front of me.

"I thought you were messengers," the man reminded him.

"That too."

A rather wide woman appeared from a door at the side of the room and bustled forwards with the tray she was bearing, unloading the goods she carried onto the top table a few steps away from us and lighting some more candles to eat by.

"Well, my weary travellers," the man said, indicating the food and drink with his hand as the woman, having laid everything out to her apparent satisfaction, disappeared back to wherever she had come from.

We ate and drank in silence; the food was functional but good and simply being indoors added flavour to the meal, as far as I was concerned. Our host sat back, indicating that any further discussion of our business here could wait until we had received the hospitality of his hall – something I was infinitely grateful for as I enjoyed sitting on the hard bench and eating real food for the first time since Oxford. I finished an extra slice of the delicious, nutmeggy cakes, flat, round and golden in colour, before our host invited us to join him back at the hearthside.

"Now, perhaps you would be so kind as to tell me what brings you to my home?" he prompted.

"We're looking for your son."

If Gideon was aiming to get a reaction then he was disappointed, as the older man didn't so much as flicker an eyelid in response.

"I'm afraid you have travelled in vain then," he finally offered in an even tone. "For I have no son."

I gasped at the denial, surer than ever that this man was Lord Rhodri. How dare he.While he was far from being a copy of his son, he had a certain steady way of looking at you that was all Devyn.

"That's a shame, for we parted company three days since

239

from a man who bid us meet him here at his father's house – or at least his cousin did, as he was not much in the way of conversation at the time."

The man threw a dark look at Gideon.

"You speak in riddles. I ask again, who are you?" The old man stood looming over an unconcerned Gideon.

"My companions are –" he hesitated "– Catriona and Marc of Oxford and I am Gideon, trusted man of the King of Mercia."

I froze as Gideon used my true name as my alias. Ass.

But the introduction told our host nothing, and his lids lowered to cover his own reaction to Gideon's dodging the true nature of his question.

"How come you here, speaking of my son?" His accent thickened as he glowered down at the smiling Gideon.

"I thought you had no son," Gideon taunted.

"Enough." I didn't know or care what game Gideon was playing. I understood that Rhodri was not a respected man in Britannia, but playing with him like this was poorly done. "We were travelling with Devyn and we had to split up. We were hoping he might have made it here before us?"

The man looked at me with a lack of comprehension that made me wonder if he couldn't understand my words; maybe my accent was too odd.

"Devyn?" He faltered on the name. "Coming here? How?"

"We were attacked, Devyn was injured, and because we were being pursued by the hounds of Samhain, we drew them off while he and Bronwyn were to come directly here. There is no sign of them?"

The man drew a shaking hand across his face.

"Devyn is on his way here?" he asked again.

"Yes."

"No, no, he hasn't arrived." He started for the door and then stopped again. "Truly?"

"Yes," I repeated and Gideon, in turn, nodded as Devyn's father looked to him too for confirmation.

He made his way rapidly towards the door and there were sounds of shouting from the yard before he returned.

"If you are lying, I will end you; I care not who you serve," he opened grimly.

"We are not lying," I assured him.

"Then tell me how this comes to be," he ordered.

"Devyn was hurt on our way here." I didn't want to reveal all, but his reaction had not included any surprise that his son was alive, despite the commonly held belief that he had died years ago.

"How?" For a man who, moments before, had been denying Devyn's very existence, he seemed interested enough now.

"He was wounded by a knife," I gritted out, not looking at my travelling companions, both of whom shared the blame for what had happened.

"The cut is deep?"

"No," I shook my head. "But we think there was something on the blade and it's made him very ill. We weren't able to help him. Bronwyn said we should come here because you have a healer who might be able to do something for him."

Rhodri paled.

"Our druid left yesterday and he is not expected back for another week at least. I should have gone with him, but I stayed here, just in case."

I shook my head, confused. "In case of what?"

"In case my son came home."

"I thought you had no son," Gideon said with a smirk.

Lord Rhodri shook his head wearily. "I did not know who you were and 'twould not be wise to tell strangers at my door that I waited... in case he might seek a night here on his way north."

"How did you know we were coming?" Marcus asked, speaking for the first time, I realised.

"Well, *Marc of Oxford*, the entire country is buzzing with news of the York prince fleeing the city with the Griffin's son, risen from the dead, leading him home. People expect Marcus Plantagenet Courtenay to go to York, but Devyn's fealty is to Mercia. Once beyond the border, he would have a duty to go there directly." The tired, dark eyes looked towards the fire. "I am an old man and I waited here in the hope that he would seek shelter on his way. I would like to see him once more."

He turned towards me. "And so now that we are all being a little more honest, I take it your name is not Catriona?"

I hesitated. I so wanted to tell him. This man had been destroyed by what had happened twenty years ago but I bit my lip and shook my head.

"Cassandra," I offered up, sticking to my promise to Callum and to Devyn to conceal the truth.

"Cassandra, it is my pleasure to host you." He bowed his head, waving in a waiting serving woman. "Now, I'm sure you are tired. Meg will take you to your room."

While it had been warm beside the fire, the temperature quickly dropped as we circled up into the tower where I was shown to my room. This room too showed signs of disuse but, like its lord, hints of former pride and grandness were still visible under the surface abandonment. I wondered what Gideon had made of the man who used to be the greatest warrior in the land, a man I recalled he had once admired, though his frame had become frail and seemed as discarded and uncared-for as his home.

I quickly washed as best I could, using the cloth and icy-cold water which had been left for the purpose, before climbing fully dressed beneath the somewhat musty, heavy covers of the four-poster bed. The throw at the bottom of the bed caught my eye, its geometric burnt reds and yellows far from the swirling blues and greens more typical of the Celts. It spoke of Mediterranean Africa; was this one of the few remnants of Devyn's mother, who had died too soon after escaping the Empire? Devyn. My mind raced in worry. Where was he? They should have made it here before us. Even delayed by Devyn's wound, their route should have been half the distance of the one we had taken. Where could they be?

I lay there, unable to relax despite the relative comfort of a bed, when the door opened again. I turned slightly, expecting the servant who had brought me here. But in the doorway, in the light of the single candle he held aloft, stood Marcus.

"Ah, yes. Thank you, I'll be fine," he spoke to someone in the hallway before entering the room and closing the door to the stairwell.

"Cassandra, I..." He hesitated.

I smiled in amusement at his consternation.

"It appears the Celts don't keep to the same rules as the city when it comes to unmarried couples," I observed dryly.

"It appears not," he responded carefully.

"I'm okay if you are," I offered quietly when he made no move to come closer.

He nodded and crossed the room, leaving his candle on the table by the bed before he too cleaned up with a fresh pour of water and the cloth I had used before him. He pulled off his outer layers of clothing, fastidiously folding them and placing them on a nearby chest before climbing in beside me. He quenched the candle with a soft huff of breath.

The room, which had been so empty before with only my thoughts rattling around in it, now felt suffocatingly small. I dragged back my consciousness from the forests where Devyn lay somewhere, suffering but still alive, I was sure. I would feel it if he were gone; he was closed off, distant, but still breathing. I knew it with the same certainty with which I drew my own breath.

Being this close to Marcus made the inevitable awareness in my blood begin to heat as the handfast went to work. We had worn the metal cuffs for months now, longer than anyone I had ever heard of and the effects were impossible to ignore – for me at least, unprotected by my lost charm or by Devyn's proximity. My fingers curled into my palms, digging into the skin to distract my mind from the attraction of the warm body on the other side of the bed.

I nearly jumped out of my skin when a hand gently brushed my shoulder.

"Are you all right?" came his voice, soft in the darkness.

I remained silent. I didn't know what to say. No, I was not all right, and his touch made me at once furious and maddened with the need to turn into his arms. I hated the cuffs with a strength that would bring down the mighty stone walls of the keep if I released it.

"I'm sorry," he said.

The darkness allowed the words to linger in the air.

"It's not your fault," I finally managed to breathe into the cold air.

"No," he said dismissively, "not for this – well, maybe a little for this, but I'm sorry for what happened."

I stayed silent. Let him say it. I wasn't going to let him off so lightly if he was actually apologising for what had happened on our way north. His part in it at least had not been on purpose. Gideon, on the other hand, I would hold accountable until the last day I drew breath.

The bed, despite its considerable substance, moved under Marcus's mighty exhale. "I shouldn't have left, I definitely shouldn't have risked exposure by hooking up with some random Briton in a village, and I'm sorry that Devyn got hurt."

Was he sorry? Actually sorry? He'd had a right to be angry that night in the barn; I could hardly blame him for wanting to put some distance between us that night. He had still been grieving for his father and the loss of the only life he had ever known for an uncertain future in this primitive and hostile land. Even without the handfast cuffs complicating everything, his storming off was understandable.

I reached up to the hand on my shoulder and put mine over it.

"Okay," I said softly. I pushed away from the chemical reaction I felt and focused on the Marcus I had known before the handfast: the caring physician, the warm friend, the charismatic social centre of every group. Someone I realised I had not seen in a while. Marcus on the road here had been quiet – not cold but solitary. He spoke seldom and interacted with others as little as possible. I knew he was still grieving, but in trying to push away this terrible handfast attraction, I realised I had pushed away my friend. My friend who was in pain.

I couldn't risk turning around to embrace him, not here in the dark with just the two of us, but I pulled his arm around me and tucked it into my body, hoping he understood that comfort was all I could offer him. He stiffened, but as I made no further move, he relaxed, and eventually his breathing evened out.

I woke the next morning, for once warm and cosy. The coldness of my nose was the only indication that something was not as it had always been... before. In the comforts of the city. I blinked my eyes open to find the wintry sunlight streaming in through the window set in the bare granite walls of Devyn's father's castle.

Devyn. My heart thumped at the remembrance that he was not here. He was not here. The dread made my body heavy in the soft grey light.

Then who...?

I twisted round in the bed and took in the handsome sleeping face that shared my pillow. Marcus.

Abruptly, I pulled myself out of his arms and with a thump found myself on the bare rug that was all that separated me from the wooden floor. A floor which I had hit with my now tender arse.

"Ow," came a laughing voice from above. "That sounded like it hurt."

Marcus's face appeared over the side of the bed above me, a genuine smile on his lips – the first I had seen there in what felt like for ever.

"Morning." I smiled back ruefully.

"Come back into the warmth," he invited. "I promise I'll find a way to restrain myself."

Disgruntled, I nonetheless dove back in; it was freezing outside the covers.

"That's what you get for being in such a hurry to escape my

arms," he teased. I looked over at him, his green eyes lighting with a warmth that hadn't been there since his father, the arena, the illness, the escape This was the Marcus I had known for only a few months of summer in the time before.

"Well, if your giant hulk wasn't taking up most of the bed…" I shot back.

"Hulk! I'm just a little tall," he said, "though not so much out here with the Britons."

"Most of the Britons we've met so far have been warriors. I'm not sure how typical they are," I reassured him, giving him a patronising pat on the shoulder.

He huffed in laughter before his eyes grew sombre.

"Lord Rhodri has it, Cassandra," he said.

I blinked, not following.

"Has what?"

"The illness."

I thought back to the man by the fireside the night before. He hadn't looked ill, a little frail maybe, but he was old so surely…?

"Are you sure?"

"Yes. He doesn't seem too far gone. His skin is a little off colour and there is a tremor in his hands. He looks older than he should; I would put him at late forties, but he seems ten years older somehow." He shook his head. "The symptoms don't match the ones I've seen in the city – there is something faded about them – but I'm certain that's what it is."

"Bronwyn knew he was ill when she came to Londinium," I recalled. "She wanted Devyn to leave then, to go home with her and make peace with his father."

"That's not possible. The Treaty Renewal was over two months ago." Marcus frowned. "His symptoms should be far worse by now."

247

I thought back to the patients he had treated at Bart's. Once the first symptoms showed, the illness progressed rapidly, the prognosis fatal in weeks, not months.

"Maybe he's sick with something else."

"No." Marcus sounded sure. "He has the illness, but somehow they are holding it off."

"You think they've found a way to treat it?" I asked, happy to see the confident medical professional in Marcus resurface.

"Fidelma spoke of a treatment," he reminded me as he braved the cold and jumped out of bed with renewed purpose.

We arrived in the hall to the sound of raised voices. A short man in a long hooded travelling cloak who stood facing Lord Rhodri fell silent as we entered the room.

"Is this why you called me back? What do they need?" He spoke gruffly and wasn't terribly welcoming at the sight of strangers in his lord's hall. "Well, what do you need? Speak and let me be back on the road."

Marcus and I looked at each other in bewilderment. What on earth was going on?

"His lordship has called back his healer." A deep voice drew my attention to Gideon's tall frame as he leaned casually against the eaves of the window, looking out onto the road leading up to the keep.

I turned back to the bearded man glowering at us.

"You're a healer?" Relief sprang inside me. Devyn might not be here yet, but at least help would be at hand when he got here.

"Yes. Now what do you need, and I'll be on my way," he said impatiently.

"It's not us. It's our friend and he's on the way," I explained.

The healer looked exasperatedly at his lord. "You called me

back for a patient who isn't even here. Are you losing what little is left of your mind, my lord? We should have made the journey to Conwy weeks ago. There is nothing in the store and you will be dead before I can make it back. Though maybe that's what you want," he finished with a scowl.

And was met with an answering one.

"Madoc," he said, in a quelling tone.

"You think I care what these strangers think? I care not. I have spent too long keeping you alive despite yourself, and I'm not waiting here for some traveller who may or not make it, who I may or may not be able to help. What I know is that if you will not go to Conwy, I will go alone and be back before the last of the supplies runs out," he spat. "I hope."

"Madoc."

Lord Rhodri's tone brooked no further complaint. His healer merely stared back at him in disgust, sending us a similarly dismissive glare before he turned and began to stride out of the hall.

"Madoc!" Lord Rhodri's bellow brought the man's exit to a sharp halt, and he turned, surprise at the force of his lord's command clear on his bristled face.

Lord Rhodri stared down the hall before explaining softly.

"It's Devyn. Devyn is coming."

The man's face fell in shock and he took a quick step forward.

"What? He has the Mallacht? Not the boy." He looked fiercely towards us as if commanding our denial at his conjecture. "But we haven't enough for you to last the week. How can I help him? If I go now, I can be back in a few days, less if your brother gives me fresh horses."

"It's not the Mallacht," I interjected, recognising the Briton term for the illness. Whatever medication it was that was running low was clearly intended to treat what ailed the father and not the son. "It's some kind of poison or infection. We think. At least, he was...."

"I threw a knife at him. I hit him. There was probably something on the blade," came a flat voice from the window.

I glared at Gideon and got an uncaring shrug in response.

"What was on the knife?" Two hard voices spoke in unison as the older men turned towards the laconic dark-haired warrior.

"I don't know," he frowned slightly. "People knew that we were going in search of them. The chances that the pointed end of my knife might scratch the Oathbreaker were probably even enough that someone took the time to apply a little something to the blade. Whether it's a poison or curse... I have no way of knowing."

Or caring, his tone communicated quite clearly.

"The scar..." Lord Rhodri's eyes narrowed. "You're the York pup the Mercians took in. You expect me to believe you don't know what was on the blade that you stuck in my son?"

The man could still move quickly when he wanted to and shoved Gideon against the wall, his elbow in the taller man's neck.

Gideon smiled darkly and pushed away from the wall against the hard bone digging into his exposed throat.

"If I had wanted your son dead then he would be dead."

Lord Rhodri sagged. "They wouldn't even let him come home. It was not his sin."

"He ate your sin, old man," Gideon said into the silence in a hard voice.

Lord Rhodri stepped back, his body seeming to diminish as he made his way back over to the chair by the fire, his alertness fading.

"He was just a boy. Just a child."

He spoke into the fire, no longer really present in the room.

I wondered if he had travelled back in time, to the frozen riverside where he had chosen to save his own life and that of his son, leaving my mother and me to our fates. I felt no hate towards the broken man by the fire. He had failed my mother and me on that day, and he and his son had been paying for it ever since. This once proud warrior sat in his empty shell of a keep, praying to whatever gods they believed in out here, to see his son one last time before he died – the son he must have thought dead this last decade, the son who had paid the more substantial price for his father's sin. A boy who could barely remember a time when his own people didn't hate him. A people who hated him for my sake. And he had come for me anyway.

I crossed over to Lord Rhodri. I didn't know him, but his pain was a palpable thing as I laid my hand on his arm.

"He's going to be okay. We will make sure that he recovers." I couldn't promise any more and I wasn't even sure I could guarantee that much. I met Gideon's dark gaze. He seemed to resolve something and pushed himself off the wall.

"Which way did you send your men?" he asked gruffly.

"What?" Lord Rhodri struggled to gather himself back. His face was pale and I noticed a flush had appeared on his high cheekbones, which were so like his son's.

"You sent men out last night, didn't you? There's no point me going in the same direction."

Gideon was going out to search for them. I don't know why the thought of him seeking Devyn comforted me, but it did.

Lord Rhodri lifted a hand and pointed south. "You said you were just outside Worcester when you parted and that your party came through Rhayader and Llanfyllin, so I sent them

251

towards Oswestry and Shrewsbury, which would have been the most direct route."

"Maybe too direct. Bronwyn is no fool. York is on the roads hunting them and if they were to try and cut her off, they would have taken that road. It's what I would have done."

"You would know," grumbled the old healer.

"What if she came on the old roads up to Ellesmere? It would be longer, which explains why they're not here yet, but it would have been safer," Gideon suggested.

"Why would a princess of Kernow ride in fear of York? Why would they be in danger from your father's troops?" Lord Rhodri had been a warrior in the service of the Lady of the Lake once; he would understand more about the tensions and alliances that made up Briton politics than I could ever hope to. What was it that seemed off to him? Since leaving Oxford we had ridden in fear of York, fortunate that when they finally caught us Callum had led them, and their focus had been on the immediate threat to all our lives rather than their original mission.

"Your son rides with her." Gideon shrugged.

"What would York want with Devyn? He is worth nothing to your father," said Lord Rhodri.

"No, but you have something that is of worth." Nobody needed to turn to look at Marcus. York was scouring the countryside for the three of us and if they found Devyn they would be unlikely to let him go. And when the steward discovered that the Plantagenet prince was sitting behind the fortified walls of a Gwynedd castle and that Callum had had us within his grasp and let us go, he would not be happy about it. Having Devyn would give him leverage.

"I don't know how that poison got on my knife, but I do

know that my father will not overextend himself to ensure that the Griffin doesn't die from a wound I gave him."

Gideon delivered this casually from where he leaned against the wall, as if he were speaking of matters which he could scarcely be bothered to discuss, but there was something about the very casual nature of his tone and posture that seemed overdone to me. It did bother him that Devyn might die of the dagger wound he had dealt. Not for Devyn's own sake perhaps, but because killing him had not been Gideon's intent and he bristled at being used that way. Or maybe it was because he wanted to ensure Devyn lived for my brother's sake, though either way it didn't really matter. I believed that if Gideon set out to find Devyn, then find him he would. That was good enough for me.

Lord Rhodri surveyed Gideon steadily.

"I have no fresh horse to give you." Apparently Devyn's father had drawn the same conclusion. "Take your own, but go through Chirk on your way. The De Laceys will give you some horses and I'll write you a letter of safe passage. Perhaps not a full introduction, though. They bear the steward little love."

"Few outside Anglia do," Gideon acknowledged.

Madoc pulled some parchment from the travel bag that still hung from his shoulder, quickly followed by a quill and a small pot of ink. Sometimes it shocked me anew how thoroughly the Britons had managed to hold off the advances of the modern age so completely. Surely ink in a ballpoint pen wouldn't be too great a concession to the technology of the Empire? It wasn't like it was a computer tablet. Was it sheer stubbornness or was there a reason why they stuck to the barest of conveniences?

There was a notable shake in his hand as Lord Rhodri wrote his letter for the family at Chirk Castle. Nobody else

253

seemed to observe the difficulty he was having as he turned away to conceal a suppressed cough. Gideon, having retrieved his cloak and sword from wherever they had been stored, accepted the completed note and with a nod to me strode out of the hall.

"Marcus?" I called as soon as Gideon and Madoc had left the hall. I might be entirely at a loss when it came to the politics of this strange and foreign land, but I had waited before calling attention to Lord Rhodri's condition until the man he considered no friend of his house was gone.

I threw a concerned look towards Devyn's father, indicating that Marcus needed to take a closer look at him while the druid was absent from the hall. Maybe Marcus's assessment of how advanced his illness was an underestimation of its progression.

"Can you help him?" I asked as Marcus checked his vitals. The older man was slumped in his chair, exhausted from the façade he had maintained in the presence of the younger warrior.

"Lord Rhodri." The healer had returned. "Out of my way, boy."

He pushed past Marcus as he bustled through, anxious to serve his lord. "Rhodri, what have you done?" he muttered to himself as he reached for his travel bag once more.

"Was trying to save... Not much left," Lord Rhodri managed to say.

I frowned. What was he trying to save?

"You damned fool," Madoc grumbled as he put whatever he had taken from his bag into a cup of water on the table nearby and, supporting his lord's head, helped him to drink.

Marcus's gasp was audible as Devyn's father revived almost immediately. I could barely believe my eyes. Yesterday I hadn't even noticed the symptoms of the illness that Marcus had managed to catch. But this morning, in the space of twenty minutes, he had gone from seeming fine if frail to fully symptomatic, displaying the signs I recognised all too well from my time in St Bart's hospital, the symptoms of one with mere days to live... to almost fully recovered within minutes.

"What—?" Marcus could barely get the words out. "What was that?"

"Ha! We have something that all your fancy medicine doesn't, eh?" the healer taunted Marcus.

"Please, I'm a doctor. There is no known cure for the illness. How did you...?" If Marcus heard the man's snarky tone then he didn't respond; in his eagerness to learn more he was practically tumbling over his words. His hands reached for the now empty cup.

He lifted it to his nose and sniffed. "Bitter. What is this?"

The healer cast a suspicious look at the outsider but finally shrugged. Who was Marcus going to tell?

"A tincture made mostly of mistletoe. The druids grow it. It's no cure but it helps. Our stocks are low. The prince distributes it to the principality over Yuletide after the midwinter harvest but we've gone through it fast this year. More and more have fallen ill of the Mallacht and we couldn't wait another month. But then news came that a Briton boy had escaped the city and his lordship hoped it was his boy, so he insisted we delay. When two weeks went by I figured he must have gone past already but Lord Rhodri would not leave, just in case."

He looked down at his lord who, though he looked much recovered, now slept in his large chair, clearly exhausted by the battle that had taken place in his body.

"I hope we did not delay too long. He hid how low our supply was and I took some for my journey in case I met

CLARA O'CONNOR

anyone in need. Excuse me while I see exactly how long our supply will last for those within the keep who rely on it to keep them this side of the grave."

I waited until Madoc left the room. Marcus was lost in thought as he watched him leave, no doubt wanting to learn more about the treatment. I had need of his attention though.

"Are you strong enough yet?" I indicated the frail older man. "The medicine he's been taking, it won't cure him. But you can."

Marcus nodded thoughtfully. "I think I could help one or two now. I will speak to him tomorrow and see if he will accept my help."

"Why would he not accept?"

"We'll see."

256

Chapter Sixteen

On the second morning after Gideon's departure, a call went up that riders were coming. The position of the tower high on a hill afforded its residents a view over the surrounding countryside for miles and miles, so it felt like an age before the two riders finally emerged from the trees close enough to be identified: Bronwyn and one of her warriors. Where was Devyn?

Bronwyn was hailed and entered through the open gates. I stumbled down the stone stairs that brought me from the top of the wall to the courtyard. I rushed over to Bronwyn as she dismounted.

Her eyes caught and held mine, her face drawn. My breath caught in my throat. I couldn't make the words exist in my mind, much less emerge from my mouth.

She caught and squeezed my hand.

"He lives," she assured me. "Where is Madoc?"

"He went to check on his supply of mistletoe, I think." I wasn't sure of his location though.

257

I trailed after her as she immediately took off towards the side entrance to the tower where Madoc's room was.

"Where is Devyn?"

She didn't falter as she answered over her shoulder through the black wing of her hair.

"He's coming behind. But we need Madoc," she said. "Now."

What did that mean? I reached for Devyn to find out for myself but could sense nothing. Surely he couldn't be too far behind. Where was he and what had happened to slow them down this much?

"Madoc," she called, and without waiting for an answer was inside.

The druid – I had been corrected when I had referred to him as a healer – was pulling some herbs down from where they hung drying on the wall. There were small pots and bottles covering every available surface. Bottles and jars of blue and green, brown and transparent, of both pottery and glass. The clear ones that I could see held liquids and pastes of various colours; some contained seeds and a large one beside me seemed to contain dirt. The benches were crowded with pestles and pots and even a series of tubes that dripped a greenish liquid into a smaller dark pot.

Madoc didn't look up as we burst unceremoniously into the room, just bustled about plucking one bottle off a shelf before returning it and reaching into a drawer and taking out two others.

"Madoc," Bronwyn repeated impatiently.

"Tsh, tsh, I hear you, girl. I'm not deaf," he said, continuing to lift and discard various bottles, peering into them and opening the stoppers to sniff at others.

Bronwyn was not a woman used to being hushed like a

child, but neither was she able to bring herself to shout at a druid she presumably had known since childhood.

"Gods, Madoc, please," she finally pleaded with him to acknowledge her.

He sniffed at one last green bottle and, apparently satisfied, put it into a bag which he then lifted over his head, settling it securely across his body.

Crossing to Bronwyn, he laid a gentle hand on her shoulder.

"How bad?" he asked.

"Bad."

My stomach jumped a little at the confirmation of what I already knew to be true.

"Is he conscious?"

"A little," she said. "That is, he wakes some, and he knows me, but then he is gone again."

"How far has the darkness extended?" he asked, referring to the dark veiny colour that we had described to him, the one that crept from Devyn's wound when we had last seen him.

"His whole chest, his arms, up to his neck."

My stomach swooped. Were we too late. Had whatever it was invaded too much of his body to be repelled by whatever concoction Madoc had prepared to fight it with? Focus. I needed to focus on what they were saying; I could process it later.

"His face?" he asked.

"No."

"Good, that's good." The druid nodded as he pulled his great grey cloak on. "When he's not awake, how deep is he gone?"

"Deep." She glanced at me. "He seems almost dead at times."

259

I bit my knuckle so hard that blood welled where my teeth cut flesh. *Don't scream, don't scream. He's not dead yet.*

"How far?" Madoc surveyed his workbench before nodding in satisfaction to himself as he patted the satchel under his cloak.

"Not far, I think. We were not far from Chirk when Gideon met us. He gave us fresh horses to come to fetch you. The rest are coming behind with Devyn. We have him in a cart but it's too slow. Gideon doesn't think he will make it if you don't treat him first."

I trailed them back out to the courtyard where the two horses waited. Bronwyn's warrior mounted one, leaving one for Madoc. Gideon and the other soldiers who had gone in search of Devyn had emptied out the stables.

I had never felt so helpless in my life. Not in Richmond watching Devyn ride away, nor on the sands about to face a justice that I knew was rigged against me. As if on a string, I followed the horses through the gate, stopping outside the castle wall as they picked up the pace along the road, watching unblinkingly until they disappeared into the forest. He was dying, and all I could do was stand here in this cold crumbling castle doing nothing. What good was all this power I supposedly had if I couldn't do anything to save him?

A fine-boned hand intertwined with mine and gripped tightly.

"He will make it, Cassandra," Bronwyn said firmly.

"Will he?" Or would he die out there in the green forests of his homeland? At least he would have that; at least he wouldn't be closed in by the urban prison of Londinium. He found me and returned me to the land of my birth; that was all he had wanted. Would he now slip away, leaving me here alone?

My knees gone, I folded to the ground.

What would I do if he never made it here? I pushed the thought away. Devyn would make it. Whatever had been on that blade would not be enough to steal him from this world.

Bronwyn spoke to me but the words were just a faint buzz, my entire body focused on the riders galloping along the road through the great trees of the forest, their horses' hooves a steady patter over the rustle of the wind in the leaves that carried me along.

They followed the road through the forest, their way littered with the debris of the summer long gone, bare saplings standing solitary under great gnarled trunks. Open fields and craggy cliffs. A babbling brook that rippled along beside the road.

Until finally they met a group of horses carrying men. One of the horses pulled a small cart, alongside which a large man rode. The horse was tired, relieved of its burden as the two groups met, and the man was lifted from the cart.

A wind curled across the bare grass, whistling through the manes of the tired horses. The robed man was tending to the one prone on the ground, whose head rested in the lap of the large, dark-haired man.

His heart was beating but slowly, so slowly. The golden liquid poured into his mouth ran over the cracked lips and slid down his pale cheek. A sliver of gold slid through the body, carrying energy in it, carrying life, pushing back the dimness that closed in on the heart, which now began to beat a little stronger, to beat a little stronger for me.

His eyes opened. For me, for me.

I smiled, and through the bond I felt the slightest stir. It was enough; he would come back to me. Gladness warmed me.

The ground underneath me felt cold, seeping up into my

bones, but I felt warm, safe, wrapped in a heavy wool cloak. It scratched at my neck while my head rested against the stone wall at my back.

I drew in a breath of the cold winter air.

"Cassandra." It was Marcus's voice. "Come inside. Help me persuade this stubborn old man to let me help him."

I nodded reluctantly; here was something I could do while we waited.

Night came and went with no sign of them. I breathed out and watched the white vapour extend across the cold air in front of me from the warmth of my bed. I searched for Devyn; I still couldn't feel him, but he was more present somehow. Had they travelled through the night or had they rested to give him time to regain his strength before attempting the last stretch?

I had no way of telling. I wasn't sure how I had followed the druid and Bronwyn's man out to Devyn yesterday, but nothing I was doing to push my consciousness out was having any more effect beyond the wool blankets than the vapour of my breath on the cold air.

I untangled myself from Marcus and, bracing myself, left the warmth and exposed my bare feet to the floor, relieved to find I was still wearing the Celtic tunic and pants I had donned the morning before. At least Marcus's behaviour as my soon-to-be husband had some boundaries. My last memory of the evening had been watching over Rhodri after Marcus treated him. Without having multiple patients to treat, Marcus was able to concentrate his efforts. He assured me Rhodri would make a full recovery once he shook off the impact of his intervention. He then spoke at length about the differences he had felt in Rhodri, fascinated to explore the effects of the medicine that made the illness chronic rather than terminal. Marcus's presence ensured that Bronwyn spent the day elsewhere. Their initial encounter not withstanding, she and Marcus weren't on the friendliest of terms.

My stomach growled. Loudly. It was protesting at the two meals I had missed while tending to Rhodri. I pulled on my soft leather boots and crossed the leather strings around them, winding the thongs up my calf and knotting them closed at the top. I pulled on my outdoor cloak to make my way downstairs.

The great hall was not unoccupied when I got there, despite the early hour. Lord Rhodri was in his usual fireside seat with Bronwyn in the deep chair opposite him, her slight figure curled up under her cloak as if she had been there all night.

"Good morning," Rhodri greeted me, as I helped myself to the little round cakes, which Meg had told me were called griddle cakes, that sat piled on a platter on the long table. I frowned at him; he didn't look well enough to be out of bed already. I took the smaller chair to his side as I wolfed down my breakfast, gratefully accepting the warm herbal tea he poured for me from a cast-iron kettle that sat on the wide hearth.

I blew on it gently before taking a testing sip; the flavoured water wound its way down my body, warming as it went. There was a tang of apples in my nose as I sniffed the cup with my next sip. The crisp, clean smell was as enjoyable as the heat of the cup itself as my fingers wrapped around it.

"Thank you," I murmured. Devyn's father looked exhausted, his face at once pale and flushed. There were deep hollows under his eyes. Marcus had assured me his treatment was working, despite appearances to the contrary, the lingering symptoms a result of how much longer he had suffered with the illness than those Marcus had treated in the city.

"No sign?" I asked softly, not wanting to wake Bronwyn.

He shook his head wearily.

"They'll be here soon," I assured him, and he nodded as if comforted, though he had no way of knowing that I had some reason for my confidence that his son was indeed on his way and not already passed on from this world.

We sat in silence for a time, watching the flames flicker and glow on the logs that burned in the open fire. The fire was three times the size of any I had ever seen in Londinium. Burning wood was a luxury in the city; there were enough logs in this fire that the cost would feed a poorer family in the stews for a month or more.

I wondered where Marina and Oban were now. Devyn had risked a lot to help them. I wondered how many more he had helped during his time in Londinium while he was watching me, trying to ascertain if I was indeed the infant this man had abandoned. An abandonment so profound and far-reaching that it had ruined his family's name for ever.

I had only known Lord Rhodri a couple of days, but what little I had seen of him reminded me in many ways of Devyn; he cared deeply for his son and he treated those around him with respect and care. Gideon had said that as Griffin he had been the greatest warrior in the land. Why had he deserted the revered Lady of the Lake? A woman whose life was his to protect. Devyn had given up everything, had risked his life for years in the hope of finding a child he barely knew. He had not been afraid for himself for a single moment in the arena. His only thoughts had been about me. I couldn't understand how this man, two decades ago, had been such a lesser version.

"Tell me about the Griffins," I said, before I realised I had intended to speak.

Tired eyes met mine, a sadness so profound in them that I had to blink against the tears that welled in mine in response.

He closed his eyes and was silent for so long I began to think he had fallen asleep.

"The Griffin," he corrected softly. "There is only one. I am the last. Where did you hear that term?"

"Bronwyn used it to refer to you." I frowned. "And Gideon uses it when he talks about Devyn."

His lips thinned.

"York," he spat.

Rhodri was less than happy at Gideon using the term, seeming to concentrate his dislike of the family in general on Gideon in particular. He had said that he was the last…

"Devyn does not inherit the name from you?"

"The Griffin is the title given to the lady's protector. He would have inherited it –" he paused "– but there is no longer anything to protect." He sighed. "Do they teach you much of our legends behind the walls?"

I shook my head. I knew a little about the Griffin but the weight of the term out here implied that there was more to it than Devyn's brief explanation in Londinium had suggested.

"Then let me tell you of the legend. Many centuries ago, the land was ravaged by war. A young man called Arthur Pendragon sought to unite the land in peace." He looked up for confirmation that I at least recognised the name. Satisfied, he continued. "Nimue, the Lady of Avalon – a mystical isle – gifted him two great prizes: a sword and her sister, Guinevere of the Lake, as his bride. The lady married Arthur, and together with his druid Merlin they made him High King of the land and peace was known, for a time. Amongst his knights was one who was more skilled, stronger than all the rest, and Arthur made him the protector of his lady wife. Unfortunately for us all, this knight and Guinevere fell in love, and Arthur, in a rage, had them both killed. Nimue cursed Arthur's poor treatment of her sister and dark days fell upon the land.

"The various Briton tribes – the Mercians, Umbermen, and Anglians – fought invaders on all sides for centuries – the Romans, the Saxons, the Northmen, the Normans – as well as each other. Many of these peoples settled, integrated, but the Romans wanted complete dominance and so generation after generation spent their lives fighting the might of the Empire. And the Empire was winning. By the time that concerns us, many centuries after Arthur, Kernow was overrun, Anglia too, the people of Cymru hid in the mountains, Mercia was almost entirely crushed. John Plantagenet of York was a king in name only, seeking refuge in Carlisle after he lost three brothers to the Romans. Henry, Richard and Geoffrey were all killed in the battle of Reeth. Mercia held on for another decade but it too was on the verge of annihilation after losing the siege of Alnwick."

He checked to see that I was still following his tales of battles and places I had never heard of. I was aware that the Empire had stretched almost to Alba but how and when the tide was turned was not something we dwelt on in our history lessons. It was pretty much summarised as the Lady of the Lake arrived and used magic to massacre the imperial legions.

"Fleeing Alnwick, King Belanore of Mercia came upon a lake surrounded by apple trees and there on its shores he met Nimue and her sisters."

"The same Nimue from before?"

Rhodri nodded. "Time moves differently in Avalon, and

Nimue and her sisters are unaging while they stay there. Belanore knew they had taken pity before so he begged their aid, vowing to be true unlike the Pendragon King. The Lady Evaine was moved by his words. She came and united the druids to their cause and they succeeded in pushing back the invaders. Belanore and Evaine fell in love, they married and she bore him four children One of their daughters, Olwen, inherited her mother's gifts when she reached maturity and their eldest son, Adelon, inherited the throne. When their parents both fell under the Roman sword they continued the fight."

His words were barely audible over the crackle of the fire, which was the only noise in the vast, empty room.

"At the battle of Leicester, the Romans cut down Adelon and had trapped the lady Olwen when the armies of Cymru took the field. John of York's daughter Joan was married to Llewelyn of Gwynedd and had pleaded with him to join the fight."

"I thought that Gwynedd and Anglia hated each other?"

"They bear no great love for each other today, but this was many centuries ago," Rhodri explained before taking up the tale once more. "Llewelyn arrived just in time and fought his way to Olwen and protected her with his own life. They won the day but the loss of Llewelyn ap Iorweth was a great blow to the people of Cymru. Avalon rewarded the prince's bravery and his youngest son, Gruffyth, was given gifts that made him the greatest warrior in the land. Gruffyth could sense when the lady Olwen was in danger and he vowed to protect her in memory of his father. He had no child, but a nephew in his house displayed similar gifts when he came of age and became Olwen's bodyguard; it has been the honour of House Glyndŵr to serve ever since. Our line has always produced a boy destined to become the Griffin and he is sent to protect the Lady of the Lake."

"Why are they called the Griffin?" I asked. "In memory of Gruffyth, who was the first?"

"Yes, in part. The Griffin is both eagle and lion, a creature born to keep safe our most precious treasure." A shadow crossed his face before he took up the story once again. "He is given various skills to better serve his lady. It is said that Gruffyth ap Llewelyn could turn into a griffin in battle."

"Then you are descended from Gruffyth? Is Devyn not the next after you?" I was obviously missing something. Why had Rhodri been annoyed that Gideon had addressed Devyn with the title.

"No, I am the last." The sadness in those dark eyes was endless, the lines in his face seeming to be carved in an expression that spoke of regret and shame. "There was a new lady, but she was killed as a baby. They had bonded, so Devyn knew what it was to feel that connection, to live in the knowledge that you drew breath in service to another. He would have become the Griffin on his sixteenth birthday but that didn't happen. He never bore the mark, was never truly made Griffin, for what is it to be a protector to something that is already destroyed? With no new lady to serve, I am the last Griffin."

Gideon had called Devyn the Griffin before he knew I was Lady of the Lake, not to show respect but to mock him, to remind him of the gaping hole where his honour and duty should be. Fury surged through me. How dare he.

He dared because the sin was unforgivable. If the legend was to be believed, the Griffin's failure to keep her safe would have ended the matriarchal bloodline.

Rhodri had shared the same bond with my mother that I

did with Devyn; he would have felt her terror and yet still he had turned tail and run, leaving her to be mowed down. I closed my eyes to hide the anger and disgust that ran through me. This was why Devyn and his father had been cast out, dishonoured; his father had broken that sacred bond and left my mother and me to die.

"He was always convinced she lived," he continued, unaware of the tumble of emotions his story was causing in me. As far as he was concerned, I was a Roman citizen and this was all myth and legend to me. It was a story he couldn't tell to people here, who would have their own opinions and judgements, those who still served him in this nearly empty keep, those who had stayed with him when all the kingdoms of Briton had recoiled from his actions, from his failure. "He couldn't sense her through the bond, but he believed it anyway. I was so full of my own grief, so angry at her for leaving us. I understood all too well why he didn't want to believe her gone. I thought with time he would come to his senses; he swore himself to her house, to her brother, but then he left to find her. If she was alive, he should have been able to find her, should have been drawn to her; I could have found my lady deaf and blind on a battlefield of thousands. But he was gone so long. Year after year I waited for word. I promised her I would keep him alive, but his fate was out of my hands. What could I do? He was gone and I didn't know where."

His head was bowed and his voice trailed off. Perhaps he had forgotten I was there and even now was following the rest of his thoughts down whatever circular path he must have travelled over and over in the years since that day.

Most of what he said fitted the pieces of the puzzle that I already understood. Most, but not all. "You said you were angry at her?"

He coughed, his eyes glazed and the sweat on his brow visible in the light.

"She made me swear to her. There is little magic in my blood, but enough as Griffin to allow her to bind me." He gripped my hand, his fevered eyes looking directly into mine. "I didn't know. How could I have known? If we hadn't been there, if she hadn't bound my vow... But she did and I could do nothing."

He was rambling now, barely audible. His exhaustion finally carried him away into the maze of his memories and regrets. He knew things I wanted to learn more about, but it seemed cruel to stir those memories when he was recovering.

"Uncle?" Bronwyn, it appeared, had no such compunction and was kneeling at her uncle's feet in a flash. I wondered how long she had been awake...

"Your vow was bound?" she asked intently.

She shook him gently but the old man had drifted into a doze.

"Bronwyn, let him be."

She scowled at me. "You don't understand. Uncle, please." She shook him again, a little more forcefully this time. "You made a bound vow? Who bound it?"

"My lady," he whispered. "I didn't know how dangerous it would be. On the road, Viviane had a vision that Devyn would live to take her home. That he must take her home. I didn't understand. I promised to keep him safe; he was my boy... of course I'd keep him safe."

Bronwyn gasped. "You made a vow to keep Devyn safe? Is that why? Is that why you ran? Is that why you left her?"

"I didn't know –" his eyes closed "– that it would be a choice. She made me choose him."

His head lolled forwards slowly on his chest. For a

moment, I thought he had died right in front of us; maybe the cure had succeeded where the illness had not. Not now, not when Devyn was so close. What if he died now before they had a chance to see each other after so many years? The anger I had felt towards the man who had deserted my mother melted away; more than anything, I wanted him to have the chance to see his son once more.

"Bronwyn, stop." I pulled her out of the way so I could lean in and check his breath. I barely felt it as I watched for the rise and fall of his chest as proof of life. I couldn't tell, I couldn't be sure… I put my trembling fingers to his neck to feel for a pulse, but between my own thumping heart and the numbness of my cold fingers, I couldn't tell.

A weary, rough cough came just as I was about to call for help. I felt weak with relief. I needed to have faith in Marcus; if he said the old man just needed time to recover from the impact of the cure then I needed to believe him.

Bronwyn looked up at me from where she had fallen on the cold tiles.

"What were you doing?" I accused. Why had she hounded him about some decades-old promise when his body was already under stress?

"Weren't you listening?"

"Yes." Of course I'd been listening. Little did she know this wasn't some fairy tale to me; this was my own history.

Bronwyn's face expressed relief at something I couldn't figure out. What was it that she had heard?

"She bound him to take Devyn away."

"I don't know what that means." These bloody Celts and their weird customs.

"You know how seriously we take a vow… any vow?" she asked me, her eyes in deadly earnest.

271

I did. I was all too aware of it. Devyn's life was owed to the King of Mercia due to a vow he had made as a child. He was desperate to get back there to face gods knew what consequence for breaking it by leaving to find me.

"The lady made him swear to keep Devyn safe."

"You mean, he abandoned her to the Empire because he had made a promise to keep his son safe? He had a duty to protect her, but he chose to leave her because of a promise. Is that what you're telling me?"

"No," said Bronwyn. "You don't understand. It wasn't like he made a decision to abandon her. If she bound him to that promise, then he had no choice at all. As soon as he perceived Devyn to be in any danger, he would have been unable to do anything to help her. He would have been compelled to leave whether she followed or not."

"People always have a choice."

"Not if a promise is bound. The lady was powerful; if she had bound his vow magically, then there was nothing he could have done."

Magic.

I looked down at the sleeping man.

"Why would she have made him promise to save Devyn?" I asked. "If they were going to Londinium, and she sensed a threat awaited them, then shouldn't her baby have been her main concern?"

Bronwyn stood, hands on hips. "You're right. It makes no sense."

"Will it help Devyn?" I asked.

Bronwyn's brows drew together as she contemplated this new information and the impact it might have on the perceived betrayal of duty that the Griffin had committed – a betrayal that his son had inherited.

"Probably not," she admitted. "Rhodri should never have sworn to put another's life before hers. And the crime Devyn returns to is his own, not his father's. Of course, he has to survive first."

"He will." He had to.

We sat in silence for a while as Bronwyn ate some breakfast.

"What was that?" she finally asked, looking over at me.

"What?"

"Yesterday. What were you doing at the gates? Marcus was most insistent that you be left alone. You were out there most of the day. What were you doing?"

"I was waiting for Devyn."

One brow quirked upwards. "I have some magic in my blood and I could tell you were doing more than just waiting. What were you doing?"

I checked that Rhodri remained undisturbed, but his sleep was heavy and he hadn't stirred.

"I wanted to see him for myself."

"You projected? Your abilities are certainly varied for a latent." Her eyes narrowed. " Neither have you shown too much concern about what happened between Marcus and me at the inn. You're lying about your relationship... but why?"

I could see the wheels turning in her mind.

"Fidelma assured us all that you had little ability, but that was another lie, wasn't it? And... that you weren't the one he sought. Is that another lie too?" she pressed.

Put on the spot, I hesitated, unable to lie to her face.

"I don't know what you mean."

"Yes, you do," she breathed. Her eyes lit. "He *did* find you."

"No, no. I..." Caesar wept, I was bad at this. Devyn trusted Bronwyn. Would he have kept this from her if he were well?

273

I shrugged helplessly and was instantly caught in her fierce, jubilant embrace.

"We must tell Rhodri."

"Shhh, we can't. I promised Devyn. He says it's best to keep this to ourselves until we are safe."

Bronwyn's eyes clouded as she looked over at her broken uncle. Her shoulders dropped. "He's right."

We couldn't move Devyn's father, but after a while I fetched Marcus down to check on him again, to be sure that despite appearances he truly was recovering. We took turns sitting with him as the long morning unwound into the afternoon. And then, as the wintry sun began its early descent, dimming what poor light made its way into the dark hall, something changed in the atmosphere... or perhaps there was a change in the noise outside, where what few people were left were going about their business at the end of the day. And then I knew.

They were here.

Part Three

THE SEA IS IN OUR SOULS

Then doth the spirit-flame
With sword-like lightning rend its mortal frame;
The wings of that which pants to follow fast
Shake their clay-bars, as with a prison'd blast,—
The sea is in our souls!

— *The Spirit's Return*, Felicia Dorothea Hemans

Chapter Seventeen

I half ran, half stumbled to the castle walls and scrambled up the stairs. The group were still too distant to recognise as they broke from the trees.

I ran along the wall to the guards, who had closed the gate and refused to open it until they were certain of the identity of the group, no matter how I threatened or pleaded with them. I eventually left the gate as it was and went back inside to enlist aid.

Lord Rhodri remained at his fireside vigil, Bronwyn frowning at me not to disturb him as I raced across the hall.

"They're here."

She followed me back outside and, after squinting at the approaching riders, concurred and commanded the guards to open the gates. We both ran out to meet them.

We arrived out of breath. Well, I was out of breath.

I scanned the grim-faced men. The warriors were in front, and we fell back to let them pass until the druid and Gideon arrived.

The warriors all looked tired and dusty from the road,

Madoc solemn as he met Bronwyn's eyes and the unasked question contained within. The cart was gone and Devyn rode in front of Gideon, but his head hung low on his chest and it was clear that Gideon's hold was the only thing keeping him on that horse.

"Devyn." I reached up to catch the hand hanging limply by his side. His skin was cold and clammy; I took his hand tight in mine and there wasn't so much as a flicker of response.

Gideon barely looked down as he kneed his stead to keep moving into the courtyard.

Two warriors came to help Devyn down, laying him out on the uneven cobbles. He looked worse than when I had seen him last. In the week since we had parted, the flesh had melted from his bones. He had always had sharp cheekbones, but deep hollows now lay underneath, and dark circles ringed his eyes.

I didn't know what to do. Bronwyn was busy thrusting her cloak under his head while Madoc checked him over before instructing the waiting warriors to take him to his rooms. I trailed behind uselessly.

Madoc's rooms were a world away from the sterile environment of St Bart's Hospital. They laid him down again, this time on a cot in the corner behind one of the druid's overcrowded benches. Devyn's breath was laboured, a dreadful catch sounding in his chest as he drew each breath. Madoc had him quickly stripped down, revealing the crawling blackness creeping under his skin and all across his torso. The druid unwrapped the bandage to reveal the small stab wound, which was now an angry, putrefying mess. A sickly sweet smell cloyed the air.

I reeled back and knocked against the shelves behind me. Madoc, reminded of our presence in the room, shooed us out despite our protests. In moments we were on the outside of the tower door.

I curled my arms around me. Devyn looked like he was on the edge of death, and this was *after* Madoc had treated him on the road. My throat felt like it was closing in on itself. He had to make it. I straightened my shoulders.

Without thinking, I rounded on Gideon.

"*You* did this,"

"No," he returned grimly. "Madoc says it wasn't my knife."

"What?" I hadn't even got started in venting my rage when this latest revelation stopped me in my tracks.

"The knife didn't carry the poison."

"How can he know that?"

"He says the wound isn't the source of the corruption. In fact, my knife wound was probably the difference between him living and dying." Gideon's lips tugged upwards in that irritating nonchalant amusement at our disbelief. "It's true. There was poison in Devyn all right, but it existed before my dagger hit him. Left undisturbed, it would have quietly done its work until the moment he drew his final breath and keeled over. The knife disrupted it, drew it to the surface rather than burying it in his organs. So you ladies should be thanking me."

He gave us a debonair half-bow as if accepting our unspoken relief.

"He was already poisoned?" I asked. "How? When?"

"Are you sure it was poison?" Marcus asked at the same time.

"You'd have to ask Madoc for more information. I'm just relieved that somebody isn't going around dipping my knives in poison without my knowing," Gideon said. "I could have used that knife to eat. It had crossed my mind to wonder if *I* had been my father's intended victim. I'm pretty sure he wouldn't miss me."

Gideon had never intended to kill Devyn. Well, Callum had speculated as much. But who then would have had the opportunity?

Callum.

He was the only person we had met on the way who knew who we were. Was that why he had been so convinced that Gideon hadn't meant to kill Devyn? Because *he* was the real culprit?

"Is it possible Cassandra or I might also have this poison in us?" Marcus asked. It was a fair question. If we had been dosed by Callum – or even earlier, before we left the city perhaps – could it even now be moving undetected in our veins?

Marcus took my hand in the Briton style, wrist to wrist, using the technique Fidelma had taught him. His eyes closed as he checked my blood before releasing me, satisfied that he could not sense it.

"Maybe we all had it. We could have burned it off," he suggested.

I supposed that was true, or maybe only Devyn had been targeted. But first things first: Devyn had to be cured.

There was no sign of the druid for the rest of the evening, though he sent some of the mistletoe potion for Rhodri, as yet unaware that Marcus had rendered the medication unnecessary.

———

Waking the next morning, I immediately made for the druid's rooms and knocked lightly on the door.

When there was no answer, I gently let myself in. Madoc lay sleeping on blankets on the floor while Devyn still slumbered on the cot behind. I surveyed him quietly; there was some colour in his cheeks and the dark hollows seemed to have lightened if not filled out overnight. My body sagged in relief.

I reached for the bond and it felt firm and real once more, either because he was close or because he was better, I wasn't sure, but it was tangible again.

But he didn't wake that day, or the next, and Madoc grew increasingly concerned. Over a week passed before I opened the door to an exhausted but happy Madoc.

Stepping past him a breath of relief sighed from my smiling lips as I met the dark-brown eyes looking steadily back at me. The smile stretched across unfamiliar muscles in my face.

"Hi."

He blinked in response, an answering smile playing faintly on his lips.

I sagged to the ground beside him, catching the now warm hand that lay on the blankets, savouring the feel of the calloused palm, the steady pulse, the natural healthy colour of the skin.

"You're okay?"

"No, he is not okay," Madoc growled from behind me. "What are you doing in here, girl?"

His brows drew together at the sight of our linked hands. I had haunted this room while he lay sick but had been careful to come with Marcus. As far as he knew, I was with the York prince; maintaining the appearance that I was with Marcus had been no great challenge in Devyn's absence, more difficult while he lay unconscious. Without Devyn to counter the pull of the handfast, I had been drawn to Marcus, the wondrous power of the cuff reversing our almost non-existent chemistry. But with Devyn now awake and within touching distance, our natural polarity was restored.

"He's better?" I asked, ignoring the druid's facial expression and tightening my hold on Devyn's hand, deeming it more suspicious to pull away than not.

"For now."

"What do you mean, *for now*?" I asked. This recovery wasn't permanent?

"I've done what I can. The potion I made has worked well enough and I threw a few more things at it overnight so you were strong enough to rouse. I've done as much as I can with the supplies I have but some of my more powerful herbs were running low. If you remember, I was on my way to Conwy to restock when his lordship called me back." He pulled me firmly aside as he turned down the blankets to check on his patient. The black tendrils staining his bronze skin had receded, but the wound, though greatly improved from the putrid mess it had been yesterday, still looked raw.

The druid nodded to himself.

"You'll do, boy," he said. "Now up you get; we have a ride ahead of us."

"He can't ride! He's been at death's door for days. He needs time to recover."

"He needs medicine I can't give him. Either he's strong enough to get off his arse and ride, or he can lie there and gamble on us making it back in time."

"I missed you, Madoc," Devyn said, straight-faced. With a groan, he levered himself up on his elbows. I put my arms around him and helped him rise until he found himself unsteadily on his feet. But at least he was on his feet.

"We need to get to Carlisle," Devyn stated after a moment.

"You won't make another day without the right herbs," Madoc said flatly.

"I guess we're going to pay a visit to my uncle then," Devyn said wryly.

Madoc looked him up and down, assessing the man he had last seen as a boy, instead of the patient he had been so far.

"Not without speaking to your father."

Devyn's jaw clenched at the suggestion.

I put a calming hand over his heart, but far enough away from the bandaged wound that I could put some pressure on it.

"He's not well, Devyn. I mean, he's better; Marcus has treated him. The illness is gone but he has been chronically ill for so long..." I clarified. Madoc frowned at me, seeing no need to take the pressure off by informing Devyn of his father's recovery. A fact which Madoc seemed to need constant reassurance of, checking up on his former patient one of the only reasons he had left this room since Devyn's arrival. "He has waited such a long time to see you again."

He looked down at me and I could feel his body unclench... a little. His eyes were dark with emotion as he looked down at me and nodded.

"Fine, I will speak with him before we go." I could sense his dread at the prospect, but before I could even offer to accompany him, he made his preference clear. "Alone."

He was much stronger but still needed Madoc's support to make it to the great hall. I went with them that far, so I saw Rhodri's face when he clapped eyes on Devyn for the first time – the hope and regret, the love and shame, all mixed together and practically pouring out of him. For a man who had lived with being shunned for decades, he sure didn't do too great a job at concealing his emotions. I guess, when you've stood at the edge of death for so long, and the person you love most in the world walks back into your life, it's time to put aside the masks that pride makes us wear.

At the other end of the spectrum, meanwhile, stood the son, also on far too familiar terms with impending death, but I didn't need to see Devyn's face to know it would be completely expressionless. Devyn did not want to do this. He believed what people said and thought about his father.

Did he know about the magically bound vow? He had never mentioned it, and I wasn't sure it would make a difference to him. I couldn't imagine a single thing I could say to make Devyn vow to put something else before my life. Every fibre of his being was tuned into what was safest for me, including his own heart. There was no part of me that didn't believe that also extended to his own life and limbs.

Bronwyn was visibly relieved at the sight of her cousin more or less standing on his own two feet, and she stood hesitantly beside her uncle, unsure whether to stay or go. This was a matter I quickly cleared up for her and the others who loitered in the hall. I informed everyone that they needed to pack as we planned to be on the road within the hour to reach the medical supplies that awaited in Conwy.

———————

And so we were. When we passed through the hall there was no sign of Rhodri, and Devyn awaited us in the courtyard. Gideon sent half the Mercians home to Carlisle with a message for the king to explain our detour. The rest of us made a beeline for Conwy.

Conwy Castle was imposing, to say the least. It loomed over the landscape, a formidable grey fortress commanding the coastline. It was a forbidding place built to repel enemies – hopefully also a place of sanctuary for those considered friends.

Would we be received as friends? I certainly hoped so. After all, the prince of Gywnedd was Devyn's uncle; he was family. But what did that prove? Those I had called family had discarded me like a trendy trinket gone out of fashion. Where once I had been the Shelton family's prized jewel, when my star had crash-landed onto the sands of the arena, they had been nowhere to be found.

Rhodri loved Devyn, but he believed – as the rest of Briton society did – that his line was disgraced and there was no way back for them. What honour Devyn had won back by pledging fealty to the King of Mercia after the death of the lady had been irretrievably forsaken when he had broken his oath to go in search of the baby he believed still lived. That these sins had been committed when he was still a child was ignored. What was I thinking? Sins? They had been no sins of Devyn's; bearing the blood of a traitor was no fault of the son. As for his crime of believing that the lost lady still lived, surely returning with me would wipe the slate clean?

I needed to speak to him, to tell him that I knew who I was... and that the secret was out and on its way to York via Callum. But I knew better than to talk about these heavy secrets while we were surrounded by warriors. That some of our companions had figured it out couldn't be helped; I wouldn't spread it further.

We had emerged from the endless forests to the miracle of the sea this morning, and Bronwyn had laughed at my delight. She had dismissed the grey-blue rolling waves that lapped the shore as so much less than the open ocean that she had grown up with in the southwest. She described sweeping cliffs and vast stretches of golden sands with waters that changed from the exquisite turquoise of the ring that adorned her finger to violent, dark swells that rose amidst the anger of storms. Apparently, the stretch we rode along was no more than a contained piece of sea trapped by the northernmost section of Cymru, by Eireann to the west, and by Mercia stretching north until it hit the land of Alba. I had a vague appreciation of the island's geography and knew that the sea here was sheltered compared to the waters that crashed against the toe of Britannia where Bronwyn was from. But to me, the reality of it was beyond anything I had imagined from photos. The vastness of the water as it stretched out to the horizon was incredible; it went on for ever. No crowded vessels bobbing on it, hustling for space at the dock, just an infinite emptiness that went on and on, shimmering and undulating in the wind. I could taste a tang on my tongue that blew away the last vestiges of the ties that bound me to Londinium. These waters were constant, as was the land at my back. Life was sleeping in the wintry forest but it endured, and so would I. Come spring, the cycle would turn.

Devyn sat tall in his saddle, his dark curls tossed by the wild winds coming off the sea, his face lifted to the castle ahead of us. The horses' heads lowered as they huffed their way in the frigid air, clip-clopping over the bridge that spanned the river and then up to the castle entrance. The winds buffeted us mercilessly as we made our way across.

Bronwyn gained us entrance after speaking softly with the guards who stood sentry at the open gates. Unlike at Dinas Brân, a party of our size was considered little threat here at Conwy Castle. The single tower in the hills was nothing to this magnificent fortress; there were towers and buildings behind massive fortified battlements behind which the entire town could take refuge. We clattered through to the courtyard, and grooms came forward to meet us and take our horses before we had even dismounted.

A small figure emerged, cloakless, from the building at the far side of the courtyard. He hurried over with a quick step as he greeted Bronwyn with a warm "Niece" and embraced her in welcome.

The Prince of Gywnedd was a smaller, wiry version of his brother. Though his curly hair was also grey, he was lighter of spirit, which made him seem younger than Devyn's father, though I was aware that Llewelyn was the senior by some years. His lively eyes surveyed us and then grew dark as they lit upon the scarred face of Gideon.

"York," he snarled. "You are not welcome here."

Gideon's chin went up as a broad grin spread across his face at the dislike directed at him.

Bronwyn laid a softening hand on her uncle's arm as he bristled at Gideon's impudence.

"Uncle, he's with us," she explained in an attempt to get him to back down from his unwelcoming stance.

"I don't care who he's with. No one from House Mortimer will spend a night under my roof," the small man gritted out, his hand lifting in a signal that brought armed guards to escort Gideon from the castle.

"Uncle, he's with me," Devyn said, stepping forwards and lowering his hood.

The Prince of Gywnedd kept one eye on the Anglian who was the target of his ire but he turned, giving his attention to the young man before him. The hard lines softened as he registered Devyn. He lifted a shaking hand to touch the gaunt face under the tumult of black curls.

He looked to Bronwyn who smiled in confirmation.

"Boy..." he whispered, dragging his nephew into a fierce embrace. Although he barely came to Devyn's shoulder I worried that he would do some damage to his nephew, so strong was his embrace; he held on to him as if by doing so he could prevent him from ever disappearing again. "So it's true. You've come back."

Devyn pulled back with a wince. "Uncle Llewelyn."

Both men stood there taking stock of the changes visible in each other. I wondered what his uncle made of the changes in the young man he had known. Were his memories of the sad, withdrawn boy I had glimpsed in my vision or of better times? He and his father must have spent time here, in this great castle. I imagined Devyn's chubby legs running across this courtyard, perhaps thwarting a nanny as he escaped to the stables. Was there any sign left of the child he would have known in the lean, sombre man before him?

A crooked smile tugged at Devyn's lips, lighting his face.

"Gideon left his father's house long ago; he's Deverell's man now," Devyn said, defending the Anglian.

"I don't care what kennel the pup crawls into at night, I'm still not letting a rabid cur enter my home."

Gideon's eyes darkened at the damning declaration, a tic appearing at his jaw. The warrior might present an indifferent mask to the world around him, but he wasn't immune to the slurs that came his way. Richard Mortimer, the Steward of York, was one of the most powerful men in the land. Why did Llewelyn despise him, and would that hatred extend to Marcus and the House of York once he discovered who he was? Marcus and I exchanged glances.

Devyn's smile broadened as he glanced at the glowering warrior, all too aware that Gideon would love nothing more than to oblige the prince and take off back along the coast. But he had promised to deliver us to Carlisle so he couldn't leave without us, and we weren't going until Devyn was fit to continue north.

A tall, fair-haired man now stood at Llewelyn's shoulder and Bronwyn looked to him to intercede for us. The new arrival smiled broadly at her and Devyn but said nothing.

"Rhys." Devyn's eyes warmed briefly in greeting before returning to their deadlock with his uncle. "He saved my life and he has got us this far. If he goes, I go."

Devyn laid down his ultimatum, putting a hand on his uncle's shoulder in a familial manner. Though apparently it landed with rather more weight than Llewelyn had expected as his gaze flicked up in alarm at his newly returned nephew.

"Dev," he said with some urgency, his other arm coming up to help brace Devyn, who wobbled before his strength gave out.

Marcus's hand restrained me as the fair-haired man, Rhys, bobbed forwards underneath Devyn's arm and took his weight as he sagged down; they moved quickly to get him inside. A quick flick of Llewelyn's hands told his guards to stand down as the trio made their way across the courtyard.

Gideon watched the guards drop back before giving Marcus and me – as usual, at a loss how to proceed in this strange world – an indication to follow. I took Marcus's hand to reinforce our status as a couple, admitting to myself that it also gave me comfort. A comfort which, with Devyn back in close proximity, was no longer tangled with other more confusing feelings.

We were led through the huge oak doors and along a hallway into a larger room where massive tables stretched the length of the hall. Unlike at Dinas Brân, here there was life: long-haired warriors looked up from their food as we entered the great room and several women bustled over in attendance as we made our way along the tapestried wall at the side of the hall. The prince called for aid for his nephew. One young boy ran off the way we had come as if his life depended on it, while others milled about in our wake, exclaiming at the return of the long-dead scion of the House of Gwynedd.

We arrived in a room with one entire wall given over to a cabinet made up of tiny drawers and bunches of herbs hanging from the ceiling like I had seen in Madoc's room. Like, and also *not* like. Where there chaos had reigned, here stood cosy order. A beautifully woven rug lay on the floor and a warm fire crackled in the hearth. Llewelyn gently manoeuvred his nephew down into an armchair, tenderly running a hand through the dark curls before turning to his niece for answers.

Bronwyn's blue eyes showed her worry as she pushed her long dark hair back over her shoulder.

"He has been ill." Her eyes flicked over to us where we hovered inside the door. How much would she reveal to her concerned uncle? He had barely allowed Gideon in the door; the whole truth at this point probably wasn't the wisest course. "We came here for help."

At this, the shrewd eyes flicked to Madoc who had just reappeared with another robed figure.

"There's something in his blood that weakens his life force," Madoc explained as the druid followed us in and crossed to the patient in long-legged strides that ate up the room. "I was able to hold it off temporarily, but it was beyond my skills to cure it."

The new druid bent down to examine Devyn, who had started to recover in the relative comfort of the warm room and bristled at the presumptuous hands that prodded at him. The newcomer turned Devyn's head first one way and then another, then tipped it back and used long fingers to stretch open his eyelids to look into the deepest corners of his eyes, while Madoc was briskly stripping Devyn of his cloak and undoing his tunic. He eased it off his shoulders to reveal the bandage on his right shoulder, before removing that too to reveal the dark stain that spread out beyond the wound. Black and purple tendrils spread like an ink stain under his golden skin.

The tall druid tsked, even as the rest of our party gasped at the return of the stain, which had receded the last time we had seen it.

"I thought it was getting better," I accused Madoc. How was this possible? Devyn had been so much stronger since Madoc had started treating him; he had ridden here, upright, on a horse.

Madoc shook his head. "I drew it away from his heart but I wasn't able to extract it. I merely routed it back to the surface wound. It was the best I could do." He spoke to the other druid, who was removing the last of the bandage from the site. "Tell me I didn't make it worse, Ewan."

The festering wound was now entirely visible to everyone in the room, the injury still as fresh as the day it had occurred but oozing more of the dark-purple matter that discoloured Devyn's skin. My stomach dropped at the sight of it; the parasitic poison was gaining territory and without thinking I used our bond to slip under his skin.

Devyn's eyes flicked in my direction as he directed me to withdraw. I stared at him mulishly. How did we know this Ewan would be any more able to help than Madoc had been? If I dropped my defence, how much more of Devyn's flesh would be invaded by the malicious spread? Devyn pushed at me as I became aware of a new flicker of consciousness entering the fray. The slithery energy recoiled as I slipped away, and I hoped the druid's focus would be on the enemy he faced and not my friendly protective energy exiting stage left.

The druid's face went blank as he mentally probed the infection. The air in the room felt strangely light and my eye snagged on the dust motes caught in the light of the fire as they danced in the warm air. The wind was beating at the windows from the encroaching night outside, as if the darkness was trying to gain entry even as that light and energy danced and swirled. The very health of the light forced away the dark, yet the dark remained, and the rain lashed at the windows as fingers dug into my wrist. I tried to shake it off and when I couldn't, I followed the offending grip up to Marcus's glaring face.

I had fallen into the druid's energy. I snapped back, and when my full consciousness was back in my body, I drew in a long shuddering breath. The druid was not winning.

I looked back to the fireplace to find Ewan looking in our direction.

"Unusual," he mused. "It's not entirely magical; there is something synthetic to it, making its progression strange. I've not seen anything like this before. If it weren't for the knife wound forcing it to the surface we never would have caught it. It appears that being pulled to the surface has drawn it out, but that in itself may kill him. Your attempts here have held it off, but not for long. It's in the blood, but it is not so far gone that we cannot do something about it."

Ewan turned to start working up whatever potions he deemed would cure whatever was killing Devyn.

He pulled some labelled bottles from their neat rows, arranging them on the clear workstation and giving the usually bristly Madoc succinct directions which he followed without hesitation.

Ewan turned back briefly and raised an eyebrow at what he deemed to be an unnecessary audience.

"We're not going anywhere," I said in a tone even I could hear was mulish. I had learned from our earlier experience that it was hard to get back in once a druid had kicked you out of the room. A slight tug of humour whispered along the bond as the druid and I had a silent standoff. I pushed it away; it wasn't funny and I wasn't leaving.

"Please," Marcus appealed on our behalf. "I am... *was* a doctor. I would like to understand more about your medicine. I am told I have some ability; perhaps I can also be of some help, under your guidance of course."

My charming, handsome princeling to the rescue! The druid pursed his lips, the glint in his eyes sharing that he was not unaware of the calculating strategy beneath Marcus's courteous approach.

"What the lad says is true," Madoc supported him. "He seems to have healed Lord Rhodri... completely."

A lone brow rose at this.

"Does he now?" Ewan blinked. "All right then. But stay out of our way."

Where Madoc's process of concocting had been a chaotic symphony of bottles and jars – lifted, put down, sniffed, tasted, a smidgeon of one, a scrape of another – Ewan's was a singularly methodical process of selection, addition and completion. He was composed and focused, doses were given in small quantities and the results contemplated, then the patient was judged and the potion was adjusted before the cycle would begin again. Over and over until I could scream from the repetition of it all. Ewan responded to Marcus's inquiries shortly at first, but as night turned to day, and the final solution continued to elude him, he opened up. His frustration was as restrained as his potion-making, but as the cycles slowed, he became even more thoughtful.

"What are you doing?" Marcus asked for the hundredth time as Ewan paused to observe the effects of his latest attempt.

Ewan's brows crinkled and he extended a hand to Marcus, who took it as he stood over Devyn, who had fallen asleep again. Since taking the potions, he had started to drift in and out of consciousness, which Ewan told us was merely a result of the base ingredient and not the lingering poison.

"Focus on his blood," he instructed his new pupil. Marcus's green eyes lost focus as he followed wherever it was the druid led him.

Not wishing to be left out, I rested my head on Marcus's shoulder as if I were tired, but with the physical connection established I was along for the ride. I had frequently assisted Marcus in Bart's, temporarily lending him power when he was mysteriously healing the ill in his hospital.

We drifted down through Devyn's body, following as the druid tracked through his limbs and organs, examining the results of the latest concoction. We wafted along, applying the essence of the potion to the greyish sections he sought out; some sections were resolved, healed, while others resolutely resisted. He stayed with one particular dark-grey area for a while, pushing and prodding at it; Marcus seemed to understand and began pushing at another side, causing it to go dark. It was his mistake, but I got it, and I nudged him to an adjacent spot and then pulsed my energy through him.

I could feel Marcus's surprise at discovering I'd hitched a ride, but it was working.

"Again," Ewan encouraged him.

I sent a pulse at the darkness and the area coloured, becoming suddenly vibrant and healthy. Marcus figured out what I was doing and we flowed through Devyn's blood at Ewan's direction, seeking out and destroying the damage that the potion couldn't beat on its own.

Finally, after what could have been either minutes or hours, we were done. I blinked as my vision returned to the workroom, where the once aloof Ewan was now regarding Marcus with a new respect.

"That was well done," he said. "How did you learn to do that?"

Marcus shook his head, catching my eye. "I don't know. It just came to me."

I made my way through the dark halls. I felt trapped; I needed air. I stumbled through the stone-flagged corridors, finally finding a door that led out into the courtyard we had arrived in earlier... or yesterday, I supposed. I just needed to breathe. I tripped on the cobbles in the dark, but regained my balance and headed for the high walls surround the keep, somehow managing to drag my weary bones up the stone steps that led up to the massive boundary wall. I felt like I was being called by the growing light in the sky. Eventually, I found myself at the top of the ramparts and saw the vast undulating sea sparkling in the distance as the sky in the opposite direction began to glow a light grey.

I breathed out into the sea air, expelling the darkness and the slimy touch of the evil that had slugged its way through Devyn's veins. Gladness filled my heart and I tasted the salt on my tongue, felt the wind whipping through my hair, and I lifted my face to the growing light in the east.

The sound of a step behind me alerted me to the fact that I was no longer alone. I didn't turn though, wanting to savour the moment for as long as possible. I inhaled the clean, open tang of the air into my lungs and through my body.

"How is he?" A gravelly voice spoke softly into the air at my back.

"Better," I said, turning to the dark shadow that now stopped at the top of the stairs.

Gideon exhaled.

"The Griffin will live?"

"Yes, no thanks to you," I snapped, out of habit more than anything, because now we knew that Gideon's knife had probably saved Devyn's life.

He arched a brow before continuing as if he hadn't heard my snarky comment. "Was the druid able to tell you any more about the poison?"

"He didn't know. Perhaps something Devyn had eaten or drunk before we met you on the road."

"Who? When?" He was immediately attempting to identify where the threat might have come from.

"I don't know. Nor do I care right now." Devyn was well again; that was enough.

"You should care, kitty cat. Why would anyone target the Griffin? What could anyone hope to gain from it? Was Marcus the target? Were you?" he mused aloud.

"Whoever it was, what does it matter now? We're safe."

"Are you? Somebody tried to kill Devyn, or one of you. Where it was worth trying once, it will be worth trying twice," he scoffed. "Was it done before you left Londinium? In Oxford? While you were travelling on the road?"

My current exhausted indifference didn't mean that my mind hadn't been worrying at the same problem. Was he right? Had Devyn been poisoned by accident or on purpose? We had travelled closely together; if it had been someone singling Devyn out, then there would have been few to no opportunities. What reason would anyone have for cutting down Devyn? Most Britons had thought him dead for nearly a decade. A few had known he lived: Fidelma, Bronwyn and the man I now knew to be my brother.

Bronwyn I believed we could trust and Fidelma seemed not to care for politics. Then there was the ruler of Mercia, my brother. I had danced with him at the ball and he had somehow known who Devyn was. But he had saved Devyn that night. Why protect someone only to kill them later? And when would any of them have had an opportunity? We hadn't seen anyone on our way from Londinium. Except for Callum…

My mind balked at the idea that Devyn's former teacher could have done such a thing. But every time I asked these questions, my mind always brought me back to Callum.

Gideon had a point though; someone clearly didn't want Devyn to return home.

Or had the poison really been intended for Marcus or me? Most likely, Marcus; I was of little value dead, whereas Marcus wasn't just a powerful healer, he was a symbol of power to both peoples on this island. The magic in his veins was either a hope or a threat, depending on which side you stood. But how would the council have got to us out here in the Wilds? Or could it have been done before we left?

My peace utterly shattered, I glared at the bearer of these unsettling questions.

"Fine, you have a point, but it could be anyone," I said.

"We should be safe here for now." Gideon was reassuring

me, and it didn't pass me by that he included himself as one of us.

"Why?" I asked. "Not why are we safe, but why are you helping us now?"

"You are my lord's beloved sister, back from the dead; your boyfriend is my own nation's true heir, returned to us at a time when power has been waning in the land, and your *not*-boyfriend, while not my favourite person, brought you both back to our people, so if he stays alive, I'm okay with that," Gideon answered. What did he mean, my *not*-boyfriend?

He smirked at me.

Damn.

I glared at him.

He moved closer, invading my space. His voice was substantially lower as he spoke again, merely a whisper on the salty wind between us.

"It is the Griffin's job to keep you safe, and if he cannot do so then somebody else will have to," he said.

"I told you, Devyn is going to be fine."

"The Griffin has issues of his own that may make it difficult for him to be your protector."

"You all keep saying that, but you never explain what you mean and I've had enough." I was fed up of never quite understanding the forces that kept us apart.

"Devyn broke his oath to the Lakes when he ran off to find you, princess. He has given up his right to be Griffin."

"But he found me," I whispered. "Surely that counts for something."

"Depends on who has him."

"How so?"

"In Anglia, he would find little mercy. My home is made up of people who would rather die fighting the Empire than live in it for one second. We are warriors first and last. My father would show no mercy to a warrior who broke his oath. You saw my reception here; House Glyndŵr has certainly not forgotten that my father voted to have Rhodri executed twenty years ago."

"York would kill Devyn?" But we weren't in Anglia. "Then just as well we happen to be in Gwynedd."

Gideon shook his head. "Not really. There's a reason I didn't want us to come here. It will provoke York all the more. My father will see it as an act of war that Devyn flees justice."

"Why?"

"House Glyndŵr has run thin. Devyn Glyndŵr is the last of their line. Llewelyn and Rhys will have no children, and his sister, Cerys, married the prince of Kernow and bore him daughters. Rhodri has only one son."

"Devyn Glyndŵr," I repeated. Not Devyn Agrestis. Just like how, to these people, I was not Cassandra Shelton.

"Just so." Gideon inclined his head. "The last son of Glyndŵr has come home. Llewelyn will want him to stay. This is also the path most likely to keep him alive. The path at your side, as protector, has a less certain future."

Gideon took a step back, looking out to the growing light

"Losing you... after Viviane died was a dark time; we have lived on borrowed time ever since, dreading the moment when our weakness was discovered. We cannot lose the lady again." He looked back at me, his face in shadow. "If you lack a protector, I will offer you my sword."

I shook my head. "I don't need you. I have Devyn."

"Do you now?" Gideon continued. "That's going to be a problem too."

I scowled. If I needed protection, I had someone bonded to

me by ancient magic. Someone I had followed to the ends of my world. Someone I would not give up.

"Catriona Deverell and Devyn Glyndŵr... It cannot be, lady. Not in this lifetime," he said in an uncanny echo of the warning I could never completely shake.

Chapter Eighteen

I n the days after the last of the poison was eliminated, Devyn finally moved from Ewan's rooms to his own; the cure had left him nearly as weak as he had been at the worst of the poisoning. I had seen Marcus only when I sat with Devyn in the druid's rooms; he had practically become joined at the hip with Ewan, lapping up all the medical knowledge he could. Unlike at Dinas Brân, either because of the greater number of rooms or a greater regard for propriety, here we were given our own rooms. Meanwhile, Gideon and Bronwyn seemed to have reached some sort of unspoken agreement to keep me under constant surveillance, ensuring any conversation I had with Devyn was chaperoned. It was worse than having overprotective parents.

I was getting frustrated at the scraps of news Bronwyn fed me. I had had enough, and if I couldn't speak to Devyn in public, then I was going to speak to him in private. I had questions and I needed answers, and nobody was going to stop me. I stormed out of my room in such a whirl of determination that I forgot to put shoes on. My feet were now suffering from my failure as they shied away from each petrifying stone that took me closer to Devyn's room. Nor had I figured out how I was going to explain myself if I was found wandering the halls in an outdoor cloak and no shoes. A midnight craving for cake, perhaps?

"Are you going to accept his offer?"

The dark shape at the window turned around at the sound of my voice as I closed the door softly behind me.

Devyn started towards me and then stopped in his tracks.

"You shouldn't be here."

"Are you going to accept?" I persisted. Bronwyn had confirmed Gideon's prediction that Llewelyn, having no sons of his own, would want to make Devyn his heir. It was an offer which would assist in both prolonging his life and restoring his name – or giving him a new title, at least.

Devyn shook his head softly.

"You could be Prince of Gwynedd." If he were a prince, surely he would be able to count himself worthy of being with a neighbouring lady.

"That is not my choice."

"What do you mean it's not your choice?"

"My life has always had one purpose: to be the Griffin… And there must be a Griffin. To become Prince of Gwynedd, I would have to give that up."

"I thought being the Griffin was part of your bloodline."

He laughed softly. "Technically no. It is a gift of spirit, not of blood, though it has been in my line for many generations. As there is no other male of my line, if I accept my uncle's offer, I would have to forsake my calling. I couldn't be Griffin and a ruling prince at the same time."

"You can pass on being Griffin?" This was news to me.

"Maybe. There is a ceremony that those at Holy Isle could do to release me."

"Then let there be another Griffin. I don't care as long as I have you."

His brow creased at that and he took a step back.

"As you say, this is my decision and my choice is to remain the Griffin. What use would I be as heir to the Prince of Gwynedd? Britannia is falling apart; if we don't pull together then the Empire will finally take the whole island. Is that what you want?"

The Empire expanding beyond the walls, the urban sprawl eating up mile after mile of green land and blocking out the sky… Governor Actaeon would crush the people here. I shuddered at the very idea, but that was a problem well beyond us.

"I don't care. What does any of that have to do with us?" I was beyond tired of all of it.

"You are the Lady of the Lake," he intoned very slowly.

"Yes, thank you. I'd figured that out." I glared at him. "No thanks to you."

"Do you realise what that will mean?"

"Yes, it's fantastic, there'll be a parade, the blood will grow strong and the land will be well. Petals will fall from the sky and the illness will miraculously be cured," I spat out. "Have I missed anything?"

"That about covers it." He leaned back against the wall, one arm behind him to help lever himself down onto the cushions below the window.

"Is it your wound?" He had been fine all day, and in the few days since Ewan had treated him he had made a total recovery, or so I had thought.

His shoulders slumped slightly. "It's the middle of the

night, Cassandra,"

Without thinking, I was beside him, leaning in to take his weight and help him back to the bed. The skin creased at the corners of his eyes as he looked directly at me, his face only inches away.

"What are you doing?"

"I'm helping you to bed."

Even as the words left my mouth, I realised I had overreacted; he did not need my assistance to get to his bed. My face warmed as the other interpretations of my words occurred to me. And just like that, the atmosphere in the room changed. He was well enough not to need my assistance to get to his bed, but here we finally were: Devyn, his bed and I all alone in this room in the middle of the night.

My eyes dropped to his lips; it had been so long since I had felt their touch. My fingertips traced their way along the place my own lips longed to be, though I couldn't recall lifting my hand. I looked up to assess his reaction, but his lashes skimmed his cheeks as he let my fingers have their way. Awareness crackled down the bond between us.

His chest rose and fell shallowly, while the fire crackled on the other side of the room. I cursed it for its loudness. He stood abruptly, towering over me, but his dark gaze met mine. I touched my lips with my tongue, my mouth dry with nerves. His gaze snagged on the movement.

He was alive, and it had been so long since we had touched like this. I reached up and ran my hands along the nape of his neck. I rose onto my tiptoes to gain some much-needed height so I could bring our lips another inch closer. I put a fraction more pressure on the hand at his nape.

"Please," I breathed.

With a groan, he swooped, and his mouth was on mine, his

arms around me. He swept me up until we tumbled together onto the bed, his hands sweeping under the full-length white cotton nightgown that I had been given by someone back at his father's house. My own hands pulled at the tunic he wore, pushing it up and out of the way to get to the warm, clean satiny skin underneath. I yanked it over his head, clearing the way to the expanse of muscular darkly golden chest beneath.

A flinch alerted me that the movement had jarred his shoulder.

"Oh, sorry, sorry." My hands froze as he stilled above me. His skin glinted bronze in the firelight as he pulled away from me.

"No." I caught his left arm in both hands, this time avoiding the still bandaged shoulder. "Please."

He stared balefully at my hands until I released him. I fell back and stared at the ceiling.

"You should go."

I sat up, my cloak spread beneath me on the bed, the nightdress hanging off one shoulder. I hoped I was cutting at least half as tempting a figure as he was, standing there all brooding and rumpled. He wouldn't even look at me.

"I came here to talk."

"We can talk in the morning." He strode over to the door and, after checking the hallway, opened it wide, letting the cold come flooding into the room.

"I want to talk now. I need you to explain to me what's going on with you." I lifted my gown to cover my shoulder in a show of good faith.

"Tomorrow," he said, continuing to hold the door wide.

I stomped over to him, or as close to stomping as could be achieved barefoot.

"Now." I meant it. I was done with him shutting me out. "

You keep saying we can't be together. I need you to explain it to me. Properly. All of it."

I folded my arms and planted my feet. I was going nowhere.

He pushed the door closed and brushed past me, but my triumph was barely a breath long as I felt the heavy fall of a cloak about my shoulders.

Then I was being propelled towards the door. I braced myself against it, and it made a satisfyingly loud noise as it slammed shut.

I swirled to face Devyn.

"You idiot. You can't be caught in here," he said in exasperation.

"Can't I? What will happen? Will my marriage to Marcus be called off? Will they think we are sleeping together if they find me here in your bedroom in the middle of the night? So what if they do? Bronwyn and Gideon suspect anyway."

It seemed a stunningly simple realisation. I was done playing by Devyn's rules. Why shouldn't everyone know we were together? What could they do about it?

The clack-clack of steel-toed boots could be heard coming down the hall.

Devyn frowned at whatever he read in my eyes and pushed me against the door, covering my mouth with his hand as the footsteps came closer. As if that could stop me, I pulled my foot back and then kicked the door with as much force as I could muster. It hit the door with an annoyingly quiet thud, but it was enough that the footsteps went silent.

Devyn's exasperation doubled and he glared down at me before his hand was gone, replaced by meltingly warm lips as he kissed me again… wholly and thoroughly. My arms wound up around his neck again, holding him to me as he began to pull away. He deepened the kiss again and I fell into him. He lifted his head and smiled crookedly down at me. The footsteps receded into the night.

I raised my foot again, and this time brought it crashing down on Devyn's. The boots the Celts wore were thankfully a soft enough leather that it yielded a small grunt.

"If I remain the Griffin, I will be your sworn protector."

I narrowed my eyes at him.

"I don't need a protector. I can stop entire troops of men in their tracks. I beat the hounds. Twice," I reminded him.

"Technically, you beat them once, and city weapons beat them off the time before that."

"What's with you and the technicalities tonight?" I glared at him. "Is that what your kisses were? A trick? Oh, I know, *technically*, you told me we could never be together. But you needed to lure the stupid city girl out of her tower and you gave me just enough so that I kept on hoping. But I was never going to get what I wanted. I could have stayed at home and married Marcus."

"This is your home."

I shook my head, my heart twisting.

"This is *your* home."

I had no home. I didn't belong here. Devyn didn't want me. Marcus certainly didn't want me. I still had a brother somewhere north of here. Would he care, or would I only be in the way? Maybe he liked being the last child of the Lady of the Lake, the single power in the north, and my resurrection would not be welcome news.

It had all been for nothing. Giving up my home, my parents, my friends, my city… my life. It had been for nothing. Less than nothing.

"It hasn't been for nothing." Devyn's voice was soft as he

appeared in front of me, his chest a blur. Had I spoken out loud? I blinked and pushed him away as hard as I could.

"It's fine. I don't need you. I don't need anyone." I had always been alone, acting the part of the perfect daughter, the good student, the sweet bride-to-be. Pretending to *be*. Until he came along. That had been real. I left my entire life behind because it had been real.

"I hate you."

His eyes met mine before he swung away. He lifted a palm to his forehead, pressing against it and screwing his eyes shut.

Then he was in front of me once more, his arms around me, whispering to me, the bond between us completely open. His emotions crashed into mine: heartbreak and hope, denial and determination, joy and defeat… It was a swirl that eddied me around, crashing through me, until I couldn't tell which were his and which were mine. I was dizzy with it. I couldn't do this anymore.

I pushed back, rejecting everything. I wanted no more of this.

"Stop, stop, Cass." I was a swirling mass of sharp pieces, but his warmth surrounded me, melding all the little shards back together. His lips kissed away the wetness on my cheeks as he lifted my boneless body and carried me over to the chair by the fire. I felt raw and wanted to push him away.

He knelt before me, his eyes anguished at the sorry sight I presented.

"You are my home."

"What?"

"You are my home."

I didn't even know what that meant, and I was too tired to care. I got to my feet, my legs taking a moment to feel solid beneath me.

He caught my hand, his fingers crushing mine.

"Please, let me explain," he said. "I'll explain."

I looked down at him. What would be different this time? I was tired of this dance. So tired.

He looked at where his hand held mine so tightly that whiteness appeared around his grip. He loosened his hand and I pulled mine away.

"Okay." I flopped back down in the chair.

"What?"

"I said, okay."

I waited while he gathered his thoughts, struggling to explain to me why he kept pushing me away. I was pretty sure I knew why but until he said it, I couldn't argue against his imbecilic reasoning.

"I know you came with me because of this thing between us," he began, his eyes downcast, not meeting mine. Not a good sign. "I should never have kissed you, especially after that night, when I realised you really are *her*. I know I said I would try and fight for us once we got here... I had no right. Out here we are simply too... You must understand my position. I am an outcast, an oathbreaker. Besides which, the lady and the Griffin can't be together. Not like that."

"Stop." I couldn't listen to this. I placed my hands on either side of his head and forced him to look at me. His -brown eyes reflected the pulse of sadness that I could feel reverberating through him. His cheeks were still hollow from the poison that had racked him, his powerful frame thinner than I had ever seen it. Almost like the frame of the insipid boy who had waited in the background of my life. Waiting for a sign that I was who he hoped, that I was the woman he was born to protect.

"No, Cass. That I found you and brought you home is

beyond my wildest dreams. To see you reunited with your family is all I have ever..." He paused to control the emotion leaking into his voice. "I can ask for no more than this."

"Ask who? The gods,? Fate? Who is it you can't ask more of? Ask me. I am the owner of my fate. I decide who I will be with. Who I love. Not the council, not the gods. Me. And I say that I want you."

"They will never allow it."

"Who is they?" I demanded. I had had enough of *they* and *them*, whoever they were.

"Society. Your brother."

My brother. I had family here, a family who would want a say in my future. But it wasn't my family who came and found me. It was Devyn.

"My family gave up on me," I said. "You never did."

"That doesn't matter."

"Of course it does. Is that not why you are outcast? Because you broke your oath in leaving my brother in order to come and find me?"

"You don't understand."

I could feel the wall building inside him, the one he constructed around himself and used to keep me distant.

"I do understand. You are the Griffin, a legacy from your father."

"One he betrayed," he said, his face forming in resolute lines.

"No, I don't think so. My mother bound him to a promise. A promise to protect you at all costs. She caused him to betray his role as Griffin. He didn't choose you over me. *She* did."

He opened his mouth to speak, then closed it again as the foundations of his world were rocked beneath him.

"That's... Why would she do that?" he asked. The secret his

father had kept all these years, the reason he had abandoned us, the single act Devyn had blamed him for – which *everyone* had blamed him for – blew up in his face. The taint upon their name was not the result of his father's failure to protect my mother. The lady herself had manipulated the events that had led to her death and my capture.

"Why?" he repeated.

"I don't know." I had no good answer.

"It wasn't his fault," he said quietly.

"Just as it wasn't your fault that I was taken. You were a child; it was a miracle that you found me. And now you can tell everyone and restore your family honour."

His face tightened.

"I refused to listen to him."

"What?"

"When we met at the castle, he wanted to tell me something but I refused to let him. What could he possibly have said that would redeem him?" His lips thinned. "Why didn't he tell anyone?"

"Perhaps he felt it was his duty to keep it secret, to hide whatever it was that motivated the lady. His final act of loyalty."

"He asked me if I still believed the baby had lived."

I looked up. I hadn't seen Rhodri before we left. Perhaps...

"Did you tell him?"

His lids dropped as he shook his head, his dark curls glinting in the firelight. His slightly longer hair made him look more like the Celt he was and less like the Roman citizen he had pretended to be for so many years.

"I was so angry. I should have told him but I've been angry with him for so long. I've blamed him for so long. I looked at him and saw everything I would be if anything ever happened to you. All I could think was that there was nothing on earth that would prevent me from keeping you safe. I will never be like him, I will never live in a world that doesn't contain you."

He was so fierce, so resolute, that chills washed over me. I forced out a laugh, dismissing the idea that he would ever be faced with such a choice.

"My mother thought it was important for you to stay alive, so let's not be crazy here."

His eyes locked with mine.

"I would give my life for yours," he vowed. "Every time."

"I'm not asking for your life. I'm only asking that you keep your promise," I said, reminding him of the discussion at hand.

"Your brother will not allow it. The Griffin and the lady can never—"

"Damn my brother. And damn you too. I decide who I love, and I choose *you*. All right, idiot?" I demanded. I'd had enough, enough of doing things that others wanted. My mother had allowed me to be taken by the council who had manipulated me my whole life, and the brother I had never even met was trying to keep me from Devyn.

I poured every bit of determination, will and love that I could down that bond. It was a white light that washed away the darkness of his shame and powerlessness as a child, the pain and blame my family and society had dumped on his young shoulders. The reflection of that shadow lifted from him, and his face lit up, softening as he finally met my eyes fully. My determination and love reflected in eyes so dark I could barely tell his iris from his cornea. His shoulders squared, as though he was physically readying to take on all who attempted to get in our way. His lips descended on mine, and he kissed me so thoroughly that I could feel its heat spreading down through my body, melting and tingling its way down to my toes.

He stood, lifting me with him, his arms filled with the strength of his renewed will.

"All right," he answered me, tumbling me into the bed that was just a few steps away, before crawling up my length until he hovered over me, his arms caging me in a cocoon of him. I inhaled the warm scent of him, that fresh smell that was all him, that reminded me of open skies and mountain ranges.

"Idiot, huh?"

I beamed up at him.

"*My* idiot."

He wouldn't back away again, I could feel it in my bones. This time, everything was out in the open. I understood why he had resisted but those walls had been torn down and they would not go back up, I vowed.

"Cass."

"Mmm?"

"We can't... Marcus."

"What about Marcus?" I rolled him over so I could explore him with my hands and lips.

"The handfast."

I frowned. Was he really asking me to respect the—? "No. Remember, unlike me, he is protected by the charm; nothing will leak out of this room. Now, can we stop speaking of—"

He stopped my words with his lips. Nicely done. That was the last sensible thought I had for a while, as those warm lips traced a path down my neck and along my once again bare collarbone as I arched up into him. The sensitive skin tingled in the wake of his path down, down, down...

My eyes opened to the breathtaking sight of a healthy sleeping Devyn. I pressed my lips softly to his before slowly levering myself off the bed.

"I'll need those." He caught me twining the ties of his soft knee boots around my calves.

"I didn't want to wake you. You need your rest."

I bounced back over to the bed and, after a much more thorough morning kiss, I floated out of the room.

The first light of day was only just beginning to creep across the sky. Unable to resist, I made my way outside to take in the light breaking over the wide-open water. There was a brisk wind coming in over the bay, creeping underneath my tightly wrapped cloak, but with my feet snug inside the multiple layers of socks with which I had padded Devyn's boots, I savoured the sensation of the fresh wind on my face. No wind in Londinium was ever this clean, this pure. This wind was untouched, having crossed miles and miles of empty sea before hitting my skin – which had been made even more tender by Devyn's stubble – on the parapet overlooking the bay.

The sky this morning was a spectacle that reflected my joy, great swathes of crimson and burnt pinky orange lighting up the sky as the sun lifted off the horizon.

My soul soared and there was an energy that flowed out of me as I laid my hands on the lichen-dappled granite wall. I felt it dance outwards in greeting to the day.

"Red sky at night, shepherd's delight, red sky in the morning, fisherman's warning." An all too familiar voice came to ruin my moment.

I frowned back at Gideon, looming behind me.

"What does that mean?"

"It's a saying the common folk use. A red sky in the

evening usually means the following day will be fine. A sky like this often foretells bad weather."

He couldn't have just let me enjoy the view. There wasn't a cloud in the sky and while cold, what did it matter when we were finally under a roof again? With Devyn on the mend, it wouldn't be long before we would have to push on to the Lakelands. I stamped my feet to put some life into them. Even the thought of being back on the road anytime soon was enough to make a shudder run through me.

"We should go inside, m'lady." There was a note of censure in his voice. I rolled my eyes. Gideon's attitude towards me had noticeably changed since he had learned who I really was. Was I now too fragile for fresh air? Not so long ago he would have happily dumped my arse on the road to walk all the way to Carlisle on my own if the opportunity had presented itself.

But the wind was more than a match for the cloak I had wrapped around my long nightdress. I made to step around him. Caesar's teeth, he was tall.

He stepped into my path.

"Your brother comes."

"What? When?" I felt suddenly short of breath.

"You think he would allow the Oathbreaker to hole up in his ancestral lands and not come to fetch him? It was only a matter of time. Word was received last night that he would be here this morning."

"Right." I braced my shoulders and pointedly stepped around him.

I clunked my way back to my room.

What should I wear? It wasn't every day a girl met her only family in the world. I ran my hand over the few options available to me. Beyond the nondescript travelling clothes Callum had donated, I had a couple of serviceable woollen dresses that Rhodri's household had found for me. Serviceable because I was pretty sure the previous owners had been in service, the rough hems and neat patching speaking of hard wear and able fingers. The dark-red one fit me better than the green and the finicky ties cinched in my waist. What did the Britons have against zips, for the gods' sake?

I pulled off Devyn's boots and the two pairs of socks I was wearing. One of the pairs wasn't too thick to fit into my own boots. If I tucked Devyn's boots under my cloak, I could smuggle them quickly back to him before the Mercians got here. No time to do anything more with my hair than drag my fingers through it to detangle it before letting the gold and copper tresses hang loosely over my shoulders; at least it was clean.

I ran back along the hallway and tapped at the heavy wood of Devyn's door. It was opened almost immediately by a servant I didn't recognise.

"I was looking for Devyn," I said unnecessarily, as I stood at his door not long past the crack of dawn, a fact that certainly wasn't passing the serving lad by. He opened the door wider to allow my entry.

Devyn sat there, loose limbs stretched before him, beside the freshly stoked fire, eating some of the delicious little griddle cakes I had become addicted to at his father's house.

"Cass, good morning."

"Ah, good morning." My cheeks heated as I bumped into a misplaced chair; his eyes were full of mischief. I was utterly thrown by the presence of the boy, who bustled about behind me, dressing the bed that I had helped to get to its current tumbled state.

I checked to make sure the boy wasn't looking my way as I bent to put Devyn's boots under a chair, rearranging my cloak to hide my activities. Snagging a cake as a reward for my task accomplished, I settled back into a chair, somewhat shy as I finally met Devyn's eyes.

Devyn's lips curled at my attempts at discretion. I took a bite of the still warm cake, the raisins bursting with flavour, the sugar a delight against the starchy goodness of the cake itself. My mind blanked at that smile. Why was I here?

Oh yeah. The cake was suddenly too dry in my mouth to swallow. I coughed as it stuck in my throat.

"Here." Devyn handed me his hot drink. I took a sip and nearly groaned as the rich coffee hit my taste buds. I raised widened eyes to Devyn.

"We are in one of the wealthiest castles in Cymru. Traders come here all the time," he explained.

"Shadowers?" I asked, thinking of those who lived in the wider imperial province. It had long been rumoured in the city that they crossed the borders unofficially to trade with the Britons, though Gideon had said that they were not permitted this far north.

"Once perhaps, but now mostly traders from Eireann, the Americas, and other free lands. I'm sure you'll find fancy fruit in the kitchen if you ask nicely. They come from all over to trade with the druids on Anglesey, and many continue here to Conwy too."

My mouth watered at the thought of fruit. Devyn's addiction to coffee was second only to my adoration of exotic fruits not native to this island, pineapples and mangoes being particular favourites. His teasing reminded me of the days we had spent in Londinium in coffee shops observing the sentinel patrols. I had loved to poke fun at his joy in the rich drink, the boyish pleasure he couldn't hide despite the reserved mask he presented to the world.

"Surely there's some cook from your youth to whom you might want to say hello?" I batted my lashes in a way any elite female would be proud of.

"We'll see." His tone was more proper than mine and he glanced at the lad, who seemed to be taking an overly long time dressing the bed.

I loved seeing Devyn like this; he was always so intense, but right now he was as relaxed and at peace with the world as I had ever seen him. His eyes were warm, his words teasing, the light-hearted morning-after of my dreams. My news would be sure to break the spell.

Right on cue, a bell rang out. Devyn was immediately on alert and reached for his recently returned boots. I laid an arm on his shoulder as he grasped them. He continued his movement and retrieved his boots, but looked up at me questioningly as he straightened.

"The King of Mercia is here."

The light dropped from his face as if a cloud had passed in front of the sun. He nodded.

I stared at him. *Don't you dare change your mind.* His dark eyes locked on mine and his lips softened. My shoulders dropped as a breath I wasn't aware I had been holding was released.

His eyes flashed to the boy now tending the fire before he said carefully, "We are agreed. We will need to wait and approach him in private. We need to give him time to take in the news first."

I nodded and swung from the room to find Marcus. I was about to meet my brother properly. I drew a new breath. I had Devyn and soon I would have a brother too.

Everything would be fine. We just had to take it one step at a time.

Chapter Nineteen

My heart fluttered like that of a tiny bird as the horses clattered across the bridge towards us. The entourage was small enough to travel fast but large enough that I could feel the tension in the Gwynedd guard as the Mercian warriors filled the courtyard.

There he was, halfway back in the group, the man from the masquerade. Today he was a blond warrior, tall and stern and dressed for hard riding. Without the mask, he was recognisable from the vision I'd had when I visited Fidelma at the forum. There was little of the laughing man I had glimpsed in my vision of the world that might have been. I looked over at Devyn, who had placed himself at my side; my hand brushed his in a whisper.

The Mercians parted to allow their leader to ride to the front, now that they were inside the walls, but they spread out ever so slightly so that he was protected on all sides. If attacked, he would be back at the heart of this force in moments.

He cut a stern figure, mounted on his horse and sweeping

his flinty gaze across the group that had assembled to meet him. And then the skies opened and rain began to spill in great droplets. I glanced towards the equally stone-faced Llewelyn. I had thought Mercia and Gwynedd were allies because they both spoke of Anglia with dislike. Was not an enemy's enemy a friend? But it appeared not – and just when I thought I was getting a handle on Briton politics.

Gideon stepped forwards to hail his liege lord but halted in his tracks as narrowed blue eyes flicked to him before travelling onwards past the Prince of Gywnedd to his nephew. They passed lightly over the rest of us before tracking back to Devyn.

"You have forgotten the way to Carlisle, Glyndŵr?" His tone was cold, expressing indifference at best on reuniting with his boyhood companion, the weeks of delay in our journey north deeply unappreciated.

"My lord." Devyn bowed his head and kept his gaze on the cobbles as Rion Deverell dismounted and came to a stop in front of him.

"You no longer kneel before your king?" queried the soft, cool voice.

Devyn dropped to his knees on the wet cobbles, his head bowing even further as the rain dripped off his dark curls. Marcus gripped my hand tightly as rage ripped through me.

"Dev," his uncle growled at Devyn, a clear indication to rise. Rhys laid a restraining arm on Llewelyn's shoulder, visibly calming him as he bristled in outrage.

Glacially cold eyes flicked at Llewelyn.

"Twysog." Rion nodded courteously, greeting Llewelyn in the local language. The wind whipped around the courtyard, the dark storm that Gideon had promised as nothing compared to the one I was about to raise.

"Breathe," Marcus said under his breath. This was their world, their customs. Don't interfere. Don't overreact.

Gideon appeared at the king's shoulder as he scanned us, his brow lifting at the unfamiliar faces in the group. "My lord, this is Marcus Plantagenet."

"Your Highness." The golden-haired Mercian reverted to the common tongue, behaving for all the world like we were standing at a summer party. His manner was formal yet friendly as he greeted Marcus, as if Devyn didn't remain on his knees at his feet.

"Rion, this is…"

I flashed Gideon a warning look; if I were to release some of the energy that burned in my blood right now, it would incinerate him where he stood. Right now, I would rather flatten Rion Deverell than recognise him as kin. Gideon glanced down at where Devyn still knelt and grimaced as he looked back at me. He was not happy at concealing my identity from the lord he served, especially as he knew my reaction was in defence of a man he did not respect. My lips thinned. Whatever Gideon did or didn't think about lying to his lord, he thought better of introducing him to his long-lost sister when she looked ready to gut him rather than embrace him.

"Cassandra Shelton," Gideon finished and then added, "His Highness's betrothed."

"Ah, yes." Rion Deverell smiled in recognition. "We met at the ball in Londinium."

I did not return his smile.

"Devyn is still recovering," I found myself saying.

His eyes went flat.

"He's still breathing," he said coldly. "I would say his health is more robust than it deserves to be."

Llewelyn's intake of breath was the only sound in the courtyard. "Rion," Bronwyn called as she tripped down the stairs towards us, her hood up against the rain as she flew into his arms. "I'm so sorry we didn't make it all the way to you."

She trailed off as she became aware of the tension in him and turned to survey the rest of us. Her head went back as she took in her cousin on the ground, her eyes widening. "Oh, Rion, please, can't you—"

Whatever she was about to say in Devyn's defence was cut off. The King of Mercia had obviously had enough of our objections to Devyn's treatment.

"Another word of this and he will stay there until the wind and rain weather his bones. Am I understood?"

"You are in my home," came a growl from the Prince of Gywnedd. Rhys's restraining hand was violently shrugged away.

"He is mine to command as I will," came the answering growl.

I was going to fry him where he stood. This... this was the brother I had longed to meet? Bronwyn laid a gentle hand on Rion's chest.

"My lord, I beg you," she started.

"By rights he should be in chains, not standing free to greet me," he said flatly, looking directly at his host. Given the severity of his crime, Devyn was considered an outlaw. As soon as he had crossed the borderlands, we had stayed out of sight as much as possible – for all our sakes. Gideon and Devyn had warned me how his return would be received. I had been lulled into a false sense of security because the first households we had entered had been Devyn's own family.

"Rion," Bronwyn spoke more firmly. "Devyn is barely recovered from the poisoning."

That caught his attention, his stiffness unbending sufficiently to ask, "What poisoning?"

"On the road north," Bronwyn explained softly. "He nearly died."

Glacial blue eyes flicked to Gideon who nodded in confirmation.

"I sent word with your men."

"I did not meet them. I received word of your detour by other means."

Without looking to where Devyn knelt, he threw his chin up in a signal to Gideon who stepped over to Devyn and reached under his arm to raise him from the ground.

"When we leave, he leaves with us." The king spoke directly to Devyn's uncle.

Llewelyn's jaw set mutinously and he neither agreed nor disagreed, indicating instead that they should all continue inside.

My chest was tight as we followed them inside. A servant took my dripping cloak as we entered the hall. My hair and face were wet, but with the heat that was burning through me, I half expected to see steam rising.

Llewelyn was near shaking with rage as he answered whatever Rion Deverell had said to him as they walked in.

"You will have the trial here." His accent was so strong it sounded as if he would trip over the words as they were catapulted violently out of him.

I couldn't hear the king's response from where I was, but it only served to enrage Devyn's uncle further.

"You will have the trial here," he repeated. "Or there will be no trial and you can be on your way now."

Everyone froze as the two lords faced off.

What trial?

323

"You would break the laws of our land?" came Deverell's low voice.

"He'll get no fair trial in the north. If justice must be done, it will be done here," Llewelyn rejoined decisively. "We can send for the High Druid from Anglesey. You can find no fault with that."

My heart thumped against my chest. What trial?

Those frozen blue eyes flicked to the spot outside where Devyn had knelt before turning back to the small, fierce figure before him.

"I agree," came that low voice again. Calm and formal.

My eyes caught Bronwyn's. She looked worried. I searched for Devyn but he hadn't followed us in, choosing to make himself scarce following the confrontation in the courtyard.

"What was all that?" I whispered to her as we followed through to the great hall.

She checked to see if anyone was close enough to hear.

"I don't know," she started. "I had hoped… I did not expect him to be so…"

It appeared that Bronwyn was as shocked at the scene that had taken place as I was. Why?

"You people never stop telling me that Devyn is beyond the pale."

"Yes, but Rion loved him once," she returned, pulling me aside into an alcove as everyone continued on. "It looks like we defied the Lakes by bringing Devyn to his family."

"Then explain," I said fiercely, "that we would never have made it to the Lakes."

"I will, but we should have sent you and Marcus ahead. He won't understand why we didn't. He's not to know that you put Devyn's life above…" She stopped, her brow furrowing. "Oh gods, we put his life above everyone else.

Above yours. When he learns who you are, he'll kill Devyn for sure."

"Devyn was barely conscious; it was hardly his decision," I protested. I followed her logic, unwillingly, but I did follow it. What Rhodri had done in saving his son instead of the lady would be deemed unforgivable. Rion Deverell would be beyond reasoning with if he felt Devyn had repeated his father's sin.

"Devyn knew who you were. So did I," she moaned softly. "Another betrayal by our house. Putting our own blood ahead of yours. What have we done? What should have redeemed him has damned him utterly."

Her eyes looked wild as the full impact of our actions hit her.

"Then we don't tell him." What he didn't know couldn't be used against Devyn in this trial. History repeating itself would condemn him in the eyes of everyone here.

Bronwyn blinked.

"No, we have to tell Rion," she began.

"We don't have to tell him anything. This would hurt Devyn at the trial?"

She nodded slowly.

"I think so. It is a miracle he found you. That alone would have saved him, had we gone north directly. But if they are gathering a court for a trial proper, the lords will never be able to look past history being repeated."

"It wasn't exactly his choice." I threw my eyes up in the air. How could I reason with people if they wouldn't listen to logic? It was the same here as in Londinium. It wasn't about the truth, it was about how the truth was presented. If leading the newly recovered Lady of the Lake on a detour was a hanging offence, then we would remove the offence.

One small snag though.

"I'll make sure Devyn agrees to go along with keeping my identity quiet," I promised. One way or another I would make sure of it. "But you two aren't the only ones who know."

"Marcus?" she guessed, her face tightening as if she had just eaten something bad. The only woman in the land who didn't like Marcus.

"Yes, but he's not the problem."

"Then who?" she asked.

"Gideon."

"What?" Her exclamation was overly loud in the quiet hallway. "How?"

"He figured it out on the way to Dinas Brân." How to explain that Gideon and I had had a brief truce? "I'll talk to him."

"We're doomed."

"Don't be so dramatic." It wasn't like it was a matter of life and death to get Gideon to continue to keep my secret from his friend to save a man he despised... Ha. "I'll figure it out."

I winked at her as I whirled out of the alcove. And I'd thought today was going to be such a good one. Red sky in the morning indeed.

We rejoined the party in the great hall, where the new arrivals were throwing down warming drinks provided by their still hostile host. I sat demurely by Marcus as the tale of our journey north was laid out for the king of Mercia, who listened intently. He gave no sign that he hadn't already dismissed the events outside entirely from his mind.

He questioned Gideon and Marcus closely, directing an occasional icy query at Bronwyn when they got to the point where we had decided to split up. Bronwyn's initial embrace outside had suggested that they were usually on friendlier terms, proving our guess that Deverell's anger at having to hunt down Devyn himself had not been well received.

His gaze rested on me with mild interest at points when I was mentioned in the tale, but he didn't ask anything of me directly. I felt Gideon's amber gaze linger on me from time to time, but I refused to meet his eyes.

Rion Deverell sat straight in his chair, deigning to turn his head from time to time and subjecting the talker to his considered gaze. His unwavering attention took in not just what they said but what their choice of words left unsaid, what their body language added, and the expressions of those around them as they listened. Here was a man used to following every move on the chessboard, one who liked to know all his available moves and the motivations of each player.

His eyes were cobalt blue where mine were aqua, and his hair lifted in a wave from a wide forehead already showing lines, even though he was only a few years older than me. Where my hair was tawny, his was caramel and gold, long in the same style as his warriors but pulled back and constrained at the nape of his neck. His strong jawline was stubbled – the only real evidence of having been on the road. Occasionally a glimmer of warmth broke through and his lips would tug slightly up at the right where I could almost see a dimple. It was barely there and, like mine, visible only on the right side. He dropped his eyelids often as he listened, concealing his thoughts, his chin always lifted at an arrogant angle. He was utterly self-contained and off-puttingly regal in his bearing. But every now and then, his eyes flicked to the door, his fingers fidgeting with a ring on his left hand.

His jaw flexed as he was told of Gideon's knife being thrown at the end of the fight with Bronwyn, his eyes flinty as he checked Gideon. It was the first sign of emotion I had spotted as I sat taking in every detail I could. Was he annoyed at Gideon's recklessness or because he had hurt Devyn?

Gideon met his lord's censure with an insouciant smirk but gave the lie to his defiance by explaining that we now knew that the knife had not been the source of the poison. Bronwyn added that had Gideon's knife not drawn and exposed the poison to the surface, we would never have known it was there until it was too late.

Those blue eyes widened slightly as the tale continued to the episode where the hounds of Samhain had pursued us.

He nodded at the decision to split up, expressing interest at the cuffs that had required Gideon to take the city pair while Bronwyn had retained his warriors to keep the slower party protected.

His head tilted slightly as Gideon told of our passage through the valleys with the hounds in pursuit. Gideon failed to mention that we had received aid from York on the road, but I had the uncanny notion that Rion Deverell was already making a note to speak further to Gideon in private. Did he deem that the decision to use the warriors to protect Devyn had put unnecessary risk on Marcus?

His lids almost concealed those sea-storm eyes entirely as Bronwyn described the events at Dinas Brân. He barely moved as he listened, almost as if acknowledging the fact that Rhodri Glyndŵr still lived would be to give him too much consideration.

"Why continue west after?" He spoke without inflection, but his hands splayed out in his lap then curled back into tight balls. His fingers again twisted the gold ring.

Bronwyn cast a glance at me then back at Deverell.

Her expression was soft and her palms came up in a gesture that begged forgiveness.

"We had no choice. There was only so much Madoc could do to hold off the poison. We needed Ewan's greater skill."

"So you carried an outlaw even further into his family's stronghold." His pinched expression left no one in doubt of his opinion on this decision.

"Rion, he wouldn't have made it to the Lakelands," Bronwyn said.

"And now he may never," Deverell gritted out as he brought himself up to his full height and without another word, strode from the room.

"What did that mean?" I asked into the silence.

Bronwyn shook her head, her eyes flicking to the servants lingering around the room. Later then, I thought, but her brow was furrowed and she looked as worried as I had ever seen her. This was not an encouraging sign considering that most of the time I had spent with the Kernowan was while we were being hunted by the vile hounds and her cousin lay on the edge of death.

Gideon rose and I hurried after him. The hall was empty when I got there and my shoulders dropped. Where did he go? I needed to speak to him before he told Deverell the truth of my identity.

I kept going and as I reached the alcove Bronwyn and I had ducked into earlier, a hard hand reached out and grabbed me.

I found myself yet again at eye level with Gideon's broad chest and had to crane my neck back.

"Why did you not tell him who you are?" He glowered down at me.

I'd had plenty of time to plan it out while they were

recounting our adventure. Saving Devyn's neck was not an argument that would sway Gideon to hold his tongue.

"I don't think it's safe."

"What?"

"You said it yourself." I hurried through my explanation. "Somebody tried to kill us. We need to find out who it was. What do you think will happen as soon as Rion Deverell learns I'm alive?"

"He will make sure you are safe."

"I'll never be safe as long as the poisoner is out there. Think about it. Whoever it was got close enough to nearly kill Devyn. Maybe they were after Devyn, or maybe it was meant for one of us. But if Devyn is imprisoned and Marcus is in York, and I'm rolled in cotton wool in a tower in Carlisle, we'll never know."

"That sounds like an acceptable outcome to me."

I exhaled audibly.

"Well, I can't live like that for ever. I *won't* live like that," I underlined before throwing down my trump card. "You said you wouldn't reveal my identity."

His eyes narrowed at the reminder.

A small tic pulsed at the corner of his jaw. He would not forgive me for putting him in this position, especially when he realised that I was doing it for Devyn.

"Unless it puts you at risk… If it becomes necessary, I will tell him."

"For now, I think it's in all our best interests to keep my return from the dead quiet," I bargained.

"Or you could tell him now."

There had to be an argument that would sway him. I went through everything I knew about Gideon. He had a mind like a steel trap; he had figured out who I was on the slightest of evidence and he could argue his way through any logic I might present. The man was like a rock, completely invulnerable... No, that wasn't true. He had a weakness.

"What about your father?"

"What about him?"

"What will he do if my brother takes me north? You know that Marcus and I can't be separated. How will the Steward of York feel about his prince being taken to Mercia? All that power back in Britannia, in the hands of your friend. What happens then?"

Gideon stilled. Who said I didn't understand Briton politics? Because I knew what would happen next and so did Gideon. York would gear up for war. Gideon's blood family against his sworn loyalty. Which side would he choose? "Bad time for Briton lords to be fighting amongst themselves." I pressed home the advantage while I sensed him weakening. "War is coming. Will you be ready, or will you be too busy fighting each other?"

"You are asking me to lie to my liege lord."

"No. I'm just asking you to delay telling the truth," I said.

"For how long?"

How much more could I reveal before I gave away too much? He wouldn't agree to this indefinitely.

"We need to find a way to get these bloody handfast cuffs off. Then Marcus can go to York and I can go to Mercia and everyone is happy.

"You'll tell him before you leave here."

I nodded.

His eyebrow rose. Damn it.

"Your word on it, m'lady."

I sighed. I weighed up my options. There weren't many – more than we'd had in the arena though. I shrugged.

"Fine, you have my word on it."

So many promises. So many secrets.

He moved fractionally closer, invading my space. I had to crane my neck further back to maintain eye contact. He was way too close. Gods, he was large.

"I give you my word that I will tell my brother who I am before I leave Gwynedd." It was the first time I had acknowledged him out loud as my brother since he had arrived. From the moment he had got off his horse and forced Devyn to the ground, he had become a threat to be dealt with – just another problem that stood between me and Devyn. But he was my brother. When he discovered how we had tricked him he would be angry. Disappointed. I was so over disappointing family. It wouldn't be the best start, but he was the one who had come here and attacked Devyn.

"I will hold you to that, city girl," Gideon stated flatly. "Interesting, though, that you're planning to separate from your dear betrothed."

"Calchas and the council put us together. We have no interest in staying together. I'm here because I'm a Briton and I want to go home."

"You have a funny way of showing it."

"Things got more complicated than when we originally planned our escape," I admitted.

"You and Devyn."

I needed to stop talking. How had we got here?

"Yes." I tilted my head, looking at him as if I didn't quite follow. "He's the one who found me and told me the truth. That's all."

"Of course it is." Gideon didn't say anything more. *Don't fill the silence*, I told myself. Nothing more I could say would help. I had got him to agree for the time being. That was enough.

I backed out of the alcove.

"I like these boots better." The taunt followed me down the corridor.

My boots. I didn't have another pair of boots.

I stopped.

A soft chuckle sounded behind me.

Chapter Twenty

"You need to convince Devyn of our plan," Bronwyn whispered to me as she took her place beside me at dinner that evening.

"I can't find him," I returned under my breath. I had been everywhere and there was no sign of him. The antipathy the inhabitants of this castle felt towards me as a citizen didn't help my search as all enquiries were met with a shrug. Devyn's room was empty. Frustration and worry fizzed through me.

"He's in the dungeon."

I gaped at her. Was she kidding? They had thrown him in an actual dungeon?

"He's under arrest until the trial," she said as if that explained everything. He was barely recovered. I couldn't help but glare in the direction of the head table where the Prince of Gywnedd was busily playing the convivial host. "It's not his fault."

I continued to glare until Llewlyn's partner Rhys caught me and I lowered my eyes to my clenched fists. They sat there merrily eating and drinking in the warm hall while Devyn rotted in some dank dungeon. At least, I presumed it was dank – weren't all dungeons? A bloody dungeon. Devyn was Llewelyn's family.

"Cassandra, never mind them. You need to talk to Devyn before Rion does or our plan is blown," she said, pulling my attention back.

"What do you mean?"

She exhaled noisily. "He is refusing to conceal your identity, even if it's the only hope of saving his neck."

Of course he was.

"Go down there and get him to do as he's told."

"What's wrong with him?" I grumbled.

"He's stubborn," Bronwyn replied equally sourly. "And too damned honourable. Now focus. See the girl over there by the door in the black skirt?"

Scanning the edges of the hall, I saw a girl with long brown hair and a black skirt watching us.

"She is supposed to take his dinner down. He is still the lord's nephew after all. She'll lend you her cloak and you can carry his tray down. Don't wait too long," she commanded. "The guards will be suspicious if the serving girl delays too long with him."

I slipped from the table before Bronwyn had even finished speaking. I got it. I wasn't an idiot. I followed the girl to the kitchen and she handed me her cloak and tray with directions to cross the courtyard and take the guarded door to the north tower before descending to where Devyn was locked up like a criminal.

I gritted my teeth as I smiled sweetly at the Mercian warriors standing by the door.

335

Unlike the cell at the arena, this was a prison more equipped for regular detention. Balls of light bobbed above my head as I went down and down.

I made my way past two empty cells before finding an occupied one. Sensing my arrival, Devyn was already at the bars.

Anger rolled off me but Devyn smiled mildly back at me.

"Calm down, Cass, it's protocol. I'm awaiting trial. I told you, I'm considered a criminal here."

He waited while I wrangled my temper under control, cursing the burn in my blood which made my emotions so volatile.

"Fine," I said slowly. "I'll be calm if you'll be quiet."

"No," he responded, catching my meaning instantly. "I will not deceive him."

"It's your best chance," I argued. "Bronwyn says you have no hope if they learn we put your safety above mine."

His eyes darkened. "That seems fair to me."

"Devyn. You promised."

"I did not promise to deceive my liege lord."

"No, but if you tell him then he will never let us be together,, and then you break your promise to me," I argued.

"Maybe." He shrugged.

Was he out of his mind?

"If you do this, I will deny it," I said fiercely, yet also as quietly as my temper allowed. This was taking too long. "I will deny everything. Without evidence of my power, why would they believe you? Which is easier for them to believe – that you've gone mad in search of a dead girl or that Marcus Courtenay's betrothed is just a lost city girl trapped by the handfast into coming here against her will?"

I could feel him steeling his will against mine.

"If they won't let us be together I will have no reason to stay. As soon as this cuff is off, I promise I will return to Londinium. Let them do with me what they will. What will I care?"

His eyes darkened at my threat.

"They will kill you if you go back," he stated starkly.

"Maybe." I shrugged.

"Touché." His lips tugged unwillingly upward.

"And what if whoever gave you that poison was trying to hurt me? Who will protect me and get their own stupid arse poisoned next time?" It was a stretch; it seemed most likely that Devyn had been the intended target. That would never occur to him though.

"Fine," he agreed. "Just until the trial is over."

I followed up, sensing him already regretting his capitulation. I heard footfall on the stone stairs – one of the guards coming to see what was taking me so long.

Devyn's lips twisted before he finally nodded in agreement with my proposal that he keep his mouth shut. I flashed him my teeth in victory and spun on my heel, apologising blithely for the delay as I passed the incoming guard.

We broke our fasts in the great hall. The tables heaved with crusty bread and tea – the herbal tea was acceptable but coffee was available if you asked really nicely. I spread strawberry jam across the bread and sank my teeth into it.

It was barely past dawn, but the King of Mercia and a number of his warriors had been halfway through their breakfast when I arrived, the golden lord sitting beside Gideon, speaking of nothing.

I waited tensely, trying to catch the eye of the serving girl in the fading hope that today she would give me a sign that I could take the tray to Devyn, when I sensed him approach. Bronwyn had pleaded with Deverell and Llewelyn for the last three nights that Devyn be allowed back to his room given the state of his health. Apparently, Rion Deverell's anger had cooled enough that they had even gone one step further and granted him the freedom of the castle. Arriving to breakfast late, he paused momentarily in the doorway. He blinked at the suddenly silent company gathered there and then the doorway was empty again.

Chatter resumed before the door had swung closed. I almost jumped a foot in the air as the clatter of a fist slamming on the table rang out like a shot. All eyes turned on the King of Mercia who had remained so determinedly relaxed all morning. The force with which he had pounded the table gave lie to that indifference. Bowls were still spinning after they found the surface of the table again.

The hum of conversation did not cover the silence this time as the door swung closed in the departing king's wake.

What did Deverell want? Was he going after Devyn? After waiting for as many minutes to pass as I could bear, I made my way to the door.

In my soft indoor shoes, I took off along the corridor, almost running, my skirts swirling around my legs. I paused at the end of the hall – stables or bedroom? There was no way anyone was going out in the lashing rain that had continued through the night.

And yet. He had been cooped up for days.

I ducked my head against the driving rain that stung my

face like needles. I ran across the courtyard, hunching against the weather.

I paused as I entered the stable, and after shaking off the rain as if I were a half-drowned dog, I centred myself and felt for Devyn. If he was here I should be able to... There.

Passing by the horse stalls to the end, I found Devyn putting a saddle on a horse.

"What are you doing?" I asked, aghast.

"Going for a ride."

"In this? What is wrong with you? You've barely recovered from the... you know, nearly dying."

"It's better for everyone if I stay out of sight. I need to be outside these walls for a couple of hours," he said in a controlled manner. I went to him as he fixed the girth, laying my hand on his arm.

"He's looking for you."

Devyn's muscles tensed. He was wound as tightly as I'd ever seen him. I recalled his face when he'd opened the door to find Deverell at breakfast. He didn't want to face his former friend, didn't want to lie to him. But lie he must.

"Are you sure?" His eyes flicked behind me to the entrance.

"Well, no. But he's been watching that door all morning, so I assume he knew you weren't in the dungeon anymore. He seemed upset that you decided not to join us and stormed out after you."

"Right," he sighed. "Now he wants to talk."

"Devyn—" I started to remind him that he couldn't say anything.

"Stay here," he cut me off abruptly, pushing me firmly back into the stall as he made his way out of the tack room.

"Leaving again?" Rion Deverell sounded bored.

Devyn gave no response that I could hear.

"What are you doing here?" Deverell sounded angry, but it was heavily laced with frustration and exasperation. "You come back and put yourself in the middle of... If you had just come to me first as I told you, I could have contained it. We could have figured it out. But now it will be public and I cannot be seen to show weakness."

I waited for Devyn's response.

"I am still your man," Devyn finally said.

"That remains to be seen." That cool, restrained tone returned at Devyn's formal but uninformative response. Silence hung in the air, filled only by the soft whickering of horses.

"I asked you a question."

"I was poisoned. It wasn't exactly my decision," Devyn answered.

"You're lying to me." Deverell spoke slowly, assessing the man before him.

Silence again. I could feel Devyn's struggle to find words that would move them beyond this. Something that would help him avoid lying further.

"What aren't you telling me?" Deverell tried again, to resounding silence. "York's bride came with him." The king tried a new tack. "As I recall you nearly got yourself killed in Londinium over her."

My heart stopped. Did he know? Was it possible that he suspected the truth? I leaned my head against the wall, begging Devyn to hold the line.

"Damn you," came that controlled voice.

Footsteps rustled through the straw, leading out of the stables until they paused momentarily before they quickly returned.

"You left me alone. He was a ghost. After you left, I had no one." I couldn't see Rion, but I could hear his pain and feel the answering pain his words stirred in Devyn.

"Why did you leave?" The words sounded like they had been torn from him against his will.

Again, Devyn didn't answer; he didn't need to this time. His boyhood friend knew the answer already. Deverell's groan said as much, as did the sound of a hand hitting a stall with a bang.

"Dammit. That cannot be your defence."

"It's the truth."

More silence as Deverell absorbed Devyn's simple reply. He didn't ask if Devyn had had any success. Whether because he didn't care if his sister was still alive or because no part of him thought it possible, it was hard to tell.

"How long will you stay this time?" No echo of the anger of a moment ago remained in his voice.

I could feel the shame that weighed Devyn down at this question. Other emotions pulled at the edges of that shame. A wish to be able to make that promise. Frustration at being unable to do so. As if the promise was not in his gift to give. I swallowed as I crouched in the tack room, the straw scratching at my ankles.

"I have forgiven you twice. There will not be a third time."

Once, when he was a child, Rion Deverell had chosen to stand in front of the boy the world hated for his mother and sister's death. When was the second time?

"Twice?" Apparently Devyn couldn't do this calculation either.

"When I saw you in Londinium, I thought…" There was a pause, as if he could not find or name the words he had felt there in the middle of the masquerade ball. "For a moment I half expected you would step forward and present…"

Would Devyn tell him now? That he had done what he had set out to do and found his long-dead sister.

There was a huff.

"You should have come directly to me."

No response again. Devyn wasn't the most liberal with words when under pressure.

"A thrice-damned trial," Deverell said. "Your uncle seeks to save you. But he… There is little I can do here."

"I know."

What did that mean? Little he could do about what?

"Will you have me back?" Devyn's question was barely audible.

"Should you live so long," came the flat reply.

There was nothing for Devyn to say in response to that. "Damn you."

Deverell ended the conversation, the crunch of straw indicating his departure. I opened the stall door to find Devyn standing there, his head thrown back and his eyes shut.

"Are you okay?" I asked. I could feel he wasn't. I knew how difficult hiding the truth had been for him.

He lifted his head and looked over at me. A smile broke across his grey face. Like the light that breaks through a bank of cloud and in shards of light illuminates a single section of countryside.

"I broke my vow but he…" His chin crumpled. His friend had forgiven him his betrayal, without even knowing that Devyn had succeeded. Irrespective of everyone else's condemnation, he had forgiven him.

I wrapped my arms around him as he sucked in great breaths to steady himself.

I knew that my brother's opinion mattered a great deal to Devyn and the fact that he had been forgiven for breaking the vow he had made to Mercia would go a long way to healing the jagged tear that I could occasionally sense in Devyn.

"This is good, right? No need for a trial now?"

Devyn shook his head.

"It's too late. Once the trial was called, my uncle acted immediately and sent out riders with a summons to neighbouring lords to convene here. Llewelyn meant well."

"What do you mean?"

"He forced Rion's hand by calling for a trial. If we had made it to Carlisle, then Rion alone would have had the power to decide my fate, and there would be little his peers could do to gainsay him, whether he forgave me or had me executed. It is his right as it was his house I broke my vow to," he explained.

Executed? Since when was that the punishment for a broken promise? I knew that Devyn had been outlawed when he left the north, but I had assumed that the punishment would fit the crime. When the others had said... I'd thought it was a figure of speech. Breaking a promise wasn't even a crime against the Code, but this felt like a massive overreaction. Surely some kind of fine would be more appropriate.

Devyn ran his hands down my arms. "It will be all right, Cass. The trial is a formality. The lords hereabouts should vote with my uncle."

"Should?" I asked, my voice coming out a little on the shrill side. "Like the King of Mercia's confidence that said you could return to his service if you live long enough to do so?"

Devyn lifted his head at the sound of approaching voices. He brushed his lips against mine.

He took the reins to lead the waiting horse outside. He was obviously still planning to go for that ride.

"It will be fine."

But it wasn't going to be fine. The first of the lords had arrived while Devyn was enjoying his ride along the coast in the wind and rain. And Lady Morwyn of Caernarfon, Llewelyn's closest neighbour, was seriously displeased when she learned of it.

The gruff old lady insisted on standing in the courtyard to wait for his return. Llewelyn waited with her, simmering at the implication that Devyn could not be trusted.

Devyn finally returned, dark curls dripping down his face as he cantered in, immediately taking in his not so welcoming committee.

He dismounted and bowed formally to Lady Morwyn, who had the guards escort Devyn directly to his room where he was to remain for the duration of the trial. An oathbreaker was not to be trusted to his word not to run. Rion Deverell watched the whole scene, unblinking, from inside the doorway and merely stood aside, expressionless, as Devyn was marched past him.

His eyes flicked to me afterwards, less out of an interest in me than merely noting the anger on my face. My reaction was worth noting. Again, I had the impression that Deverell was assessing me like a piece on a chessboard.

Between my response now and his recollection of Devyn's reaction at the ball in Londinium, he clearly had suspicions about our relationship, but whatever triangle was going on, while noteworthy, was no concern of his. I gnawed at my lower lip. For now.

It took some days before the Prince of Gywnedd announced that with six lords present they had a quorum ready for the judge. Llewelyn himself, the King of Mercia, his neighbours Lady Morwyn, Lord Arthfael and Lady Emrick, who came from somewhere in the mountains. And an Anglian,

Lord Montgomery, who had been visiting Emrick when the summons had arrived. Two more days passed waiting on the druids even though they were nearby at Anglesey, the approaching solstice the likely cause of the delay. The arrival of the High Druid elicited a great deal of fuss. I watched her arrive from my window. Garbed in the same long cloak as the others I had met so far, she looked like something out of myth with her long, fine white hair and a flowing white dress.

When I went down to dinner later, I discovered to my delight that the High Druid was none other than the wisewoman Fidelma. She caught my eye as I went to greet her, shaking her head slightly. It would be better if our acquaintance was not common knowledge; I nodded faintly in compliance if not complete understanding.

The High Druid had not travelled alone; there were several white-robed druids seated at a high table in the hall, one of whom caught my attention and who I definitely was not going to pretend not to know.

Having spotted her first, I made my way around to her table. When I was at her shoulder, I leaned down to whisper in her ear.

"Hello, Marina."

She let out a squeal and quickly extricated herself from the bench before wrapping herself around me, her delight abundant.

"Cassandra! Oh, I wanted to come and find you straight away but Fidelma said it wouldn't be the thing to wander around the castle and we were waiting and waiting for you to come down, but you didn't. But you're here now."

"We?" I asked, bemused.

"Me and Oban." Her older brother was hovering behind her, looking a little disquieted at the amount of attention we were attracting. I hugged him and he smiled back at the warm reception.

I took them both in, Marina in a green version of the druid's robes and Oban in a plain but immaculately cut tunic in the Celtic style.

"You came with Fidelma?" I took in Marina's flushed, healthy colouring and her lustrous hair swept up in braids. "You look wonderful."

"Yes, I'm a novice now but I'm training to be a druid."

"In Anglesey?" I asked, struck by the coincidence that they had also ended up in this corner of the wilds.

"No, we're in Glastonbury. Fidelma was visiting the Holy Isle for the harvest when the summons came. Druid John remained at the Holy Isle for the winter solstice so we came to Conwy instead; she's more important anyway. She was supposed to be back for solstice at Stonehenge but she said we would come here instead. I really wanted to see Stonehenge, but obviously it's so much better to see you here instead. Have you ever seen such a place? It's huge, isn't it?" She indicated the castle, her eyes wide in appreciation.

"Damp though."

"It does rain a lot." Marina sighed heavily.

"What do you mean, Fidelma is more senior? Isn't she just a wisewoman?"

"No," Marina laughed. "She's the High Druid at Glastonbury Tor. She's like the boss."

"She's healed you?"

Marina frowned. "I'm way better. Did you know that the Mallacht – that's what they call it here – has been around for ages? It's a curse caused when the energies of the earth aren't cared for. That's what druids do. Not the curse – though apparently that's what the Romans say – but they know the old ways and they look after the land. I'm taking some of the medicine that Druid John produces so mostly I feel better but I can't take it while I'm training because then I can't sense the ley. But I can't train on the road anyway."

"But when you aren't taking this stuff, you still have the illness? The Mallacht?"

"Yeah, but I ain't dead," she pointed out, winking.

I smiled back at her. It was unspeakably good to see them here. I was so tired of being surrounded by new people. And Marcus should be able to do better for her. He was showing the druid here his technique and Marina could be added to those he was using to demonstrate to Ewan and Madoc how he cured the Mallacht.

"How are you?" I asked, turning to Oban, giving the high table a glance over my shoulder; my presence at Marcus's side was overdue.

"I'm well, my lady," he said politely. I frowned at his polite response. "I... uh, I'm well enough," he said. "P'raps not as useful in a druid community as I might be elsewhere."

I surveyed their companions' simple robes. "No, I suppose not. But if you're looking for an occupation while you're here, I could do with some help," I said, indicating my plain woollen dress.

Oban grinned, his pleasure at being able to make himself useful evident. "Can do."

At the high table, there was no real discussion of anything more than the recent harvests and the spread of illness in their communities. It was as if Devyn didn't exist. Marcus, of course, was of great interest to the new arrivals, and they went to a good deal of trouble to engage him and solicit his thoughts on any and all topics that arose. Marcus was used to being the centre of attention in most gatherings in Londinium, so he took it in his stride and was effortlessly charming in return.

I, on the other hand, had little desire to charm anyone. Even my lifelong training to be the sociable beauty on Marcus's arm wasn't enough to entirely mask the dread that leached out of my sullen mood.

Chapter Twenty-One

The trial began on the evening of the day after Fidelma's arrival with a great deal less ceremony than a Mete occasioned in Londinium. Each day, after the evening meals, tables were pushed back, Devyn was brought in, and was made to stand alone in the centre of the room.

He was never afraid. Every evening, for an hour or so, he calmly answered their questions about his life following his departure from Carlisle. According to their laws, everyone had a right to speak in their own defence, the goal being to understand events rather than spin evidence against the accused. Devyn was honest and respectful. He told them of his life in the Imperial Province. Marcus remained rigid as Devyn described his skills with technology, his friendship with Linus and other dissidents, and their efforts to help latents. He made it clear to everyone that he was quite willing to accept whatever the court decided, and that this was an eventuality he had foreseen from the moment he had decided to leave the Lakes.

Since I was denied access to Devyn, Bronwyn kept me

occupied by teaching me how to ride properly; otherwise I kept to my room as much as possible, though I was regularly joined by Marina, who bubbled over with enthusiasm for her new life. She was full of talk of the ley line she tended at Glastonbury and the druids' delight in the strength of her ability. Oban also took to sewing in my rooms when Marina was off being treated by Marcus.

After Devyn was done with, others were called upon to fill in the events of our journey north, most particularly from the point when Devyn had become ill. Bronwyn answered clearly and placed emphasis on Devyn's incapacity during the critical decision-making part. Gideon was called on to recount the events on our side after splitting from the main group. His responses to the High Druid, even for Gideon, were spectacularly insolent.

Oban lured me to his room the next day for a final fitting of my soon-to-be replenished wardrobe, having procured cloth from Rhys, with whom he had quickly become friendly. Returning to my rooms, I almost collided with Gideon as he burst around the corner. His hands shot out to catch me. He steadied me and seemed about to hurry on when a dark gleam suddenly lit his amber eyes.

Gideon stiffened and leaned his body further into mine, his hand on my lower back holding me to him when I tried to pull away.

He leaned down and whispered in my ear, "If you want me to keep your secret then grant me this one thing."

What one thing? What was he doing? Gideon could have any woman in the castle; I had seen them throwing themselves at him.

"What thing?" I asked somewhat breathlessly. I was confused and annoyed but there was a reason every woman between ten and a hundred threw themselves at him. He was gorgeous and slightly dangerous... and his large body curving intimately about mine was making me think of things I had no business thinking about.

"Gideon." A woman's voice came from somewhere behind him.

He had known she was following him – that had to be it. This was what he had wanted from me, a cover to put off some woman he had grown tired of. I was surprised he was going to such lengths; I'd never seen him have any trouble before telling anyone they were no longer welcome in his company. It appeared to be his default setting.

"Gideon," the voice came again, an insistence that suggested she was not leaving without speaking to him.

"I'm a little busy right now," he said, stepping fractionally closer to me so that his body was pressed against mine as he held me against the wall. One leg was nudging between mine in a way that was all too suggestive and way out of line. I stiffened and began to push him off.

His body was hard and strong and his breath was warm against my ear as he breathed a word of warning into it. "Do we have a deal?"

I scowled at him but let my body melt. Whatever game he was playing was not about me but about the woman behind us; the more I went along with it, the sooner it would be over.

I lifted my arms and embraced him, moaning as he placed his lips against my neck in response to a kiss he wasn't giving me. His hands roamed through my hair and cupped my head. I gritted my teeth against the invasion. He was barely touching me and only in the least intimate of places but his hands were talented. Given the practice he had, by all accounts, notched up, they should be. I couldn't take much more of this.

A featherlight touch ran up my face, the tender investigation of a lover's features. I bit my lip as I felt my breath hitch. I could feel his breath expand in his chest.

"Gideon," the voice came a third time.

His dark head lifted and he turned his head to eye the woman rounding the corner.

"What do you want?" he growled, conveying his displeasure at the interruption. I winced for the poor discarded fool who continued to chase him.

"I would like to speak with you." The voice was cool and calm, if somewhat annoyed. "You make it difficult."

"Well, as I said, I'm a little busy at present," he said, turning to face her and bringing me around as he did so. One hand was on my shoulder, the other laid possessively just above my chest – not inappropriate enough for me to protest, but enough that anyone looking at us would be in no doubt of our intimacy.

Fidelma's face was genuinely surprised as she took me in.

"Cassandra?"

The High Druid was who he was avoiding? My face burned. What must she think of me? Despite our brief previous acquaintance, we hadn't really spoken since her arrival. I had hoped it was because she didn't want to be seen to favour Devyn, though I was aware she was also working with Ewan and Marcus in the healing chamber. I couldn't meet her eyes now. What could she want with Gideon? Surely not... She was ancient.

"What are you doing?" she asked. I looked up to see which of us she was addressing as I squirmed inwardly, but her gaze was directed over my head.

"What does it look like?" came the insouciant answer. I was going to kill him. What was he playing at? I was mortified.

"It looks like you play childish games," she sighed sadly.

"If you say so, druid," he said dismissively.

She stepped towards us and took his hand off my chest, for which I was grateful, despite the odd fleeting moment of—

No, there was no fleeting moment of anything. The sooner this oaf was no longer touching me, the better. The fact that even a corpse would welcome his clever touch was irrelevant.

My relief was momentary as he rested his hand back on my stomach.

"The time for childish things ends soon."

With one last look at the man behind me, she was gone.

As soon as her footsteps faded, I threw off his hands and whirled about.

"What in Hades was that?" I hissed. But I pulled up short as I took in the expression on his face. Gideon, whose impassive features rarely revealed more than his usual cavalier smirk, looked like a crushed little boy as he stared in the direction Fidelma had taken.

"Gideon?" Without thinking, I lifted my hand to his face to soothe the pain I saw there.

His hand caught mine before it could reach him though, a more familiar arrogant expression now in place.

"What's this? You interested in a little more, Cat?" He stepped closer to me once again, this time for nobody else's benefit but his own.

"Aargh." I ground my teeth, refusing to acknowledge that his proximity was bothering me. "My name is not Cat."

"You wish me to call you by the name the Romans used for you? No, my lady. I will not. The Griffin calls you Cass; it is not so dissimilar and you don't object to him?" An eyebrow challenged me to explain why Devyn was allowed to be the exception. "Besides, I like it. You are a hissy little thing."

"Get off me." I had never felt more in need of hitting anyone in my life. The desire to knock the knowing smirk off his face was overwhelming.

"As you wish, m'lady." He stepped away. "But if you ever need a little warming on a cold night, I'd be happy to oblige."

And with a knowing wink that said he was well aware that I wasn't as indifferent to him as I pretended, he was gone. Insufferable, odious, arrogant—! My brain couldn't supply the adjectives fast enough for my fury. What was that all about? I loathed him. Whatever was between him and Fidelma baffled me but was not my greatest concern.

The lingering warmth of his touch on my belly was wearing off and I rubbed the heel of my hand across my front just to wipe away the last traces. The whole thing had been strange. Druids. The only thing even more incomprehensible than a Celt.

That evening, there was a change in tone from the almost casual question-and-answer sessions of the preceeding evenings.

"Lords and ladies, you were assembled here to judge the case of Devyn Glyndŵr who broke his oath to the Lakelands. Lord Devyn, you gave your oath to Mercia following your father's exile, is this true?" the High Druid asked.

"It is." Devyn stood tall and alone in the centre of the room.

"What was that oath?" Every bone in my body tightened at Fidelma's question. They had spent the last few evenings concentrating on what had happened since Devyn left, and now they were going back to the beginning to discuss the offence itself.

"To serve the Kingdom of Mercia until my last breath."

"An oath you then broke?"

"Yes."

Even though everyone in the room was more than aware that Devyn had left his lord, there was still an audible intake of breath as he responded.

"Why did you forsake that oath?" Fidelma's attempt to remind the court of his good intentions was cut off as Lord Montgomery interjected. As an Anglian, his stance had been much more martial than the others' throughout the trial, focusing on obedience and allegiance and so on.

"What does it matter why he broke his oath? His word was given – the highest bond in our society. If I cannot believe in the integrity of the fealty and promises given to me or the loyalty that I owe to my people in return, then all would fall asunder."

"He was a child when he gave his word," Llewelyn objected.

Fidelma leaned across the table, raising her palm for silence.

"Devyn Glyndŵr, do you feel you were too young to be bound by the oath you gave?"

"No."

What was she doing? Dammit, why wouldn't Devyn say anything to defend himself?

"Why then, did you forsake it?" the druid probed.

"I believed I had a prior obligation."

"What was that?"

"My duty to the Lady of the Lake is gods-given and, as such, I believe takes priority over my sworn word," he replied matter-of-factly. He wouldn't lie to this court, I realised, no matter how crazy his answers would appear to them.

The lords looked at each other.

"What duty could you owe to the lady so many years after her death?" Fidelma had tested me in Londinium and had deemed me no more than a powerful latent. She had no idea that he had succeeded in his quest. This line of questioning about why he had abandoned his oath to chase ghosts would make him look reckless at best and utterly unhinged at worst.

"I did not believe her to be dead." Devyn's tone was implacable and it was easy to visualise now the intractable boy he had once been, whose insistence on the impossible had so maddened a grief-stricken court.

Rion Deverell's face was stony as he became the centre of attention, all curious to see what he made of Devyn's insistence that his mother and sister weren't murdered all those years ago.

"You believe the lady was captured and kept in Londinium all these years?" Fidelma clarified.

"Yes."

This time, the High Druid herself looked at Deverell for his reaction.

"If the lady were alive, your father would have said so. As the Griffin, he would have been able to sense her. He would have been driven to go to her," she reasoned with Devyn. "He wouldn't have faded into his exile under house arrest."

"My father's duty was over. Mine is not," Devyn stated blandly.

"Are you saying that the lady's daughter is alive?"

"I believed she was," Devyn answered, stepping around the question.

"You felt her and you were compelled to go to her?" the druid asked.

"No. I couldn't sense her, but I knew she was still alive."

"How?"

"When I was sixteen, some of the gifts of the Griffin manifested. I believed it proof that she lived."

"So, you went to Londinium," Fidelma completed for him.

Devyn bowed his head, his back straight but his head lowered in deference to the court.

"Yes."

"Where you have stayed until now."

"Yes," Devyn answered simply.

"And in these many years you searched for the new lady, did you find any trace of her?" Lady Emrick asked.

"I thought I would be able to sense her once I was in Londinium, but no, m'lady, there was no trace that she was alive through the bond we had shared when she was a baby," Devyn answered carefully. For years, he hadn't been able to sense me, the bond between us having been broken since the day my mother died. His only clues had been non-magical ones he found inside the city's databases, something in the perfection of the records alerting him that they were manufactured. It had been enough to give him the belief that there was more to me than met the eye, despite my lack of magic.

"Yet you did not return home?" Lady Emrick pushed.

"I had to be sure." Despite all the evidence to the contrary, he had refused to give up on me.

"And are you sure now?"

"Yes, m'lady."

Gideon's eyes flashed across at me, deeply frustrated at the farce playing out in front of us.

"Your participation in the tragic events that took place in the borderlands stripped your family of all honour. The King of Mercia took pity on you and allowed you to foster in his home and learn alongside his son so that you might still have a life worth living. You swore that oath of loyalty freely and it is to your shame that you walked away and broke what was left of the lord's heart. He did not live long after your desertion," Lady Morwyn recounted.

Devyn had remained rigidly controlled but this was news to him, and he swung jerkily to face Deverell, looking for confirmation. The King of Mercia did not even deign to flick his eyes in Devyn's direction, but that was confirmation enough.

Nobody had thought to tell him. Deverell had chosen to say nothing, though he must have known what a blow it would be to the boy who had grown up in their home.

As for myself, I dismissed the flicker that ran through me. I didn't have time to deal with learning how my father had died, right now.

"Do you have anything to say in your defence?" Fidelma asked, her eyes flicking lightly to me.

Still stunned at the blow, Devyn said nothing. Our hopes were pinned on his transgression from years ago being blamed on his youth and his commitment to his responsibility as the Griffin. Bronwyn's eyes locked with mine, her grim expression telling me to stick to the plan to avoid adding the complication of my resurrection and our subsequent decision to prioritise Devyn's health over my safety.

But surely once they knew he had succeeded in finding me, his transgression of leaving would be forgiven? It certainly sounded like his being the Griffin, and the responsibilities that came with that, overrode any other promises of loyalty he might give.

The jury of peers removed themselves from the room to deliberate.

They were not gone long, and on returning they were sombre and difficult to read.

The High Druid, lords and ladies lined up behind the table and remained standing.

"The court has reached a decision."

My stomach sank as I took in their grim expressions.

"Hear me out first, I beg you," Llewelyn interjected. "I have no son. Give my nephew into my care and I will—"

The druid lifted her hand and Llewelyn was forced into silence.

"I have already heard your proposition, Lord Llewelyn. Your appeal is refused."

What was she doing? Why wouldn't she let him appeal? He was Devyn's last chance. Fidelma looked to her left and right to make sure none of the other nobles planned any further intervention.

"As Lord Montgomery and Lady Morwyn have said, integrity and fealty are central to our laws and society. Devyn Glyndŵr, you have repeatedly broken this most fundamental pact. Your word cannot be trusted and you sit beneath the worms in the ground. We all live in service to a higher goal – to the gods, to the land, to the water, to the air. You serve none of these and so none will serve you. You will be taken from this court and the axe shall end your life, whereupon you shall be burned so that no trace of you remains to burden the earth. That is the court's decision. Sentence to be carried out immediately."

I couldn't have heard correctly. Death? My hands pushed the hair off my face and I looked up, but I couldn't see. My skin felt as if... They couldn't do this. I wouldn't let them do this.

I stepped forward. Marcus's hand tried to restrain me but I pulled away and swung myself out onto the floor.

"No!" I was fairly vibrating with anger. My voice was shaking with it.

Devyn attempted to stand up and speak, but I couldn't hear anything over the roaring of surf and thunder in my ears. I would bring this castle down on top of the lot of them.

All eyes were on me as a wild wind whipped through the hall.

"You cannot kill the Griffin," I stated.

Lord Montgomery laughed dismissively. "Griffin? There is no Griffin. "

"Devyn Glyndŵr *is* the Griffin," I repeated.

Llewelyn barely reacted, his hollowed eyes still registering the verdict. The King of Mercia watched remotely from an expressionless face. The other lords looked at each other in confusion.

"My child, you don't understand. That title is no more; it was given to the protector of the Lady of the Lake." Lady Emrick hesitated. It was a heavily guarded secret that the lady had died all those years ago. It was a subterfuge Devyn owed his life to – that all the Britons relied upon to protect them from the council and the imperial legions. Killing the Griffin and his son would only have added substance to any rumours of the lady's death. The Britons had managed to keep it quiet for years, to ensure that knowledge of it never made it as far as the walls. Or so they had thought. I was more convinced than ever that the praetor knew all too well that the Lady of the Lake was dead because he was the one who had killed her.

"The lady is dead, and her line is broken. There is no new female heir to her power," Lady Morwyn explained gruffly. "With no lady to protect and his oath broken, the Griffin's life is owed to no one but himself."

"And this court finds that an Oathbreaker has little use for it himself," Lord Montgomery said, his lip curling as he spoke.

"His life is owed to me. He is my Griffin."

I turned my back on the nobles and crossed to Devyn. His intense, dark gaze burned into me as he stood and we locked eyes for a moment before he nodded. My life might still be in danger, but he would not lay his neck bare for the axe if it meant leaving me unprotected. The storm of shouting and speculation was no more than a murmur to us, background noise inside our private bubble.

I turned, my hand taking Devyn's as I faced the crowd. A deathly hush fell.

Rion Deverell had left the high table and now stood in front of us. He was preternaturally still.

"*Your* Griffin?" he said tonelessly.

I met the stormy eyes that were the only indication of the emotion swirling inside him. Gideon had made his way onto the floor and stood at his lord's shoulder, his face stoic, showing no indication that he knew anything.

"My Griffin."

"I found her," Devyn said from beside me, his hand squeezing mine as he finally delivered the news to my brother that he had succeeded in the mission he had set out on almost ten years earlier. The mission that had caused him to break the very oath for which he had just been condemmed.

"It's true, Rion," Bronwyn added as the wind died in the hall. "He wasn't sure when we were in Londinium. He's sure now."

"How?" Just one word, chipped in ice.

"The bond has returned."

Deverell's eyes narrowed.

Gideon stepped forward, his mouth twisted. "I've seen it.

She has powers. The hounds didn't drown the way we said; the Severn took them for her. She pulls in more energy than I've ever seen before. The air, the water... the earth itself responds to her. "

The blue eyes in front of me locked with mine as he froze. Then his eyes flicked to our interlinked hands.

Suddenly, our hands were wrenched apart as Devyn went flying across the floor as a result of Deverell's fist connecting with his face.

Gideon reached for the king as he yanked Devyn to his feet in apparent preparation for striking him again. Gideon held Deverell back, whispering in his ear, his muscles bunching as he restrained him. I swear it felt as if the ground shook from the forces contained in that embrace.

Deverell's eyes cooled, his steely control in place once more as he thrust Devyn away from him before striding out of the hall. People stumbled over one another in their rush to get out of his way.

Llewelyn called for order, and the court consulted with each other as the seconds drew out into minutes. The crowd whispered urgently at the shocking revelation and Devyn was ushered from the court by the guards, who at a nod from Llewelyn escorted him back to his room.

The castle was in turmoil after all the drama of the trial. Oathbreaking was a serious crime here, and not everyone was happy that he had been released, especially following Rion Deverell's violent reaction.

There were still guards posted outside his door. But were they there to keep Devyn in or others out? Their lord's nephew had been convicted of oathbreaking and condemned to death, then moments later hailed as the hero who had returned their lady to them against all odds. People needed time to process it. Llewelyn had acted swiftly to remove Devyn, which ensured that the mood didn't escalate and allowed people time to absorb the news. This also left me a window during which everyone was too busy talking about us to notice us and I slipped away.

I marched purposefully up to Devyn's door and proceeded to open it without knocking. Surprised by my boldness, the guards were slow to react. One had watched me coming, so had had a little more time to gather his wits and he attempted to block me. But I gave him the most incredulously haughty expression I could dig up and carried straight on through the door before confusion gained the upper hand on his caution. Right now, the repercussions of the revelations had yet to be evaluated and new orders had not as yet been given, so who was he to block me from my sacred protector?

Devyn sat slumped against the far wall as if he had come into the room and, without pausing for breath, found a wall and sunk down against it.

I turned the key in the lock, no doubt to the chagrin of the guards outside, but as they had no way of knowing if this was against the new rules, they didn't challenge it. After all, I had identified myself as one of the most senior figures in the land. Who were they to challenge anything I did?

"Devyn," I called, when he failed to look up at my entrance. I was uncertain how to proceed.

"Hey," he said. I crouched beside him and took his head in my hands, lifting his face towards me so I could see him.

"It's over," I said softly, when he refused to meet my eyes. I

363

gently placed a kiss on his lips. "You're free. It's all going to be okay."

I kissed him again, trying to tease a response from him.

"You're free," I whispered between kisses. "You're alive."

He pushed me away and I sat back with a bump, off balance from crouching on my toes.

His dark eyes were turbulent.

"At what cost?" he snarled, suddenly alive again.

"Cost?" I shook my head. What was he talking about?

"We didn't want the world to know you were alive yet. That was all very public; the whole island will hear about it.What if the poisoner comes for you again?"

Ah, it was his usual trigger that we had somehow endangered my safety. "Stop it. Stop whatever crazy self-flagellating nonsense is going on in that head of yours. The main thing is that you are not going to be executed. You think your death would have kept me safe from whoever poisoned you? They no doubt already knew who I am. And they might not even have meant the poison for me. You believe that because you think the world revolves around me. It doesn't, you know." I glared at him. Did his life mean so little to him?

"It does for me," he growled back.

My eyes widened at his words and I couldn't help it. My mouth trembled as I tried to suppress it. He was in deadly earnest. A giggle popped out. Was this snarl the declaration of love I had waited so long for?

He was on me in seconds, his fury giving him momentum until he loomed over me, his dark eyes sparking down at me. As if by sheer force of will, he was going to make me see that revealing myself to the court to save his life had been the wrong move.

It was ridiculous, and the ridiculousness bubbled out of me

as the relief and joy and sheer happiness at his reprieve washed through me.

"I love you too," I laughed up at him.

He snarled down at me. An actual snarl – and then it was gone as he took me in. I was there in his arms and he was going to live. I could feel the series of realisations hit him.

He swooped down on me and kissed me hard and fast and completely. The flames whooshed over us as we ignited. His mouth swept mine and our breaths entangled. My fingers looped in those dark curls as I crushed him to me. It was all I could do to remember to breathe, and I wasn't sure I even did that anymore.

His hands pulled at the intricate lacings of my Celtic dress, releasing me more skilfully than I managed to every night, his early stubble sweeping across my bare shoulder. Sensation tingled my skin as I came to life beneath his touch. My neck arched away from him as he curled into it, his mouth tracing its way across the tender skin there.

I pulled in a deep breath as his lips moved further down my body.

He backed away and looked down at me as my eyes struggled to focus on the mischievous curl of those talented lips.

"Not laughing now, are you?" He nipped my lower lip with his sharp teeth, the sensation twanging through the haze his earlier onslaught had created and ratcheting up the heat that was building inside me.

I groaned as I clung to him. No more thoughts, only sensation, touch, heat.

I scrabbled to release his shirt, yanking it over his head, in a hurry to lay my hands on his warm, velvety skin. Removing his shirt revealed black ink and raw skin over his heart.

I paused at the sight of the tattoo and the inflamed skin around it. Devyn looked down at the pattern that had caught my attention. It was a Celtic swirl, of course, but still it was recognisably the emblem worn by the Mercians: red roses and lakes. I had been forced to look at it every day of the trial as it sat front and centre of the jury's table. Since the prosecuting lord and highest ranking individual was lord of Mercia, the Mercian arms had dominated the table. This was a similar design but woven into a Celtic knot.

"Why?" I asked, tracing the air above it.

He sat up, pulling me with him. His eyes darkened as he pulled my dress up over my shoulders once more.

"When I left, I was too young to bear ink. I was glad of it when I got to Londinium as a tattoo would have all too easily revealed my origins. But tattoos are what we on this island use to proclaim our history, our affinities, our loyalties, our lives. My skin was unmarked. I did not want to enter the afterlife with no story." His eyes locked with mine. "I have a story."

I traced the roses and the lakes etched over his heart, careful not to touch the tender-looking skin. He said nothing as I contemplated what he had chosen to represent himself in what had so nearly been his final days. My brother's coat of arms.

His vow to Mercia was how he had defined himself.

"Oh." I felt a little jealous. He had chosen my brother over me.

His brow furrowed as he took in the disappointment I was helpless to conceal.

"The form is a dara knot, signifying my oath to Mercia… to him. And for us…" He took my fingers in his and lightly carried them across a swirl that branded his arm, the curves

366

winding up and down through the tattoo in a vaguely recognisable pattern before ending in a Celtic symbol.

"The Tamesis," I smiled. He had included the river, the one which had separated us and on whose shores we had found each other again. "The river flows into a triquetra, signifying life, death and rebirth."

I felt his answering smile through the bond.

"And for you…" He turned his back and my eyes almost fell out of my head. He must have really missed being able to ink himself while living in the city. He certainly couldn't be identified as anything other than a Celt now. Across his entire back was etched what, from Rhodri's description, I knew to be a griffin. Celtic knots and swirls looped across his back in flaring wings while the watchful eyes of the eagle looked straight at me and the powerful lion's body was poised. And there, at its heart, was a crown. Me.

He turned back to face me. This time it was Devyn who caught my face in his hands and I turned my gaze from the ink on his skin to his eyes.

"I love you," he said and kissed me again. This time it was warm and deep as it reached into shadowed parts of my heart that had existed in darkness for so long that they barely recognised the light he brought with that kiss.

When he pulled away again, I felt an all-encompassing warm haze, as if sunshine had bathed my soul. He smiled at the state his kiss had reduced me to.

"That good, huh?"

I blinked.

"That must have taken some time?" I asked inanely, giving myself a moment, as I pushed at his bare shoulder so I could examine his back again. "How did you do it?"

He laughed at my question. So, my brain wasn't firing on all cylinders in that moment. I was aware of this.

"Llewelyn was not so confident of the trial's outcome that he would deny my request. It is a tradition and is unveiled when the chosen Glyndŵr takes his place at his lady's side," he explained. "He sent some of the best artists he could summon at short notice. They weren't entirely happy about doing the griffin; one refused to work on me at all. But Hari knew me as a child and he said that if I had dedicated my life to serve as the Griffin despite everything, then that was a story I had a right to own."

I exhaled in awe at the intricacy of the tattoo, at the sheer size and power of it. The eagle's eye that seemed to capture something of Devyn's watchful gaze that had followed me for almost half my life. The integrity and loyalty shone in every line.

I looked again at the one on his chest that signified Mercia.

"He's angry," I said. It wasn't exactly news, but with Devyn's cheek starting to swell from the punch that had landed there, it also wasn't something we could ignore for ever.

"Yes." Devyn was resorting to monosyllables. Never a good sign.

"Because we didn't tell him straightaway." In fact, we couldn't have found a worse way to tell him what should have been good news.

"Yes."

"And he didn't like us holding hands."

"No, he didn't." I had to restrain myself from rolling my eyes. I understood that these were painful subjects for him, but a little insight here on how we could resolve this wouldn't go astray.

"You don't think he will allow us to be together?"

"You heard him. He will not forgive a third betrayal."

"Us being together would not be a betrayal."

"In his eyes it would be." His tone had gone flat, deadened, the words all too familiar, the start of a downward cycle that he repeated over and over.

"Enough. We've talked about this. Give me a chance to talk to him. I'll make him listen." I smiled at him.

I stood, straightening my dress and composing myself in order to hide all evidence of the recent activities that wouldn't help our cause. Unlocking the door, I said before exiting, "Anything is possible. You found me, after all."

Chapter Twenty-Two

The hall was busy with people decorating every available surface with holly and ivy for Yuletide, which began on the Winter Solstice less than a week away, when Gideon found me the next morning, his familiar expression of lazy arrogance something of a relief. Since the dramatic ending to the trial and the revelation that Devyn had succeeded in his quest to find me, people had been acting strangely around me. I wasn't just risen from the dead, I was the new Lady of the Lake; people looked at me as if I was a legend come to life which, I supposed, to them I was.

I hadn't seen Devyn since yesterday. I had tried to get in to see him again, but the guards posted at the entrance to the lower part of the castle now clearly had new instructions. And they were Mercian guards.

Gideon had come to escort me to the King of Mercia's rooms where I had been summoned to speak to Rion.

"That was quite the scene," he said with a smirk as I scurried to keep up with his long legs.

"Yes," I said, my stomach churning. I was grateful to have

370

finally upgraded from the second-hand clothing to a fantastic Oban creation. The dress was cut in the Celtic style but it had a flavour of something else to it, something unidentifiable. Like me.

We walked in silence for a few minutes.

"The High Druid, she..." he started slowly.

"Fidelma." I frowned slightly. She had sentenced Devyn to death. I supposed she had no choice but to carry out the duties of her office. She had concealed our previous acquaintance and I could only assume that she had been overruled by the majority behind closed doors. Even though she hadn't been able to sense who I really was, she had warned me that Devyn was not for me. Had she in some way foreseen what was to come?

"Hey," he snapped at me.

I jumped, startled.

"What?" I put a hand to my heart, which had already had a rough few days.

"I need you to listen to me."

"I am listening," I said tartly. We were nearly at Rion Deverell's room. We were finally going to meet as... family. He had barely looked at me yesterday, beyond that moment where realisation had sunk in.

"Dammit." A large hand circled my upper arm, bringing me to an abrupt and unexpected halt.

I scowled up at the manhandling oaf. We were back to this?

His jaw had a tic jumping at the side; the careless Gideon was really worked up. I tilted my head. How curious.

He exhaled roughly.

"Fidelma is..." He ran a hand over his jaw roughly. "You shouldn't trust her."

""Why not?" I asked. Where was this coming from?

371

"I'm not saying she's your enemy, just that she..." He shrugged. "She has her own reasons for doing things. I see how you... Just be careful."

Be careful? Out of all the Britons I had come across, she was one of the few who had ever helped me. The High Druid had been the only person apart from his uncle to have tried to give Devyn a fair trial. I frowned as Gideon knocked on the door and the call to enter came from within.

Rion Deverell hadn't paid me a great deal of attention since his arrival; I'd had a chance to study him though. But I couldn't even guess at his reaction to his sister's return from the dead. My existence shifted the balance of power in Britannia, but would that bother him? Would he be glad?

He was sitting at a desk when I entered the room and made no move to come around and greet me. It felt like I was entering the principal's office for a dressing down for some sort of misbehaviour.

He looked up at me, his expression collected and formal as he gestured with a snapped wave of his hand for Gideon to leave. Ouch. No wonder Gideon was off with me. Helping to conceal the truth of my identity must not have gone down well with his liege lord.

"I apologise for not summoning you sooner," he started, his composure even.

"Summoning?" I echoed. Seriously?

He stood, shaking his head slightly.

"I didn't mean... that is, yesterday I was angry. Not at you. That is, I was taken by surprise." He stopped, a wry smile tilting at his lips while his blue eyes met mine. "In all these years... He always said... I never allowed myself to really believe... To dream..."

I stared as the oh-so-dignified and regal Rion Deverell

372

disintegrated in front of me. I had had time to think about what this might be like and had been observing him for nearly two weeks. This was clearly a shock for him.

I smiled back, a goofy, lopsided thing that spoke to everything swirling around inside me. He returned it and got up to come around the desk.

His eyes surveyed me intensely, taking in every feature, every expression, as I did the same to him.

"I can't believe after all these years you will really be coming home." He hesitated, a flash of uncertainty crossing his face. "Fidelma would like you to join her community in Glastonbury, to train to tend the leys as the lady has done for generations. I was hoping that first you might come home."

Home. The word thrilled through me. I nodded.

"I'd like that," I said, and a broad smile lit up his face. "What is it like? What was it like to grow up there?" I had so many questions.

"Beautiful," he said, his smile fading. "Empty."

He had grown up without the family that should have been his.

"How old were you when...?"

"I was four when Mother died. Father held on until I was in my teens but he was a ghost after she died. He was all heart, and when she was gone, so was he, really."

"Do you remember her?"

"A little," he confirmed. "Feelings mostly – her laughter, her sheer force of will. You have her temper, and her way of... I don't know how I didn't see what was right in front of me." he exhaled. "Catriona."

He pulled me into his arms and it felt right. It felt like the welcome and security of home. Finally, a home. He was family, someone who would love me unconditionally, simply because I existed.

I pulled back. I wanted, needed, to see his face. Did we look alike to others? Did we look like brother and sister.

"Rion and Catriona?" I asked.

"Yes, my— *our* mother liked the way they paired." He smiled again, as if unable to hold his happiness to himself. "Ridiculous, I know. The Lady of the Lake usually has a more traditional name."

"Like what?" I asked, only vaguely focused on this conversation. Most of my mind was still marvelling that this was really happening. I felt giddy with it.

"Like Nimue, after the lady who aided Arthur back in legend, or Evaine, or Viviane, like Mother."

"Viviane," I sounded it out just to feel it roll off my tongue. "Catriona, Cat... Devyn calls me Cass. Do you think it's because it sounds similar?"

His face clouded at mention of the disgraced Griffin.

"There can be nothing between you and Devyn Glyndŵr, do you understand?"

Okay then, we were clearly done with the "I'm so glad you're alive" small talk. I was more than happy to be direct as well.

"No."

"He is an Oathbreaker. His father failed my mother. *Our* mother," he corrected himself. "He was just convicted of it and sentenced to death. He may be your protector, but I own his life."

"They can't possibly mean to kill him now?"

"The sentence can be lifted." He straightened into his full height. His expression was carefully blank once again. "He will be allowed to exist in the shadows, but that is all. If I do not reverse the decision of the court then he will be shunned. Am I clear?"

"You can't do that."

"I am the King of Mercia. He is my subject." His blue eyes were glacial in his regal formality. "If you want him to continue to breathe, you will do as I command."

"As you command?"

"You will marry Marcus Plantagenet and unite the north."

I stared at him. I felt as if I had been punched. All the air left my lungs in one go.

Queen to king. Checkmate. His move was final, but I didn't have to play on his board.

"You do not get to command me to do anything. I am your sister." But my voice shook; he was my only family and all he was concerned about was what he might use me for – like everyone before him. "I am not your subject. I will marry who *I* choose. Not the Empire. Not you."

My anger was met head on.

"You will do as I tell you. " He looked down at his desk, his voice still cool. I had noticed that it was something he did when his control was starting to slip. I was beginning to sense that his temper was every bit as volatile as mine; he just hid it better. And my refusal was definitely triggering him. He was not used to being defied.

He took a deep breath before rounding the desk and resting back on it, his body leaning towards me as he granted a single concession.

"He can remain your protector. But he is an outcast. He ranks lower than the cur at my heel. And you will accept that, or I will have his head separated from his body."

His face was utterly expressionless. He was in deadly earnest. The power of life and death lay in his hands and here in the Briton world, there was no mitigation by the commons. His word was law.

My hand was shaking as I held it out to him. A denial, a plea, I couldn't think. My vision blurred.

What could I say to make him change his mind? He couldn't do this to us.

He took my hand in both of his and pulled it to his chest. His face softened.

"Catriona." He caressed the name in awed tones, as if now that the hard part was out of the way, he could take a moment to acknowledge me as his sister again.

"Please, don't do this." My voice cracked.

His jaw flexed.

"I warned him that I would not forgive him a third time," he ground out. "I warned him. And he lied to me."

"He didn't lie," I rushed. "He just couldn't tell you yet."

"And why, dear sister, could he not tell me?"

He knew precisely why. This was why I hadn't seen him last night; he had been cooling off. Thinking. Examining the moves on the chessboard. Deverell had figured out the reason for our delay, thus compounding our initial mistake. I hadn't thought through to the next move on the board. He had. I said nothing.

He flung my hand away and kicked the chair beside him, sending it crashing into the wall. I could feel the suck of energy. By this man's side was where Gideon had learned to soothe the powerful; the icy control was a veil my brother drew over a power that felt as wild as my own untutored kind.

"He has deceived me for the last time. I never want to hear his voice again." He was vibrating with emotion. "It is enough that I allow him to stay with you. He is the Griffin; it is his gods-bound duty, and I will not break that. But no more shall he have."

I saw my life stretching out in front of me. Locked into marriage with Marcus as yet another regime manipulated us for their own purposes while Devyn was consigned to the shadows of my life. At least in the city I had been trapped in a cage spun with sugar and pretty promises. Here, I was being propelled into the same future against every fibre of my will. Blackmailed into submission by threats against the one thing I cared about. At least my parents had pretended to love me, even though we shared no blood. Yet here stood my full-blood brother, destroying me with every word. My parents had disowned me and I had understood that somehow. But this action by this man whom I did not know inspired more heartbreak than my abandonment by the parents who had raised me. In this moment, I had never hated anyone more.

"I regret that this is hard for you, but my decision is final."

I left the room without another word, making my way to find Marcus. He wouldn't agree to this. He needed to tell them.

I found him in Ewan's room, messing about with potions. When I told him what had happened, he didn't seem surprised. "It seems that everyone wants us to marry except you and me."

"Tell them you don't want to marry me. They can't marry us if you refuse," I urged. How had I not thought of this before? Marcus was the Prince of York; he could not be forced into this against his will.

"Devyn will be pardoned as long as you go along with this," he reminded me. "I will agree because it will buy us some time. We'll figure out the rest."

"How?"

"You doubt that I can fix this? Here in the Wilds, where we

know no one and understand even less, with these infernal cuffs tying us together and everyone watching us?" His lips twisted wryly. "I'm hurt."

A laugh bubbled inside me. He was right, but we had been in tighter spots before.

I finally pulled myself together and answered him.

"Okay, husband-never-to be, let's get us out of this."

That evening I ate alone in my room, pleading a headache. The next day, Bronwyn and I met as usual for our morning ride, barely out of the bailey gate before she rounded on me.

"Cass, I need to talk to you. About you and Devyn," she started.

"Did my brother send you?"

"What? No." Her face was heavy with concern under her deep hood. "When I told you before that you and the Griffin can't be together, I thought that you understood."

"I do understand," I said tightly. Marcus was going to figure it out. I just needed to appear to accept it. To pretend, even to my friends. "Rion has made it perfectly clear. I'm to marry Marcus, just like the Empire wanted."

Bronwyn brows drew together, even as her shoulders relaxed at this news. "Oh."

"Yes. So if we could just enjoy our ride...?" I nudged my horse forwards into the grey wet day and there was little further conversation.

Day after day dragged by, while at night I was forced to face everyone again and sat at the high table, stiffly aware that I was the subject of everyone's gaze in the hall. Everywhere I went, servants and guests alike watched me with bated breath as I walked by. Where previously I had been subject to a kind of veiled resentment, now they all looked at me like I could walk on water and light the sky with my touch. And what did

I know? Maybe that was something within the gift of the Lady of the Lake.

For now, I just felt awkward and watched, like an exotic animal from the far reaches of the Empire sitting in a cage in the forum. Unlike everyone else going about their normal life, I was a useless marvel whose only purpose was to be pointed and wondered at. Marcus sat on one side of me, effortlessly engaging his neighbour in conversation; he had lived his whole life in the spotlight and probably didn't even notice the attention he attracted here, never mind the extra that my new status attracted. Rion Deverell sat on my other side, giving up after his attempts to engage me were frostily rebuffed. I looked out across the great hall. Long tables were filled with people laughing and talking loudly with each other, and servers bustling between the tables. As always, no matter how hard I tried, I realised my gaze wasn't aimless but scanned the room with purpose. Searching, always searching... Where was he?

I hadn't seen him in the days since the trial. The Mercian king had issued a reprieve of the capital punishment but had not forgiven the crime, so every time I asked anyone where Devyn was, they either acted like I hadn't spoken or replied that they had no idea who I was referring to.

There. He was leaning against the wall in the shadows, an absence rather than a presence. He was so still he was barely detectable except for the fact that the noise and bustle of the hall seemed to be repelled in the few feet surrounding him. Just as the nobles ignored him, so the lower social strata also gave him a wide berth. His outcast status was a tangible thing. No longer using the skill which had allowed him to blend in with any crowd in Londinium, here he was a beacon in every room. His intensity and sheer physicality were impossible to ignore and yet they clashed so severely with his lowly status

379

that as soon as he entered a room it was like a loud bell going off, as everyone studiously persevered in their efforts not to acknowledge him.

It made me furious, but that didn't make it any easier for Devyn to bear either. I took another sip of wine, watching him from beneath lowered lashes. As I watched, a rather shapely server crossed into the no-go zone around him; apparently not everyone steered clear of him. I saw him return her smile and had to stop myself from clenching my teeth.

Devyn had been physically avoiding me for days, but he'd also been blocking me out. Did he plan to comply with the law of the lands he had returned us to, despite all his promises? Was he giving up? But what I had learned over the course of our trials so far was that if an emotion was strong enough, it could cross any barrier he put up. And this far into the handfast with Marcus, nearly all my emotions were strong.

Concentrating, I recalled the first time we had danced together – or nearly danced together – at my father's house. I had tried to flirt with him – my way of getting past the mask he showed the world – and I'd hoped that a kiss would induce him to drop that mask. My body warmed at the memory. I followed it by recalling our first frantic kiss in Londinium's stews, the fire that had ignited between us, leaving us both shell-shocked. My breath shortened as I began to sift through the memory of the night before my handfast, the night Devyn and I had… I drew a lazy hand across the bare skin of my neck, retracing the path of his fevered kisses.

Devyn's lazy stance against the wall changed. His body became alert and even though he steadfastly refused to turn in my direction, I could tell his face bore a scowl. I squirmed in my seat; my attempts at provocation had rebounded back on me and I was every bit as affected now as he was. I saw his lips twitch in hidden salute to the change in emotion as my desire became tinged with frustration. I stifled the giggle that suddenly bubbled up through me, hiding it by taking another hasty sip of wine. I snuck another glance in time to catch a warrior walking past Devyn startled at finding himself on the receiving end of a full grin from the usually serious Griffin.

I sat back satisfied and caught Gideon watching me.

"More wine, my lady?" he asked, leaning across Rion and giving no indication that he had watched the interplay between me and the disgraced Griffin at the end of the hall.

"Thank you," I said demurely and smiled my best society smile.

At the end of the meal, Prince Llewelyn stood and the hall hushed to hear him speak. I felt rather than saw Devyn stiffen. I had no idea what was coming next.

"Ladies and gentlemen," he began, "as you all know, the Lady of the Lake has been returned to us. Her brother has graciously accepted my invitation to remain with us for the Winter Solstice festivities to welcome in Yuletide and celebrate in her honour."

A cheer went up around the hall, and I smiled stiffly. Rion Deverell stood and raised a cup in my direction. I refused to meet his eyes. He could say whatever he liked but I would not make this easier for him. He had decided. But I had never agreed.

"Twenty years ago, my mother and sister were lost to us, and the legacy of the Lakes was snuffed out. My sister's return is indeed a blessing I could never have hoped for. To have her returned safely to us is a boon to my house, my country and our entire island. With her, she brings another bloodline we had thought lost to us. With the joining of Lakes and York, we honour the gods who bestowed their great gifts on our blessed people. Such a tie can only strengthen all our lands and bring to an end the warring between our tribes. To the marriage of Catriona of Mercia and Marcus of Anglia."

The announcement fell a little flat in a hall full of Celts of Gwynedd who had no cause to celebrate such a union.

He stepped back and made his way to the end of the table where Bronwyn was now standing. I felt Marcus stiffen beside me.

"Before the twelfth day of Yuletide we shall also celebrate the joining of my house with House Cadoc of Kernow. The lovely Bronwyn has consented to become my wife when we return to Carlisle."

Deverell wrapped an arm around her and dropped a kiss on her cheek as the hall erupted in approval. Bronwyn hadn't told me. But then, I hadn't exactly given her an opportunity since I had lied to her face about my relationship with Devyn.

How neatly he had united all the great tribes south of Hadrian's wall. No wonder he had been furious that I might disrupt his plans by refusing to marry Marcus. With his announcement, for the first time in centuries, the major houses of the province of Britannia had been neatly brought together, concentrating power and uniting the various forces. Londinium and the council would hear of this.

I could barely think as I sat there, trapped, at the high table. He couldn't do this. I didn't want this. My blood boiled in my veins. My earlier silent flirtation with Devyn had been crushed by my brother's high-handed announcement.

At the end of the meal, Fidelma came over to me and took my hand in her delicate ones, attempting to give me comfort.

"The Griffin is not for you," she said. "It is better if you accept this."

"Better for who?" I asked bitterly, shoving my chair back

from the table. I was tired of everyone telling me I couldn't be with the man I loved. I stumbled from the noisy hall and down an empty corridor. I needed to be anywhere but there.

Then suddenly my shadow was there, tangled around me as we crashed through an open door into a chamber off the corridor. We kissed, lips hard against lips, his fingers tangling in my hair and pulling it back, the better to expose my throat to him as his teeth grazed across the vulnerable skin. His mouth returned to mine, taking, owning, demanding, and I met him stroke for stroke. His anger met with my ferocity.

He lifted his mouth and pulled me tight against him, his muscular body taut and coiled against mine. I needed to bring him back and so I softened my body into his. We were one. We would find a way out of this together.

"I thought you had given up on us again," I said accusingly into his warm neck.

"I told you I wouldn't," he reminded me. "I thought we would have time. I thought that if we let Rion cool off, he might come around. But it looks like we are out of time. There is no way out of this."

"There is. There has to be," I insisted.

"No. He has announced it publicly. For you to break it off now would be a political disaster. He has promised you to York and York will not let you go."

"Marcus *is* York and he will be happy to release me."

"Not yet he isn't. The steward has ruled since the last Plantagenet died. Gideon's father is ruthless, and having a Plantagenet on the Anglian throne again gives him power and it is to York's benefit if you marry Marcus."

"There is still a chance for us. I haven't had time to work on Rion." He was my brother; surely I could persuade him against adding to York's power? "I was caught by surprise before, but I'll—"

"You don't understand. Allowing me to live is as far as he can push it. To break the betrothal in my favour..." Devyn stepped back from me, running his hands through his hair. "It would be suicide for the King of Mercia even to consider such a thing."

I shook my head, my breath coming fast, as his initial reaction had cooled to resignation. I could feel him closing himself off.

"No, no, let's talk about this. There must be a way."

"There is a way." Marcus appeared in the doorway, his abrupt intrusion scaring the daylights out of us both.

Devyn's expression revealed nothing, but he waited for Marcus to speak.

"Get married."

"What?" I asked. What on earth did he mean?

"You and Devyn. Present them with the deed done and then Rion can't be blamed," he suggested. "It's one thing to pressure you into fulfilling a contract already made, but it's another for him to force you to break a more serious one, no matter how fresh it is."

"But how? No one here would dare defy the the King of Mercia's announcement."

"We'll go to the Holy Isle before everyone departs after the Winter Solstice. They can do it there."

"What about the handfast cuff?" We knew it was supposed to come off when we married, but until then it couldn't even be cut off.

"I've been looking into that. Ewan took a look at mine. He was very interested to examine one up close. They don't use them out here," he said, referring to the Britons, as he always did, as they, as *other*. "Apparently the cuffs just drop off upon marriage. He thinks it's a contract charm and he's fairly certain that the marriage doesn't have to be to each other. Once the contract has been completed by one of the parties, the cuff is released."

"He wasn't suspicious of you asking him that?"

"He had no reason to be." Right, because as men of science, discussing possibilities about how things worked didn't necessarily mean there were ulterior motives. If only all people worked like that.

"No." Devyn had heard enough.

"The druids in Anglesey won't know you," Marcus reasoned.

"It's not about the druids. I will not defy my lord in this," Devyn stated.

Marcus's green eyes met mine. He was as good as his word. He had found a way, and now all I had to do was persuade Devyn. Marcus would be ready.

Devyn observed the look between me and Marcus and his mouth set in a flat line.

"I'm telling you, it's over," he said resolutely, blocking me so I could feel nothing of him as he strode from the room.

"We'll see about that," I shouted to his retreating back. He had explained why Rion couldn't forgive him, and he was clearly torn in two by his divided loyalties. He loved me. He had shown me that enough times now. But he was also sworn to serve Rion, and persuading him to publicly humiliate his king would be next to impossible. But I wasn't ready to give up yet.

Chapter Twenty-Three

The bonfire to celebrate midwinter lit the courtyard from early evening, and from my window high up in the castle I could see out across the town and countryside where more fires glowed. I leaned against the cold granite wall, which cooled my heated skin. I felt exhausted as I emerged from yet another day hiding in my room. Despite the days spent cooped up in this castle doing nothing, my energy felt lower than it had when we were on the road.

In the days leading up to the beginning of the Yule festivities, Devyn was a ghost. He haunted the shadows but made it impossible for me to engage with him. He would slip away at any attempt to try to talk him round.

This morning I had felt strangely off and utterly defeated, merely curling into the warmth of my blankets against the icy winter air and wishing for the comforts of home. There was no point in getting up. Devyn continued to avoid me, the castle's inhabitants wore me out with their whispers every time I walked past, and there was no chance of being allowed outside the castle walls. I had managed to convince the maid who came to stoke my fire that I was feeling peaky so couldn't attend the dawn service to greet the Solstice and she had all too readily brought me my breakfast, delighted to be of service. I'd hardly touched the unappetising porridge and barely nibbled at the edge of the griddle cakes that I normally enjoyed, and this had earned me lunch in bed too.

I'd finally managed to pull myself out of bed at Marina's urging when she and Oban arrived to deliver the creation he had made for me. Marina was in an odd mood and disappeared quickly, leaving me with her brother as he made the final adjustments to the beautiful dress. The sounds of laughter and music and the smell of crackling woodsmoke wafted in from outside.

I entered the celebration on Marcus's arm – an oddly familiar role. The stage might be different, but our roles within it were strangely fixed. A harpist had arrived from across the sea to celebrate the feast at Conwy. I'd never heard a harp before, and my mind snagged on the sweet ribbons that floated melodically on the air. The notes were haunting and lonely. Even as other instruments joined in, I could feel the winding central tenet of the music as if it was always set apart, intrinsic to the tune but never entirely of it.

This feast was in my honour, apparently, and as Marcus moved me from group to group with his usual natural ease, I felt observed and judged. I looked the part – the velvet dress was divine, moulding and flowing around my body in all the right ways. Its intricate cut and painstaking embroidery were a testament to Oban's artistry. My hair was plaited and left long, and a gold circlet was placed around my crown to denote my status.

The room was festooned with holly boughs heavy with red berries, which Marina, fountain of all kinds of new knowledge, had told me was the sign of a long winter. There was also some precious mistletoe dangling over the doorway where we had entered. Marina had also informed me that this was a traditional decoration. With so many ill who needed it, to have even this small amount being used for this purpose was an extremely decadent gesture. Yet Llewelyn had some put over the doorway anyway, allowing everyone to walk underneath and have its blessing of love for the year bestowed upon them. Yay.

I had been forced to stand under it for longer than most, as Llewellyn toasted my return and the impending nuptials.

As our genial host, he had swirled me out onto the dancefloor when the music picked up, the beat of the drums and the tempo of the music proving a temptation impossible to ignore for many guests. For a moment, I was in the arms of the only other person under this roof whom I knew to be as frustrated as I at Devyn's fate. I let my mask drop, allowing myself to become one with the music, and followed his light-footed lead.

When the tune ended, he thanked me and bowed deeply.

"Prince Llewelyn, I will do what I can to help Devyn."

He raised a brow. "Lady, he found you, he restored honour to his name, and I hope it will lift some of the heaviness from my brother's heart. What more could I ask for him?"

"You offered him your title?" If the offer still held, maybe I could persuade Devyn to accept and we could stay here.

"I would be glad to have the boy rule once I am gone, but it was always a fool's dream. It was an offer made to remind people of his blood, but it could never be. He broke his oath. No man or woman would ever trust him enough to swear their allegiance to him."

"But he did it to find me."

"Yes, lady." He looked puzzled at my lack of comprehension. "The duty he owes you is beyond the laws of man. He did the right thing, but he broke our laws to do so. He broke his word to his king. You might trust him in all things, but no other in our lands ever will."

He smiled sadly and took his leave.

I frowned at the gap he had left. Especially since Rion Deverell stepped into it.

"Will you dance with me?" He grimaced at my failure to respond. "It is expected."

His hands were sure as he moved me in the correct steps of a courtly dance which, once again, had the mournful harp as the pre-eminent instrument.

"You are avoiding me," he said, sombrely pushing me away before twirling me back in.

"What do you expect?" I had waited a lifetime to have family, and the disappointment was crushing me. Not only had Rion taken Devyn away from me, he had taken something much more fundamental, something I had never dared to hope for myself.

"I had hoped to get to know my sister." His voice was soft, careful.

He thought I would get past this.

"What? Before you send me off to York with Marcus?" He had spoken to me of the home that should have been mine then moments later informed me of his plan to send me away.

His eyelids dropped, concealing his emotions. "Catriona," he began.

"My name is Cassandra." I glared at him. He did not get to tell me who to marry and who to be as well. Catriona did not exist; the girl who they all thought had died on the banks of the Tamesis outside Londinium had not come home. I had.

He winced, his eyes lidded again as he inclined his head in acknowledgement.

"I would wish that we had more time but I understand that the handfast has already gone on dangerously long."

I maintained a stony silence as he twirled me across the hall.

"I would like us not to be enemies," he tried again.

"Then don't force me to do this."

He paused long enough for me to hope, to dream that he was considering my wishes, that we could rewind and begin again. That we could be family first before pieces on a chessboard, to be moved about in political manoeuvres.

"These are dangerous times. For the battle to be won, this is the game that must be played," he finally said. This was the philosophy he lived by, and now apparently expected me to live by too. "It is for the best."

"For you. Not for me. Not for—"

He stopped cold.

"Do not say his name. I do not know what has occurred between you, but he does not get to have this. After everything, this is too much. He has no right to reach so high."

"If our lives had been different... If our mother had not died...?" I pushed.

His eyes took in the observing crowd and he swung me round to the tune once more.

"But she did die. And Devyn and his father were at fault. The Griffin failed her."

Our mother had played her own part in what had happened. Why should she condemn Rhodri to shame for all eternity and leave four-year-old Devyn to be held accountable? I hesitated for a moment. Devyn's father had made a confession that I was reasonably sure no one else knew. There was probably a good reason he had never told anyone before. More likely, knowing his son, the reason was foolish pride, but I couldn't keep it to myself. This man had a right to know. Her death, and the events surrounding it, was one of the defining moments of his life; he should have all the facts.

"She bound him. Our mother bound him with a vow that he would keep Devyn alive at all costs."

"What? Why would she do that?" His eyes flickered as his quick brain worked through the angles of this new information.

"I don't know, but you see, he didn't betray her. Rhodri followed her wishes, despite what he wanted himself."

He rolled his shoulders.

"I don't know why she would have done such a thing. But it changes nothing," he said finally. "Devyn still lives. And tomorrow you wed Marcus."

"Tomorrow?"

My chest felt tight, so tight that it could crush the very life out of me. "The druid tells me that the handfast has already gone on too long. The Steward of York arrives in the morning. Why wait any longer?"

My vision blurred as I looked past him, searching the room. He couldn't do this. I wouldn't do this. We were out of time. My sight cleared as I sought the shadows of the room. There. My eyes met intense dark ones across the merry music. Could he sense my panic? His eyes were like those of the eagle on his back as he tracked our movements and I knew he could tell that something was wrong.

I broke free of my brother's arms. I needed a moment to breathe. A large form materialised beside me, sheltering me from the crowd, manoeuvring me as I stumbled blindly to the exit.

I found myself at the walls of the castle, the sea air whipping through me, blowing out the panic that Rion Deverell's words had brought about in me. My knuckles were white in the dark as I gripped the battlements.

"Breathe," the gravelled voice behind me commanded.

I pulled the fresh tang as deep into my lungs as I could, feeling the oxygen reach the depths of my mind and body. My soul lightened in response.

Trapped. I was trapped as surely as I had been in the cells beneath the arena.

"I won't do it."

"Won't do what?" asked Gideon.

He tracked my eyes as I contemplated the other side of the castle where freedom lay.

"Hey." Gideon pulled me around by my arms to face him. "What did Rion say to you?"

"Your father arrives tomorrow," I informed him. Surprises were the worst. The least I could do for Gideon in return for getting me out of there was to warn him that the steward was on his way.

"Right." His tone was bleakly expressionless at the news.

"In time for the wedding." My tone was equally bleak, but with a tad more expression than Gideon's stoic response to the news of his father's imminent arrival.

"Ah," he said in understanding. "To Marcus."

It wasn't a question.

"Rion means well. He has been preparing for war ever since your mother died. Our protection from the Empire rested on the pretence that his mother lived and the magic was strong. Both of those protections are gone now," he said in defence of his lord. "You are known to Londinium, and they do not fear you. Your magic is new and unmastered, and the

392

powers your mother wielded may never be in your gift. He is acting swiftly, doing what is in his power to ensure our survival."

I understood all this and more. Of course I knew I wasn't strong enough to defend the Britons as my mother might have. Though what use had her powers been to her when she had fallen so easily under the hooves of the sentinels' horses? She hadn't been able to protect her baby daughter, much less an entire island.

"I have waited my entire life for a family of my own."

"You will have that," he assured me gently in the dark, his body moving closer to mine as if to warm me. "You will have a brother and a husband. You have a family."

I didn't trust myself to speak as a wave of self-pity washed through me.

"Like you do," I said, tracing the scar that slashed down his right cheek.

He huffed a breath in acknowledgement of the hit. "Your brother is not my father," he said quietly. "You've just got off on the wrong foot."

I exhaled in disbelief. The wrong foot was if I had accidentally spilled something on him, or been rude before I knew who he was. Rion Deverell had put the love of my life on the ground and then threatened to kill him. Repeatedly.

"Isn't he?" I asked. "What did your father do to you, Gideon? Because a man I've just met is forcing me to marry someone against my wishes because it is to his political advantage."

"You don't understand. It's not as simple as—" Gideon spoke quickly to defend his friend, displaying no surprise at learning that I did not want to marry the man everyone believed I was happily betrothed to.

"Cassandra?" The call came from the bottom of the stairs. Marcus's form took shape in the moonlight as he came up the steps and emerged from the shadows.

"Your brother sent me to find you." His eyes snagged on my hand at my neck, reaching for my absent pendant, and Gideon's position so close to me. I summoned up a small smile in greeting that I knew failed to reach my eyes. Gideon, of course, didn't move an inch.

"You can go now," Marcus said to Gideon in dismissal. Marcus had always been top of every pecking order, his position here even higher than it had been in the city, and he knew how to use it to his advantage.

Gideon's lip curled in response. I was pretty sure he knew Marcus and I only played at being together in order to hide my relationship with Devyn. But we were officially to be married now so he could hardly refuse to leave us alone together.

"Okay?" He waited for my consent before he left us, his route ensuring that he took his taller, broader frame closer to Marcus than the battlements strictly required on his way past.

"Ass," Marcus said, as Gideon made his way slowly down the stairs before casually sauntering across the courtyard, back into the light and music and laughter that emanated from the great hall.

"You know he enjoys pissing people off."

Marcus grunted.

He took my cold hands in his before shrugging off his jacket and wrapping it around my bare shoulders, sheltering me from the biting breeze. "We need to go."

"What?"

"Rion tells me we can finally get these bloody armbands off tomorrow." He spoke in a low voice, his words for my ears only.

"I know." The words felt as heavy as lead. "He told me."

"I spoke to Rion earlier today about us. I tried to persuade him, but Fidelma has advised him that it's dangerous for us to remain handfasted any longer. We need to leave tonight."

"We can't."

"You want to be with Devyn, don't you?"

"He won't do it. Rion Deverell will never forgive him."

The consequences of our actions would be too high a price for him. Devyn had refused to give up on me but he had also made it clear that he would not easily break his word to his liege lord. Not again. Not even for me.

"Would you rather be married to me and living in York? The Anglians are hardcore; Devyn's life would be a living nightmare. You saw how Gideon treated Devyn. He stabbed him on sight. You see how it is now. He's a non-person, and he's only allowed to skulk about in the shadows near you because they consider it his sacred duty." He spoke urgently. "They won't kill him for marrying you, you know that. You'll be able to live together here or in the Lakelands. I'll go to York and they'll get over it."

Marcus's words were convincing but I wasn't so sure. I had heard my brother in the stables that day. Devyn had cost him his family and been forgiven. He had then become the closest thing to family Rion had left and Devyn had abandoned him. Rion Deverell was an unyielding man; he asked and gave no quarter and yet he had loved Devyn beyond forgiveness. Twice. There was a reason Devyn had tried to push me away; he'd known this would be the thing that broke them for ever.

"We can fix it. Once the deed is done and you are married, they will have to accept it. I will be the King of Anglia and your brother will come around." His tone was softly persuasive. "We need to get to the druid community on the

Holy Isle of Anglesey; the druids there can marry you. Hopefully the news won't have reached them yet."

"Devyn will never agree." Nobody wanted this. Not even Devyn. Maybe I should stop. Maybe it was for the best. "If we do this, whatever alliance exists between Anglia and Mercia will be destroyed. It will be a fracture down the centre of this island. If the council comes for them when they are too busy fighting each other, they'll be annihilated. Maybe Devyn is right."

"You're giving up?"

I shrugged. I had resigned myself to marrying Marcus once before and maybe I could do so again. The wrongness of it threatened to choke me. To have come so far, and to end up living this half-life anyway... The irony was killing me.

Marcus took hold of my shoulders. "I will speak to Devyn. He has to do this now, before it's too late."

"You think you can persuade him? How?" I had barely even seen him all night. A single sighting, that was it. Did he already know what we had just learned? Was that why he was avoiding me? Delaying the inevitable of telling me for the latest and final time that we could not be together. Was this what my future would be like, knowing he was nearby but unseen, waiting on the edges of my life, and appearing only when I was in danger? Watching me be married to Marcus?

"I will find a way. We have to go tonight. I will have horses waiting at the back of the herb garden." Marcus looked determined. "Be ready; we leave after midnight with or without him."

A strange laugh escaped me. "Without a groom?"

"You think if you leave Conwy he won't follow?" Marcus's eyebrow lifted, making clear his scepticism at such a possibility. "Now, come inside before you freeze to death."

"I've been looking for you everywhere." Marina skidded to a halt in front of us at the entrance back into the castle, dismay written large on her face when she saw Marcus was with me. "Can I speak to you alone?"

"Later," I promised her.

"No, now." She hopped from one foot to the other, her tone beseeching in spite of her stubborn position.

Marcus gestured towards the great doors and the festivities within.

"It's fine. I need to find someone myself," he said, taking his leave.

"They are saying that you will marry Marcus tomorrow," she started, as soon as we found an empty room to talk in. "You can't."

"I can't?" I tilted my head. "You're the only one who thinks so."

"No, really, you can't. You and Devyn, when we was in Londinium, I thought that maybe you liked him..." Her eyes narrowed. "I saw you kissing him in the hallway."

I pulled in a shaky breath. "I can explain..."

"You don't need to explain nothing. But well, I think you and him have been... together. And I noticed you haven't been eating much the last few days. My mum, she couldn't eat either early on. So I asked Madoc if there was any way of telling for sure. Don't worry, I ask him loads of things so he won't think nothing of it."

"Nothing of what?" I interjected. I didn't have time for this. I didn't have any time. I needed to think. Was Marcus right? Should we go tonight and damn the consequences?

"Oh, you haven't realised. I thought maybe you knew and were going to marry Marcus anyway, but then I thought maybe you didn't and that's why I had to ask Madoc how—"

"Marina," I ground out.

Her eyes rounded.

"You haven't maybe missed your time of the month recently?" she asked, biting her lip.

"What does that have to do with...?" A hand stole to my mostly flat stomach. I had put on a little weight but I'd blamed the griddle cakes. Was it possible? My mind scrambled to calculate the weeks that had passed since I last had my period. It had been in the city before we left. I hadn't even thought of it; we had been on the road for most of November, I had been distracted with the poisoning and then the trial, and it was midwinter now. "I'm pregnant?"

Marina gave a crooked smile. "I think so."

"How?"

Her eyebrows shot up, that cheeky smile creasing her face. "You really want me to explain?"

"Ha, ha," I replied weakly. It had to have been the night in the city before the handfast. "Did Madoc tell you how to check?"

She nodded and put her hand out to me, taking it in the traditional grip. Her inner wrist pressed against mine as she closed her eyes. A slow smile spread across her face.

"Congratulations," she offered, her face twisting, knowing as well as I did how complicated this made everything.

A child.

I took a deep breath. It certainly helped focus the mind.

"Find Devyn. Tell him." My voice trembled. Would he be pleased? It put him in a corner but I knew him; his duty to me would compel him to defy Rion once more. "We need to leave tonight. Tell him to meet us out the back of the kitchen gardens after midnight. I will let Marcus know that Devyn will be coming. He has a plan."

"What plan?"

"For Devyn and me to marry before anyone can stop us."

Marina clapped her hands, hopping up and down on her toes. "Really?"

"Yes, hurry. And don't tell anyone else." She rolled her eyes at me, already halfway out the door.

I spread my hand across my belly and the new life that was contained there. A life that Devyn and I had created.

Marcus had a plan already in place. It had to be tonight.

We would figure everything else out tomorrow.

Chapter Twenty-Four

The mood was merry in the kitchens as the staff were finally able to enjoy the fruits of their labours and eat all the food they had cleared from the great hall. After an hour or so of drifting around the party looking increasingly wan, I had finally made my excuses, blaming a headache for my early exit. I made my way through the feasting staff, some still busy carrying fresh platters and jugs out to the celebration beyond.

I smiled and nodded at their happy greetings to the long-lost Lady of the Lake until I thought my face would crack from the strain. My exit through the kitchens might be more public than using one of the quieter doorways, but in the hustle and bustle I was also less likely to be challenged. People were in and out of the door all night. The main doors had sentries posted who were a lot more likely to take note of the guest of honour going outside and not returning to the party.

I finally made it out into the clear night, my heels clicking across the flagstones as I kept close to the walls, hoping the shadows would conceal my passing as I made my way to the kitchen gardens. The door was closed but the latch opened, and I slipped silently through.

And was immediately caught around the waist and pulled back against a broad iron chest.

"Well, well, kitty cat, out for a midnight stroll?" His breath was warm in my ear. My stomach plummeted. Gideon.

"Let go of me." I pulled at the velvet-encased band of steel that had wrapped itself around me.

"Of course, my lady." In a fluid motion he spun me around and, taking my hand, bowed low over it, his lips touching briefly on the backs of my fingers.

"Allow me to escort you back to the festivities. Your brother will be so relieved that your headache has cleared," he added drily, his gleaming eyes meeting mine in the moonlight. "And I am relieved that I have not missed the opportunity of a dance."

He didn't believe me, not for a moment. What had given me away? Why had he followed me? I didn't for a moment take his presence here to be mere coincidence.

"Did he send you?"

"Your brother? No, Cat. What reason would he have to think your journey to your room after such a big day would take you via the gardens?"

My mind raced. What possible reason could I give to explain why I was here?

"I wanted to gather some peppermint to make a tea… to help clear my head. "

"Of course you did."

Why was it every time Gideon said *of course*, it sounded like he was calling me a liar? I was lying, but that he saw right through me was damned inconvenient.

Well, damn them all. My spine straightened.

"Let me go, Gideon," I said softly into the night. He knew

where I was going. I was suddenly sure of it. That amber gaze missed nothing.

"Don't do this, kitty cat." His voice was equally low, the gravel in his tone making my heart sink. Gideon behaved as though he answered to no one, and the only person to whom I had seen him show any loyalty was my brother.

I swayed, unsure if my legs would hold me. Tears sprang unwanted into my eyes and my lower lip trembled. There was no way I could speak without betraying my despair. I took a deep breath to steady myself.

Devyn was waiting. If I didn't make it to the meeting place, he would come in to look for me. Or would he assume I had come around to their way of seeing things and accepted the inevitable? Everyone was against us. His family, my family, even Devyn himself.

But there was a tiny life inside me that needed a father, and I would give it all the security, and family, and love, that I had never known. Whatever it took. Even if it meant lowering my pride in front of my least favourite Briton.

"Please…" Damn. Despite my best efforts, my voice broke on the word.

Gideon stood unmoved.

"I'll come back," I promised.

The door to the kitchen garden opened behind me and I turned at the noise. Marcus stood frozen in the open doorway.

I looked back to see Gideon blink in confusion. It confirmed my long-held belief that he had seen through our pretence, and the fact that Marcus was the one who had come out here to meet me had him stumped.

I couldn't help the smile that tweaked my lips. Even in my desolation, having got one over on Gideon was gratifying.

"He's outside already," I explained.

Gideon's lips thinned. Seeing Marcus would only have reminded him of the enormous political repercussions of letting me go. Marcus and I were city-born so we were less invested in the political machinations of the Briton world, but Gideon was keenly aware of the shattering impact my union with Devyn would have.

I was messing this up. I could see Gideon's resolve hardening, his fingers tightening on my hand which he had never released. I had nothing to lose. I pulled his hands to my belly and held it there, revealing the truth that my body had only just begun to share: the bump that sheltered the life that beat inside me.

Gideon's eyes widened as his hand warmed my abdomen.

"Cat..." he breathed. His eyes glowed hotly at me, nostrils flared as his eyes shuttered. He drew in a controlled breath before lifting his eyes once more to mine.

"What have you done?"

"She was conceived long before any of this. She should have both her parents – a real family." Somehow, I was suddenly sure I carried a girl; I could practically feel her pleasure at being acknowledged. A soft smile touched my lips at her fledgling emotion and, looking up, I caught the sudden conflict in Gideon's gaze.

"Please," I breathed again, pressing his hand closer to the life that I had just introduced for the first time. "Gideon."

His muscular body stilled. I wasn't even sure he was still breathing. I reached up and laid my hand over his heart, which inside that immovable body beat steadily. It was a comforting, grounding beat.

"I'll be back. I'll owe you a dance," I said and then, "I promise."

I knew how he felt about promises. I knew he had no faith

in them and that he gave none himself. And yet I gave him mine. I would be back to face the consequences of my actions, but I would do this first. If they weren't all so bloody rigid in their ways, then I wouldn't need to run away with Devyn. I had to believe that Rion Deverell would forgive me after the fact.

"Go," he commanded.

He removed his hand and took a step back into the shadows. I hesitated for a moment. Was he really letting us leave?

"Go." His tone, this time, had an edge of exasperation to it.

I whirled around and was through the door to the waiting Marcus before he could change his mind. Marcus took my hand and we hurried along beside the well-tended herb beds and under the bare fruit trees.

At the far wall, Marcus pulled me to a stop as he retrieved two packs from behind a low-lying bush. The warm cloak was a welcome sight.

"Devyn told me they'd be here," he explained. "Marina, and her brother."

"I told her not to tell anyone."

"I'm not sure she counts her brother as anyone." He smiled, wrapping the fur-lined cloak around me.

"I thought for sure it was all over," he said of the scene at the far side of the garden.

"Me too."

"Why do you think he let you go?" It was a reasonable question. Marcus hadn't been close enough to see or hear the interplay that had made Gideon step aside.

"I told him about the baby," I said, smiling.

Marcus's face changed, and if it weren't for the darkness, I would have said it greyed.

"What?" His voice was off.

"Marina figured it out," I explained. "How do you think we got Devyn to agree to this?"

He opened his mouth and closed it again. He pushed a hand through his hair. I was taken aback at his reaction. Gideon had been angry – that I could understand. My pregnancy by the disgraced Griffin was a major upset to the expectations that his lord, my brother, and everyone else the length and breadth of the island, had for me. Marcus didn't want me; we had never felt like that about each other. Maybe it was a lingering effect of the handfast, the news catching him unawares.

"All the more reason for us to do this," I said. "They'll have to agree to let us marry anyway; this means we can just skip the arguing part."

"Yes, of course," He shrugged off his surprise. "Let's get you two hitched then."

He bent down, taking up both our packs, and then we were out of the gate, through the outer wall, and down to the treeline and the waiting Devyn.

Devyn was there with two horses. The last time I had met him like this, in the moonlight under the trees, it had been in an attempt to run away to a new life. This life. A life together. Last time our plan had been scuppered by the handfast tie to Marcus, so this time we were bringing him with us. There had, of course, been the small matter of the armed soldiers who had been in pursuit, so hopefully this time would be nothing like that night in Richmond.

Devyn slid off his horse at our approach and lowered his

face to mine for a slow, lingering kiss full of promise. His hand went immediately to my belly.

He leaned his forehead down against mine.

"It's true?"

"Yes," I said.

His eyes were bright with a light that went all the way through to the core of him, as he laid a palm against the tiny bump. He kissed me once more before stepping back.

"You're late," he growled. "I thought you might have changed your mind."

"Ha. Me?" I scoffed. I was the steadfast one here. He was the one who was always trying to do the right thing and leave me. "As if. It's hard to slip away when you're a miracle brought back to life, you know."

"I wouldn't know." If I was the rainbow, then he was the dark cloud that people only suffered because they couldn't have me without his sacrifice. It was a mantle he donned all too readily for my liking.

"Gideon caught me," I said, as much to distract him from his train of thought as anything.

He looked past me up the path we had arrived by, immediately on alert.

"He let me go."

Devyn looked at me in disbelief. To be fair, it was a fairly unlikely turn of events. If everyone else wished that Devyn would disappear accidentally, then Gideon would be more than happy to provide the accident.

"He let you go," he repeated, still surveying the treeline. "I don't suppose you asked him to be best man while you were at it?"

"You made a joke!" Devyn was always so serious. Was this a sign that he was happy at last?

He huffed and handed me the reins of my horse.

"Maybe we can make him godfather while we're at it," he added.

I almost fell back mid-mount.

"Ooh, two in a row," I teased, as he actually chuckled aloud at my ungainly stumble.

The night was magical as we rode through the countryside, a thing of silk and possibility, an ebony coverlet full of stars on a perfect crisp winter's night. For once, we were dressed appropriately for our journey. It felt strange to be just the three of us again. Strange, but right. And so we rode on, uninterrupted.

It was near dawn before we arrived at the Menai ferry to take us over onto the island of Anglesey. The moon had started to slide away, but the sky was lightening in front of us as we made our way westward through the thickly forested hills. The smell of bonfires from the various celebrations still lingered over the land.

As we approached the bridge that would allow us to cross over from Anglesey onto the holy isle, the sky had finally begun to lighten, casting a red-gold light out across the crashing shoreline. The salty scent of the sea mixed with the smoke...

Smoke that was far too dense to be the lingering residue of the previous night's midwinter bonfires.

"Devyn?" Something was off.

He had already halted.

"Stay with Marcus," he commanded shortly as he rode ahead at a gallop.

"Damned if I will," I muttered, and urged my horse forwards in pursuit. The druids were under attack, but who would dare to touch the holy men and women? They were

407

deeply respected, and more than a little feared.

I had my answer as we reached the top of the hill and looked down on the fleet of tall ships anchored in the bay. They were flying the flag of the Empire, and Londinium.

The community below us was burning, and the sentinels were showing little mercy to those who tried to flee, striking them down with gun and blade. I would show them no mercy either. I jumped down from my horse as I centred myself and reached for the power in the forest around me, just as Callum had taught me. I willed the elements to come at my command.

As so often happened when I consciously tried to summon the energy, it failed me. But no, this wasn't that. It was gone; it wasn't there.

This I recognised from before. "I can't feel anything. I'm blocked."

Marcus looked at me with widened eyes. "Me too. It's gone."

"We've got to get help," But how? We were many hours' ride from Conwy. The ferry – they could send someone to Conwy to raise a resistance force.

"I'll go to the ferry. They'll be able to raise the alarm."

"Let me go," I countered. "If there are any injured people down there, at least you can be of some assistance, even without your magic."

"No," he said. "You stay here. It's too dangerous. Stay out of sight. I won't be long."

I watched him mount and ride away and then looked about for a place to hide. My saddled horse would give me away if any of the soldiers came this way, so I took off the saddle and bridle and shooed her away. Free of the tack, she was happy to be gone.

The growing dawn light overtook the firelight visible in the sky. Devyn hadn't returned. He should have been back by now. The bond between us was wide open; but with the handfast cuff curbing it the thrum of his anger on seeing the fire in the sky had quickly faded once he rode away.

The trees were bare in the winter landscape, making me feel vulnerable and exposed. A thick holly bush was my best option and I crawled into its hollowed centre, feeling like a coward as I waited for Marcus to return.

But I couldn't touch my power no matter how hard I tried, so what use would I be to anyone? I felt blocked, but how could that be? It had to be something I ate or drank last night at the feast. In all the excitement of the night and the revelations about the baby, I had failed to notice it, but now I felt that same slightly blunted edge that I had experienced at the hands of the council in Londinium. I had been surrounded by friends – well, maybe not quite friends, but not enemies either. Who at Llewelyn's table could have slipped something into my food or drink to cut me off from my powers?

"Cassandra," the hushed call came from nearby. Marcus was back. I extricated myself from my hiding place.

"Marcus," I hailed him as he walked further on in search of me. I ran over to him. "Did you raise the alarm?"

"Yes. The ferryman has a way of signalling along the coast. They'll be on their way now."

"How long before they get here?"

"I don't know. They'll be faster than us once they're on the move because they will be travelling in the light, but it'll take them time to gather their forces."

"They'll be too late."

"We could go closer," he suggested. "Whoever attacked the druids is probably gone by now. I should check to see if I can help."

Anxiety was gnawing at me now. Devyn had been gone so long. I needed to know what was going on. Even if the attackers were still there, we could keep out of sight until help came.

"I'm coming with you," I stated. I would not be talked into staying behind a second time. Marcus's eyes met mine. Something flickered in his – a moment of hesitation. I readied myself for an argument. He seemed to resolve it for himself and put his hand out for me.

With my own horse having gone gods knew where at this point, I had to clamber up in front of Marcus. The light of the burning buildings scorched the dawn sky as we made our way closer to the community by the beach.

We climbed a hill to the sound of flames crackling and cries of pain, eventually coming to a circle of great oaks at the crest of the hill. It was the centre of druidic ritual and bodies lay fallen by the great rock in the centre.

I made to get down to see if we could help, but Marcus restrained me.

"They are beyond our help," he said.

"You can't know that." I squinted at the forms on the ground. In the low-lying mist of dawn, it was impossible to tell whether they were dead or if we could still aid them. I pulled free and slid off his horse, racing across the clearing to where several druids lay. I turned the first one I came to. Dead. His face was frozen in a grimace of pain that was clearly visible in the pale morning light.

"We need to get down there," Marcus urged, still not engaging with the fallen bodies. I had moved to the next body and the next. They were all far beyond our help.

I hesitated, assessing the site below. We were useless without our magic. We were close enough to see the buildings now and they were almost burnt out. Soon there would be nothing left but the wreckage of what had once been a druidic centre of learning and healing. Where was Devyn? The anxiety that had been nagging at me since he left now scraped its way up my insides and screamed for attention. Whatever had happened here, it was over. Some of the tall ships out in the bay had started to set sail. Several boats piled with what must be half a legion of sentinels were making their way out to them with what was likely the last of their troops.

"We're too late," I managed to get out, surveying the catastrophe that had unfolded beneath us.

"What about the mistletoe supplies?" Marcus asked. "We should check if they can be saved."

I surveyed the scene of nearly total devastation below. Most of the buildings were burnt out and bodies lay strewn on the ground. We were far too late. Nothing had survived down there. I scanned around for Devyn. Where was he?

"Dammit, Cassandra." Marcus exhaled. "We've got to get down there."

"There's no point. The mistletoe will already be burned. We'd be putting ourselves at risk for nothing."

"I'm afraid the point is that we have an appointment to keep," he explained grimly, advancing towards me.

I backed away on instinct, my mind struggling to comprehend what was happening, but aware that I needed to put space between myself and my friend.

I shook my head, backing up until I hit the central altar stone. I raised my hand as though I could prevent him from coming any closer by sheer power of will.

Marcus had betrayed us. Marcus had done this. I didn't know how or why but I knew.

I whirled around and started to run, hampered by the

gown I had worn to the ball and in which I had planned to be married. I was betrayed by the cloak that had warmed me as I rode through the night to a wedding which had never been part of Marcus's plan.

My cloak was caught, and the abrupt stop choked me about the throat and pulled me back. I landed on my back, stunned by the momentary strangulation. Marcus was on me in seconds, and while I was still blinking, had pulled my wrists together and tied them as I started to thrash. He was going to take me, take me to those murdering legions, back to Londinium.

I screamed through the bond. *Devyn, where are you?* In the borderlands the bond had conveyed my fear to him despite the handfast cuff's interference.

Marcus pulled me from the ground as I continued to thrash and do what I could to make it difficult for him to propel me along.

"Shh, Cassandra. Hush, be calm."

Marcus held me still and waited, waited for me to submit to his wishes. To realise I had no choice. Without my magic, I was defenceless against his superior strength.

"I need you to come with me. It's for the best."

I let myself go limp, allowing him to pick me up off the ground before I did the only thing I could think of and lifted my knee to where it would do the most damage. I took off as he curled to the ground with a suffocating noise. I ran as fast as I could through the circle and down the other side of the hill, back the way we had come. I ran but I wasn't fast enough. He was already behind me; I could hear his horse gaining on me. I took a look behind me to see how close he was, but he was already right there. My foot caught on something in the ground and I fell clumsily. I sobbed in frustration.

He dismounted and came to stand in front of me.

"Cassandra, it's time to go home. It's for the best."

"The best? For who?" I snarled as he pulled me up again only to throw me headfirst over his horse. He mounted behind me and clicked the horse into a trot.

"I'm sorry," he said over my back. "I did what I had to do."

"Traitor!" I accused, my voice muffled as I spoke from my ignominious position thrown over the horse like a sack of wheat, watching the ground as the horse made its way up and then down the hillside. I wriggled and pushed in an attempt to dislodge myself from its back.

"Stop," Marcus ordered, lifting me by the waist of my dress to rebalance me in a way that left me less leverage to get off this blasted nag. "You'll hurt yourself."

Hurt myself. I'd bloody kill him.

Marcus had set us up from the beginning. It was no coincidence that we were here this very morning and that Devyn and I couldn't reach our magic. Marcus had planned it. He had prepared our bags, and no doubt every drop of water we had consumed on the way had been spiked – if not at the feast itself too, where he would have had every opportunity. Just like when we had travelled out of Londinium. I gasped. Was he the one who had poisoned Devyn?

Step by step, we got ever closer to those waiting ships. The fire from the burning buildings heated the very air we passed through. The churned-up ground that was all I could see showed traces of blood and debris, bearing witness to whatever had happened here. I caught sight of an outflung arm, blood trailing along it and pooling underneath its owners unmoving hand.

"Damn," Marcus breathed, momentarily stilling the horse before he picked up speed. The motion unbalanced me slightly, and there was suddenly more weight on my front; with each bounce I managed to put a little more of my body over the horse. If I could shift my weight a little further over... Hopefully, I wouldn't break my foolish neck. I timed my effort with the bouncing of the horse and then, with everything that was in me, I launched myself off the side of the horse. I landed on my head, my body tumbling heavily in the mud.

Winded, I checked to make sure I still had use of all my faculties. *Hurry, hurry, get up,* I urged myself as I felt rather than heard the horse's hooves slow down as Marcus reacted to my near suicidal tumble. No time to think – no time for anything. I needed to get away.

I scrambled to my feet and, gathering my wits, tried to figure out my next step. Buildings were burning all around me, collapsing, sparks flying, with bodies lying still outside what remained of their homes. I snatched a glance behind me. Marcus had wheeled his horse around and his face wore an expression of shock and annoyance at my escape. But, surprisingly, most of his attention was focused beyond me.

I checked behind me in the direction of his gaze.

Gideon, my brother and a handful of warriors were careening down the hill towards us.

Marcus could come for me, but could he manage to bundle me back on that horse before they arrived? Unlikely. His horse whickered, pulling his head against whatever Marcus was doing to his reins. Marcus cast a glance behind him to the beach and the pier where a lone rowboat waited – for him. For us. My mind scrambled to process it. He had known they were here all the time. He had lied and he obviously hadn't raised the alarm while he was gone. Where had he been? What had he been doing? And where in Hades was Devyn?

Dread was a stone in my stomach. There was no one else

coming. My brother was here with just a handful men to stop Devyn and me; Gideon must have told him after we left. But they were alone. There weren't enough of them, and if the Empire had a chance to kill the poorly guarded King of Mercia...

Marcus wheeled around and rode towards me. I stumbled out of his reach and he halted, putting himself between me and the approaching Mercians.

"Cassandra," Marcus said as he dismounted carefully from his horse, "come with me."

"What have you done?" How could he have brought such destruction down on this community? And why?

"The mistletoe." He edged towards me. "I have to help the people. This illness kills so many in the city. I have to use it to help everyone."

I shook my head, again stumbling back and watching the oncoming riders behind Marcus. They were coming, they were coming. I just needed to stall him a little longer until they got to us. If Marcus decided to make for those ships and let them know that the ruler of Mercia was here, protected only by a paltry guard, it would be a disaster. I needed to keep him with me, to make him feel like there was enough of a chance that he could take me before the Mercians reached us. As long as those troops were on their boats, we would all be away before they could get back to shore and pursue us.

"That's why I'm here. The Britons aren't dying from it and we needed to figure out how," he explained gently, coming closer and closer, even as the shouts of the men riding on horseback towards us could be heard. They were coming.

"You got what you came for then. What do you need me for? Just go. Leave me here."

"I can't. I promised that you would return with me."

"Promised who?" Who had he planned this with? The council? The praetor? They had killed his father. Why would he have continued to work with them? "I don't understand... You were lying? From the beginning?"

He shook his head, still edging slowly towards me. "No, that night in the tower... You were right. Calchas planned to have Devyn attack you. My father was brought in to bear witness, but instead he convinced the praetor of a new plan. He persuaded him that if we could discover how they were treating the ill here in the Wilds, he would be able to end the plague in the city. Calchas agreed but only if I brought you back too."

"How were you ever going to do that? I would never return there. I would never leave Devyn."

"I know. I think... my father was the one who gave Devyn the poison. I'm sorry, I didn't know at the time, but it must have been him. It acted slowly enough to allow Devyn to see us north, but quickly enough to ensure that he would not live to see midwinter."

And without Devyn and my charm I should have all too easily complied with Marcus's desire to return to Londinium, if only the handfast still worked the same here.

I backed up a little further, swallowing down the bile that threatened to choke me. Another minute, that was all I needed. "So Calchas defied the governor in letting us go? But as soon as we return, Actaeon will have us killed."

"No, with the medicine to help those afflicted by the Malledictio, Calchas will be more powerful than the governor himself. He will protect us."

"How could you?" I indicated the broken, bloodied bodies strewn on the cold ground around us. "You exchanged our lives for those of our people."

416

"These are not our people," he sneered. "Our people are dying in their hundreds in the city. All you care about is your precious Devyn. And *your* magic, and *your* family. All you ever think about is yourself."

He looked behind him. The riders were nearly at the outskirts of the buildings. With a grimace, he mounted his horse, ready to ride to safety before my rescuers reached us.

"What about all the people you left behind? Did you ever once spare a thought for anyone beyond your gods-damned self, Cassandra?" he accused.

"Catriona!" I could hear Gideon and my brother shouting now. They were here. I was safe.

I shook my head at Marcus, but was he so very wrong? I hadn't looked back on my old life once, not really.

"You can't leave," I raised my arm, the sleeve falling back to reveal the cuff. He looked back to see what I meant, his face flashing a momentary concern.

"They can remove it," he informed me, and with a glance at the quickly approaching horses, he offered his hand to me to go to him. "You have to come with me."

I shook my head in disbelief. An almost hysterical laugh escaped my lips. "I don't think so. I'll go ahead with our plan and get it off by marrying Devyn."

He looked to the boats waiting at the pier. He took hold of his reins as the sound of the approaching horses grew louder.

"Cassandra, they have Devyn."

"No, no, you're lying."

I searched inwardly, reaching for Devyn. It was faint but I could sense him now, he must be nearby. His emotions were a steady beat of anger and tension. He was trapped. Marcus was right; they had Devyn.

I twisted to look over at the shore, blinking at the sight

before my eyes. No, it couldn't be. A dark figure stood amongst the sentinels on the pier. Matthias. Marcus's father was alive.

And in the last remaining boat, bound with his arms behind him and held by two guards, was Devyn.

They had Devyn.

I ran, ran towards Marcus and away from the warriors riding to my rescue. Marcus's strong arm swept me up and we were away and galloping along the beach.

The thud of the horses in pursuit was close behind. They were gaining but we were already pulling up and jumping off the horse at the pier.

I was tackled to the sand, and the air went out of me as the solid weight of my assailant flattened me to the ground. I tore at the hands holding me, struggling to get away, fighting to get to Devyn.

"No!" I screeched, tearing, writhing to get free of the arms that loosely held me. Gideon's grimly determined eyes snagged with mine and I managed to scratch my way free of him. Gideon. It was always Gideon getting in my way.

Pulling myself to my feet in the dragging confines of the ruined velvet gown, I had barely made it two more feet before the same set of arms wrapped themselves around me, caging me in. I stilled. I was no match for the thickly corded arms that held me tight.

Matthias's voice boomed out across the water as the boat was held at the end of the pier.

"An exchange. We'll give your man back, but we want the girl."

My brother's voice rang out behind me.

"Never."

Matthias raised his gun and pointed it at his prisoner.

418

"Last chance."

Gideon remained silent, unmoving as I clawed like a wild thing to get free of him.

"No, wait!" I screamed.

Matthias fired... and the world paused.

There was the crack of gunfire and Devyn's eyes catching mine. There was a pulse of pain through our bond and then I saw Marcus reaching for Devyn.

Blood. Lots of blood.

The guards pushed Devyn over the side of the boat as I watched in horror. The splash as he was submerged beneath the water.

I reeled at the images. My soul splintered. I couldn't feel. I couldn't think.

Chapter Twenty-Five

Gideon was running, and there were more shots snapping as the rowboat pulled away from the pier. I collapsed unsupported. The pain I felt through the bond was immense. Panic. Despair,. Was it mine or his? It was impossible to separate them.

I felt sand under my knees. Saw Gideon running along the pier. More shots. The waves were impervious, closing over Devyn. Gideon was in the water, another warrior was diving in, and the sentinels' shots were too far away to hit them now. Rion was leaving me, wading out into the water. Bodies came in on the waves. Came closer to the beach.

Devyn, they had Devyn.

I was on my feet, fighting the waves to get to them. They half lifted, half dragged him onto the beach. There was so much blood, red on the sand.

"Devyn…" My hands were reaching up to capture his face. He was still here, still with me. His eyes fluttered open. My hands pulled wide his shirt, tracking down his chest to that great gaping wound just below the Mercian sigil.

A moan escaped me. I looked at the men kneeling in the sand beside me. Their faces told me the news I would not, could not, hear. They didn't believe he could be saved.

I reached inside for something, any faint smudge of power to help him. Nothing, there was nothing. A hand took mine, gentling with its touch, calming me as only he could.

"Cass," he whispered.

"Devyn." I got out a broken, ruined approximation of his name.

"Sorry."

"No, don't you dare," I warned him. He couldn't leave me. He couldn't...

"Do something," I screamed at the silent, unmoving figures keeping their useless vigil beside me. Gideon's amber eyes met mine in anguish before he nodded and hurried away.

"Shhh," I hushed Devyn's attempt to speak. "It's going to be all right. Everything's going to be fine."

Blood was welling out onto the white sand. We had to stop the blood. I held a hand over the wound and pressed down. "Help me," I pleaded to someone, anyone.

And then there was another older gentle set of hands there, pressing a cloth on the wound. It was small and there was so much blood. I looked up into the sorrowful eyes of a druid.

"Please, fix him," I begged.

The druid placed a hand on Devyn's forehead, pushing away his dark glistening curls. He started to speak, an incantation, but it was all wrong. No, no, this wasn't right. He wasn't healing, he was helping him pass. Helping him pass away from me, away from this world.

I snarled, pushing at the druid. I put myself between them. I held the blood-soaked cloth to the wound, shaking my head. No. No. This wasn't happening. Not now. Not here. We had come so far. He couldn't die. He couldn't leave me. Not yet. Not...

"Protect." The word was faint, pleading. Devyn's dark eyes rolled from the men around him back to the druid. "Griffin."

The druid leaned in to catch the words that were more breath than speech.

"Last."

The druid looked at me for an explanation but I couldn't connect anything. I looked back at Devyn; he was fading. He was leaving me. I didn't understand.

"He's the last Griffin," Rion Deverell interpreted.

Devyn's gaze locked on Gideon who blanched, shaking his head.

"Do it." The King of Mercia's tone was all command.

Nobody reacted. Rion groaned above me.

"It can't be me. My house has a different destiny." His voice broke. "Please, Gideon."

I didn't understand. Gideon's face was without expression as he looked at me, then back to my brother, before giving the druid a sign of assent.

He dropped to his knees. The druid took a knife and pulled it across the inner side of Gideon's wrist, then, taking Devyn's hand, he did the same.

No, he couldn't lose more blood... What were they doing? The druid joined their wrists together and bound them with a cloth.

"Stop." I tried to grab their wrists and tear the cloth off, but again, strong arms held me.

"Catriona," came my brother's voice, soothing and sorrowful in my ear. "Peace."

A pulse beat strongly through Devyn. Whatever they were

doing, it was working. I smiled at Devyn and he smiled back at me, clear-eyed.

I let out a huff of air. He was going to be all right. The druid's incantation continued over the bound wrists as the steady pulse built and grew stronger.

"Cass..." Devyn's other hand tightened on mine. "I love you. It has been the greatest... You have been *all* in my life. To have found you, to have brought you home... that was all I ever wanted. And I got so much more."

What was he saying? We had plenty of time for this, but I was so grateful for the steadiness of his words that I smiled back.

"I love you too."

"You are everything, you and our child." He looked at Gideon, then at my brother, whose face showed no surprise at news of a child. "Protect them."

His gaze drifted slowly back to me as the druid's incantation grew slower, the light fading in those dark eyes. The druid unwrapped the cloth and they all stepped away, leaving us alone. He had promised me the skies of Cymru. Here we were. We were here. Together.

I gripped the hand in mine.

Tightly. Not tightly enough.

Love and warmth passed along our connection, but it was duller, fainter as the light dimmed in his eyes. Blood welled out of his mouth as one last burst of joy and strength and honour pulsed through the bond.

And then was gone.

His eyes were empty.

He was gone.

I threw my body on his as if I could stop his soul from escaping. From leaving me. My hands reached up to cradle that face, those cheekbones that had broken my heart, my fingers caught in his curls as I sobbed and rained kisses on his face.

But he was gone. Where once had been life, the central sun of my universe was now only darkness. No, not darkness. Nothing.

I lay across his unmoving body. But he was not here. I sat up – at least I think I did. I wasn't across him anymore. I looked down at my blood-covered hands and at the dark, wet patches on the velvet of my gown. The dark stain of his blood sank into the sand.

Through the dullness, a sharp pain hit my arm. I looked out across the water. The imperial ships were growing smaller on the horizon. Marcus was on those ships. Getting ever further away.

Good. It would all be over soon.

I held Devyn's hand. It made no sense to me. We had been about to get married; this morning, we'd had a lifetime ahead of us. It was still morning, and only moments ago we had everything before us. We were going to be together. To stand together against whatever came at us. My brother. The Britons. We were going to fly in the face of the traditions and customs of this world, and even take on the Empire if they came for us again. Whatever happened, we would stand together.

But now we would fall together. The pain in my arm was spreading. I closed my eyes against it, the physical pain spreading and merging with the tear inside me that promised to take me first. It was the wound that would never heal, the one that Matthias had put in Devyn's chest. He had put a matching one in my soul. And now, one set of sensations engulfed and melded with the other; I couldn't say which was worse, and it didn't matter anyway.

With a moan, I lay down beside Devyn. It would stop soon. I wasn't wearing my pendant, so I was more vulnerable to the effects than Marcus was. Once Marcus was far enough away, it would overwhelm me, and I too would be gone. I didn't have time to wait until they removed his cuff. Would the agony even stop then, if I still wore mine? The pain tore through me. And I didn't even care.

"Catriona." My brother's concerned voice came from above. If he hadn't rejected Devyn, we wouldn't have been here today. We wouldn't have been anywhere near the sentinels who had devastated this town and captured Devyn.

The pain from my arm was rippling through me now, and my body jerked against it. My eyes opened wide as it went up another notch.

The sky was still blue above me and the figures standing around me were a blur I couldn't focus on. My body went rigid as a new wave rippled through me.

"What's wrong with her?"

"The cuff. She's still wearing the cuff." Gideon knew. He had been with us and he knew that Marcus and I couldn't be separated. But it didn't matter. Nothing mattered.

"What?" My brother's voice was sharp, staccato, afraid. Maybe he would be sorry to see me go. It would have been nice to have had a brother. There was a rumble of voices answering him, explaining.

The pain receded and my body went limp. The brother I barely knew picked me up and cradled me in his arms. At least I wasn't alone. At least I had family at the end.

Another wave ripped through me, stronger this time, more intense than the last and I screamed, unable to keep the pain inside.

"Help her," Rion's desperate plea came again. "Help her."

There was no way. However the Empire was removing Marcus's cuff I didn't know.

"Take her hand," Gideon said. There was the sound of a sword being drawn. Of course. Violence. The answer to all life's problems in his mind.

"No." I tugged at the grip that caught my arm. Freed, I pulled my arm away, bringing the agony, the source of the pain, in closer to me. I didn't want to be saved. Certainly not if it meant taking my arm.

"Look at me." Hands cradled my face. "Can you hear me?"

Gideon. Was he looking for permission? He would not have it. I would not give it. I curled into a ball and shook my head, attempting to dislodge his calloused hands. Another wave tore through me and again I arched up in my brother's arms, rigid against the pain. I couldn't take much more of this. Not too long now.

Devyn would be waiting. He wouldn't be gone too far.

Gideon's hands took my face again.

"Dammit, Cat, listen to me," he commanded. "We have to try. I know you don't want to be here, but what about your baby? We have to try for the baby."

The baby.

I opened my eyes and met the blast of Gideon's fierce golden ones. So alive, so full of vitality. Not like Devyn's dark eyes that were now blank and emptied of his soul, fixed in a kind of faded brown; it had always fascinated me the way his eyes had seemed to change colour, from a rich coffee brown to a black so dark I could fall into them for ever. Endless depths. No more.

Gideon took hold of my hand and began to extend it.

Would I die from blood loss before the pain took me?

426

One of the other soldiers took hold of my hand as Gideon raised his sword.

"No, don't want…" I mumbled, but Gideon didn't so much as glance my way as his sword descended on my outstretched arm and bounced off. Putting the great lummox on his arse where he belonged.

The pain blasted through me again. Was it hurting the baby? I pulled my hand free of the stunned warrior who was still holding it and wrapped it around my belly as I curled into a foetal shape around her. It wasn't right; this wasn't right. I needed to protect her. Devyn would have loved her. I could see her: dark curls like her father, but would her eyes be a rich brown like his and her skin bronze? The pain was receding again, and then it came back even harder. Could she feel it? Was it scaring her?

I could feel fear and despair coming at me. Not my own. Was it hers? Our little girl's.

I could save her. I could still save her.

"Married," I mumbled. My lips felt so dry I was sure they must be cracked.

Rion leaned over me. "Did you say something?"

His face was streaked with tears. I wondered which were for me and which were for his childhood friend.

"Married… falls off," I pushed out, the words so faint I could barely hear them myself. It was so loud, the waves, the burning, the smell of smoke and the grit of the sand. How was the world still here when all I had loved was gone?

"What is she saying?" Gideon asked, his tone so deep I felt it reverberate through the air as he dropped to his knees in front of me once more. Again he was manhandling me, lifting my face to his. I wished he would stop… The pain struck again and I barely had the strength to react to it now.

No. I was strong; they just needed to act.

"Marry. Me." It was all I could do to grit out the words.

"Marry you?" Gideon echoed.

And finally the druid seemed to understand, his babbling words explaining to them what I already knew. A marriage vow would release me from the cuff. Any marriage vow, not just a marriage to my intended. It was a basic contract charm, and once the contract was completed by marriage or death, even for just one of the parties, it would be enough to satisfy the charm. It was a technicality, but certainly an important one when one of the parties was sailing off into the horizon.

"But who...?" began my brother. What did it matter? Any of them would do.

My hand was taken and gripped by another; the cloth that had so recently bound Devyn's wrist to Gideon's now bound mine. Blood stained the cloth; I couldn't look away from it, the red on the white. I felt so distant, the pain now an almost constant thrum through my body.

The druid started to intone what I presumed was some wedding rite. Then I heard Gideon's deep rumble. Gideon. I couldn't marry Gideon, no matter how short-lived it was.

Before I could answer, another wave of pain ripped through me. I pulled in a breath. Gideon's eyes were liquid amber. Amber, the strange substance that held moments forever frozen in time. Would this moment be frozen in time?

I lay in my brother's arms. The velvet of my long skirt reached out to touch where Devyn's body stretched out, for ever immobile, on the sand. He would never rise, never breathe, again.

Gideon knelt beside us, looming over me, his heavy cloak whipping in the cold wind. I heard the druid's voice asking again for my consent to this union. I struggled to lever myself up, my brother helping me until I was sitting upright, supported against his broad chest. They too were still clothed in last night's finery.

Only hours earlier we had danced in these clothes. Music had flowed through the air.

Last night.

It seemed like another world.

I reached a hand out and placed it over Gideon's heart, where it had rested as I pleaded with him in the castle garden to release me. His hand slowly came up to mine and held it there.

"Cat, please..." His heart beat steadily, I could feel it. My head fell forwards on my chest. I was so very tired. But the pulse of life in him was strong and sure. The new life in me fluttered. I could do this.

"Yes. I do."

All went quiet. It was done.

The bloody cloth was unwound and fluttered to the sands.

There was stone-like stillness as everyone waited. Then I felt hands grabbing the silver cuff on my arm but the damned thing refused to budge.

I moaned at the pulse of pain there. The vows had stopped it from being agony, but the band was still intact. I had done this for nothing. I had betrayed Devyn with these words. For nothing.

Gideon looked from my arm to the druid.

"It hasn't worked." His tone was flat. Final.

The druid looked nervously at me then up at Gideon before clearing his throat.

"The marriage is not... uh... not complete."

Gideon   stared   down   at   him,   frowning.   His

incomprehension finally cleared as he met the unwavering gaze of my brother.

My numb, overwhelmed brain stuttered at the suggestion. I shook my head. No. Not now. Not ever. I couldn't. Whatever Gideon saw in my eyes as he watched me had him withdrawing, his entire body stiff as he turned his back on me.

"My lady," the druid began, "you understand? You and his lordship, you must consummate the marriage."

I shook my head again. "No. Seen it. At weddings. Falls off."

His words seemed to be coming from very far away. The druid looked worriedly between us. There was Gideon, the warrior, striding away along the shoreline as if to put as much physical distance between us as possible, his body stiff and unyielding. My brother going to him, angry, commanding. Insistent.

Then he was in front of me, the golden lord who had been Devyn's childhood friend – though I had seen little sign of that friendship in the way he had treated him. I reached out and held Devyn's hand. So cold already. If I held it in mine could I delay it somehow?

"Catriona. Catriona. " Rion's voice repeated the name he insisted on calling me over and over until I looked back up at him. "Does your arm still pain you?"

I nodded. It had lessened to a dull throb, but it was still there. Perhaps if I answered, he would go away.

"You and Gideon must consummate the marriage. Do you understand?"

"I don't care." My gaze didn't move from Devyn. I wanted to memorise every curve and hollow of him.

"What?" He seemed confused at my answer.

"I don't care," I repeated. "I tried. He'll know I tried. What happens now? I live. I die. What does any of it matter?"

"It matters," he started again. "Do you understand me? You have to live, for the baby. We think that because Gideon does not wear the corresponding cuff, you must be married fully. You must be joined. Physically. Do you understand?"

I turned to him, focusing on his austere face.

"You must do this. We don't know how long you will have before the pain begins properly again. And then... it will be more difficult."

"More difficult?" my numb lips repeated. I looked at him wonderingly. Did he even know what that meant? Devyn was still here. I held his hand in mine but I had just married another man. A fresh wave of anguish tore through me. He was gone. "I can't leave him."

Rion's blue eyes pleaded his cause from his frozen face. "Catriona, you... I will see to Devyn. He won't be alone. But you must live."

"Why? Why must I?" I asked softly again. That idea was taking hold again. I had tried. What if I just let go? What if I let the handfast band take me into nothingness. "It would all be over."

"It is not over," a rough voice said behind me as a large hand encircled my upper arm. "Do you hear me?"

I looked up at him angrily, pulling at my arm until he released me.

"This is not how it ends." Gideon's face was set in grim determination.

If his will alone could make it so, I would have believed him.

"Do you want to live?"

I did. For Devyn. For our baby.

I placed Devyn's icy hand back on his chest and got to my feet unaided. The pain had indeed receded, but I could feel it there waiting, waiting to return.

Gideon held his hand out to me and I took it.

I let Gideon lead me off the beach, through the glade, and up a path into the forest. I let my mind go numb again and simply allowed myself to be dragged behind him until we came to a small cabin.

"I spent some time here as a boy. It's a place for the novices to come to spend time in nature," Gideon said as he pushed open the door. The inside was bare – just a small table with a couple of chairs and a pallet on the floor. My new husband had found a place for us to consummate our marriage.

"Were you going to be a druid?" I asked idiotically. Anything to distract myself from why we were here.

He looked at me blankly.

"What?" He shook his head. "No, no, my mother came here a lot to study. She had little interest in me but I was dragged along."

"You have a mother?"

He snorted. "Yes, I am born of woman."

"I meant... You've never mentioned her."

His brows pulled together. "She and I are not on the best of terms, but I don't want to talk of her now."

I stared vacantly at the pallet.

"I can't."

My words drifted out into the cold air. I felt exhausted, the words more effort than I had to expend. I continued to stand as Gideon sat heavily in one of the chairs. I doubted the novice druids were as large, and absently I worried for the chair.

"So you'll die, then."

"I suppose."

"And your child?" His words were like stones, each one hitting me sharply.

A spark lit inside the dense fog of my mind, but it was small and the fog was comforting. It protected me; it was heavy and obscured everything. Devyn would be in there. I would find him.

Gideon stood up and in one stride had enveloped me, his hands like bands around my shoulders as he shook me.

"Live, damn you!"

"Why?" My voice was flat and dead, but a part of me was genuinely curious at his answer. What did Gideon care? He had little use for anyone, much less me. I was surprised he had done this much.

"Because it doesn't end like this. *Live.* If not for your brother then for Devyn. You carry his child. Does that mean so little to you now?"

The spark caught and spread, the glow spreading and thinning the edges of the fog. It did matter. Suddenly, the pain in my arm registered again. It was coming back.

I could do this. I could do anything for this child.

I nodded.

Gideon stepped back from me, then after a moment turned away and started a fire as I stood listlessly behind him.

"Can we just do this, then?" I asked peevishly as he failed to return to take up his task.

Gideon turned from the fire. His face was dark in the backlight.

"Kiss me."

I jolted. What? No. I shook my head. "Can't you just...?" I waved a hand aimlessly. This wasn't anything... special. It was just an act and it needed to be done. It didn't matter how perfunctorily the deed was performed.

"No. I can't just…"

His hand gently traced the edge of my face and I pulled it away. Tenderness was not part of the deal.

"What do you mean?" I stared stonily at him. Gideon was not immune to me. There had always been an awareness that rippled between us. An awareness that disgusted me now. Had Devyn known? Had he seen? Was that why he had asked this of Gideon? No, he had asked him to be Griffin. *This* had happened after. The fog moved in again.

"Dammit, Cat." Gideon commanded me back from the fog that threatened to engulf me. He stepped towards me, gently turning my face up to his.

I pulled away.

"No. Just do it."

"I cannot just do it," he gritted out in a hard voice.

I looked at him in bewilderment. What did he…? Oh. I looked down at his trousers. He was right. Nothing.

Fine. I tugged at the laces on my bodice. The blood on my fine velvet dress caught in the firelight as it fell to the floor.

Finally, I stood before him in the all but transparent chemise I wore underneath. "Come on, then."

He hadn't moved. I knew I wasn't making this easy for him, but this was as much as I could do. He scrubbed his hand over his face.

"Maybe we can wait," he said.

I felt frozen. Like I was made of ice from my core out. Ice was good; it kept everything firmly in place. It wasn't just the pain in my arm I couldn't stand, it was the pain tearing through me that Devyn was gone. I had to keep saying it to myself to remember this new truth, this unbearable reality that had come into being.

Reality. It had to be faced. For Devyn. For the new life inside me. I could do this.

I took his hand and drew Gideon down with me towards the pallet.

We sat looking at each other for a moment and then I lifted my hand and traced his features with my fingertips. Not Devyn. Where Devyn's cheekbones had been sharp, his were blunt; where Devyn's eyes had been dark brown, Gideon's were bright amber. I ran my hands through hair that was long and uncut in the fashion of a Celtic warrior. I pulled the tie that bound it and it fell loosely over his shoulders.

He had hard stubble across his jawline; he would last have shaved yesterday, before the party. How long ago that seemed now.

I pulled his face down to mine and rested my cheek against his scratchy one, breathing him in – his newness, his differences. His breath expanded and deflated his chest.

I pulled back, our eyes meeting in the flickering light as I loosened the ties of his tunic then tugged it off. He helped me remove it. His shoulders were broad, his arms so much more muscular than Devyn's. Of course, he had spent his life training, not in the city. I let my hands trace down the contours of his upper arms, along the vein-rippled inner forearms as he sat still with his palms facing up. I lifted my hand to trace the bramble of white roses twisting around a sword over his heart where Devyn had worn the Mercian sigil. His chest rose and fell with his breaths, shadow and light moving across the golden expanse. Still, he did not move.

Again, the pain throbbed through my arm, insistent, reminding me. The intensity of it was building again. It was now or never.

I pushed Gideon down onto the pallet and he went,

435

unresisting. We worked together to pull off his trousers but it was awkward. I noticed the tree that I had glimpsed before, at the inn, stretching out in a swirling pattern across one thigh. I traced my fingers across it lightly and he shivered. His hands were gentle on my body as he pulled me to him, as if I was a thing that would shatter at his touch. I took another moment, focusing on his full bottom lip, then on his hooded eyes which were watchful beneath my gaze.

Finally, I lowered my lips to his, pressing my frozen ones to his heat. A whisper, a breeze of a touch, then another. His chest expanded under my hand. The beat of his heart was the only sound, its strength lending some to mine. It pulsed within me, sending warmth through my body, bringing me back to life. He pulled his head back, his eyes glittering in the dark as he surveyed my expression. His tattoos were a swirling pattern across the width of his shoulders in the half-light. He turned us, so that he was on top and looking down at me.

And then he met me.

He was a mass of Celtic tattoos swirling above me and around me. Devyn had borne none until recently, his whole adult life having been spent hiding his heritage, unlike the proud, arrogant Gideon who had sneered at Devyn.

There was touch, sensation, in the rude warmth of the pallet as he joined with me.

And then heat and flame tore through the ice and fog, exploding in my mind as I cried out.

And as I came down, I cried out again. His muscular arms and legs cocooned me as though he could shield me bodily from my pain. But my grief could not be thwarted and my tears fell and fell, until finally, there were no more.

I woke, stiff and wrecked in both body and mind. Lifting my head from the shelter of a broad shoulder, my heart leapt and then fell as Gideon's lashes lifted and I remembered it all. Their golden glow froze as he saw my expression.

Heart and soul empty, I untangled myself and rose from the thin pallet. Stepping over the gaping maw of the handfast bangle which lay broken open on the floor, I pulled my bloody, smoky clothes back on.

I went out into the misty morning and put one foot in front of the other, my steps carrying me down the hill.

To bury Devyn.

Acknowledgments

This book is about a search to find a place to call home. As I worked on it over the strange summer of 2020 I have never had more cause to be grateful for the friends and family who make up mine. This book is dedicated with love and thanks to all who offered to share theirs when this crazy pandemic struck at the worst possible time. Una, Ger, Liam and Lucy – for the best summer ever. Eilish, Mickey, Muireann and Joe – for autumn weekends and all our Christmases. Kim, Tom and Emily – who I could not reach, and dearly missed. Ida and Ashley, who kept the flag flying in the sunshine. And of course, Mum and Dad – for everything. Special shout out to Joy and Chutney, who shared my fate.

This trilogy had a home very early on, though as this strange year unfolded, many launch dates. So many industries came under pressure, and I have such admiration for those I watched in the publishing industry fight to do right by their authors and booksellers while dealing with the stresses and pressures we all faced in one form or another in the Spring and

Summer of 2020. For many, reading and indeed writing was a form of escape.

Thank you to all the publishers who kept the wheels turning. Particularly to Bethan and Charlotte for your encouragement when the world was mad, Melanie and Claire who managed to make a splash in a crazy book year, Lydia and Tony for your focus and clarity, and Laura and Andrew for your creations. To everyone at One More Chapter for powering on in challenging times.

A special thank you to the bookshops and booksellers who kept us supplied, especially those who fight hard to keep their doors open every year… but never harder than this one.

And most especially thanks to you – the readers who have chosen to stick with me as I explore this world. Hope to see you again soon!

Cx

Author Q & A

What were the most difficult world-building challenges when it came to creating Curse of the Celts?

The Celts and Technicalities

Technically, the Celts aren't so much a race as an identity. A culture intertwined with a way of living and experiencing the world. Art, language, religion, music, these are the things which tie the Celtic peoples together. The Romans thought the Keltoi wild and uncivilized, and slowly but surely conquered them, though some strands of this culture remained strong, broadly across the north western fringes of the Roman Empire. In my world more of Britannia stayed free, or rather fought to win back their lands, remaining essentially Celts across the centuries, arriving in the modern day still with tattoos, torcs, druids, festivals and mythology.

Speaking of technicalities. I created an alternate history and world but sometimes made a decision in the interests of keeping it simple, because occasionally the truth is stranger than fiction.

To give just a few instances of this – the Celts actually started their day at sunset but including this truth didn't add anything but confusion.

I used the name Samhain instead of Halloween to make it more Celtic than the Christianised variant – coming from the day before Hallows' Day or All Saints' Day – choosing the Irish name despite my story being much closer to Wales and its Calan Gaef, as it already has some wider recognition.

There are also some truths which could have gone one way or another. My Romans swear by Hades, which was the name of hell in Ancient Greek mythology. The Romans had Tartarus, but by the time Virgil was writing the *Aeneid* he gave Tartarus as the lowest level of… Hades.

Also, the "Americas" – I looked to find a more Native name for the continent, and found while many North American nations used the Great Turtle or Turtle Island there is also evidence to support the concept of the name "America" (variations in Old Norse, *Ommerike*; Mayan, *iq' amaq'el*; Algonquin, *Em-erika* etc), predating "Amerigo Vespucci" by some centuries, which is wild. There is some research which suggests that Vespucci's first name just fit the discovery narrative. So, in the interests of keeping it simple I went with the name we know today.

Ultimately, this is a work of fiction and I am no scholar, but if you are, and your better knowledge or my interpretations of elements have been twisted here in a way that pulled you out of the story, then I beg your forgiveness. But then I expect you will already be all too aware that all research and all interpretations of the past are imperfect. As it is inevitably no more than a collection of events told by people – storytellers all.

What were some of your foremost sources of inspiration?

Calendar and Festivals

I've always enjoyed how thinly papered-over the pagan calendar is by Christian festivals. Our month names are happily a mash of pagan and Roman names, which allowed me to keep them too.

Most ancient calendars simply followed the sun and the seasons, and in the world outside the Empire it was easy to peel this back and include the first two familiar festivals the Celts celebrate here.

Samhain

Arriving in the Celtic world on October 31st meant we crossed from the tech world to the pagan world with a bang.

As a child I was terrified of Hallowe'en, trick-or-treating hadn't really swung back across the Atlantic, and it certainly didn't entail dressing as a movie princess.

I was taught that this night was when the veil between this world and the next was thin, and anything could cross over. We were encouraged to disguise ourselves so the *púca* wouldn't take us. The candle in the pumpkin so popular today originated in the US with Irish immigrants who had carved out harder roots to place that all important light in the window to keep dark spirits out even as it welcomed the spirits of departed family and friends for whom a place was laid at the table.

Beyond the otherworldly who prowled outside in the dark, inside we bobbed for apples and told fortunes. And ate a fruit cake called Barmbrack, the delight of which as a child was finding the hidden futures within, a coin or a ring wrapped in paper that foretold fortune or love. This inspired the autumnal apple cake Devyn eats – my sister was given an apple cake recipe years ago that my family adore. (Odlums.ie have a version of it. Yum.)

Yule

The Winter Solstice or midwinter arrives between the 19–22 of December. Current holiday celebrations are a mix of the festivities of the ancients – the Roman Saturnalia before the Winter Solstice and the Norse Yuletide, which covered the twelve days after. Many elements of our December holiday season are drawn from those festivities. The druids cut mistletoe on the Solstice, Celts lit bonfires and the Norse lit Yulelogs to brighten short days. The wheel of the year turned and began anew, marked with wreaths of holly and ivy. Wassail or in Ireland going on the Wren and singing for treats is today more familiar as carolling.

Basically eating, drinking and making merry in the darkest days of winter has changed little enough over the millennia.

Wales

I originally mapped Cassandra, Devyn and Marcus a fairly direct route north to Cumbria, and was utterly shocked when everyone veered off course into Wales. But Devyn needed to go home – at first I wasn't sure why...

But much of Devyn and the Griffin were gifts of Welsh

history and lore. The Griffin is more classically from Greek and Middle Eastern legend but Welsh lore contains a creature called the Adar llwch gwin, which is very similar.

In book one, I played with the history of the Tudors, which rooted my inspiration in Wales. I think this came about because as a teen I read *Crown in Candlelight* by Rosemary Hawley Jarman and was blown away to learn that a penniless Welsh archer, Owain Ap Tewdwr, a lowly descendent of the Princes of Gwynedd, became lover (and possibly husband) to Henry V's French widow, Catherine of Valois. Two generations later a Tudor was on the throne of England. I adore the tangle of intention, bloodline and outcome...

The Griffin origin story here begins with 12th-century Llewelyn Ap Iorweth, one of the most beloved Princes of Gwynedd, which I threaded through the centuries to the Glyndŵr line for the 15th-century Owain Glyndŵr, another celebrated Prince of Wales. In the bloodlines of the princes of Gwynedd, Powys and Deheubarth, it's not beyond the realms of possibility that these bloodlines merged... and if not, well... fiction.

Exploring the World of The Once and Future Queen

THE JOURNEY NORTH

Henley and the Chilterns

Living in west London, this was a favourite walking destination – this part of England is spectacular, the winding river Thames here dotted with small islands, the rolling hills, the deep forests.

Oxford

The city of dreaming spires is Mecca for the bookishly inclined.

The history and learning, the beautiful grace of its architecture. The home of walled colleges, cosy pubs, hidden lanes...

The Severn

Crossing the Severn feels to me like the Shannon in Ireland, something about home being west of it. As it was here for Devyn.

The Shannon has a goddess and, I was delighted to realise, so too have offerings been discovered from ancient sites to the Severn Goddess.

I also managed to include the Bore, the lunar tidal wave which surfers jump on to ride up the river.

Dinas Brân

Originally, I was going to use a castle which was less of a detour. But this, this was Rhodri's home.

Austere, bare, standing guard over a desolate craggy part of North Wales, it dragged everyone further into Wales and once there they kept heading west.

Conwy Castle

My earliest trips to Wales were fleeting at best, visits to the Hay Festival or whipping across the northern coast on my way home to Ireland via Holyhead.

Further explorations of the Welsh countryside gave me many castles to choose from but the sight of this forbidding fortress on the water's edge makes a lasting impression.

Many of these castles were built to keep the Welsh under the Anglo-Norman heel, but the number and sheer defensive nature of them stand testimony to the ferocity with which the Welsh withstood conquest.

Anglesey and the Holy Isle

When searching for a place near Conwy to stage an attack on a Druid community, inspiration was easily found.

Anglesey was a sacred place to the Druids and a key target

of the Roman conquest of Britain. The Roman attacked it not once but twice, the first recorded by the historian, Tacitus, as the Battle of Mona, an older name for Anglesey, where in 60 AD the Romans under General Gaius Paulinus attacked the Druids here and destroyed their sacred sites.

Recipe: Griddle Cakes aka Welsh Cakes aka Pice ar y maen

Recipe: Griddle Cakes aka Welsh Cakes aka Pice ar y maen

A friend's aunt introduced me to the wonder that is "Welsh Cakes" and her journey back to London after a trip home to Hereford was often accompanied by an ice cream container full of these little beauties.

Do try them – fresh and warm, they are a treat!

Auntie Sue's Welsh Cakes

225g/8 oz of plain flour
½ tsp of baking powder
110g/4 oz of butter, chilled cubed
85g/3 oz of sugar
2 oz of currants or sultanas
½–1 tsp of mixed spice (nutmeg and cinnamon)
A pinch of salt
1 egg
A dash of milk, if needed

Recipe: Griddle Cakes aka Welsh Cakes aka Pice ar y maen

1. Rub butter into flour until crumbly.
2. Stir in dry ingredients
3. Mix in egg and milk, if still dry, until you get a stiff dough (similar to short crust pastry)
4. Roll out to ½ cm thickness and cut into rounds 6-7 cm wide.
5. Fry on each side 2-3 mins until golden.
6. Sprinkle with caster sugar. Eat hot or cold.

Thank you, Sue, for sharing the family recipe!

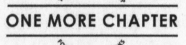

YOUR NUMBER ONE STOP

ONE MORE CHAPTER

FOR PAGETURNING BOOKS

One More Chapter is an
award-winning global
division of HarperCollins.

Sign up to our newsletter to get our
latest eBook deals and stay up to date
with our weekly Book Club!
Subscribe here.

Meet the team at
www.onemorechapter.com

Follow us!
@OneMoreChapter_
@OneMoreChapter
@onemorechapterhc

Do you write unputdownable fiction?
We love to hear from new voices.
Find out how to submit your novel at
www.onemorechapter.com/submissions